Chapter One

London, 1816

"I cannot promise His Grace will see you this morning, Miss Darracott. Last night was . . ." The butler lifted one bushy white brow. "Last night was a particularly exhausting evening for His Grace. But I shall do my best to impart the urgency of your request."

Isabel Darracott gave the elderly retainer the same smile that had won her admittance past two footmen and into the Duke of Marlow's London town house. "Thank you, Fromsby. I trust you shall not fail me."

"I shall do my best, miss."

Isabel sagged against the back of a leather chair after Fromsby closed the library door. She could only imagine how the duke would take the news of her uninvited appearance in London. Especially after he had experienced an exhausting evening. He probably suffered from gout, as many men on the shady side of fifty did. He would probably be furious with her.

Silently she chided herself. She was five and twenty, far too old to act missish. She forced starch into her back and drew a deep breath, catching the soft scent of leather from the morocco-covered chairs and sofas. "I have every right to be here," she whispered, trying to prop up her sagging courage.

Indeed, the duke ought to be ashamed of his actions. Still, she could not stop feeling like a country mouse about to do battle with a lion. She smoothed her hand over the wrinkles in her apple green wool pelisse. Nine hours riding in a crowded mail coach did not do much for a woman's appearance.

She hurried toward a pier glass hung on the mahogany-paneled wall above the fireplace, hoping to improve her appearance before her first encounter with the elusive duke. If she could only—

"Dear heaven!" Isabel froze, her breath halting in her throat at the sight that greeted her near the hearth. A man lay sprawled on his side on the carpet near one of the sofas. His left hand was flung out toward the fireplace, resting against the burgundy-and-ivory carpet, palm up, long, elegantly tapered fingers curled inward.

She stepped closer, approaching him as warily as she would a wild animal she thought might bite. He was tall, his long legs encased in close-fitting black wool trousers. He certainly was not one of the servants. She might not be acquainted with London fashion, but she recognized expensive cloth and expert tailoring when she saw it. The duke had two sons. She suspected the man lying on the floor might be one of them. Still, why the devil was he sleeping on the floor of the library?

He shifted, rolling onto his back with a lazy growl.

His white silk shirt spilled open across his chest, drawing her attention to the black curls shading his skin. It certainly was not proper to notice a man's physique. Yet this man demanded her attention. Since there was no one to notice her impolite stare, she indulged herself. He was so starkly masculine, so splendidly proportioned, broad across the shoulders and chest, with a lean waist and narrow hips. How any man could manage to look commanding while sleeping on the floor, she didn't know. But this man definitely managed. Even in repose he radiated a barely restrained aura of power.

"Are you all right?" she asked softly.

His nose twitched, his only response. She knelt beside him, with every intention of making certain he wasn't injured in some way. He certainly did not appear injured. He seemed to be sleeping as peacefully as a babe in a cradle.

An odd, simmering warmth rippled through her as she absorbed every detail of his features. Black waves of hair, overly long, framed a face sculpted with bold lines and curves—a fine, straight nose, sharply chiseled cheekbones, and full lips that lent a moody expression to his countenance. Thick black lashes rested against his cheeks; the color of his eyes was a mystery. The night had painted his lean cheeks with an enticing shadow of beard. Surrendering to a wayward nudge from her curiosity, she touched his cheek, just a graze, a soft brush of her fingertips against that fascinating rasp of black stubble.

He stirred, a low growl emanating from deep in his chest. She snatched back her hand as he opened eyes the color of an ocean at sunrise, gray and green blending with a startling beauty. Heat shimmered across her skin. "I hope I didn't disturb you."

He blinked, as though trying to bring her face into

focus. A lazy smile curved those sensual lips, transforming a handsome face into a devastating weapon.

All the moisture evaporated from her mouth. "You must be curious to find a stranger at your side. You see, I'm here to, ah, I was waiting for . . ."

Her words dissolved in a squeak as he wrapped his powerful arms around her and pulled her down against his hard chest. Before she could utter more than a startled gasp, he captured her lips with his. His lips moved against hers, firm, demanding, as though he could not get enough of her. His tongue plunged into her startled mouth tasting of fine brandy. His beard rasped her soft cheeks. Excitement surged within her, sparking along her every nerve.

Life at Bramsleigh had never provided her much excitement. At the country assemblies and house parties she had attended, never once had she met a man who had aroused her desire. Although she considered herself practical in most aspects of her life, since practicality had become a necessity after her mother's death, she had never completely abandoned her dreams.

Passion and romance. A love that sparked legends. She had read about such things in books. She had dreamed about such wonders at night. She had feared she would live her entire life and never taste desire. Yet this was desire, raw hunger, unrestrained passion. Dear heaven, she could not breathe.

He rolled with her in his arms, pinning her against the thick wool carpet. The weight of his big body pressed against her. Powerful muscles shifted against her breasts, her belly, her legs, each touch a confirmation of potent masculinity. His scent—sandalwood soap and an intriguing musk that defied identification—flooded her senses. The heat of his body soaked through the layers of their clothes, drenching her skin.

She struggled beneath him, pushing against his

broad shoulders. Yet he didn't seem to notice or care. Instead of releasing her, he slipped one hand between their bodies and caressed her breast. She stiffened at the bold touch. Through wool and muslin her skin tingled at the warmth of his large hand on her. He squeezed the sensitive tip between his long fingers, sending sensation shooting through her. She gasped against his mouth. In desperation, she swung her reticule, smacking the side of his head. That caught his attention.

"What the bloody hell!" He pulled away from her.

Isabel scrambled away from him, tripping over her skirt as she came to her feet. She caught the back of a chair and steadied herself.

He sat on his heels, rubbing the side of his head, glaring at her. "Do you mind telling me why the devil you did that?"

She drew a shaky breath. "It seemed the only way to convince you to stop attacking me."

He rose, his movements filled with the powerful grace of a born athlete. "Attacking you?"

Her lips still tingled from his kiss. Her entire body trembled from his embrace. "Are you going to deny you attacked me?"

"What the hell do you expect? Bothering a man while he's sleeping."

She bristled at his continued vulgarity. "Are you in the habit of sleeping in the library?"

"I sleep where I bloody well choose." He frowned, his gray-green gaze raking her from the top of her green velvet bonnet to the tips of her black half boots. "Who the devil are you? And what the hell are you doing in my house?"

She met his brusque demand with a direct look she hoped would disguise the trembling in her limbs. "I'm waiting to see my guardian, the Duke of Marlow," she said with as much dignity as she could manage.

"Your guardian?" He looked surprised, and then a glint of humor lit his stunning eyes. "Clay put you up to this, didn't he? His idea of revenge for that tart I sent him last week."

"I have no idea what you're talking about." Isabel folded her hands at her waist, her reticule dangling from her wrist. "I'm Isabel Darracott. And if I didn't need to speak with the duke, I would not stay another moment in your company."

He studied her a moment, his lips curving into a lazy smile. "So you're here to speak with your *guardian,* the Duke of Marlow?"

She really didn't like the glint in his eyes. It made her feel too much like a mouse confronting a hungry lion. "Fromsby has gone to announce my arrival to the duke. I expect he shall return directly."

He moved toward her in slow strides she suspected were designed to make her wonder what might happen when he reached her. It worked. She took a step back, and bumped into the back of a chair. Unless she wanted to run past him like a frightened schoolgirl, she was trapped. He drew near. She held her shaky ground.

In spite of her every attempt to quell her attraction to the rogue, her skin tingled with the same excitement she had experienced earlier when she lay pinned beneath him. He stepped so close his legs pressed against her pelisse. Far too close. Certainly no gentleman, even in London, would stand so close to a lady. Yet this man evidently followed his own rules. "You are being quite impertinent."

One thick black brow rose. "Am I?"

"Yes," she said, her voice escaping in a thread of breath.

He leaned forward. A warm scent of sandalwood

soap drifted from his skin and swirled through her senses. She stared up at his handsome face, her heart pounding against her ribs while a voice in her head screamed *Run!*

"Where did my brother find you?" he asked, his breath warming her cheek. "At Covent Garden?"

"I have never met your brother. And if he is as disagreeable as you, I hope I never have the occasion to meet him. I've come here to speak with my guardian. I doubt the duke will appreciate the way you have treated me."

He slid his hand around her neck, his long fingers pressing against her nape. "Come now, my sweet. We both know I'm the Duke of Marlow. And I'm certainly not your guardian."

"You!" Shock speared through her. "You can't be Marlow."

"You aren't the only one with those sentiments. Unfortunately there is no hope for the situation."

"You're the duke's eldest son?"

He laughed softly, a dark sound filled with an odd note of self-mockery. "Justin Hayward Peyton Trevelyan, at your service."

The blood drained from her limbs as cold reality took its place. "And you mean to say something has happened to your father?"

"Even he couldn't command the hands of fate, or the course of his disease."

Isabel closed her eyes, blocking out his compelling image, snatching desperately for a slender thread of hope. "You're hoaxing me. Aren't you?" She looked up at him. "Please tell me you really are *not* the Duke of Marlow."

"That would be a lie. And I don't like lies of any kind. I am the Duke of Marlow, Marquess of Angelstone, Earl of Basingstoke, Baron of Campden, Trowbridge, and Arden. Now may we end this little farce?''

Isabel swallowed hard. No matter how much she wanted to deny the truth, it stared at her from a pair of exquisite gray-green eyes. ''You really are Marlow.''

''I have been since my worthy sire died fourteen months ago.''

''What a complete disaster,'' she whispered.

''I'm certain he thought it was.'' He pressed his fingers against the back of her neck, urging her upward toward his lips. ''Now, where were we before you interrupted me? Ah, yes, I believe I was about to make love to you.''

His dark voice coiled around her like a magnetic current, coaxing her near. She pressed back against the chair. He leaned closer. The warmth of his body beckoned her, promising more of the tingling excitement she had found in his wicked embrace. Desire slithered through her like a fiery serpent, leaving a trail of steam in its wake, threatening to melt her brain. ''Take your hands off me,'' she said, appalled at the breathless sound of her voice.

He brushed his lips against the tip of her nose. ''I must come to see you onstage sometime. You play the wounded innocent to perfection.''

''Oh, let me go, you big brute!'' She pushed against his chest.

His full lips tipped into a crooked grin. ''How long do you plan to play this little game?''

''Stand aside!'' she demanded, keeping her voice low.

''As you wish, *milady*.'' He stepped aside and executed an exaggerated bow.

She put several feet between them before she turned to face him. ''I realize it's too much to hope any logic will pierce that thick skull of yours, but circumstances demand I try.''

Justin leaned back against the chair, folded his arms over his chest, and grinned at her. ''I can think of better things to do.''

''Will you listen to me? I am Isabel Darracott. My father, Lord Edward Darracott, Baron Bramsleigh, died fourteen months ago, leaving your father as my guardian, as well as the guardian of my two younger sisters.''

''I shall have to come up with a truly inventive way of showing Clay how much I appreciate this little play of his.''

''You are the most infuriating . . .'' She clenched her hands into fists at her sides, clutching her composure. ''I am not an actress. And I have never met your brother.''

''Is there a second act to this play?''

''Don't you see the implication? You could very well be—'' She broke off, unable to voice the unspeakable thought. ''Oh, this is a disaster. A complete disaster.''

Justin frowned, his expression growing uneasy. ''You're not going to start weeping, are you? I haven't much patience for women who turn into watering pots.''

''I intend to see your attorney, Mr. Yardley, before I leave London this afternoon. Perhaps, under the circumstances, the situation can be rectified. And I need never see you again. We can only hope that is the case.''

Justin leaned back against the chair, watching Miss Isabel Darracott—or whatever her name might truly be—march across the room, while he tried to ignore the heat simmering low in his belly. He wanted noth-

17

ing more than to toss the tart on her lovely backside and finish what they had started. Still, he had never chased a woman in his life. He was not about to start now. Even if the creature in question was one of the most intriguing females he had encountered in a long time—a tart who looked and sounded like a starchy governess.

A thick lock of hair had fallen free of her pins. The glossy, light brown coil swayed with each step she took, brushing her green overgarment right where the small of her back was hidden from his sight. Images rose in his mind, of soft brown hair sliding over the sleek curves of this woman's naked back. Lust jabbed low in his belly.

He swore under his breath. Damn the wench for intruding on his slumber, for enticing him, but most of all for turning into an icy little prude. Trust Clay to send a whore who refused to perform. At least the whore Justin had sent to his worthy brother last week had managed to bed him—not leave him hard and aching and frustrated enough to slam his fist through a wall.

She turned at the door. "Good day, Duke."

Innocent indignation shone in eyes as blue as his childhood dreams of heaven. A maiden's blush painted her smooth cheeks a dusky rose. If he didn't know better he would have believed she was every bit as pure as she appeared. Yet he had abandoned his faith in innocence a long time ago. "Come back again, sweetheart, when you're in the mood for some real entertainment."

"One day you shall regret those words." She closed the door behind her with a soft click. A very ladylike exit for a woman at the height of her anger. Justin had to compliment his brother. Clayton had devised an ingenious means of revenge on his wicked brother. He sat on the arm of the chair and contemplated her performance. An icy sensation brushed the nape of his neck, like a ghostly hand. *If* it was a performance. How did she know about Yardley?

He shook off the chill. It must all have been part of Clay's little game, he assured himself. It was absurd to think her story was true. He certainly could not have inherited the guardianship of anyone, especially not three females. Even the Almighty, who had dealt him more than one unpleasant blow during his thirty years on this green earth, did not have that twisted a sense of humor.

Still, there was something about the woman, some horrible aura of sincerity that prickled the base of his spine. He quickly dismissed the sensation. It was the aftereffects of too much drink, he assured himself.

He rubbed the back of his neck, easing muscles stiff from sleeping on the floor. Although he was usually competent in holding his liquor, last night things had gotten out of hand.

Last night he had left the party his grandmother Sophia had given in honor of his and Clay's birthday. He had decided to celebrate in a less genteel fashion, in one of his favorite dens of iniquity—Madame Vachel's. In deference to their grandmother, Clay had remained at the party, enduring the boring company of three hundred of London's most fashionable members of the ton. Unlike Justin, Clay could always be depended upon to do the proper thing.

As Justin recalled, he had left Vachel's establishment near dawn, after having his fill of three plump tarts and a bottle of Irish whiskey. He remembered arriving home and sitting in the library with a decanter of brandy. From there, his memory failed him. Apparently he had never made it to his bed.

It was not the first time he had awakened away from his bedchamber. It would not be the last. As his father had often told him, the only thing Justin was truly good at was overindulgence. His muscles tensed, as they always did, when he thought of his father. Still, nine years ago, much to his father's chagrin, after the duke had cut off all of Justin's funds in an attempt to bring his son under rein, Justin had discovered another talent.

With a small loan from Sophia, Justin had managed to accumulate a considerable fortune by playing the Exchange. Insult to injury, as far as his father was concerned. Yet Justin had long ago stopped trying to please his father. It had been a brutal lesson, learned at a young age, but Justin had discovered that he could never please the man who had sired him. No matter how hard he tried.

He stood and stretched, easing the tension in his limbs. Guardian to three females. Clay could not have thought of anything more absurd. Yet if the woman had been playing a game, why hadn't she stayed to finish the performance? And the look in her eyes— could anyone truly counterfeit such astonishment, such utter sincerity? He sank back onto the arm of the chair, the prickling sensation at the base of his spine rising until the back of his neck tingled as well.

It could not be. Yet he had never read his father's will. He had been in Italy when his father died, and he had stayed out of the country through the proper period of mourning. Donning black for George William Justin Emory Trevelyan was not something he had cared to do. These past three weeks, since returning to England, Justin had avoided every attempt Sophia, Clay, or his father's attorney had made to discuss the terms of his father's will. Justin didn't give a damn what his father had bequeathed his eldest son. Yet could part of his inheritance include a blue-eyed virago and her two sisters?

He stood, his heart pounding against the wall of his chest. Perhaps it was time to see just exactly what was in his father's will.

Chapter Two

The fragrance of rose potpourri mingled with the sharp scent of burning coal in the drawing room of Marlow House on Park Lane. After his father's death, Justin had seen no reason to use his father's London residence. Instead, he had allowed the elegant mansion to remain in his grandmother's control. He stood beside the carved gray marble mantle, facing his grandmother, tense with the realization of the disaster that had befallen him. "Did you know about this?"

"Of course I knew of it." Sophia, the dowager Duchess of Marlow, sat near the hearth on a gilt-trimmed sofa. Sophia was one of those rare women who made a mockery of the passage of time. Tall and slender, she had golden blond hair that revealed only a glimmer of brass from the artful hand of her hairdresser. With classically carved features and brilliant blue eyes, her beautiful face still captured the attention of many gentlemen, including the Marquess of Hempstead, a man of nine and fifty who was her current lover.

"Edward Darracott and your father were friends since their days at Harrow. In fact, dear Edward was here to visit your father a few days before George died." Sophia stroked the sleek ocelot lying on the sofa beside her, his regal head resting on her lap. She slid her elegant fingers through Perceval's long, spotted fur, earning a deep-throated purr in response. "As if matters were not bleak enough during those terrible last days, that night, after they left here, Edward and his son Stephen were murdered, attacked near their hotel by common footpads."

Justin's chest tensed with the reminder of Miss Darracott's tragedy. "I suppose you didn't think it was important to tell me I had inherited the guardianship of three females."

Sophia lifted one finely arched brow. "If you had allowed Mr. Yardley to impart to you the terms of your father's will, you would have known."

"Damnation, Sophia . . ."

Sophia lifted her hand, her ruby-and-diamond ring catching the fire of candlelight. "I shall have none of your vulgarity, my boy. Speak civilly, or do not speak at all."

Justin inclined his head in a silent apology. "Father must have taken leave of his senses. This is beyond everything. Me, the bloody Devil of Dartmoor, a guardian for three females."

"I do wish you would not banter that horrible epithet around. Really there are times when I think you actually revel in being thought the most dangerous man in London."

Justin grinned. "A poor reputation has its advantages. I can't remember the last time some matchmaking mama shoved an ambitious chit in my way."

"No, dear. Now they hide their daughters when you

are near." She gave him her sweetest, most sarcastic smile. "Quite an accomplishment on your part."

Justin ignored her barb. After all, it was the truth. He needed only to examine his behavior with the prim Miss Darracott to confirm the fact that he was an unprincipled, disgusting debauchee. "Father should have considered my black nature before trying to foster three chits into my care."

Sophia absently scratched the silvery gray fur beneath Perceval's chin. "You were your father's heir, Justin. I'm certain he felt the Darracott ladies would be in good hands."

Justin laughed bitterly. "He is still trying to manage me, isn't he? Even from the grave. What did he think, the guardianship of three females would rehabilitate my black soul? Well, I'll be damned before I'm saddled with a pack of brats."

Sophia tilted her head, holding him in a direct gaze. "Pity George didn't name Clayton as guardian. He would readily have accepted the responsibility."

The barb stabbed his heart. Yet he managed to keep his expression composed. He had learned how to maintain his composure through far worse than a few barbs shot by his grandmother. "Don't try to twist me around your finger, Sophia. I'm well aware Clay is everything I'm not."

"Justin, my dear boy, your father would not have entrusted you with Edward's children if he thought you incapable of handling the task."

"Father thought the only thing I was capable of handling was a glass of whiskey."

"I'm afraid you did not always see the best of your father." Sophia lowered her eyes, staring at her cat, stroking his silky fur a long moment before she spoke. "My son was not always a harsh man, Justin. If you tried, you could remember a time when he was warm spirited and affectionate—everything he shunned after your mother's death.''

Justin curled his hand against the smooth mantel. He stared into the coals burning on the polished andirons, fighting the tremors that had commenced deep inside him, in a place where a small, wounded boy still dwelled. That boy had known affection—a mother who had preferred life in the country with her family to the glitter of London, a father who had adored his wife and two sons. But it had all changed when Justin was nine, on a terrible day in December, when his mother had died.

''Near the end George spoke of a great many things he regretted in his life.'' Sophia's voice, soft with emotion, brushed against Justin's back. ''Including his relationship with you and Clayton. He realized he had made dreadful errors in judgment when you were boys. Mistakes that cost all of you dearly.''

Justin drew the bitter scent of burning coal into his lungs. ''I'm certain he went to his maker with a clear conscience.''

''I want you to know that your father truly regretted what happened to you at the hands of that dreadful man. He spoke of it many times near the end.''

Justin squeezed his fist against the mantel until his knuckles blanched white, while inside he clamped down hard on the lid of the coffin containing brutal childhood memories. ''The only thing my father regretted was the fact that he failed to mold me into his own image.''

''If you could only understand how he felt after your mother died.''

''Felt?'' Images from the night his mother had died rose in his memory. Justin had gone to his father, seeking reassurance. Instead, he had received a cold reprimand for his boyish tears. *Affection is for the weak, remember that. The nobility do not show their sorrow.*

Emotions must be controlled. His father would repeat that lecture over and over again in the passing years, pounding the words into both of his sons, as though he could erase all of the emotion in them. "In case you didn't notice, George William did not condone emotion of any kind."

"It wasn't lack of sensibilities that made him behave the way he did. It was because he felt too much. He adored your mother. He adored you and Clayton."

He thought of the icy stranger who had sired him. No matter how hard he tried to forget, the past remained. The cruelty his father had sanctioned stayed with him, lurking in his deepest memories buried in an all-too-shallow grave. "If that is true, then he was certainly a master of disguise."

Sophia was quiet for several moments. When she finally spoke, the tremor of sorrow that had colored her words was once again washed from her voice. "It was guilt that altered him, Justin. He didn't know how to deal with it after your mother died. It was easier to hide from his feelings than to face them. It was easier to keep you and Clayton at a distance. If you had only seen him those last few days, I'm certain you would have forgiven him."

"Forgiven him?" Justin glanced over his shoulder at his grandmother. "I find it difficult to believe my father actually sought my forgiveness on his death-bed."

Sophia shrugged her slender shoulders. "Perhaps not in words. Still, I know how much he regretted the past. I know he wished he could go back in time and alter his decisions."

Justin eased open his clenched fist. "It's best to leave the past behind us. It cannot be altered or reclaimed. We all must live with the decisions we make."

Small sounds filled up the quiet that stretched between them—the rattle of rain against the window-panes, the rustle of spent coals tumbling through the andirons, the deep-throated purr of a contented ocelot. Justin could feel Sophia's gaze upon his back, the insistent stare she gave to demand his attention. Yet he refused to turn and face her, not when she had managed to push his composure to the brink.

Sophia released her breath in a long sigh. "What did the Darracott child want from you this morning?"

An image of Isabel Darracott's face burned through the ugliness of his memories. Something dangerously close to guilt pricked him in the vicinity of his belly at the thought of her. Since he had long ago decided guilt was a useless emotion, he quickly dismissed the sensation. "Miss Isabel Darracott is hardly a child. I would judge she is at least three and twenty."

"Did you even discover what she wanted before you chased her back to Bramsleigh?"

Justin glanced over his shoulder, frowning at his grandmother. "I didn't exactly chase her back to Bramsleigh."

"I can only imagine the impression you made, refusing to believe her. You must have shocked the poor child dreadfully. As far as I know she has never even been in London before today. Edward seldom came to town, unless he was attending an auction or a lecture, and he never brought any of the girls. After his wife died, he was quite oblivious to society."

After seeing the innocent Miss Darracott, Justin could well understand why a father would keep her in the country, safe from the dangerous influence of rakes such as her current guardian. "Kept his daughters wrapped in cotton wool, did he?"

"I doubt dear Edward even thought of bringing the girls into society. He was primarily a scholar, fascinated by anything medieval. Although when he was here, I recall he did mention he was going to look for a house in town. His eldest daughter was insisting he give her sister a Season. I think Isabel had convinced him it was time to leave the seclusion of Bramsleigh.''

''Miss Darracott no doubt had grown bored with the country and decided to badger her father until he did what she wanted. No doubt she was the one who wanted all the nonsense of the Season. She probably came here to badger me into giving it to her.''

''Not all members of my sex are manipulative little schemers, Justin.''

Justin laughed. ''Every female tries her best to manage any male within her orbit.''

Sophia lifted her brows. ''Pity you haven't met a female who could manage you. Your life might be a great deal more settled.'' With a grin, Justin bowed to her. ''I like my life just as it is.''

Sophia stroked her hand over Perceval's head. ''Edward was such a handsome man. Tall and dark, with startling blue eyes. His son certainly favored him. Did his daughter also benefit from her handsome father?''

''She is attractive, though nothing out of the ordinary. Certainly not a great beauty. I doubt I would have noticed her in a crowded room.'' Still, he could not deny that the chit had managed to heat his blood. Even now, the thought of Isabel warm and supple in his arms turned his blood to liquid fire. If that was not enough of a shock, he had discovered that no matter how much he tried to banish her, he could not get the image of her face out of his mind.

''I really wish you had met Edward. He was a very likable man. And his son, so charming, so full of promise.''

Justin had seen little of his father since the day he and Clay had been sent to Harrow. Certainly their strained relationship had not presented many opportunities for Justin to meet his father's cronies. "I shall have to be satisfied with meeting his daughters."

Sophia smiled, her eyes filling with a glint of amusement. "So you plan to visit your wards."

Justin frowned as he acknowledged the reasons he wanted to visit Bramsleigh. In spite of his better instincts, he wanted to see Isabel Darracott again, if only to assure himself this ridiculous infatuation with the woman was nothing more than a momentary aberration. Virginal chits were hardly to his taste. He made a practice of avoiding them the way he would avoid the pox.

Long ago he had learned that money and position could stake a man out like a lamb. Behind every innocent face lurked a lioness on the hunt, eager to drag her prey to the altar. Not this man. Marriage did not reside in his future. He would never tame his wild ways for any female. And even though he knew he was well beyond redemption, he still maintained a few precious principles, honesty among them.

He would not live a lie. He had no intention of setting up a nursery for the sake of continuing the noble name of Trevelyan. London society provided too many examples of marriages of convenience: men who sought comfort from their mistresses while their wives took lovers to console them. He refused to participate in that hypocrisy. "I assure you, Duchess, I have no intention of playing nursemaid to a pack of females. I plan to dispatch any obligation I might have to the Darracott ladies as quickly as possible."

Sunlight played against her eyelids, coaxing Isabel from slumber. She nestled deeper into her pillow, breathing in the scent of clean linen that had been stored with sprigs of lavender, resisting the bright intrusion into her dreams. Still, once broken, the delicate thread of sleep could not be repaired. She opened her eyes and stared straight into the face of her twelve-year-old sister, Phoebe.

"Finally." Phoebe turned and yelled toward the open door. "She's awake, Eloise."

Isabel flinched at the shriek. "Phoebe, dear, do be careful. You'll shatter the window glass. Not to mention my head."

Phoebe hopped onto the bed, her golden brown curls bouncing against her back. She sat beside Isabel, dangling her feet over the edge of the bed. "I was beginning to think you were going to sleep through the day."

Isabel sat up against the pillows and glanced at the recently opened blue cotton drapes. "And so you came to rescue me from that terrible fate."

"I wanted to stay up last night to see you when you came home, but I fell asleep. I simply could not wait another instant to hear all about London and the duke." Phoebe's dark blue eyes glowed with excitement. "What was he like? Very elegant? Was he cold and distant, or did he make you feel welcome?"

Isabel hugged the patchwork quilt of colorful chintz against her chest. The Duke of Marlow had invaded her dreams last night, holding her, laughing at her every protest, until she crumbled beneath his sensual advances. Heat shimmered inside her at the memory of his hands on her body, his lips moving against her mouth, his splendid body pressing warmly against hers. She had never realized one could harbor such a powerful infatuation for a man who did not possess a single shred of decency. It was shocking to discover how shaky her scruples could be. "The Duke of Marlow isn't exactly what we expected."

"Phoebe, I told you not to bother Belle," Eloise said as she entered the small room. She paused beside the bed, her hands clasped at her slim waist, and her green eyes filled with disapproval. Dark brown curls framed an expression far too mature for her seventeen years. "She needs her rest."

Phoebe crinkled her nose. "It's nearly half past eight. I'm certain Belle doesn't want to sleep away the entire day. Do you, Belle?"

"Certainly not." Isabel smiled warmly at Eloise. "I wouldn't want to be thought a lazy dolt."

"Well then, if you truly don't mind." Eloise grinned as she drew a wooden armchair near the bed, the wooden legs scraping against the bare oak planks of the floor. She sat on the edge of the chair, like an excited child waiting for a present. "Please tell us all about your trip."

Isabel looked from one expectant face to the other, wishing she had better news for her sisters. Since Bramsleigh, their father's country estate, was entailed to the nearest male relative, fourteen months ago Isabel and her sisters had lost the only home they had ever known, as well as their loved ones. Since the tragedy, they had tried to make a home of an old cottage on the same estate where they had once lived in comfort, subsisting on a meager portion provided in the deed of settlement. Yet it could not continue this way. Her sisters deserved a better future than what Isabel could currently provide. Eloise would be eighteen in November, and Isabel was determined she would have a London Season. She had hoped to improve their situation with a small amount of help from their guardian. Now that possibility seemed bleak.

Slowly Isabel related the events of her trip to London, omitting the more salacious details of her meeting with the infuriating Duke of Marlow. Still, she could not banish the memories, or dismiss the sparkling excitement that tingled through her at the mere mention of his name. "According to Mr. Yardley, the circumstances do not alter the situation. The present Duke of Marlow shall control our lives for as long as he sees fit," she said, concluding her story.

"You mustn't worry, Belle." Eloise squeezed her elder sister's hand. "We shall do fine without any help from the duke."

"That's right." Phoebe lifted her small chin. "Once we find the old baron's treasure, we shall not need help from anyone."

Isabel lifted a soft brown curl from Phoebe's shoulder. She and her sisters had grown up believing that the legend of the Baron of Bramsleigh's treasure was nothing more than a fairy tale, until the day workmen had discovered the old baron's journal. Along with other books, the tome had been found hidden in a secret alcove in the library uncovered during her father's latest renovation project.

Unfortunately the journal had been discovered two days before Edward's planned trip to attend an auction of medieval artifacts in London. He had taken the journal with him to work on the translations. After his death, it had not been found among his belongings.

"I am afraid we have very little chance of finding the old baron's treasure without the journal," Isabel said.

"We will find the treasure," Phoebe said, her eyes bright with hope. "All we need do is search for it."

Isabel shook her head. "If the treasure truly does exist, it could be anywhere. The baron may not even have hidden it at Bramsleigh."

"The treasure exists. Papa said it did." Phoebe's lips drew into a tight line, her expression growing mulish. "And Cousin Gerard thinks it exists as well. He has been searching for it since he moved into Bramsleigh."

"Perhaps. Still, I doubt we shall ever find it without the journal," Isabel said softly. "Think of how many people have searched for it over the years. And no one has had any luck."

"I've been thinking." Phoebe stared toward the window, her expression growing thoughtful. In the distance the stately walls of Bramsleigh Hall rose from the brow of a hill overlooking the sea. "I'm certain the old baron must have hidden the treasure in the caves. It would be a wonderful place to hide the jewels."

Isabel tugged on Phoebe's hair. "Even if he did hide them in the caves, we have no idea where to start looking. Those caves meander for miles beneath the cliffs."

Phoebe turned to her sister, her expression set with determination. "We have to search for it."

"Not in the caves." Although Isabel hated to extinguish the glow in her young sister's eyes, she had long ago assumed the role of parent as well as sister.

Phoebe clasped her hands in her lap. "If we took lamps and went in pairs . . ."

"We shall not search the caves," Isabel said. "It would be far too dangerous."

"But Belle, if the duke won't help us . . ."

"We shall manage, Phoebe." Isabel touched her young sister's smooth cheek. "I shall find a way to get what we need from the duke."

Phoebe slid off the bed. "I only want to help, that's all. I'm not as much a child as you think."

Isabel leaned back against her pillows as Phoebe ran from the room, her booted heels pounding the bare floor. The weight of her responsibilities pressed against her chest like a slab of granite, until her lungs ached. There were moments when she dearly wished for someone with whom she could share the responsibilities of raising her sisters. Moments when she wished someone would touch her hand and make her believe everything would be all right. She had hoped that someone might be their guardian.

"We shall be fine, Belle," Eloise said, as though she could read her sister's thoughts. "I know you want to give both Phoebe and me a Season, but I don't need to go to London. And by the time Phoebe is old enough, perhaps we shall have saved enough for her to have one."

"It takes a great deal of money to finance a Season, dearest. We could never save that amount. It's all we can do to keep food on the table."

"Then we shall all stay here."

Isabel squeezed her sister's slim hand. "What future do you and Phoebe have if you are hidden away in this little cottage?"

Eloise glanced down at their clasped hands. "*You* never had a Season, Belle."

Isabel released her breath in a soft sigh. "And I'm a spinster, with little chance of ever altering that state."

"That isn't true. One of these days the right man will come along and discover you."

The right man. What would Eloise say if she confided the way she had reacted to the very improper advances of the Duke of Marlow? He was hardly the right man. Yet he had aroused something in her that she had never dreamed existed.

"He shall be handsome and rich, and brilliant," Eloise said. "And he shall have a kind heart and a noble spirit."

Isabel laughed softly, silently comparing the wicked duke to the lofty ideal Eloise thought appropriate for her sister. "And will he be atop a great white charger?"

34

Eloise smiled, her green eyes warming with the fantasy. "All dressed in silvery armor. Nothing but the most valiant knight shall do for you."

Isabel suspected Eloise's ideal man would also be a horrible bore. No one could say that of the Duke of Marlow. He was neither an ideal nor a bore. But he was the most infuriating man she'd ever met. "I'm afraid we should all grow gray waiting for this paragon. It's far better if we find a way to remedy our situation. I'm certain, if I apply to the duke in a manner he can readily accept, we shall get what we need."

The fresh scent of baking bread drifted up from the kitchen. Her stomach grumbled, reminding Isabel she had not eaten anything except a slice of bread and a cup of coffee the day before. Although the mail coach had stopped for meals, the waiters at the inns never delivered the food in time for the patrons to eat. At each inn, they had slapped her food in front of her just as the coachman had called "All ready." Since food wasn't allowed in the coach, she had gone without.

"Do you think you shall be able to convince the duke to help us?" Eloise asked.

"I certainly doubt the duke wants to be saddled with our guardianship any more than we want him to have control of our lives." Isabel tossed aside the covers and rolled from bed. She shivered in the cold room; coal was at a premium these days. "I intend to present him a suitable alternative to the situation."

Eloise frowned. "He didn't sound like a man who is easily persuaded."

"I doubt he is," Isabel said, slipping into her blue wool wrapper. "Still, I suspect he will be anxious to dispatch any obligation he has to us." Not that he ever took that obligation seriously, she thought. No, the Duke of Marlow would certainly agree to her plan. "I shall present him with a simple way to be rid of us."

With any luck, the duke would dispatch his obligation to them, and she need never see the infuriating rogue again. An unexpected sense of despair settled over her at the thought of never again seeing him. Isabel drew a deep breath as she left the room. In time this dreadful infatuation would die, she assured herself. It was nothing more than a momentary aberration. A foolish reaction of a maiden past her prime to the intoxicating masculinity of a rogue. In no time at all she would forget the man ever existed.

Isabel rapped on the wooden door leading to an old barn that her youngest sister had claimed as her own private domain. When she received no answer, she opened the door and stepped inside. "Phoebe, are you here?"

No answer. Still, Phoebe might not respond if she was still angry and hurt. And Isabel had little doubt her sensitive young sister was both. Lavender and herbs stirred beneath her feet, releasing a pleasant fragrance as Isabel walked toward the ladder leading to the loft—rushes spread across the floor of an ancient keep. Over the past year, Phoebe had transformed the homely little barn into a virtual castle, where she ruled as queen.

"Phoebe?" Isabel climbed the ladder hoping to make peace with her sister.

Banners adorned the rough wooden walls, some features charging unicorns, others with stags holding shields. Morning sunlight spilled through the narrow glass windows their manservant had cut into the walls of the loft. The sunlight slanted across a long, low table, where six knights sat staring across the polished oak at six ladies, all awaiting the arrival of their queen.

Isabel touched the smooth green velvet kirtle of one of the dolls. Each of the two-foot-high figures had been fashioned by a master craftsman in London, especially made for the tenth birthday of Edward Darracott's youngest daughter.

Human hair sold to a wigmaker adorned their heads. Their faces and hands were crafted of fine porcelain. Their clothes were fashioned from the finest silk and velvet. They were not only a portrait of a bygone era: they were a legacy of another day, when Isabel and her sisters took comfort and luxury for granted. Her throat tightened when she thought of all the things she wished she could give her sisters. They had little chance for marriage if they remained here. No chance for families of their own.

She rested her shoulder against a rough wooden wall and stared out across the lush green park to where Bramsleigh stood, its stone walls made golden by the sun. At first, the shock and pain of the deaths of her father and brother had eclipsed all other emotions. Then, as reality slowly closed in around her, she became aware of other losses. She had not realized how much she would miss her home until the day fate compelled her to leave it. She never thought the day would come when she would have to sell her beloved horses, when she would worry about the price of beef, when her life would be controlled by one infuriating man.

Silently, she shook off the blue devils. She did not usually indulge in mournful, sentimental musing. One must look to the future, not the past. And one must take care of the present. Which reminded her of the reason she had come here. Where was Phoebe?

Isabel turned to leave and nearly jumped out of her skin. Justin Trevelyan stood near the ladder, his gray-green eyes narrowed like those of an angry lion, lines drawing a frown on his face. He looked at her as though he wished very much to be anywhere but here.

Heat swept over her skin, as though she had suddenly plunged into an open fire. Her heart sprinted into a headlong race that stole the breath from her lungs, robbing her of any chance of forming a single syllable. Tall and commanding, the man was far more devastating than she remembered. She could do nothing but stare.

Chapter Three

The swift heat infusing his blood caught him off guard. Justin clenched his teeth, annoyed at the insidious attraction this woman held for him. "Do close your mouth, Miss Darracott. You look like a trout leaping for a fly."

Isabel snapped her mouth closed. A look of acute discomfort flickered across her delicate features before she regained control of her composure. "You startled me."

"Then we are even on that score."

She did something unexpected then; she smiled, warm and generous, completely without artifice or guile. The impact of that smile hit Justin like a clenched fist to the belly. "I shall have to remember never to disturb sleeping lions."

Sunlight poured through the window beside her, eager to touch her face. The little sleep Justin had found in his coach on the journey to Bramsleigh had proved restless. Last night Miss Isabel Darracott had had the audacity to invade the sanctity of his dreams. She had come to him, soft and willing, drawing him into her warm embrace.

In that treacherous realm he had known a satisfaction that eluded him when the sun dawned. He had awakened aching and frustrated from a ridiculous infatuation with an untouched maiden, of all things—a woman who had spent her entire life in the country, wrapped in cotton wool. And right now he could not get the thought of taking this woman in his arms out of his mind.

Still, he could not ignore the appalling fact that the intriguing creature standing before him was a lady, innocent as the day she was born. Worse, the infuriating female was under his protection. "What the devil were you doing in my house without a chaperon?"

The smile vanished at his harsh tone as quickly as if he had slapped her. "I am well past the age of needing a chaperon," she said, keeping her voice level.

"You are a child, Miss Darracott. A green girl who has no idea of the consequences of running all over London without benefit of a chaperon."

Sparks flashed in her blue eyes. "I'm five and twenty, Duke. And I've been managing my father's household since I was fifteen."

"Bramsleigh is not London. A woman's reputation is as delicate as a fine crystal vase. Once broken it cannot be repaired." The irony of the situation was not lost on Justin. Here he was, the bloody Devil of Dartmoor, lecturing about propriety. Under other circumstances he might have found the ludicrous situation amusing. As it was he wanted to stomp his feet and howl in frustration.

Isabel stiffened, her expression revealing her anger,

though her voice betrayed only a hint of her outrage. "I have never done anything to injure my reputation."

"No young woman of quality would ever call upon an unmarried gentleman."

"At the time I believed I was calling upon my guardian."

"Even so, you should have brought your maid, at the very least."

"I no longer have a maid. And I couldn't see the point of forcing our housekeeper to make such a trip. Mrs. Tweedbury is a bit flighty, and not at all fond of long trips. And if she had accompanied me, it would have left my sisters here with only our manservant. I couldn't do that."

He stared at her, a dreadful suspicion contracting his stomach. "Who accompanied you to London?"

She folded her hands at her waist, her chin lifting a fraction as she spoke. "There was no need for anyone to accompany me."

He moved toward her, closing the distance between them in long, predatory strides. Her eyes grew wide as he drew near. For a moment she looked as though she might take flight, like a frightened rabbit, but then she set her jaw, lifted her chin, and met his angry glare with cool defiance. "Do you mean to tell me you traveled to London alone?"

"I already told you, Mrs. Tweedbury certainly could not have made the trip."

"What of your sisters?"

"I saw no reason to subject one of my sisters to the discomforts of a mail coach. Even if we could have afforded the ticket."

"You traveled by the mail?"

She swept open her arm. "As you can see, we no longer maintain a coach, or horses. The mail was a great deal more acceptable than walking."

41

Guilt was not an emotion that settled easily on his shoulders. Yet as much as he tried to shake it off, Justin could not deny the weight of it pressing against him. A half hour ago he had arrived at Bramsleigh, only to discover that the Darracott ladies had been dispossessed of their family home, victims of primogeniture. The Duke of Marlow's wards were currently housed in a dwelling that wasn't fit for his horses. "You should have stayed at home, where you belong."

"I needed to address certain matters with my guardian. When Mr. Yardley informed me the Duke of Marlow had returned to London, I decided it was time we met to discuss the small matter of my sisters' future."

That small matter weighed as much as Gibraltar, and he felt every stone of it pressing against his chest. "You should have written to me rather than go flying off to London like a wet goose."

"Since my father's death, I have corresponded several times with Mr. Yardley. He informed me you were out of the country and nothing could be done about my concerns until you returned. He assured me he would speak with you concerning our guardianship upon your return to London. His last correspondence indicated you had returned, but were far too busy to address the small matter of your wards. Still, he assured me, you would soon give us proper consideration."

The smell of lavender drifted past his defenses, tempting him to brush his lips against her neck. He frowned. Certainly this appalling reaction to the chit was merely the usual animal attraction he felt for any attractive female. "Instead you decided to take matters into your own hands and barge into my house?"

"My father has been gone for fourteen months. I thought it was time I met my guardian."

He cringed inwardly at the condemnation in her beautiful eyes. "You can stow the recriminations, Miss Darracott. I didn't know about you or your sisters until yesterday."

Her eyes narrowed with suspicion. "Do you mean to tell me Mr. Yardley never informed you about us?"

"Suffice it to say that I wasn't interested in the terms of my father's will until a certain young woman barged into my house and bothered me."

She studied him a moment, as though searching for the pieces of a puzzle she had only just stumbled upon. He held her inquisitive look, certain he presented an impenetrable mask. "Under the circumstances, I can see how my appearance in your library might have caught you at a disadvantage."

A lock of hair had fallen free of the pins securing the thick roll at the nape of her neck. The lustrous curl now spilled over her shoulder, brushing the blue wool that hugged the curve of her breast. She was certainly not as well endowed as the women he usually chose to share his bed. Her figure was almost negligible by comparison. Yet the memory of the weight of her nestled in his palm flickered in his brain, kindling a warmth that swept across his skin. He clenched his jaw. "It would seem my father's demise was a greater disaster than I imagined."

"Precisely." She stared up at him, and he had the uneasy feeling she was assessing him with those candid eyes, evaluating the best tactics for attack. "Obviously the situation must be altered. You cannot possibly act as our guardian. I cannot imagine how you were ever placed in this position in the first place."

Although Justin regarded the role of guardian to the Darracott females in the same light as pestilence and plague, he bristled at her quick dismissal. "I take it you think me incapable of handling the position," he said, smiling at her, while inside he fumed.

"You are a bachelor."

"That does not preclude me from being a guardian."

She moved away from him. "You cannot mean to say you actually wish the task."

The last thing in the world he wanted was to be this woman's guardian. Yet a perverse streak of obstinacy welled deep inside him, forcing him to argue with her. "At the moment I see no alternative."

"Then allow me to give you one. Turn the guardianship of my sisters over to me."

The impertinent little chit actually thought she could do a better job than he could. "You expect me to place an infant in charge of the nursery?"

Her eyes narrowed like those of a cat about to strike. "I have been looking after my sisters since I was fifteen."

"As I understand, your father was alive and well until last year. No doubt he oversaw all of your decisions."

She planted her hands on her slim hips. "Papa trusted me."

He rolled his eyes toward heaven. "I doubt he would have approved of an unchaperoned chit taking a mail coach to London on a whim."

"I never would have had to take that journey if my guardian had taken any interest in his wards."

"Damnation, woman, I didn't even know you existed until yesterday."

"Precisely. You are not even responsible enough to read your father's will. And yet you expect me to believe you are to be trusted with the guardianship of my sisters."

He stalked her, his hands twitching with the anger boiling inside him. "It really doesn't matter what you think, Miss Darracott. I am your sisters' guardian. And as much as it might be distasteful to both of us, I am also responsible for you."

"I'm not a child."

"No. You certainly aren't." He was much too aware of the slender curves hidden beneath that simple blue gown ever to mistake this woman for a child. He leaned forward until his nose nearly touched the tip of hers. He was accustomed to intimidating people. His title alone was enough to send the weak at heart scurrying for safety. Miss Darracott stood her ground, meeting his tactics with a firm resolve. "From this day forward I expect you to behave with the proper decorum of a lady of quality."

Her startled gasp brushed his lips with a damp heat flavored with a trace of hot chocolate. "I've never behaved with anything less."

"That has been proven otherwise." He smiled in the face of her fury. "Do you think you can manage? Or should I hire a governess to tutor you in social etiquette?"

"Why you . . . you . . ."

"Belle!" A young woman shouted as she burst into the barn. "Are you here?"

Eloise's frantic cry dragged Isabel's attention from the infuriating duke. She hurried to the edge of the loft and looked down at her sister. "What is it? Is something wrong?"

Eloise stared up at her sister, her eyes wide. "I've looked everywhere; I can't find Phoebe."

Of all days, why did her young sister have to choose this day to throw a temper fit? It was hardly the impression she needed to make if she were to convince the duke she was indeed a proper choice to become her sisters' guardian. "I'm certain she'll return when she is over her pique."

"Have you managed to misplace one of your sisters, Miss Darracott?" Justin asked, his deep voice dripping sarcasm.

Isabel cast the confounded rogue a dark glance. Although she had never raised a hand in anger in her entire life, she caught herself wanting to strangle this man. At the same time she had never wanted more to throw her arms around him. She wanted to kiss those brooding, sarcastic lips, to slip her hands into his silky black hair, to feel the heat of his body against hers. Oh, goodness, she really had taken leave of her senses. "This is none of your concern, Duke."

He lifted one thick black brow, a combative glint filling his stunning gray-green eyes. "On the contrary, I believe it is very much my concern."

"Belle, is there a gentleman up there with you?" Eloise asked.

"Not exactly." Isabel met Justin's scowl with a smug smile. She tried to ignore the thudding of her heart as he moved toward her. "The Duke of Marlow has come to pay us a visit. A very brief visit."

"The Duke of . . ." Eloise's voice dissolved into a soft gasp as Justin stepped to the edge of the loft and looked down at her.

"You must be Miss Eloise Darracott," Justin said, smiling down at the stricken girl.

Eloise nodded, her eyes fixed on his handsome face, her lips parted, her expression revealing her astonishment.

"You surprise me." Isabel managed to keep her voice level, in spite of the tingling excitement that swept through her at his nearness. "I didn't realize you even knew my sisters' names."

"I am a most surprising fellow, Miss Darracott."
He grinned at her. "At times I do not even know what
I shall do until after I have done it."

She stared up into his eyes. What lurked behind that
all-too-confident exterior? Undiluted arrogance? No
doubt he had been pampered and coddled from the day
he was born. He was accustomed to getting what he
wanted, and woe to anyone who might get in his way.
Well, he would soon discover he could not cow her.

"Belle, Mrs. Tweedbury told me one of the lamps
is missing."

Isabel flinched at her sister's voice. She stared down
at the girl, the implication of Eloise's words seeping
like ice into her blood. "One of the lamps. Is she
certain?"

Eloise nodded. "She noticed one missing when she
was cleaning them this morning. When I returned from
searching for Phoebe, she told me about it. Belle, do
you think Phoebe went to the caves?"

Isabel had no doubt her sister had decided to explore those caves. Alone. "Oh, that little wretch."

Justin grabbed her arm when Isabel reached the ladder. "What is it?"

Isabel looked up into his hard expression and
wished him anywhere but here. "I'm afraid my sister
may have done something reckless."

"Such as?"

"I'm sorry, I don't have time to explain." Isabel
pulled free of his grasp and rushed down the ladder
as quickly as her skirts would allow.

Justin caught up with her as she left the barn. Although he did not say another word, he obviously was
not pleased. Isabel stopped at the house long enough
to grab a lamp and a tinderbox. After insisting Eloise
stay at home, she left the kitchen. Much to her chagrin,
Justin fell into step beside her as she rushed along the

path leading to the cliffs and the beach below.

A breeze brushed Isabel's face with the tangy scent of the sea. She glanced up at Justin's sharply chiseled profile, dreading the inevitable lecture that would come from this. "There is no need for you to become involved in this."

"I am already involved." The breeze tossed a thick lock of hair over his brow, making him look less like an arrogant aristocrat and much more like the devilish rogue she had met the day before.

He took the lamp and tinderbox from her hands. "I take it your sister has made off with a lamp to explore the caves along the beach," he said, shoving the tinderbox into his coat pocket.

Isabel smoothed a lock of hair back from her face. "I told her to stay away from those blasted caves, but she can be rather strong willed."

"I suspect it's a family trait." Justin took her arm as they started down the path leading to the beach.

In spite of everything, she was glad he was with her. The man had a way of taking command of a situation, of making her feel he could set things right with a wave of his hand. At the moment, she needed all the reassurance she could find.

Long strands of grass growing in sparse clumps along the steep path swayed with the breeze. Gulls glided over the silvery strand of beach, their shrill cries in sharp harmony with the low crash of waves against the shore. When they reached the beach, Justin soon found the small footprints in the damp sand that marked Phoebe's trail.

"It looks as though she has passed this way." He glanced out to sea, then glanced at Isabel, a wealth of meaning in his eyes. The sea lapped upward toward those small footprints, rising slowly with the incoming tide.

Isabel's heart crept upward as she hurried to keep up with Justin's long strides. They followed the footprints toward the dark openings of a series of caves opening to the sea. The small footprints led them to the first cavernous opening. He paused at the mouth of the cave to light the lamp. The sound of flint against steel echoed in the cave, like a skeleton's bones rattling against stone.

"Phoebe!" Isabel called as she stepped into the cave.

Sunlight slanted a few feet past the yawning stone entrance before succumbing to the blackness. She walked to the edge of the light and called once more to her sister. Above the steady crash and roar of the sea she focused her attention, straining to hear her sister's response. Yet nothing rose above the rumble of the sea.

Without waiting for Justin, she ventured into the darkness, keeping her hand on the rugged stone wall. She called to Phoebe, her voice echoing through the darkness ahead of her, reverberating on the stones. Still she could hear no response above the voice of the sea.

Light from the lamp flickered on the stones in front of her. Justin paused beside her, so close his sleeve brushed her arm. The simple contact scattered sparks along her skin. She glanced up at him. He stood like a statue, staring into the blackness that hovered just beyond the feeble light. Golden lamplight bathed his face, illuminating the tension carved upon his features. He looked like a man staring into the face of death itself.

Isabel touched his arm and felt thick muscles taut beneath the smooth dark blue wool. When he glanced at her the sheer terror in his eyes stunned her. "Are you all right?"

He glanced away from her, staring once more into the darkness. "The tide is coming in. You should wait on the beach. If Phoebe is in here, I'll find her."

"I'm not leaving here without her."

"Stubborn females." He moistened his lips. When he spoke his deep voice was oddly strained. "We'd better find her. Quickly."

Chapter Four

Justin couldn't move. He clutched the smooth metal handle of the lamp, cursing the weakness inside him. He shivered as though he were a child stranded in an ice storm. His shirt clung to the chilling sweat spreading across his skin. Deep inside him, childhood memories beat against the lid of their tomb, threatening him.

Sunlight glowed behind him, beckoning him to run from the darkness. From the corner of his eye he could see Isabel staring up at him, lamplight illuminating the confusion etched on her features. Not now, he thought. He could not surrender to the ancient fear. Not in front of this woman.

He stared into the darkness, fighting old demons, struggling for control. An image penetrated the terror clouding his brain—a little girl trapped inside this black hell. That image broke his paralysis. He forced his legs to move.

Golden lamplight flickered over the rugged stone walls, a blessed oasis in this demon's lair. In his memory he saw the flicker of a single candle in the darkness, a sliver of golden light seeping beneath a locked cellar door.

"Phoebe!" His voice bounced against the stone walls, mocking him. Still he tried again and again, calling her name, throwing her a lifeline, just as his brother had held out that golden sliver of light for him so many years ago.

Isabel grabbed his arm, bringing him to a halt. "Did you hear that?"

Justin held his breath and waited. For a moment he could hear nothing over the sound of his pulse pounding in his ears. And then it came, a thread of sound cutting through the roar in his ears, a soft cry for help.

"It came from there," Isabel said, pointing toward a connecting passage.

He grabbed her arm when she bolted toward the dark passage. "Take care, Miss Darracott. I don't need to lose both of you in here."

"You're right, of course." She gripped his arm.

Did she need comfort? Or did she sense his own need? For now he didn't care. The grip of that slender hand helped keep the demons at bay.

Phoebe's cries for help grew louder as they turned into the passage. Lamplight glittered on small pools of water trapped in pockets in the stone floor. This part of the cave would be underwater during high tide. A soft glow shone from a pit in the floor of the cave a few feet ahead of them.

"Phoebe!" Isabel broke free of Justin and hurried toward the pit. Her foot turned on a rock. She cried out as she stumbled.

Justin grabbed her arm and dragged her back from the precipice of the pit. "Take care!"

She leaned against him, shivering in his arms while she regained her breath. Justin pressed his cheek to her hair, breathing in the scent of lavender, while a fierce sense of protectiveness swept over him.

"Help me!" Phoebe wailed from the depths of the pit.

Justin lifted the lamp high, spilling light into the pit. About twelve feet below, Phoebe stood in a small pool of light cast by the lamp at her feet. Yellow light from his lamp fell upon her face, illuminating her wide-eyed stare.

Isabel knelt on the edge of the pit. "Are you all right, Phoebe?"

Phoebe choked back a sob. "I'm so sorry, Belle. I didn't mean to cause any trouble."

"It's all right, dearest. The Duke of Marlow is here with me."

"The duke?" Phoebe asked, her voice revealing her surprise.

"Yes, dear. Together we're going to get you out of there."

Justin could not remember the last time anyone had put any confidence in him. At least confidence that he could do something constructive. To his surprise, he discovered an overwhelming desire not to disappoint her. He set the lamp on the stone floor beside Isabel. After stripping off his coat, he stretched out on the floor beside her. "Hold my legs."

Isabel hesitated a moment before resting her hands on his calves. Her touch sent a shiver of awareness rippling through him. He clenched his jaw against the infuriating reaction of his body to this woman. He dangled the coat like a rope into the pit. "Grab the coat, Phoebe. I'll pull you up."

Phoebe stretched with her right hand, keeping her

close to her side. She snagged the hem of the coat.
I have it.''

"Grab it with both hands," Justin commanded.

"I can't. I hurt my wrist."

Justin swore under his breath. If she couldn't maintain her grip while he hoisted her out, he wasn't sure
how he would get her out of there. "Hold on, Phoebe.
Hold very tightly."

"I will."

Justin grabbed the wool and tugged Phoebe off the
floor. Hand over hand he dragged her upward, one
precious foot at a time. The light from the lamp flickered upon her features, revealing the strain of her effort. He could feel her hand slipping down the length
of wool. "Hold on, Phoebe!"

"I . . . can't!"

"Hold on, dearest!" Isabel shouted.

"I . . ." Phoebe's voice ended in a gasp as the coat
slipped from her grasp. She fell back to the bottom,
landing on her feet. She stared up at them, tears glittering in her eyes. "I'm sorry."

"It's all right, Phoebe. We'll get you out." He sat
on the edge and faced Isabel's concerned expression.
"I'll have to try something else."

"I'll go back for a rope," Isabel said.

Justin glanced at the wall behind Isabel, where
lamplight glistened against damp stone. "There isn't
enough time."

Isabel's eyes grew wide. She stared into the pit.
"We have to get her out of there."

"We will." Justin swung his legs over the edge,
and tried not to think of the possibility of becoming
trapped in that pit. "Press to one side, Phoebe. I'm
coming down to get you."

"You can't." Isabel grabbed his arm. "It's terribly
steep. You won't be able to get out."

He stared into her eyes, stunned by the concern for him he saw shimmering in the blue depths. "I will make it out."

Before she could protest, or he could come to his senses, he eased over the edge of the pit. He caught a narrow foothold with the toe of his boot and started to lower himself, searching for purchase. Rocks shifted beneath his weight. His footing disappeared.

"Damn!" he muttered, clawing at the smooth rock. His heart slammed against the wall of his chest as he fell. Pain flared in his shoulder as he rammed against solid stone at the base of the pit.

For several moments he sat wedged against the damp wall, dragging air into his lungs, trying to clear the pounding in his head. When he opened his eyes, he stared straight into a pair of dark blue eyes.

"You're like a knight from a fairy tale," Phoebe whispered, her soft voice filled with awe. "Charging to my rescue."

In another time and place he might have laughed. How ludicrous to imagine anyone would consider the Devil of Dartmoor a knight. Unless of course he was the blackest, most vile knight in the kingdom. Still, a part of him warmed to the child's praise. He glanced up at Isabel. Light from the lamp she held cast a golden nimbus around her head. She looked like an angel beckoning him to heaven.

Mentally he shook himself. He would not allow his brain or his backbone to turn to mush. He stood, cringing at a sudden twinge of pain low in his back. Tomorrow he would feel the full extent of his foolish act. "We'd better get you out of here."

"Thank you. I tried crawling out that hole," Phoebe said, gesturing toward a crevice at the base of the pit to Justin's right. A distant roar emanated from the dark mouth of the crevice, like a beast on the prowl—the sound of the tide stalking the shore. "It must be the way the water recedes during low tide. But it got too narrow for me to pass."

A shiver slithered through him at the thought of entering that narrow passage. "We shall take the high road."

Phoebe glanced up at her sister, then looked at Justin. "How?"

He gripped Phoebe around the waist and hoisted her to his shoulders. "Use the wall for balance, and stand on my shoulders."

"Like court tumbler," Phoebe said, with all the excitement of the foolish or the very young.

She drew up her legs. He steadied her as she balanced for a moment with her knees on his shoulders. Her first attempt to stand landed one booted foot upon his head.

"Terribly sorry, Duke," Phoebe said, poking Justin's nose with the side of her boot in her second attempt to find his shoulder.

Justin grabbed her errant foot and planted it on his shoulder. "See if you can climb out."

He heard shuffling sounds above him. Pebbles showered his head and shoulders.

"Give me your hand, Phoebe," Isabel said.

Justin slowly released Phoebe's legs, as Isabel pulled her to safety.

"I have her," Isabel shouted.

He stepped back and looked up, assuring himself both sisters were safe.

Isabel hugged Phoebe close and peered over the ledge. "Can you climb out?"

"Excellent question," Justin muttered. He glanced around at the walls. The rock was smooth from the rush of water swirling over them. The low roar of the ocean echoed from the black crevice at his feet. How long before the tide would fill this space? As he turned in the small space, searching for a means to escape, the walls seemed to close in around him. His vision blurred. A cold sweat soaked his shirt.

He sagged back against the stone, drawing in deep drafts of the salt-tinged air, fighting the fear clawing at his chest. He stared at the flickering flame behind the cracked glass of Phoebe's lamp. When he was certain he once again had control of his voice he spoke. "I suggest you take Phoebe and get out of here, Miss Darracott."

"I cannot leave you here," Isabel said, her voice breaking with barely concealed tension.

He looked up at her and managed a smile. "Go for help. I'll need a rope to get out of here."

Isabel studied him a moment, determination carved into her features. They both knew help would never arrive in time.

"Go to Bramsleigh." Isabel thrust her lamp at Phoebe. "Tell them we need help. Tell them to come quickly."

Phoebe glanced over the ledge. "I'll be back in no time at all."

"Hurry!" Isabel said, her voice raw with emotion.

Justin glared at the woman. "What the bloody hell are you doing?"

Isabel sat on the edge of the pit. "I'm not leaving here without you."

"I order you to leave this instant."

In the feeble light of the lamp glowing at his feet, he could see the glimmer of her smile high above him. "Phoebe took the lamp. If I tried to leave now, I could get lost and never find my way out."

Water surged from the crevice near the base of the

pit, splashing his boots. "If you don't get out of here now, you could get caught by the tide. Have you thought of that?"

"It has occurred to me." She dangled his coat over the edge. "So I suggest we get you out of there as soon as we can."

"Don't be a fool." He grabbed the lamp and tied the handle of the precious light source to the dangling sleeve of his coat. "Pull that up, and get the hell out of here."

Justin leaned back against the wall as Isabel hauled the lamp out of the pit. Darkness closed around him. He closed his eyes, clamping down hard on the lid of his memories. Blood pounded in his temples. An ancient fear slithered like a viper inside him, threatening to humiliate him in these last few moments of his life. He clenched his fists at his sides, summoning his will.

"Grab the coat."

Justin glanced up at the sound of Isabel's voice. She lay on the floor above him, bathed in the flickering light of the lamp. She had one sleeve of his coat wrapped around her slender arm while she dangled the rest of it over the side. "You're not strong enough to hold my weight. I will only pull you down if you try to pull me out of here."

"I am not leaving here without you." Isabel hooked her free arm around a low mound of stone. "So you might as well give it a try."

"Damn stubborn female." He grabbed a handful of wool and pulled, testing her strength. She held the coat tightly. Still, he hesitated.

"Climb! We don't have a great deal of time."

Justin stared up into her face, saw her determination, and knew she intended to stand by her conviction, even if it meant drowning beside him. He drew in his breath, braced his feet against the wall, and gripped the sleeve with both hands. He began to climb out of the pit. With each tug he made on the coat he was aware of the slender arm keeping him from falling. With each hard-fought foot, he prayed she would not tumble headfirst into the pit.

Isabel clenched her jaw against the pressure of his weight against her arm, the terrible tension tugging her shoulder. She squeezed the superfine wool of his coat, fighting with all of her will for balance, for the strength to keep them both from a fall. The roar of the sea echoed in the cave, growing louder, stalking them. Moments stretched into a lifetime, while she clenched the wool and watched Justin's slow rise from the pit. After an eternity, he crawled to the stone floor beside her.

Isabel collapsed against the smooth stone, clinging to Justin's coat, still too afraid to release the lifeline. Strong arms slid around her, lifting her from the damp floor. Justin cradled her in his arms, holding her against his chest, while he unwrapped his coat from her trembling arm.

"Damn foolish female."

The harsh words brushed her face in a dark caress. Each hard thud of his heart pounded against her cheek. "Your gratitude overwhelms me."

He rubbed her arm, his long fingers massaging her strained muscles. "No more than your foolishness astonishes me, Miss Darracott."

She stared up into his face, seeing the concern behind the fierce mask. Warmth radiated from his big body, wrapping around her, chasing away her chills. The threat from the growling sea receded, leaving only her awareness of this man. She had the strangest feeling, as though nothing in the world could harm her as long as he cradled her in his embrace.

He touched her face, a soft brush of long fingers

against her cheek. She imagined seeing a deep well of longing in his eyes, a loneliness that mirrored her own. It must be an illusion, a trick of light, she thought, for in an instant the reflection hardened into an impenetrable mask.

He glanced toward the opening to the main passage. "I suggest we get out of here before we're fish bait."

His words snapped her foolish musings. If she were not careful she would be pining over this man, as though she were some silly schoolgirl afflicted with her first infatuation. Unable to eat. Unable to sleep. Wasting away like a besotted, mutton-headed dolt. She scrambled from his arms, only to pitch forward when her foot tangled in her gown.

"Damnation!" He grabbed her arm, saving her from a long tumble into the pit. "If you fall into that hole, I'm going to leave you there."

She did not believe him for an instant. "If I were to fall into that hole, I would deserve to stay there."

He squeezed her arm before snatching the lamp from the floor. "Let's get the hell out of here."

He held her hand in a tight grasp as they dashed into the main passage. Water swirled around their ankles as they hurried down the sloping stone floor toward the mouth of the cave. The water rose with each successive wave. Sunlight glowed at the entrance, only a few yards away, but the encroaching waves seemed to add miles.

Waves crashed against the mouth of the cave, plunging inward. The cold salt water slammed into Isabel, knocking her off her feet, dragging her back toward the belly of the cave. Salt water flooded her nose. She clawed at the water, fighting against the relentless tide.

"Isabel!" Justin dropped the lamp and grabbed her arm, his fingers biting into her skin. She heard his curse over the roar of the waves. She clutched his shirtsleeve like a lifeline, her heart hammering against the wall of her chest. It wasn't enough. The sea was sweeping her back into the cave.

Justin hauled her through the churning water, pitting his strength against the raging waters. She caught a glimpse of the fierce expression on his face before he clasped her against his chest—shelter in the midst of the angry sea. He held her for a brief moment before he shifted and tossed her over his shoulder. The hard thrust of his shoulder rammed into her middle, slamming the breath from her lungs.

She felt his body straining beneath her as he fought the tide, like a powerful hunter plowing through a muddy field, carrying her into the sunlight. He staggered a few yards away from the cave before lowering her to a narrow strip of sand against the embankment.

She leaned back against the rocky slope, dragging deep drafts of salt-tinged air into her lungs. He leaned against her, his back to the sea, his brow on her shoulder. His breath warmed her cold skin through her wet gown. His body shielded her from the wind whipping off the water. In spite of the cold, heat shimmered through her.

She stared at the damp waves curling beneath his ear, resisting the urge to twist the ebony strands around her fingers. *Foolish, foolish woman.* She suspected any female who entertained romantic notions about Justin Trevelyan would soon regret them. Yet, for the life of her, she could not prevent them. This harsh man had a way of plowing through her defenses.

She wanted to cup his face in her hands, kiss those sarcastic, sensual lips until all the stones of his castle defenses crumbled at her feet. Unfortunately, she suspected it might take something close to a battering ram to accomplish that feat.

He straightened and looked down at her. The harsh,

sarcastic expression had been washed from his features. He looked younger, more approachable, and in some unfathomable way terribly vulnerable. "I trust you are unharmed?" he asked, his voice not quite achieving his customary harsh tone.

"I'm fine," she said, her voice sounding oddly strained to her own ears. "Thank you."

He stepped back, his gaze sweeping over her, as though he wanted to assure himself of her well-being. The cool breeze buffeted her wet clothes, wool and muslin clinging to the curves of her breasts, her belly, her thighs. A voice in her head commanded she cover her breasts with her arms. Yet she didn't move. Suddenly she felt a temptress, a siren on the beach, calling to this dangerous man.

He lifted his gaze and looked straight into her eyes. A magnetic current arced through her, sizzling along her nerves, melting until only sensation remained. Her lips parted with the memory of his mouth moving against hers. Yesterday he had given her a taste, a tempting glimpse of the excitement she could find in the arms of a man driven by primitive instincts. A man governed by his own desires. A man of fire and passion. Since that one heated moment in his arms, she had thought of little else.

His own lips parted. He looked for a moment as though she had caught him unaware. Then those stunning eyes narrowed with the recognition of the desire she could not conceal. He lowered his eyes, his gaze brushing her breasts with a look so sultry she felt as though his hands had caressed her bare skin. Her skin tingled. Her breath stilled. Excitement thrummed through her veins until she felt giddy and trembling.

One corner of his mouth tightened. He tore his gaze away from her and dragged a deep breath into his lungs. "Shall we return to the cottage, Miss Darracott?

I prefer not to catch a lung fever from standing out in the cold while I'm soaking wet.''

Isabel flinched at the harsh tone in his voice. Her skin warmed with the realization of her own wanton thoughts. She did not want to imagine what the man thought of her.

In spite of his air of indifference, he took her arm in a gentle grasp and guided her along the narrow beach and the cliff path. They met Phoebe and three of the grooms from Bramsleigh at the top. At the moment she could scarcely even ponder how to deal with her sister. The man walking beside her presented a much more compelling dilemma.

She glanced up at the harsh set of Justin's profile. Even now her heart thudded against the wall of her chest. Something had to be done. He could not possibly continue as their guardian. In fact, the less she saw of this man, the better. She had a dreadful feeling this infatuation would only worsen. It was only a matter of time before she made a complete fool of herself with him. She had to put an end to it. Now.

Chapter Five

Strange little female. Justin looped a starched length of white lawn around his neck, trying to concentrate on the intricacies of his cravat. Yet his mind kept wandering, as the pile of wrinkled white lawn neckcloths lying on the floor at his feet could attest.

He frowned at his image in the mirror above the washstand in his room at the Royal Arms Inn. Dark, sardonic, his face issued a warning to any female who stumbled into his path: *Danger, proceed at your own risk.* Apparently Miss Isabel Darracott could not read.

This morning she had stood on that beach as bold and seductive as a siren, luring him into her arms. And he had almost tumbled straight into disaster. The woman was as pure as a babe. Not to mention the appalling fact that he himself was responsible for protecting that innocence. Did she have any idea how easily she could tempt him?

Behind him, Fielding, his valet, cleared his throat.

"Would you like me to tie that for you, Your Grace?"

Justin glanced over his shoulder at the short, slender man who took pride in seeing that his master's appearance was always impeccable. "I can manage to tie my own cravat, Fielding."

"And quite exquisitely, Your Grace. Why, just the other day Archer, Lord Shipley's valet, was inquiring about the method you employ to achieve such an original style." Fielding rubbed the side of his long nose. "I only ask if you might need some assistance this afternoon because His Grace seems a bit . . . distracted. And that is the last neckcloth starched and ready."

"His Grace can manage just fine." Justin clenched his jaw, glaring at his image in the glass. Only a fool allowed a pretty piece of muslin to warp his brain. He was many things, but he was not a fool. And no woman would make a fool of him. He concentrated on his cravat, ignoring a knock on the door while he carefully crossed the ends of the starched strip of lawn.

Fielding opened the door. A moment later the voice of one of his footmen sliced through Justin's concentration. "A Miss Darracott is here to see His Grace."

White lawn crimped beneath Justin's fingers. He closed his eyes with a silent oath. What the devil was Isabel doing here? He had told her he would return to the cottage at four to discuss the matter of his role of guardian with her. Apparently the woman was not very good at taking orders. It was just one of the things that needed to be addressed. She had been allowed to run wild long enough. A strong hand on the reins, that was precisely what the chit needed.

Fielding turned toward Justin. "A Miss Darracott is . . ."

"I heard." Justin smoothed his crumpled neckcloth between his fingers, trying to ease out the creases.

"Tell John to show the lady into my private parlor. I shall be with her directly."

Fifteen minutes later, Justin strolled into the private parlor he had engaged, prepared to do battle with a blue-eyed siren. He took two long strides into the room and froze. Phoebe sat in a chair by the hearth, nibbling a cherry tart. Isabel was nowhere in sight. "What the devil are you doing here?"

Phoebe jumped from the chair, her boots plunking against the wooden floor. "I wished to thank you for rescuing me."

Justin frowned, uncomfortable with the adoration glowing on Phoebe's young face. "Does your sister know you're here?"

Phoebe brushed crumbs from her gown. "She didn't say I couldn't come here."

Apparently lack of sense ran in the Darracott blood. "How did you get here?"

"I walked."

"It must be five miles."

Phoebe shrugged. "I like to walk."

He lifted one black brow and pinned her with a disapproving glare. "You like to get into trouble."

Phoebe glanced down at her half-eaten pastry. "I didn't mean to get into trouble. But I did so want to find the treasure. I know I ought to have listened to Isabel, but I thought if I could find the old baron's treasure, then we wouldn't have to worry about getting any help from you. Since you didn't seem to want to help us."

She peeked at him. He maintained his stern mask, ignoring her jab to his conscience. "You disobeyed your sister."

"Isabel worries so much about Eloise and me. I only wanted to help. You see, the treasure would solve all our worries. I had to try to find it. You do understand?'' She coughed into her hand. "Don't you?''

He did understand, at least in part. As a boy he had often disobeyed an order to follow some silly piece of whimsy. And all too often he had dropped straight into trouble, of a far different kind than Phoebe had. "I do not see how I can understand when I know nothing of this treasure,'' he said, his voice losing some of the harsh tone he had earlier employed.

She smiled, her small face lighting with excitement. "Back in 1649, the Baron of Bramsleigh took all of his wife's jewels and hid them, including the Bramsleigh emeralds. You see, he did not want them to fall into the hands of Cromwell. Well, *he* fell into Cromwell's hands instead. And then he died—hanged, actually—without telling anyone where he had hidden the treasure. I do think it was most inconsiderate of him to have died without telling anyone where the jewels were. Don't you?''

Justin suspected that a man facing the gallows had other things to occupy his mind. He sank into a wing-back chair near the fire and motioned for her to sit in the chair across from him. He managed to keep the humor from his voice as he spoke. "A terrible addle-pate, this old baron. Any man facing the noose should definitely reveal the location of his treasure.''

"Of course he should.'' Phoebe sat on the edge of her chair. "It would seem the mannerly thing to do. Not to mention it would have saved me a great deal of trouble.''

Justin planted his elbows on the arms of the chair and pressed his palms together. "Of course, if the old baron had revealed the location of his treasure, then it wouldn't be lost, and you wouldn't have even the chance to go dropping into pits in your quest to find it.''

"I hadn't thought of that. So perhaps we ought to

thank the old baron for not telling anyone.''

Justin rested his chin on the steeple of his fingers. Two days ago if anyone had told him the Devil of Dartmoor would find himself listening to the rambling conversation of a twelve-year-old, he would have laughed in his face. Yet, to his own astonishment, he discovered that the child amused him. ''I shall leave that communication up to you.''

Phoebe smiled at him, then took a small nibble of her tart. ''You're not at all what I expected.''

He rubbed his fingertips together, wondering how Isabel had described him to her sisters. ''What did you expect?''

She brushed crumbs from her light blue gown. ''I thought you would be older, but you're not really so very old.''

Justin's lips twitched in a smile he managed to suppress. ''I have a few good years left to me.''

Phoebe licked cherry juice from her fingertips. ''And I never expected you to be so handsome. You really could have stepped straight off the pages of some book, a knight of King Arthur come to life.''

Justin had been called handsome before. It was something he took for granted. It certainly was not an exceptional accomplishment since he had nothing at all to do with it. Trevelyan men were notoriously attractive to women. His looks had become an asset of seduction, much as wealth and power were assets to be wielded against his opponents. Yet seeing the innocent admiration in Phoebe's eyes caught him by surprise.

He could not remember the last time anyone had seen more than a black-hearted scoundrel when they looked at him, except of course his grandmother and his brother. But they were relatives. Blood had been known to cloud a person's judgment, and youth had a way of blinding one to the truth. Phoebe's adoration attested to that.

She coughed, covering her mouth with her hand. He pulled out his handkerchief and handed it to her. "You are probably catching cold. That's what happens when you go around tumbling into pits."

"Thank you." She sniffed and dabbed at her nose with the white linen.

"How is your wrist?"

She lifted her left hand, showing him the white linen bandage wrapped around her arm. "The doctor said it isn't broken. Just bruised."

"You are a very lucky girl."

She smiled. "I am lucky you were here to rescue me. I was hoping you might come to Belle's rescue the way you came to mine this morning."

Justin stiffened. "What the devil do you mean? What has happened to her?"

"Oh, she is all right. It's just our cousin Gerard. Gerard Witheridge. His father was the one who inherited Bramsleigh. Only he didn't want it, since he has a big house of his own in Hampshire, so he gave it to Gerard. And Gerard keeps bothering Isabel."

Justin set his jaw. "How is he bothering her?"

"He keeps trying to convince Belle to marry him."

An odd emotion coiled inside Justin at the thought of Isabel with another man. He curled his hands into fists against the green wool covering the arms of the chair. "He wants to marry your sister, does he?"

"He certainly does. I thought you could scare him away. I'm sure he would leave if you just gave him a severe look." Phoebe narrowed her eyes and sent him a dark glance, mimicking one of his quelling looks. "You're so very good at it."

"Thank you. I practice."

"Really?"

He nodded. "I send little children screaming for their mothers on a daily basis."

She stared at him a moment, as though she weren't quite certain what to make of him. "You're hoaxing me. Aren't you?"

He lifted one black brow, allowing her to ponder his wicked nature. "I take it your sister doesn't want to marry this cousin?"

"Oh, no. Belle doesn't want to marry anyone, unless of course it's a grand passion of the heart, like Isolde and Tristan."

"And this Gerard isn't her Tristan?"

Phoebe's expression puckered like that of someone who had just bitten into a sour apple. "Not at all. But Belle is so worried about us. I'm afraid she shall do something noble, like marry Gerard so she can get her inheritance and move us all back to Bramsleigh. It would be like her to sacrifice herself for us."

"I've never had much patience with noble sacrifices. They usually end very badly." Justin rose from his chair. "I believe it's time I met your cousin Gerard."

"This is scandalous! Justin Trevelyan, your guardian?" Gerard paced the length of the small sitting room in Bramsleigh Cottage. He pivoted at the arched entry and stared at Isabel. "Why didn't I know of this?"

"I'm certain if your family had remained in London at the time of Marlow's death, you would have known his son had succeeded to the title." Isabel sat on the sofa near the hearth, watching her cousin pace back to the windows. "But we all had a great deal to attend to during that time. I'm told the duke died a few days after Papa was murdered."

"My dear Isabel." Gerard sat beside her on the

70

sofa. Sunlight streaked through the windowpanes, glinting on his golden hair. "Something must be done. You and your sisters cannot be exposed to a man like Justin Trevelyan. He isn't fit to be in the same room with a lady of quality."

Isabel bristled at the insult to her guardian. Yesterday she might have agreed with Gerard. Today she had glimpsed a different side of Justin Trevelyan. If not for Justin, Phoebe might have drowned. "I realize the situation is a bit awkward, with the duke being a bachelor, but—"

"A bachelor! If that were the only problem." He studied her, his blue eyes filled with concern. "My dear Isabel, I do hate to speak ill of the man, but I feel you must have your eyes opened to his true nature. The truth is, Justin Trevelyan is notorious. A libertine. Why, the man keeps a dozen mistresses. And it still doesn't prevent him from dallying with any opera singer who catches his eye."

"A dozen . . ." Isabel giggled; she could not help it. Gerard looked so severe as he spoke such nonsense. "You don't actually believe any man would keep a dozen mistresses at once? Can you imagine the expense? And how would he ever find the time to dally with each of them?"

Gerard's lips tightened. "They call him the Devil of Dartmoor for good reason."

Isabel wondered how Justin felt about the title he had been given. "How very colorful."

Gerard's eyes narrowed. He had always possessed a serious nature; even as a boy he had been inclined to look down his nose and judge those around him. "Mothers warn their daughters about him."

"He is young, wealthy, and possesses an old and respected title." Not to mention the fact that Justin Trevelyan was one of the most attractive men she had ever glimpsed, Isabel thought. "I suspect more than a few mothers have pushed their daughters into his path."

"Isabel, this is a serious situation. If you have no thought for your own safety, then you must think of Eloise."

"You don't mean to imply that the Duke of Marlow would try to seduce a seventeen-year-old girl?"

"Precisely."

"Rubbish!"

Gerard sat back as though she had slapped him. "I don't think you realize the extent of this man's villainy."

She did, however, appreciate the full extent of Gerard's priggish nature. "I seldom judge a person based on rumor."

Gerard huffed. "His exploits are legendary. Any woman who has a care for her reputation would not be seen with him."

"Have you ever known the duke to have ruined an innocent female of good family?"

Gerard frowned. "Not that I'm aware of."

"Since we are innocent females of what I trust you would agree is a good family, you have nothing to fear for us."

"But I do fear for you." Gerard took her hand between both of his. "I see only one possible solution to this dilemma. You must marry me, and come to live at Bramsleigh Hall where you belong."

Tall and slender, with golden hair and blue eyes, he had the look of a fairy-tale prince. Unfortunately, this particular prince was also as exciting as a well-worn riding boot. "Gerard, we've discussed this before."

"Circumstances have altered. I realize I may not be the most stimulating fellow, but I shall make you a reliable husband."

"Gerard, I—"

"It would seem you have company, Miss Darra-cott."

Isabel started at the sound of that deep, familiar voice. She turned and found Justin standing beneath the arched entry. Sunlight slanted across one broad shoulder, leaving his face in shadow. His presence filled the small room, crowding the sunlight, the air, until the raw power of the man pressed against her.

Gerard squeezed her hand so hard it ached. He too was staring at Justin Trevelyan, his eyes wide, his mouth slightly slack in shock. Justin moved toward her, a king entering his castle. He glanced to where Gerard clutched her hand and then fixed her cousin with a dark glare. Gerard immediately released her hand and shot to his feet. Isabel gathered her wits and introduced her cousin to her guardian. Justin met Gerard's stiff greeting with cool cordiality.

Gerard waited until Justin had taken a seat on an upholstered armchair near Isabel before once again sitting beside her. "I was quite surprised to hear you were guardian to my cousins," he said, a note of censure in his voice.

Justin rested his chin on the steeple of his fingers and met Gerard's cool stare with one of his own. "When I entered the room, I got the impression you still weren't aware of the fact that Miss Darracott had a guardian."

Color rose in Gerard's cheeks. "Isabel and I have known each other since we were children. We are cousins. I'm certain you can understand why there would be an easy familiarity between us."

Justin's lips curved into an icy imitation of a smile. "Few people can be certain of what I shall think of any given circumstance. Fewer still can surmise what I shall do about one."

How could anyone manage to look so menacing with a smile? Isabel wondered. Beneath that chilling smile, Gerard froze into a portrait of righteous indignation, for once at a loss for words. She touched her cousin's arm. "The duke and I have a great deal to discuss. I hope you don't mind."

"No, not at all." Gerard snatched the opportunity to leave, as she had hoped. After a brief and very formal farewell to Justin, he left the house.

Sunlight streamed through the window near Justin, illuminating the smug curve of his smile. He looked like a lion who had just polished off a plump rabbit.

"Do you practice trying to intimidate people, or is it a natural talent?" Isabel asked.

Justin shrugged. "I was only doing what Phoebe asked me to do."

"Phoebe?"

"She was under the impression your cousin was bothering you, so she asked me to come to your rescue. She is the one who suggested I frighten him away with one of my severe looks."

"Phoebe came to see you?"

Justin leaned back in his chair, a ruler passing judgment. "It would seem you have a difficult time controlling the child."

Isabel squeezed her hands in her lap. "This has not been the best of days, but I assure you Phoebe is usually quite manageable."

He planted his elbow against the arm of the chair and rested his chin on his open palm. "From what I understand, you've been managing this household since your mother died ten years ago."

"Father was a scholar, not inclined to practical matters. It was only natural for me to help him manage the household."

"And now you assume you should continue managing the household. Without interference from me."

She rose, too agitated to remain sitting calmly before him. She moved to the window beside his chair. "I can't imagine any reason why you would wish to remain in this awkward position."

His gaze touched her, as intense as the sunlight streaming through the windows, and every bit as warm. "When you came to London yesterday, what were you going to ask of my father?"

She hesitated a moment, uncomfortable with discussing her situation with this man. Yet she did not have a choice. "I assume you know the restrictions placed upon our inheritances."

He nodded, his expression revealing none of his thoughts. "You must marry to receive the money. And you can only marry with your guardian's consent."

She could not imagine ever asking Justin Trevelyan for permission to marry another man. "I'm not at all certain what Father was thinking when he had that entered into his will. I am certain he never dreamed we would be in this situation."

Justin glanced around the small room. "That is safe enough to say."

Isabel stared out the window, looking past the narrow lawn to the immense black traveling coach in the lane, the elegant conveyance at odds with the humble setting. "The will gives our guardian the freedom to bestow upon us any amount of pin money he sees appropriate. I was hoping your father might turn the entirety of my inheritance over to me."

"To what purpose?" he asked, his deep voice colored with a trace of surprise.

"I thought I might invest most of the money on the

Exchange. With the interest, we could afford a more suitable house. And next year I hope to have enough to finance a Season for Eloise.''

From the corner of her eye she could see him frowning at her. ''What do you know of investing on the exchange?''

''Gerard has had some success in his investments, and he is more than willing to help us.''

''I'm certain he is.'' Justin slowly rubbed his palms together. ''If I were inclined to dispose of your inheritance in such a manner, you would be left without a dowry, Miss Darracott. A definite deficit when you decide to marry.''

She waved aside his words. ''I'm well past the age of worrying about my dowry.''

''Hmm, you consider yourself a spinster.''

His casual use of the word pricked her pride. She focused her attention on the ducal crest painted on the door of his coach. She stared at that pouncing golden lion on a field of scarlet and suppressed a scream of frustration rising up inside her. ''Not every woman is destined to marry. Some of us were meant to be aunts.''

''And here I thought you were waiting for your Tristan.''

She glanced at him, appalled to see him smiling at her, as though he found her terribly amusing. ''Tristan?''

Justin left his chair. His arm brushed against hers as he leaned against the window frame, the brief graze scattering tingles along her skin. ''Phoebe sees you as Isolde waiting for Tristan.''

''I'm afraid Phoebe has a horribly romantic nature.''

He lifted a lock of hair that had fallen from her pins and tumbled over her shoulder. Since she no longer had a maid to dress her hair, it seemed part of it was

76

forever coming undone. Usually it didn't matter to her. Today, with this man, she certainly didn't want to appear a dowd.

"And you, Miss Darracott? Do you have a horribly romantic nature?"

"Perhaps, when I was her age, I indulged in romantic notions."

He drew the strands of her hair through his fingers, the soft caress whispering across her skin. "You have had a great deal of responsibility for a woman your age. When you should have been going to parties and balls and acting as silly as a schoolgirl, you were taking care of your family."

"You make me sound a martyr. I'm not."

"Modest. Generous. Not to mention brave enough to save my life." He stared down at the lock of hair lying across his palm, a wistful smile curving his lips. "Miss Darracott, you terrify me."

The dark currents in his voice swept around her, tugging on her in unseen ways. "I doubt there is much that terrifies you."

Thick black lashes lifted, revealing emotions in the turbulent depths of his gray-green eyes—undisguised desire, the same raw hunger she had tasted in his kiss. The warmth of his body filled the space between them, beckoning her. The intriguing scent of sandalwood soap swirled around her. He stood so close, all she need do was raise up on her toes and she could touch her lips to his. The warmth of his breath touched her cheek. She felt herself lifting toward him, like a flower reaching for the sun.

He lowered his head toward her. Excitement rippled through her with the certainty of his kiss. He halted, like a man who had just bumped against an unseen barrier. Muttering an oath under his breath, he turned away from her. She flinched, as if she were a sleepwalker jerked from slumber.

He marched away from her in long strides. She stared at his broad back, bewildered by his mercurial moods. What had she done to anger him? One moment she felt a warm current coiling around them, drawing them together. The next he was marching toward the door, leaving without so much as a word.

He turned at the entry and fixed her with a stern stare, all the warmth washed from his eyes. "I shall send two of my footmen to you this afternoon. I expect you and your sisters to be packed and ready to leave by ten tomorrow morning."

She blinked, stunned by his autocratic command. "Leave? And may I ask precisely where we may be going?"

"I have decided you shall come to London and live with my grandmother."

"We could not possibly impose on your grandmother."

His full lips tightened into a narrow line. "You shall do as I decide. And I have decided this is the best course of action."

Blood surged through her veins with her mounting anger. "If you think you can simply march in here and order us about as though we were—"

"Children?" he supplied, smiling at her.

She glared at him. "Slaves."

"You and your sisters are under my protection, Miss Darracott. I certainly do not intend to allow you to continue living in this hovel."

She planted her hands on her hips. "And what about my proposal?"

"Your proposal? My dear Miss Darracott, only a fool would drop twenty thousand pounds into the hands of an infant who has been wrapped in cotton wool all of her life.''

"I am not an infant. And I am fully capable of handling my own finances.''

He laughed, the sound a deep rumble of pure sarcasm. "Start packing. We leave precisely at ten tomorrow morning.''

"Ooooh.'' She stamped her foot as he marched away from her. She ran after him, catching him at the door. "And what of Mrs. Tweedbury, and Roland? They came with us when they could have done better at Bramsleigh. Do you expect me to turn them off?''

He shrugged. "Take them with you, if you like. I'm certain Sophia will find a place for them.''

Her heart pounded a steady beat of indignation against her ribs. "You really are the most infuriating creature I have ever met.''

He grinned at her. "I don't know why you say that, Miss Darracott. I am giving you precisely what you want. A comfortable home for your sisters. Security. A glittering prospect for the future.''

"I don't want you to give us anything. I am quite capable of taking care of my family, if you will only give me what is properly mine.''

"You are my responsibility, Miss Darracott.''

She would rather boil in oil before she became a responsibility to this man. "You know very well my father never intended you to be our guardian.''

"Unfortunately my father did not share your father's views.''

"If you would only agree to name me as guardian, you could wash your hands of us.''

"That I cannot do.''

"May I ask why?''

"I have already given you my answer. You and your sisters have been placed under my protection. I shall see you tomorrow morning precisely at ten. I trust you will be ready.''

Although she recognized the opportunity he presented for her sisters, she refused to be dictated to as though she were a schoolgirl. ''I will go under one condition.''

His eyes narrowed. ''You will go, Miss Darracott. End of discussion.''

''Are you prepared to carry me out of this house kicking and screaming?''

His lips pulled into an icy smile. ''I will see you and your sisters settled with my grandmother, Miss Darracott. If you had any sense you would not be arguing with me, unless, of course, you are prepared to accept the consequences.''

She stepped closer, ignoring this man's attempt to intimidate her. ''If your grandmother does not wish for us to stay, I would ask you to allow me to set up my own establishment with the money set aside for my dowry. I refuse to be a burden to anyone.''

Justin released his breath in an agitated huff that touched her face with warmth. ''There is no need for such histrionics. My grandmother will be delighted to have you.''

''You're quite certain of yourself, aren't you?''

His smile turned devilish. ''In all regards. Be ready by ten, Miss Darracott.''

An unspoken threat darkened his words. Isabel had little doubt the brute would toss her over his shoulder and carry her from the cottage if she defied him. She stood on the threshold of the cottage and watched him climb into his elegant black coach. Heart hammering against her ribs, she watched as six gray horses pulled the coach away from the cottage. Only when the coach had disappeared from view did she step back into the cottage and close the door. She turned and found Eloise and Phoebe standing in the hall, watching her.

"Are we really going to London?" Eloise asked, her voice betraying her excitement.

"Yes, it looks as though we are," Isabel said, a thousand thoughts spinning in her head, most of them revolving around a handsome, infuriating devil. She was tempted to tell the arrogant aristocrat to go to blazes, regardless of the consequences. Yet no matter how satisfying that might be, she had Eloise and Phoebe to consider. It would not do to allow them to see their sister hauled out of the cottage like a sack of potatoes.

"But what about the treasure?" Phoebe asked. "I thought the duke would stay and help us find it."

"He probably is not fond of falling into pits," Eloise said.

"It was only the first time I ever fell into a pit. And the duke handled the situation like a true knight of legend." Phoebe coughed into her hand.

"Are you feeling all right?" Isabel asked.

Phoebe shrugged. "I'm just a little achy."

"From falling into a pit," Eloise said.

Isabel thought of what had happened this morning. Justin had been ready to sacrifice his life for Phoebe. A few hours later he was dictating his commands like a king dealing with a nettlesome peasant. The man was a constant contradiction. A puzzle where all the pieces didn't fit.

The Devil of Dartmoor. According to Gerard, the Duke of Marlow was a scoundrel with no chance for redemption. Yet she suspected there was a great deal more to Justin Trevelyan than his reputation would lead one to suppose. She had witnessed his bravery. She had also witnessed his harsh, high-handed arrogance.

"I'm certain if we were more careful, we could find

the treasure. Especially with the duke's help," Phoebe said.

"We need to forget about the treasure for now." Isabel slipped her arm around Phoebe's small shoulders. "We must think of all the exciting things we shall do and see in London."

Phoebe's expression brightened. "The Tower! Do you think the duke would take us to see it?"

"I promise we shall see it, regardless of whether or not the duke chooses to accompany us." It would be better to see as little of the Duke of Marlow as possible, Isabel thought. No matter what the puzzling pieces of his personality might be, one thing was a certainty: he was very dangerous. Only a fool would try to shave the beard from a lion to see what was hidden beneath. She had no intention of allowing the man to sink his claws into her.

Chapter Six

"I'm sorry, Your Grace; Miss Darracott said you weren't to be coming in."

Justin set his jaw. His expression revealed nothing, he assured himself. Even though he felt as though he had been backhanded across the face. He glared at the short, gray-haired woman who stood like a plump terrier in the doorway of Bramsleigh Cottage. "I assume you are Mrs. Tweedbury."

She eased a little behind the door. "That I am, Your Grace. Miss Darracott told me that when you came here this morning I was to have you wait out here while I go fetch her."

"Should I assume Miss Darracott and her sisters are not planning to leave for London this morning?"

"I'm afraid they aren't."

For the first time in his life he had actually attempted to be responsible, and Isabel Darracott had thrown all of his good intentions back in his face.

Well, so be it. If the ungrateful chit wanted to stay in this hovel, then she could very well stay. But he would have a few choice words with her first. "Step aside."

Mrs. Tweedbury's eyes grew as round as pennies as she stared up at him. "But Your Grace, Miss Darracott said you should—"

"Unless you want me to pick you up and move you, Mrs. Tweedbury, I suggest you step aside."

"No, Your Grace." She jumped back when he took a step toward her. "I mean yes, Your Grace."

He strode into the narrow hall. "Where is Miss Darracott?"

"Upstairs, Your Grace. She'll be in the room that's the first to the left."

His booted heels tapped the rough oak planks as he marched to the stairs. *Confounded female.* He took the stairs two at a time. She did not have the sense to see what was best for her. Well, he intended to wash his hands of her.

She would regret this. She would wither away here, doom her sisters to her fate. They would all end up dried-up old spinsters. Or worse, they would end up married to farmers. He smiled. Yes, that would serve Isabel well. He threw open the door without knocking. Yet the caustic words burning his throat lodged there at the sight that greeted him.

Isabel rose from a wooden armchair near the bed and hurried toward him. An icy hand gripped his vitals as Justin took in the scene. Although the curtains were drawn, there was enough light in the room to see Phoebe. She lay asleep in the bed, snuggled beneath a colorful chintz quilt. As he watched, she rolled her head on the pillow, a pitiful moan escaping her lips to twist around his heart.

Isabel took his arm and ushered him out of the

room. "You should not be here," she said, keeping her voice low.

"What the devil is wrong with her?" he asked, matching her low tone. "Have you summoned a doctor?"

Isabel closed the door. "The doctor was here shortly after midnight."

"Is it serious?"

She looked up at him, her brow furrowed in a frown. "Have you ever had measles, Duke?"

"Measles?"

"The doctor said once you've had them you generally do not get them again. I had them when I was six. But Eloise has never had them. I've told her to stay away from the sickroom, but I'm afraid it's too late. She started coughing and sniffling this morning. I wouldn't be surprised if she is still too ill to leave her bed by tomorrow."

Justin released his pent-up breath. "At least it's nothing serious."

She rubbed her temples. "Have you had them?"

Justin could not recall ever suffering from this particular ailment. Still, he was a grown man. He was not about to succumb to some childhood malaise. "There is nothing to worry about."

"The doctor said it's very contagious."

Justin smiled. "Is that why you stationed Mrs. Tweedbury at your door? Were you protecting me?"

"I was trying. I do hope you didn't terrify poor Mrs. Tweedbury."

He shrugged. "I imagine she shall recover."

She crossed her arms at her waist. "I suppose it was too much to ask of you to do as I requested."

"I saw no reason behind the request."

She shook her head. "I would imagine that one of

these days, your arrogance will cause you great harm.''

Justin was unaccustomed to having anyone, except his grandmother or brother, speak to him in such a candid, if not entirely impudent manner. His rank did have its advantages. Still, oddly enough, he found Isabel's candor intriguing. ''And has your sharp tongue ever caused you great harm, Miss Darracott?''

Her lips tipped into an unexpected smile. ''I would rather be harmed by the truth than by a lie.''

''Honesty is a quality I have seldom associated with the female of our species.''

A glint of humor filled her eyes. ''Perhaps you've been associating with the wrong females.''

In her own direct manner, she was flirting with him. She had a guileless quality about her he found utterly enchanting. Still, she had no idea the trouble she could get into by tempting a devil. But he did. He should turn around and leave before he caught himself doing something unforgivably foolish. He should walk out of this house, climb into his coach, and not stop until he was back in London. He could send a coach for Isabel and the girls when Phoebe recovered. Still, something anchored him here. ''You look exhausted.''

She shoved a loose curl back from her face. ''I was up most of the night with Phoebe.''

''Get some rest, before you find yourself ill.''

She shook her head. ''I don't want to leave Phoebe unattended. And Mrs. Tweedbury has enough to do without asking her to take over my duties in the sick-room.''

''I'll sit with Phoebe.''

Her lips parted with her sudden surprise. ''I couldn't ask you to—''

''You're not asking. I'm telling you to get some rest.''

Her brows lifted. "Must everything be an order with you?"

"It's part of my arrogant nature." He grinned at her. "Get some rest, Miss Darracott. I shall look after your sister."

"I'm certain I leave her in capable hands." She touched his arm, and he experienced an odd constriction in his chest.

Startled by his strange reaction to this woman, he stared after her, watching as she walked down the narrow hall. He was still staring when she turned at the doorway of her chamber and smiled at him. He turned away from that siren smile and escaped into Phoebe's room. Still, he could not escape the warmth flooding his blood.

It must be lust, he assured himself. Certainly it wasn't anything to concern him. He knew lust. Understood it. He frequently lusted after attractive females. It was his nature. This attraction was no different, except of course that he could do nothing to appease it. Until he reached London and Vachel's. An enthusiastic tumble with a pretty whore would cure him.

"Is that you, Duke?" Phoebe asked.

"It is." Justin went to her side. In the dim light he could see the flush in her cheeks.

"Could I have something to drink?" She licked her lips. "I'm very thirsty."

Justin found a pitcher of barley water and a glass on a small table near the bed. Although he had no experience dealing with ill children, he knew he could certainly handle the situation. He filled the glass and offered it to the girl.

Phoebe struggled to sit. "Could you help me?"

"Of course." He slipped his arm around her narrow back and propped her up so she could sip the water.

When she finished, he lowered her once more to her pillow.

"I'm sorry. I wanted to go to London today. I would have been ready. We all would have been ready."

"Are you looking forward to going to London?" Justin sat in the chair by her bed.

She smiled. "Oh, yes. I want to see the Tower. And all the museums. Everything."

He smoothed his hand over her feverish brow. "Then you shall see them."

She closed her eyes. "I'm glad you're here."

He stroked her hair, hoping to lull her back to sleep. It wasn't until he heard her breath ease into a slow, steady rhythm that he realized he was smiling.

A single lamp burned on the small pedestal table in the sitting room of Bramsleigh Cottage, casting a soft, flickering light over the man sitting in the chair near the windows. Isabel handed Justin a glass of brandy and settled on the sofa near his chair. For the past several days, the duke had shared the duties of nursing her sisters. If she had not seen for herself the care he had given Eloise and Phoebe—reading to them, fetching drinks, and coaxing one or the other to eat—she might never have believed the worldly Duke of Marlow capable of such tenderness. Still, she suspected there was a great deal more to Justin Trevelyan than he allowed the world to see.

"I don't know how I would have managed these past few days if you hadn't been here." She lifted her glass to him in a salute. "Thank you."

He frowned, looking uncomfortable with her gratitude. "A poor guardian I would be if I ran off and left you here with two invalids."

Sensing she would only force him further into a

defensive posture, she neglected to mention the fact that he could have sent her one or more of his servants to help. She lifted her brandy snifter. The rich bouquet flooded her senses before she sipped the amber liquid. Heat poured across her tongue, sliding downward with the potent liquor, spreading warmth across her chest.

Justin's long lashes swept downward as he sipped his brandy. "Excellent."

Lamplight glinted on the sheen left upon his lips. Warmth curled in her belly as she remembered what it was like to taste brandy upon his lips. "I kept a few bottles from Father's cellar when we moved to the cottage."

"And Witheridge didn't object?"

"Only the house and land were entailed to Gerard's father. My sisters and I inherited the furnishings, the books in the library, and the contents of the wine cellar. After his father gave him Bramsleigh, Gerard gave us the cottage in exchange for most of the rest."

"How generous of him," he said, his voice dripping sarcasm.

Justin had removed his coat and cravat soon after dinner. His shirt had fallen open at the neck, revealing an intriguing shadow of dark curls beneath the hollow of his neck. It seemed so intimate sitting alone with him at this time of night, while the girls slept soundly in their beds. It made her imagine things she should not. "Gerard has actually been very kind. If he hadn't given us the cottage, I'm not certain what we would have done."

Justin looked down into his brandy. "If I had known of the situation, I would have taken care of it long ago."

"You mustn't feel we've been completely miserable here. We've managed."

A muscle flickered in his cheek with the clenching

89

of his jaw. "You've managed to go without."

"There are only a few things I truly regret doing without."

He looked at her. "Such as?"

She hesitated, not wishing his pity for her loss. "I wish we could have kept our horses."

"I'm surprised Witheridge wouldn't allow you to keep them in the Bramsleigh stables."

"I'm certain he would have. But I didn't wish to rely on his charity."

Justin rolled his glass between his palms. "I can understand why you wouldn't like to be in his debt."

"I prefer not to be in anyone's debt." She lifted her snifter and took a deep breath of the heady fragrance before savoring a sip of the aged liquor.

Justin tilted his head, his lips tipping into a grin. "I never would have guessed you would enjoy brandy, Miss Darracott."

"At times I used to enjoy a glass at night, with my brother and father." She looked down into her glass, seeing her reflection cast by candlelight in the amber liquid. A familiar ache tightened in her chest when she realized she would never again see her brother's smile, or hear her father's gentle voice. "We would sit in the library, talking for hours after the girls had retired for the evening."

"You were very close to them," he said, his dark voice barely lifting above the rattle of rain against the windowpanes.

Isabel slid her fingertip along a bevel cut into the heavy crystal glass, one of the few treasures she had kept from her home. "There are times when I wonder why things happened as they did. My father and Stephen had years ahead of them. All of that time was stolen from them. From all of us. And for what? They

90

were murdered for the sake of a few coins. It just doesn't make sense to me.''

Justin had leaned forward, and now he cupped her cheek in his big hand, his long fingers brushing warmth against the sensitive skin beneath her ear. She glanced up, meeting his gaze. She saw a wealth of understanding in his eyes, as though he had felt pain as deep as her own.

''There is very little in this world that makes sense. But the strong somehow manage to survive. You're a survivor, Miss Darracott.''

''There is strength in you, Duke. I imagine you could survive anything set in your path.''

He smoothed his fingers over her cheek, his touch so gentle it tore a ragged sigh from her lips. Something shifted in his expression, exposing his emotions. She saw a lingering sadness behind his carefully fashioned facade, an ache of loneliness and pain that made her want to curl her arms around his neck and draw him close. Yet the glimpse behind the mask was fleeting.

He drew back his hand and glanced away from her. A muscle shifted in his cheek with the clenching and unclenching of his jaw as he stared out through the rain-swept windows. ''Why did your father go to London that last time?''

She leaned back against the stiff sofa, trying to ignore the warmth his touch had ignited in her blood. ''He was going to attend a private auction of medieval manuscripts. One of the collectors he knew, a man named Rennison, had died unexpectedly; apparently he broke his neck in a fall from his horse. His widow decided to sell the manuscripts. I remember Father was particularly excited about the auction because he knew the Philistine would be there.''

Justin lifted one thick black brow. ''The Philistine?''

"His most fierce rival, Eldridge Belcham. For years they taunted one another whenever they would acquire a new treasure."

Justin swirled the brandy in his glass, a thoughtful expression on his handsome face. "Which one of them walked away with the Rennison collection?"

"Father died the night before the auction. Belcham bought the collection." Isabel drew in her breath, easing the growing tightness in her chest. "When Belcham discovered Father had died, he raced to Bramsleigh to buy his entire collection."

Justin frowned. "Did you sell it to him?"

Isabel shook her head. "You will probably think me foolish, but I couldn't stand to have him take Father's collection, for any amount of money. The girls and I decided we would keep it, as a sort of memorial."

"I understand."

"Belcham didn't. In fact, every couple of months he comes by to see if I've changed my mind."

Justin grinned. "I believe that will soon stop. Once he realizes I am in charge of that collection."

"I am not accustomed to having someone handle my affairs."

"You can rest assured, Miss Darracott, that I can manage things."

His air of command made it easy to believe he could handle anything. Somehow, in the past few days, she had grown accustomed to relying upon his strength. It was the first time in a very long time that she felt she did not carry the entire weight of the world upon her shoulders. "I'm certain you can. You seem a man of remarkable resources."

A curious expression crossed his features, as though she had surprised him. "I trust you shall be ready to travel the day after tomorrow."

"Yes. The girls are looking forward to the trip."

He glanced at her. "And you?"

"I've always wondered what it might be like to live in London."

"Anxious for balls and parties and all that nonsense?"

"I'm not unlike any other woman. I enjoy dancing and conversation."

"You're wrong, Miss Darracott. You are not at all like the women in London. And if you should try to ape them, you shall become a simpering bore."

The bitterness coloring his voice surprised her. "I was under the impression you enjoyed the women of London."

He rolled his snifter between his palms, and she caught herself staring at his hands. His hands bespoke strength and elegance; they were lightly shaded with dark masculine hair, his fingers long and tapered. She wondered what it might be like to feel his hands against her skin, brushing her arms, drawing her into his embrace.

"I see Witheridge has been telling you tales of my disreputable ways."

Although his tone remained light, she sensed a barely restrained anger behind his words. She wondered what he truly thought of being considered one of the most notorious men in London. "I'm curious. You don't actually keep twelve mistresses at a time, do you?"

He blinked. "Is that what Witheridge told you?"

"Yes. But I discounted the tale." She resisted the urge to ask him if he currently had a mistress—a woman who had the pleasure of holding him through the night, of touching him, of kissing him. "I mean if you had a dozen mistresses, you wouldn't have time to do anything else but spend time with them."

He laughed, the sound a deep rumble in the small

room. "I've never found it wise to keep more than three mistresses at any one time."

Three! Isabel maintained her smile, hoping she appeared much more sophisticated than she felt. "What do you do if they attend the same party at the same time?"

Mischief glinted in his eyes. "Pay each of them an equal amount of attention."

She could not imagine sharing this man with any other woman. "And does it cause any amount of animosity among them?"

"Only if I've made the mistake of giving one of them a more elaborate piece of jewelry than the others. I'm usually careful."

He had such a cavalier attitude toward women. Cold. Calculating. As though he had reduced the entire relationship of man to woman to the most primitive level. "Have you had much trouble with them lately?"

Justin grinned at her. "Are you asking me if I currently have a mistress, Miss Darracott?"

Heat crept upward across her neck. "I assume you do."

He lifted one black brow. "I do not."

She silently gave thanks to heaven. "Then you must be looking. What type of woman do you choose as a mistress? How do you go about it?"

He swirled his brandy in his glass again, staring into the amber liquid, his expression as hard as his voice. "There are any number of women who flit about on the fringe of the ton. Born with beauty and ambition, they manage to catch the eye of men who are wealthy enough to satisfy their greedy little hearts. Then there are the widows of the ton, those who prefer discreet affairs over shackles to another man."

Physical liaisons. The coupling of bodies. Nothing more. She felt as though she belonged to a different world. She could not imagine giving herself freely to a man without a sense of connection to him, without giving her heart as well as her body.

He looked up at her, the expression in his eyes as cold as the North Sea. "And of course, there are those women who adore their husband's wealth and position, but despise the man."

"You have had affairs with married women?"

"I see I have shocked you, Miss Darracott."

"I suppose it shouldn't surprise me. But it does. I have always thought a husband and wife should share their lives in such a way that there would be no room for infidelity."

He studied her as though she were some rare species he had just plucked from the far side of the world. "I didn't think you had any romantic notions left, Miss Darracott."

"Is it so romantic to believe in affection between a husband and wife? To give your loyalty, your respect, your love, and expect the same in return?"

His smile lacked the cutting mockery she had seen before. "Romantic and rare."

"I realize you think me naive, but my parents shared that kind of devotion. They loved each other dearly. After my mother died, my father never even considered finding another wife."

Justin's expression altered, the smile slipping from his lips. He looked past her, as though he could see something more in the shadows, something that filled his eyes with a haunted sadness.

"Is something wrong?" she asked, touching his forearm. Powerful muscles tensed beneath her palm. "Have I said something to offend you?"

"No." He pulled away from her and rose from his chair. "It's getting late. I shall see you tomorrow."

Isabel watched him walk toward the door. The man

was a puzzle, and more than a few of the pieces were hidden. A wise woman would leave him be. A wise woman would not even think of uncovering the man hidden behind his arrogant mask. "You really aren't what you appear, are you?"

Chapter Seven

Justin froze at her soft statement. He turned to face her and found her smiling at him. "That depends on what you think you see."

"I see a man who would like people to think him harsh and unyielding. Arrogant. Selfish. Rude."

Justin placed his hand over his heart, hiding the true sting of her words behind a smile. "Be careful, my dear Miss Darracott, I might swoon from the flattery."

Amusement glittered in her eyes. "Oh, but I'm not finished."

"I was afraid of that."

Isabel glanced down into her glass as though in it she could see all of his secrets. He watched her, assuring himself he didn't care what this woman thought of him. Still, he could not deny the anxiety churning in his gut at what she might say.

"When I look at you, I see a man who would like the world to think him devoid of kindness. A man who does what he pleases, when he pleases, and the rest of the world can go straight to blazes.''

''You paint a pretty portrait, Miss Darracott.''

She looked up and smiled at him, a hint of mischief in her beautiful eyes. ''But not an accurate one.''

''What is that to mean?''

She placed her glass on the table and rose from the sofa. ''Although it's the last thing you would like anyone to know, you're really a very kind, exceptionally generous man.''

She caught him unaware, as she often did, hitting him straight in the solar plexus with one of her candid remarks. ''I never realized you had a propensity to see saints where there were only sinners.''

''Don't worry, your secret is safe with me. I shan't tarnish your reputation by telling anyone that you have a noble heart.''

''A noble...'' He tossed back his head and laughed, the deep sound rumbling like thunder in the small room. ''You're a pretty little sapskull if you imagine me some kind of saint.''

''Oh, I don't imagine you a saint. But you have been all kindness to me and my sisters. You shall have to forgive me if I hold you in high esteem.''

''What if all my kindness were merely a ploy, Miss Darracott?'' he asked, keeping his voice dangerously low. ''A means to get you into my bed?''

She blinked. Her lips parted without a word before she regained her composure. ''You're trying to shock me.''

''They call me the Devil of Dartmoor for good reason. I'm a debauchee, my dear, a disgusting beast who cannot be trusted around lovely ladies. Mothers hide their daughters when I enter a room. Keep that in mind next time you start to see saints where there are only sinners.''

Isabel's soft mouth pulled into a tight line. Her eyes

filled with a hard gleam. "From what I have heard, Duke, you have never once in your life seduced an innocent female."

Justin managed a smile, hoping the mockery he had cultivated over the years would not fail him. "There is always a first time."

Doubt flickered over her features before succumbing to grim determination. She moved toward him. "Are you trying to frighten me?"

"I am trying to warn you, Miss Darracott. Do not tempt a devil. You will get burned."

She paused a scant few inches in front of him, so close he could smell the delicious fragrance of lavender warmed by her skin. Much too close. "A woman can only be seduced if she wants to be seduced."

"And you are impervious to the devil's charm?"

She glanced away from him, hiding the expression in her eyes. "I am not as naive as you think. You would never involve yourself in some careless affair with an innocent female of good family. You prefer women of the world, those who would not be injured by a casual dalliance. You said as much yourself."

The warmth of her radiated against him, threatening his resolve. He wanted nothing more than to take her in his arms, to kiss those sweet lips, to bury himself deep within her warmth. "You have a great deal of faith in my honor. More than you should."

She looked up at him and smiled, warm and generous without a glimmer of artifice. "I have seen your bravery. As well as your kindness. I know you have a noble heart, even if you would prefer that no one knew you have a heart at all."

Justin touched her cheek, absorbing the warmth and softness of her skin. He could not deny it; he burned for Isabel. Lust was not new to him, even if his desire for this woman burned deeper than any flame he had ever felt. Still, this affliction would pass. He knew himself too well to believe he would ever be faithful to one woman.

If he were a different kind of man, if he truly had a noble heart, he might have considered a future with this woman. But a devil could not be redeemed, even by a blue-eyed angel. "I have no intention of ever entering that constrictive hypocrisy known as matrimony, Belle. If you have any thoughts about trapping me with your innocent wiles, consider yourself warned. You will get hurt."

Isabel stepped back as though he had slapped her. "Not every woman is out to trap a man into marriage."

He shrugged, knowing he appeared harsh. Yet it was his only defense against this beguiling female. No matter how much he wanted her, he hadn't fallen so low that he would destroy her to enjoy what in the end would be a momentary pleasure. "I learned a long time ago how the prospect of obtaining a husband with a title and wealth could bring out the huntress in members of your sex. You should know this: I have decided that any female who throws herself into my path deserves what she gets."

She marched toward the windows, where she stood and stared out into the rain-swept night. "You cannot abide anyone thinking you honorable. Or generous. Or kind. You must have everyone just a little afraid of you. I actually believe you enjoy being called the Devil of Dartmoor. You certainly wouldn't want anyone to know you are really very amiable."

"Amiable?" A word reserved for elderly gentlemen, tamed cubs, and drawing room dandies. Certainly not one to describe the Devil of Dartmoor. "I am not amiable. I have never been amiable. Nor shall I ever be amiable.''

She turned to face him. ''You are very dear, actually.''

''Dear?'' He stared at her, his heart pounding an appalling rhythm against the wall of his chest. Did she think he was some stripling lad? A drawing room ornament? Some puppy sniffing after her skirts? Or did she think of him as some doddering old uncle?

''And incredibly chivalrous.''

He cringed at the insipid thought. The blood pounded so loudly in his ears, he could scarcely hear her next words.

''You are also terribly gallant.''

''Gallant!'' He would show her just how gallant he was. He closed the distance between them, employing a purposeful, predatory stalk. A flicker of surprise touched her features. Yet she stood her ground, facing the devil without the good sense to fear him. ''Let's get this straight, Miss Darracott. I do not possess an amiable or sweet bone in my body. Neither do I coddle any gallant or chivalrous aspirations. And I assure you, I never shall.''

She smiled up at him. ''Did I mention you also have a truly heroic spirit?''

''Enough!'' He wrapped his arms around her waist and hauled her up against his chest and off the floor. He clamped his mouth over her lips, intent on teaching her a lesson. He would show her just how dangerous he was. Heroic. Chivalrous. Gallant! He was a scoundrel. A rake. A libertine with no hope of redemption.

He slanted his mouth over hers, forcing her to taste the raw hunger burning inside him. This was what happened when pretty little girls toyed with nasty men who spent their nights wallowing with prostitutes and expensive society whores. He meant to shock her. To frighten her. To teach her to keep a safe distance. Perhaps then he would be safe from her.

Yet instead of fighting him, as any intelligent maiden with a thought of maintaining her innocence ought, this strange female threw her arms around his neck and returned his kiss. She held him as though she had no intention of letting him go in this lifetime. Her mouth moved beneath his, soft and eager, like sweet spring rain dripping from the petals of a rose.

The warmth of her skin brewed the flavor of lavender and the fragrance of wool into an intriguing essence that was hers alone. The scent spilled into his lungs, intoxicating his blood with every breath he took. The fury evaporated from his kiss, stripping him of his defenses. Unguarded, he fell beneath her innocent assault.

He tightened his arms around her, seeking her warmth as a man trapped in the endless depths of winter. The gentle curves of her body nestled against his hardened frame. His muscles dissolved into marmalade.

He staggered back, his calves colliding with the sofa. She clung to him, her arms clasped around his neck, her lips moving sweetly against his. His tight grip on her waist slackened. She slid down the length of him, her delicate curves gliding warmly against him, until her toes touched the threadbare carpet. Still she held him, as though she would still be holding him when the last star faded from the sky.

He could not remember a time when a woman had felt like this in his arms: incredibly innocent, burning with her first taste of passion. Blood pounded through his veins, singing out a horrifying truth—he needed her. He slid his trembling hands down her back, gripped her slender waist, wanting her in a way he had never wanted anything before.

She kissed him as though she cared for him. Not his blasted title. Not his money. She kissed him as though she truly believed all that nonsense about his sterling nature. As though she needed him as much as he needed her.

The part of his brain still functioning loudly recounted all the reasons he had never in his life become involved with an untouched maiden. All the infinite reasons he could not become entangled with Isabel. This had to stop. Now.

A soft, silken sound issued from deep in her throat as she slipped her hand inside the edge of his shirt. She glided her slender fingers over his chest, as though she loved the feel of his skin. His muscles tensed and quivered at her touch. He grabbed her waist, intending to push her away.

Her curious fingers found his nipple. Heat slithered through his blood, searing sense until it crumbled into an ashen heap. His fingers flexed against her waist, drawing her close when he should push her away. Thoughts of consequences withered in the fire she ignited in his blood. He tugged at the ties of her bodice, wanting to feel the soft warmth of her breasts against his face.

He kissed her deeply, slanting his lips over hers, touching her mouth with the tip of his tongue, while he slid his hands over her shoulders, peeling her gown, chemise, and petticoat from her shoulders. A part of him expected her to protest, to end this before it was too late. Yet she was kissing him as though she wanted his hands on her skin, as though she needed him as much as he needed her.

He swept her up in his arms and sank to the sofa, settling her across his lap. The soft weight of her bottom nestled intimately against the pounding ache in his loins. He touched her neck, feeling her pulse beneath the softness of her skin.

Lamplight flickered golden against her skin. It slid with loving adoration over her pale shoulders, her breasts. Her nipples rose with each breath, taut little berries, tempting him. "I knew you would be this beautiful."

"I want to be beautiful to you. Only you." She drew her arms from her gown and undergarments and snuggled closer into his warmth, brushing her bare breasts against the white cambric of his shirt. A moan rose from deep in his chest, startling him with his own blatant desire.

He nipped her chin and then slid the tip of his tongue down the column of her neck. She dragged her hands over his shoulders, his chest, as though she could not keep from touching him. She was a flame in his arms, scorching him, warming him in places he had long ago thought frozen forever.

She curled her arms around him. He dragged his mouth over her collarbone, rubbed his cheek against the swell of her breasts while he lifted her against him. He felt connected to this woman, as though the threads of her life twined inexplicably with his.

He claimed her breast, closing his mouth over the tight little nub. She arched in his arms, a startled gasp tearing.

"Easy," he whispered against her skin.

She drew a shaky breath. "I find it all so . . . startling."

So did he. Startling to discover he could want like this, with a hunger that sank into the very marrow of his bones. He brushed his cheek against her breasts, breathing in the scent of her skin. He flicked his tongue over a taut, raspberry-colored nipple. A soft sob escaped her lips, as though dragged from her throat by a tight tether of need. Soft, pleasured sounds rose from her throat to curl around him, while he lavished his attention on her breasts.

He had never felt this way, as though he could slay dragons if she asked it of him. He pulled back and looked into her eyes, savoring the sultry look he had kindled within them.

''Kiss me,'' he demanded, the harsh whisper betraying his need.

Without hesitation, she slipped her hands into his hair and dragged him close until her lips touched his. A shudder rippled through his body. She kissed him without reservation, a kiss filled with such innocent enthusiasm it stole his breath. He plunged his tongue into her mouth and she welcomed him, meeting his raw hunger without shame.

He slid his hand under her skirts. Her skin bathed his in a silky warmth, feeding the fever in his blood. The iron grip of desire tightened in his loins. He drew his hand upward, over her cotton stocking and the garter tied above her knee. She shivered as his fingers brushed the silken warmth of her inner thigh.

Somewhere in the back of his mind he acknowledged that this had escalated far past the point he had imagined. Yet he could no more deny the inviting feminine heat than he could deny his need for his next breath.

He touched her, an intimate stroke of a bold male hand against that most secret part of her. Instead of a proper denial, her hips arched, instinctively reaching for him. He complied, rubbing that hidden source of sensation he had discovered long ago, until she writhed beneath him, soft, whimpering sounds escaping her tight throat. Her body oiled his finger as he slipped inside her.

Even as slick as she was, her feminine sheath barely accommodated his finger. He had never in his life touched such glorious innocence. Blood pounded in his loins, his sex pushing against the barrier of his trousers, hungry for a taste of her. Somewhere in the heated muddle of his brain, he acknowledged all the reasons he should not be doing this. He should stop. Now. Yet he could not stop caressing her.

Her body shuddered and tensed, innocent flesh clenching his finger. A soft cry escaped her lips, the sweet song of feminine release. When he felt her ease in his arms, he drew his trembling hand away.

His hand burned, as though the damp heat of her body had branded him. She lay nestled against him, her cheek turned into his shoulder, her eyes closed, her lips parted. He lowered his gaze. Her breasts rose and fell in a soft rhythm, each exhalation warming his skin through the thin layer of his shirt.

Her warm bottom snuggled against his lap, torturing him. He was painfully aware that he need only flip open his trousers and plunge into her to find relief, to experience heaven—to tumble straight into hell. God Almighty, what had he done?

A virgin! He had entangled himself with a virgin. Worse, he was responsible for her honor. What should he do now? Challenge himself to a bloody duel?

"Bloody hell!"

She turned her head against his shoulder and looked up at him with sleepy blue eyes. "Is something wrong?"

"What the bloody hell do you think you're doing?"

She blinked. "Pardon me?"

He slipped out from beneath her so quickly he knocked her off the sofa. Her bottom hit the floor with a thump. He started to reach for her, then stopped himself. He wasn't sure what the hell he might do if he touched her again.

Stunned, she sat in a crumpled pool of muslin and

wool, staring up at him. Lamplight flickered against the pale swells of her breasts. He turned his back to her. "Cover yourself!"

"You need not be cross with me," she said.

He dragged air into his constricted lungs and tried to snatch the reins of his runaway emotions. "Why the bloody hell didn't you stop me?"

"Why are you so angry?" she asked, her voice filled with confusion.

He understood how confused she felt, because he was suffering his own confusion. "It would seem one of us should have the good sense to be angry."

"I suppose I've shown a terrible lack of propriety. You shall have to pardon me. I found the experience . . . overwhelming."

Dear heaven, so had he. He glanced over his shoulder and found her standing by the sofa, struggling with the laces of her gown. He turned to face her, all the anger he felt at his own actions spilling into his voice. "What the bloody hell did you think you were doing?"

She flinched. "I thought it was obvious. I wasn't thinking."

"Too obvious." Yet not as obvious as the simple fact that he should have known better.

"I don't understand why you are being so disagreeable." Although she held her chin high, light from the lamp glittered on the unshed tears in her eyes.

"Isabel." He took a step toward her, wanting to take her into his arms, and bumped straight into all the reasons he should keep his distance. If he touched her, if he took her into his arms, if he felt her warmth radiate against him, he would never be able to control the beast inside him. Without another word, he pivoted and marched from the room.

He reached the end of the walkway in front of

Bramsleigh Cottage before he realized he had left his coat and greatcoat hanging on pegs in the hall. He kept walking, marching toward the small storage building that currently served as shelter for the horse he had hired in town. He lifted his face to the rain, welcoming the cold rush against his flushed cheeks.

A chill shivered along his limbs, yet he had no intention of going back into that house. He had already spent every ounce of his control to leave. If he went back now he would take her. He would tumble Isabel back against that stiff sofa and bury himself so deep within her he would never again find himself.

He did not look back. He forced his legs to carry him farther and farther away from the temptation of Isabel. His blood was still pounding when he reached the storage shed. He pressed his brow against the wet wooden door, pushing until pinpoints of pain shot through his head. Still he could not drive images of Isabel from his brain. She remained, taunting him with her innocent passion.

Soft lips swollen from his kisses. Pale breasts damp from his mouth. Soft, pleasured sounds filling his ears. So incredibly innocent. He could still taste her. Her fragrance still lingered in his senses. Pain ground his groin, like a millstone grinding grain, pumping with each surge of his still-heated blood.

He leaned back against the door and lifted his face to the driving rain. Water coursed in rivulets down his cheeks. Cold rain soaked his shirt, his trousers, chilling his heated flesh. Still, he could not ease the need pounding in his blood.

Isabel.

He had ruined her. Destroyed her innocence. An honorable man would marry the girl. Yet would the cure only cause more harm?

He closed his eyes against the rain. He had given

parties that would have made Romans straight from their orgies blush. He had tasted the most tempting fruit in every elegant brothel in London. Still, it was more than the countless whores he had used, more than the hundreds of loveless affairs he had wallowed in that made him a poor candidate for Isabel's husband. His profligate ways might be altered if he were a better man.

Yet Justin had no delusions about his character. His heart was as bleak as the moors near the home where he was born and bred. Cold. Harsh. Unyielding. His soul was no better. Every ounce of goodness had been beaten out of him when he was a boy. A better man might have retained some grain of kindness. He had not. Isabel deserved a great deal more than he could ever give her.

Isabel. What the devil am I going to do with you?

Chapter Eight

"Isabel!"

Justin's voice swept through the open doorway of the tree house, carried on a chilly breath of wind. Isabel's heart tripped. He could not possibly know where she was, she assured herself. She crept on all fours toward the doorway. The tree house was perched in an ancient oak, which stood with several others near the edge of the cliffs. Her vantage point provided her an excellent view of the tall, dark-haired man prowling the cliff path. He was no more than fifteen yards away from her sanctuary, a marauding warrior ready to destroy the wounded remnants of her pride.

Lightning carved a jagged streak across the morning sky, plunging into the gray water of the channel. Six seconds later thunder rumbled over her head. In the distance, sheets of rain fell like a pale gray veil from the sky to the rolling gray waves. The wind brushed her face, thick with a damp, salty taste. The storm was headed this direction. Certainly Justin would soon turn around and head for shelter, she thought. He paused on the path and scanned the area. The wind buffeted him, sending his thick black hair into waves, whipping the tails of his dark gray coat, plastering his white shirt to the broad plains of his chest.

She crept closer to the open doorway. Would Justin notice if she closed the door? She hesitated a foot before the opening, afraid the movement might betray her. Instead she sat on the wooden floor, wrapped her arms around her shins, and hugged her knees to her chest.

This had once been one of her favorite places. The tree house had been maintained over the years, kept for each of the Darracott children. When she was a little girl she would come here to escape into a wonderful realm of make-believe, where the tree house became the deck of a sailing ship. She and her brother would pretend they were pirates, or explorers, or travelers to far and distant lands. She wished she could escape into that make-believe world this morning. Yet she knew she would have to face Justin sometime. She had only hoped it would be later. Much later. When she had pulled together the shreds of her dignity.

"Isabel!" Justin shouted.

Isabel shrank back into the shadows. Justin's face had filled the few hours of sleep she had managed the past night. She had relived every moment in his arms, and more. She had awakened just after dawn with a pounding headache, and a clear understanding of her own foolishness.

A hot pot of tea and a few scones had helped relieve the pounding in her head, but nothing could salve her wounded pride. Last night had been the most foolish episode in her life. The man had warned her and she had still thrown herself at him, like a demented moth flying into a flame.

She was a woman who faced facts straight in the eye, no matter how disturbing they might be. The responsibility for what had happened last night lay squarely on her shoulders. She had goaded Justin into his actions. She had poked and prodded until she had gotten exactly what she wanted. There existed only one explanation for her actions: Justin was a virulent disease. He seared away her sense, turned her into a reckless fool, an idiot who would risk almost anything to be held in his arms.

Foolish, besotted imbecile.

Justin turned and stared straight up at the tree house. Isabel's heart crept upward, until each beat throbbed at the base of her neck. Oak leaves rustled in the wind, whipped about in the fury of the approaching storm. He could not see her, she assured herself. The shadows would hide her. And he certainly would not think to look for her in a tree house. She glanced at the rope ladder she had hauled up after her. Even if he did think to look for her here, he had no way to reach her.

He moved toward the tree, in that lazy stride that whispered of barely constrained power, his gaze fixed on the doorway fifteen feet above the ground. She scooted back until she collided with the far wall. Had he heard her? She huddled against the wall, holding her breath. *Go away. Please just go away.*

Thunder rolled overhead. Her quick heartbeats marked each passing moment. He would notice there was no way up and go away. He would—

A hand smacked the wooden floor of the doorway. A moment later Justin hauled himself over the threshold. Bits of bark clung to his dark coat and his buff-colored breeches. Isabel scrambled to her feet as he drew up onto his knees. She pressed back against the wall, trapped. "You climbed the tree."

He slanted a glance at the rope ladder piled near the door. "Apparently you didn't hear me calling you."

Her chest tightened, squeezing the air from her lungs, as her body acknowledged its undeniable attraction to this dangerous male. "I'm not in the mood for company."

"I noticed." Justin rose and bumped his head on the ceiling. "Damnation!" he whispered, ducking his head. "Why do I always seem to end up bruised when I'm around you?"

"I didn't invite you here."

"No, you did not," he said, rubbing his head. "Still, I'm afraid we need to talk."

She would rather hang by her thumbs than discuss what had happened between them. When she thought of how she had revealed herself, she wanted to scream. Yet it seemed she could not escape the inevitable.

He glanced around the small room. "Did the tree house belong to you?"

"My father had it built for me and my brother a very long time ago," she said, appalled at the breathless sound of her voice.

"My brother and I built one of these when I was a boy. We took wood from my father's timber yard, without telling anyone. For a long time no one knew about it. I used to think no one could find me there."

A wistful quality colored his voice, a thread of sadness that she might have missed if she were not so aware of this man. She recalled the bitterness in his voice and in his eyes when he had spoken of his father the first day she had met him. "I suppose all children like to hide from their elders every now and then."

He looked at her, and she caught a glimmer of bitterness in his expression before he pulled his features

113

into a sardonic mask. "Unfortunately there are some things from which we cannot hide."

She could feel the blade of the guillotine pressing against her neck. Cold. Inescapable. "True."

He leaned back against the wall, cocking one knee at a decidedly masculine angle. "I've given what happened last night a great deal of thought."

"I think it would be best for us both to forget about what happened last night."

He lifted one black brow. "Is that what you propose we do, Miss Darracott? Forget it ever happened?"

She would never in all her years forget last night. Facts were not always easy to face, such as the fact that what had happened last night meant as little to him as any encounter he might have had with any female. She hugged her arms across her chest, fighting a chill from within. "Yes."

He rubbed a tear in his breeches over his knee. She stared at his elegantly tapered fingers and tried not to remember the way he had touched her. "Can you so easily forget you lay half naked in my arms?"

She squeezed her arms tighter to her chest. "I need not be reminded."

"And do you not need reminding that I very nearly took your maidenhead last night?"

Nothing in his expression betrayed his thoughts. He regarded her with an unnerving reserve. She only wished she could match his icy composure and control this horrible pounding of her heart. But then this all meant far more to her than it could ever mean to him. "There is no need to try to humiliate me, Duke. I've managed quite nicely without your help. I do wish you to know I've never before in my life behaved in such a manner."

"If I suspected for a moment that you made a habit

of giving yourself so freely to men, I would never have decided to marry you.''

She flinched. ''Marry me?''

''That's right. Soon after we reach London.''

She stared at him, torn between stunning joy at his proposal and utter contempt for his arrogance. ''Strange, but I don't recall your having asked me. And I certainly do not remember accepting your offer.''

He grinned. ''The matter was decided when you seduced me last night.''

''When I seduced . . . Why, you . . . I did no such thing!''

''I warned you what would happen if you tempted the devil. Under the circumstances, marriage is the only solution.''

''Are you implying that I allowed you those unfortunate liberties to trap you into marriage?''

He drew away from the wall, bending slightly at the waist to keep from bumping his head on the ceiling. ''It doesn't matter. I learned long ago every woman has a price. I want you, and I'm willing to pay the proper fee.''

She stared at him, stunned for a full twelve beats of her heart. He wanted her. Although a part of her found that knowledge gratifying, another part of her, the part still able to think, suspected his definition of *want* fell to the most primitive of levels. ''And according to you the proper fee is what, exactly?''

Thunder rattled the walls of the tree house. ''I offered you marriage, Miss Darracott. I am willing to make you my duchess. It's more than I've been willing to pay to have any other woman.''

She pressed her hand to her heart. ''My goodness, your generosity leaves me positively breathless.''

He touched her cheek, a warm slide of his bare fingers against her skin—the gentleness in his touch a sharp contrast to the harsh tone of his voice. "If you're expecting me to drop to one knee and start spouting romantic platitudes, you shall have a long wait. I will have no hypocrisy between us."

"You're suggesting we marry to satisfy your lust? And nothing more?"

"Are you suggesting you don't feel the same for me?"

Lust was such an insignificant part of what she felt for him. Yes, an animal attraction burned in her, undeniable in its intensity. Yet that attraction was all tangled up with infinitely more tender, terribly foolish feelings. "I would think lust is hardly sufficient reason for marriage."

The corners of his eyes crinkled with his grin. "Don't underestimate its power, my dear. Thrones have tumbled for its sake."

Isabel turned away from him. She rested her hand on the wooden frame of the doorway to steady herself. "Lust has a way of burning out, doesn't it?"

"It always has," he replied, his voice colored by a trace of wariness.

"And after this fire of your lust dies, then what? When you grow tired of your wife, will you turn to a mistress?"

"I've never pretended to be anything other than what I am. If you marry me, you'll do it with your eyes open."

"I see."

He muttered an oath under his breath. "No matter what I do, you would still be a duchess."

Isabel glanced at Justin over her shoulder. "And would I also be accorded the same freedom? When your fancy had strayed to another woman, would I be free to choose a lover to warm my bed?"

His expression altered, the self-confident mask melting like wax under a flame, revealing a look so fierce that the back of her neck prickled. "I'll kill any man who touches you."

Her heart tripped with the harsh tone of his voice. Still, she could not safely attribute his possessiveness to anything more than male pride. "I would think it wouldn't matter to you, as long as I was discreet."

"Damnation, woman! We aren't even married and you're asking permission to take a blasted lover."

She turned to face him. "I don't want a lover. I want a husband. A man who cares for me in a way that is more than some animal attraction that will burn itself out and leave nothing but ashes behind. I want to feel free to give all of my affection, my loyalty, my life, without the fear he will throw it all in my face."

He stalked her, until he stood so close she could smell the tangy scent of sandalwood soap on his skin. "I want you, Isabel."

"Do you?"

"I've wanted you in my bed since the first moment I saw you. Isn't that enough?"

"The first moment you saw me, you thought I was a prostitute. It would seem you still think I am. Only now you think I come with a much higher price."

"I offer you all I'm capable of giving. I can offer no more."

He offered her marriage. A chance to live with him, to hold him, to make love with him. A chance to watch him make a mockery of her love for him. Rain spilled through the leaves overhead, pounding on the roof. "You may find this a surprise, but I don't want your wealth, your title, or your arrogance. I'm afraid I shall have to decline your offer."

"Confounded woman." He gripped her waist,

dragged her against him, and clamped his mouth over hers.

A simmering current coiled through her, igniting a hunger inside her. Heat slithered through her blood, collecting in a smoldering pool of need low in her belly. In spite of all the sane, logical reasons she should protect herself from this man, she could not keep from throwing her arms around his neck and holding him. As though recognizing the master of her senses, her body melted against his, snuggling into his hardened frame, too steeped in memories of recent pleasure to resist.

Hunger filled his kiss. She tasted it on his tongue, more intoxicating than brandy. Prudence, sanity, wisdom, withered in the searing inferno of his kiss. She matched his hunger, claiming his mouth as he claimed hers, ravaging as he ravaged, wanting as he wanted. He held her so close she could not tell the pounding of her heart from his. This was where she longed to be, in his arms, for the rest of her life.

Thunder cracked like a whip over them. He released her so suddenly that she fell back against the wall. He stared down at her, his eyes narrowed, his breath as sharp and ragged as her own. "Tell me you don't want me as much as I want you," he demanded, his voice a harsh whisper. "Tell me I wouldn't find you warm and wet if I slipped my hand between your thighs."

She could not deny the truth. Yet no matter how much she wanted to marry this devastatingly handsome, terribly complex man, she could not. "I want much more than you do. That's the problem."

Justin glanced away from her. A muscle flexed in his cheek as he clenched and unclenched his jaw. "I will give you until ten tomorrow morning to alter your decision. After that I shall consider the matter closed. In any case, I shall expect you and your sisters to be ready to leave for London at that hour.''

Her answer really did not matter to him, she thought. He had offered for her out of a sense of honor. The honor he would never admit he possessed.

He hooked the rope ladder with his foot and kicked it out of the doorway. The planks unfurled against the tree trunk with a clatter. Although she wanted to put some distance between them, she did not want him to catch a lung fever in the rain. ''You will be soaked to the skin if you try to leave now.''

''Are you always so quick to point out the obvious, Miss Darracott?''

She set her jaw. ''Perhaps you should wait until the storm passes.''

''I have things to do this afternoon.'' He sat on the floor, swung his long legs over the edge, and climbed down the ladder. He strode back the way he had come, as though oblivious to the driving rain.

She leaned her shoulder against the wooden door frame, watching him march away from her. Rain poured over him, soaking his coat, plastering his hair to his head, molding his breeches to his muscular legs. Yet he didn't seem to notice or care. Apparently even a storm could not intimidate the Duke of Marlow.

The man was the most arrogant, infuriating creature she had ever had the misfortune to meet. She refused to worry about him. And she certainly would not regret her decision. She would not be treated like a whore no matter what price he offered. She would show Justin Trevelyan. She was not for sale.

The next day, Justin stared out the window of his coach, blind to the dark green rolling expanse of pasture spreading out from the stone fence at the side of the road. At half past nine this morning he had arrived at Bramsleigh Cottage. At ten he and the Darracott ladies had boarded his coach and struck out for London. That had been two hours ago. He glanced at Isabel. She sat beside Eloise on the black velvet squabs across from him. She sat there reading a book, of all things, as though she had not just made the biggest mistake in her life. As though she had allowed his offer of marriage to expire without a second thought.

Confounded female!

It didn't matter, he assured himself. He had never planned to marry in the first place. He could get along just fine without Miss Isabel Darracott as his wife. He had been insane even to ask her. An imbecile to lie awake half the night wondering if she would come to her senses. A cretin to sit here fuming about her refusal. It did not matter. He would not allow it to matter.

Blazes, he wanted to slam his fist through the polished mahogany lining the inside of the coach. It took all his will to keep from tossing back his head and howling his rage and frustration. What the bloody hell did she want from him?

This was what he got for trying to do the proper thing. Well, he had learned his lesson. The regent would welcome Napoleon to London with open arms before he would ever again ask that infuriating female to be his wife.

No one in his life had ever brought him to his knees. He had withstood beatings that had left him raw and bloody. He had survived the dark pit of hell. All without begging for mercy. He would be damned before this slip of a spinster would bring him to heel.

She would regret it, he assured himself. When she was old and withered she would look back on this day and weep. On her deathbed she would wish for a chance to go back and change the past. She would die a spinster, her innocence taken to her grave, a feast for the worms. Still, as much as he tried, he found no comfort in the appalling images filling his head. Nothing eased the horrible tightness in his chest.

Phoebe tugged on his coatsleeve. When he looked at her, she smiled. "Do you think we might come back to Bramsleigh soon and go treasure hunting?"

He stared at her, sorting through the muddle Isabel had made of his brain, trying to make sense of what Phoebe had asked.

"I think the duke has heard enough about the treasure, Phoebe," Isabel said.

"But Belle, we can't just forget all about the old baron's treasure, not when we know it's real."

Isabel shook her head. "We have no idea of where the treasure might be. And I won't have you putting yourself in danger again."

Phoebe turned to look up at Justin. "I'm sure the old baron must have hidden the treasure in one of the caves. If we were very careful, we could search without getting into trouble."

Justin shook his head. "If you think I'm going to go tumbling into any more pits after you, think again. From now on I expect you to stay out of trouble. Is that understood?"

"Yes, Duke." Phoebe sat back, her lower lip plumping into a pout.

Justin shifted on the squabs. He felt as though he had just kicked a puppy. He glanced at Isabel and found her studying him, a thoughtful expression on her face. He couldn't tell if she approved of the way he had dealt with Phoebe or not.

Why the devil should he care what Isabel thought? He was Phoebe's guardian. He didn't give a farthing what Isabel thought. And if he kept saying that to himself long enough, he might actually start believing it.

He leaned his head against the upholstered back and

closed his eyes. It was only a matter of time before this hold she had over him faded. Lust always faded. When he got back to London, he would pick up the threads of his old life. Soon he would forget Isabel even existed.

Chapter Nine

Isabel had not realized that nine hours in a coach could seem like nine years. Although spacious, the conveyance did not provide enough room to escape Justin's brooding presence. Still, she could have been on the opposite side of Westminster Abbey and still have been aware of Justin.

He had not spoken of his proposal once all day. Apparently he was content to allow the matter to crumble silently into dust between them. It didn't matter, she assured herself. She would not accept the arrogant scoundrel if he fell to his knees and begged for her hand. Still, she could not dismiss him as easily as he had obviously dismissed her.

By the time they reached London and Marlow House, she was fuming inside, as angry at herself for caring about the rogue as she was at him for his nonchalance. She loathed him for proposing with such terrible honesty. For wanting her only for the most primitive of reasons. For shielding his heart when she had so foolishly lost her own.

Isabel followed him down a wide hallway of the huge mansion, trying to ignore the pounding of her heart. She knew he meant to dump her and her sisters into his grandmother's lap, then wash his hands of them. If it weren't for her sisters she certainly wouldn't care what the rogue did. As far as she was concerned she never wanted to see the beast again as long as she lived. If she kept repeating that to herself she was certain she would soon believe it.

Eloise and Phoebe walked on either side of her, glancing about the elegant hallway like children with their first glimpse inside of a sweetshop. Isabel scarcely noticed the paintings hanging upon the mahogany-lined walls, the porcelain urns and dishes placed on polished rosewood tables, the delicate-looking chairs and settees placed against the walls. Her mind was in too much turmoil. What the devil would they do if the duchess did not want them here? What would the lady think of them, barging into her home without so much as a minute's warning?

The scent of rose potpourri welcomed them as they entered a large drawing room. Candlelight spilled from a crystal chandelier high above them. Flickering flames burned behind the etched crystal globes of the wall sconces, lending a golden glow to the room. A slender, golden-haired woman sat on a gilt-trimmed sofa near the hearth. Yet she looked far too young to be Justin's grandmother. Isabel's heart slammed against the wall of her chest when she noticed the animal stretched out on the sofa beside her.

Eloise grabbed Isabel's arm. "Is that a—"

"A leopard!" Phoebe hurried toward the sofa. "You have a leopard. How marvelous!"

Sophia smiled at the girl. "He is an ocelot, actually.

A friend of mine brought him back from South America last September.''

''May I pet him?'' Phoebe asked.

''Phoebe, dear, perhaps you should wait until you are properly introduced,'' Isabel said.

''It's all right. Perceval doesn't stand on formalities.'' Sophia glanced from Isabel to Justin, a hint of mischief in her blue eyes. ''Like most males, he will allow any pretty girl to pet him.''

Justin grinned at her. ''Spoken with the authority of experience.''

Sophia crinkled her nose at him. ''I see you have decided to bring your wards to London.''

While Justin introduced Isabel and her sisters to his grandmother, Isabel watched Sophia's face, looking for any sign of annoyance. She found only a genuine warmth in Sophia's lovely face. The duchess actually looked pleased, even after it was clear Justin intended to leave the girls with her.

Justin stayed only a few minutes. Apparently he was only too eager to rid himself of them, Isabel thought. Fortunately Sophia seemed as equally content to have the Darracott sisters come to live with her. Before dinner she personally gave Isabel and her sisters a tour of the huge mansion that ended by her showing each sister to her new bedchamber. After Sophia had shown Eloise and Phoebe to their new chambers, she led the way to a large bedchamber at the back of the house.

''I thought you might like this chamber, my dear.'' Sophia beckoned Isabel to join her at one of the windows in the huge room. ''It has a nice view of the gardens.''

Crescent-shaped beds of newly awakened roses spread out from the stone terrace. Beyond the roses, a brick-lined path wended through a shrub garden, where tall walls of yew formed geometric patterns around a large stone fountain. At the far end of the gardens, a white marble pavilion in the shape of a Greek temple rose like a phantom from another time and place. "It's beautiful."

Sophia looked pleased. "I'll send you a maid to help you prepare for dinner."

"That's very kind, but I've been seeing to my own toilette for more than a year. You needn't go to any trouble for me."

Sophia smiled. "It's no trouble at all."

Isabel took comfort in the sincerity in Sophia's face. "I really must apologize again for appearing on your doorstep this way."

Sophia waved aside her words. "Nonsense. It is I who should apologize. I had no idea you had been driven from your home. If I had, I would never have waited for my grandson to accept his responsibility. I do hope you can forgive him for taking so long to get around to you."

"I doubt the duke is a man who seeks forgiveness from anyone."

Sophia lifted one golden brow. "You're a very perceptive young woman. As well as candid."

Isabel sighed. "I'm sorry. I didn't mean to be impertinent. I'm afraid I have a terrible habit of saying what is on my mind."

"I find your directness remarkably refreshing. You and your sisters have brought life into this empty house." Sophia cupped Isabel's cheek in her smooth palm, the scent of spicy flowers spilling around her. "I'm very glad you're here."

"Thank you, Duchess. For everything."

"I do hope you will call me Sophia, my dear. There is no need for formalities. After all, you're part of the family."

Isabel leaned against the window frame when Sophia left the room. *Part of the family.* She wondered what the duchess might think if she knew how close she had come to actually becoming part of her family. She stared out at the gardens, trying desperately not to wonder where Justin might be, or worse, who might be with him.

It was none of her concern. He could do as he pleased. Yet no matter how hard she tried to banish them, images kept taunting her. She kept seeing Justin surrounded by beautiful courtesans, all intent on pleasing him. With the images came a dull ache near her heart. Oh, she wished she had never met the scoundrel!

He wished he had never met the infuriating spinster! Justin stood at a cabinet in the library of his brother's town house on Grosvenor Square. He sloshed whiskey from a decanter into a crystal glass, then drained it in two swallows. The heat of the aged Irish liquor warmed his throat and chest, and the rich scent flooded his nostrils. The mellow taste scarcely permeated his tongue.

"Justin, do you want to tell me the reason you are abusing my whiskey?" Clayton asked.

Justin turned to face his brother. Clayton sat in a coffee-colored leather wing-back chair near the hearth, with his feet propped on a leather footstool. Dressed in a black evening coat and trousers, Clay might have been a likeness of himself, if Justin had ever been able to look that reserved.

"I assume your vile mood has something to do with your wards."

Justin dropped the crystal stopper into the decanter, a loud ping ringing through the room. "The next time I even think about accepting responsibility for a pack of infants, shoot me."

"From what you said of the eldest the day you accused me of sending you a prudish prostitute, she was hardly an infant. What was her name, Arabelle?''

Justin squeezed his glass. ''Isabel.''

''Ah, Isabel.'' Clayton grinned. *The lady has captured your interest.*

Justin could easily read the thoughts behind his brother's arrogant smile. Since they were boys they had never been able to keep a secret from one another. They shared more than the same mold of features and form. They shared a bond neither of them had ever truly been able to explain to anyone else. When Clay had been wounded at Waterloo, Justin had fallen to his knees with a sudden stab of pain in his side. They had been linked in this fashion since the first day they had drawn breath. ''I'm so glad my misery amuses you.''

Clayton planted his elbows on the arms of the chair, clasped his hands, and rested his chin on his knuckles. ''Hasn't Isabel forgiven you for thinking she was a prostitute?''

''The blasted chit *still* believes I think she's a prostitute.'' Justin slammed his glass on the cabinet and stalked to the hearth.

''Tell me, brother, what have you done to give her that impression?''

''Nothing.''

Clayton lifted his brows. ''Nothing?''

''Only a female could manage to twist a situation the way she did.'' Justin grabbed a poker and jabbed at the fire on the hearth, sending sparks shooting from the stack of burning coals. ''If Phoebe and Eloise hadn't contracted measles, I wouldn't have been there that night.''

''Measles?''

Justin nodded. ''I was taken by the insane notion to help tend the girls. One night, when they had recovered, Isabel and I were sharing a brandy in the sitting room. The girls were asleep upstairs. Isabel and I were arguing about something, and the next I knew, she was in my arms.''

''Good God, Justin. Are you telling me you made love to her? A woman under your protection? A virgin?''

Justin clenched his jaw. ''Not precisely.''

Silence stretched between them, filled only by the quiet hiss of flames consuming coal. When Clayton spoke, his voice held the weight of a judge. ''What do you mean to do about it?''

Justin glared at his brother. ''I already proposed marriage, so you needn't take that sanctimonious tone with me.''

Clayton stared at his brother in that way he had of stripping away the defenses Justin might have sustained against any other human being. ''She refused you?''

Justin shoved the poker into a brass holder with a clatter of metal. ''She's obviously a fool.''

Clayton smiled. ''Obviously.''

Justin threw himself into the matching leather wing-back chair across from Clay. ''No doubt she would have contrived to make my life miserable.''

''No doubt.''

''I never realized the Almighty even remembered I existed until the day she refused me.''

''I can see you shall be attending church every Sunday, giving proper thanks.''

Justin propped one foot on the footstool. ''She shall regret it.''

''I would wager she is weeping at this very moment.''

Justin frowned at his brother's sarcasm. ''I like my life just as it is. When I want a woman, I pay for her.

When I'm through with her, it's over. And there is no looking back.''

Clayton nodded his head slowly. "You have escaped the hangman.''

"Exactly. I am relieved about it. I must have been insane ever to have asked that sharp-tongued, waspish little termagant of a spinster to be my wife.'' Justin shook his head. "Responsibility can twist a man.''

Clayton smiled, regarding Justin with the certainty that only came when one could share the thoughts and feelings of another. "Are you trying to convince me, or yourself?''

Justin shifted under his brother's steady regard. He had as much chance of hiding anything from Clay as his brother did from him. "It isn't the first time I've been intrigued by a beautiful face. I find the better I get to know a woman, the less fascinating she becomes.''

Clayton glanced at the hearth. The soft glow from the coals touched his face, revealing the sudden seriousness of his expression. "Not all women lose their charm over time, Justin. Some actually become more potent as the years pass.''

Justin did not need to ask to know what woman had managed to sink her claws into his brother. Seven years ago, Marisa Grantham had managed to confirm what Justin already knew: women were not worth the trouble they inevitably caused. "A female no doubt invented marriage. I prefer not to play by their rules.''

Clayton tilted his head and looked at his brother. "What are you going to do?''

Justin smiled. "I'm going to exorcise the woman from my blood with a little help from Vachel and her ladies.''

A smile tipped one corner of Clayton's lips. "Sometimes that particular cure does not work. No matter how many women you bed, you won't satisfy your hunger for that one infuriating female who has managed to sear her image into a part of your memory that you just can't destroy.''

Justin knew his brother spoke from experience. The wounds Marisa had inflicted were still there, hidden beneath a cool mask of indifference. ''Isabel may be a fire in my blood. But it will cool, especially with a little help from a few of Vachel's tarts. Care to come with me?''

''No, thank you. I'm not in the mood for theatrics tonight.''

Justin frowned. ''Theatrics?''

''I always feel as though I'm moving through a play when I'm at Vachel's. The entire house is a stage, and everyone there has a role. We are the wealthy aristocrats, insatiable in our appetites. The women are there solely to satisfy our needs by bedding us and pretending to enjoy every moment of it. When it's over, we line their pockets with gold for their performance. Then they move on to the next play.''

Justin tapped the edge of his fist against the arm of the chair, uncomfortable with the blatant honesty in his brother's appraisal. ''Where are you going instead?''

''The Trenton musicale.''

Justin grimaced. ''You really are serious about finding a bride this Season. It's the only explanation for suffering an evening at the Trentons'. If I were you I would take the Trenton chit off my list right now. If you were to marry that little piece of ice, you would be spending most of your nights at Vachel's just for the chance of touching a female again.''

Clayton shrugged. ''One of us has to assure the succession.''

''Damnation, Clay, I've seen your little list of prospective brides. Every one a beauty and a dead bore. Not one of those chits will keep you satisfied. Don't go off doing something reckless for the sake of some blasted title. Let it fall to the cadet branch before you put your neck in a noose.''

''I am the reliable brother, remember?'' Clayton grinned. ''When have I ever done anything reckless?

''When you bought a commission five days after Marisa called off the engagement.''

Clayton's lips pulled into a tight line. ''That was a long time ago.''

Justin rubbed his fingers against the smooth leather arm of the chair. ''I always wondered what happened. Why she cried off.''

Clayton shrugged. ''She changed her mind.''

Justin stared at him. ''Changed her mind?''

''Yes.''

''Marisa never married. To tell you the truth, even though plenty of men have tried, I've never known her name to be romantically linked with any save yours.''

Clayton straightened his cuff, a gesture of nonchalance wasted on Justin. ''I suppose she has never found her ideal.''

''Marisa loved you. I know it. Yet on a whim she ended your engagement?'' Justin released his breath in a long sigh. ''Women are not merely another sex. They are an entirely different species. I'm not certain they are from this world at all.''

Clayton grinned. ''Isabel must be a rare breed indeed. I look forward to meeting the only woman who ever managed to twist a marriage proposal out of my brother.''

Justin laughed, the sound bitter to his own ears. ''That's what happens when responsibility gets its hold on you for the first time at the ripe age of thirty.

Before you know it, you're proposing marriage to a woman because you want her in your bed, and that's the only honorable way to have her.''

A frown creased Clayton's brow as he studied Justin. "I suppose you told Isabel precisely why you wanted to marry her.''

"I can't tolerate hypocrisy.''

Clayton leaned back in his chair. "Well, I can't understand why she didn't leap at the chance to become your bride, after you told her you wanted her only to warm your bed.''

Justin stood. "I'm not like you, Clay. I'm not worthy or steadfast. My attention lasts only so long, and then my eye wanders. I'll not pretend to be something I'm not.''

Clayton rubbed his fingertips together. "I wonder if you aren't underestimating the attraction she holds for you.''

Justin smiled. "I've never doubted what I am. A piece of stone replaced my heart a long time ago. I'm not capable of remaining loyal to any female. It's only a matter of time before I'm completely recovered from my malady.''

Clayton shook his head. "You are a better man than you have ever admitted to yourself.''

Justin made an elaborate bow. "I'll leave sainthood to you. For me, I'm going to enjoy all the delights of Vachel's pastry shop. And forget I ever met Miss Isabel Darracott.''

The drawing room of Madame Orlina Vachel's was decorated completely in white and gold. The walls were paneled in oak painted white and accented by elegant gilt trim. Sofas and chairs sat upon a white-and-gold carpet, all upholstered in white silk brocade highlighted with gold threads. It was nearly nine, and the room was already crowded with gentlemen who had come to partake of Orlina's supper before sampling one of the elegantly attired courtesans who roamed the room.

Justin smiled at the beautiful dark-haired woman moving toward him. The daughter of a French Count, as a child Orlina had escaped the Revolution with her head firmly attached and her pockets entirely empty. At fifteen she had become the mistress of the Marquess of Wansford. Ten years ago, his money had financed the beginnings of her current establishment. Her French chef had immediately made her suppers famous. Her selection of only the loveliest, most genteel women had ensured her success with the men of the ton. Although most of the residents of St. James's Square were aware of their neighbor's profession, no one spoke publicly of Orlina's drawing room.

"It has been too long since we have seen your handsome face." Orlina said, slipping her arm through Justin's. She smiled up at him, mischief glinting in her dark eyes. "I was beginning to despair, thinking you were too busy with some new mistress to come see us."

"I've been out of town." If anyone knew how he had actually been spending his time, no one would believe it. He scarcely believed it himself. Was it only yesterday he had proposed marriage? He could only blame the pressure of responsibilities for his strange behavior.

"I have a new girl. Her name is Susannah. I think you will like her."

Justin nodded to several of the girls he had enjoyed in the past, and greeted a few of his friends as Orlina led him toward a group of three women standing near the white marble hearth. Two of the women he recognized. He had bedded both of them. The third, a tall, buxom brunette, was new to him.

Justin had spent many an evening under Orlina's roof. It had always been comfortable. Yet tonight he felt he was out of his element. He was too aware of the predatory looks of the women. He had always appreciated those looks before, taken them as a compliment. He was generous with his whores. They knew they would be well compensated for their best efforts. It was one of the reasons he always had an enthusiastic bed partner.

"Susannah, look at the handsome man I have brought you," Orlina said.

Justin nodded as Orlina introduced Susannah to him. Susannah slipped her arm through Justin's and leaned toward him, pressing her ample breasts against him. The cloying scent of her perfume stabbed his senses. Although she smiled, the expression in her green eyes remained cool. He could almost see her calculating the bank notes she would earn for the evening. "Your prowess is legendary, Your Grace. I'm looking forward to becoming better acquainted. Perhaps we could slip away from this crowd?"

"Perhaps." He hesitated only a moment when she tugged him toward the hall. As he approached the door, a tall, fair-haired man crossed the threshold. Justin tensed when he came face-to-face with Gerard Witheridge. Yet he masked his surprise behind a composed facade. Unlike the shocked expression on the other man's face.

Justin molded his lips into a chilling smile. "Witheridge. I didn't realize you were in town."

Gerard snapped his gaping mouth closed, then swallowed so hard Justin could hear his Adam's apple click. "Good evening, Duke. I came to town last week."

While he and Isabel had been caring for her sisters. With a slight inclination of his head, Justin dismissed Witheridge and continued on his way. As he left the room with Susannah attached to his arm, Justin wondered how Gerard would manage to tell Isabel where he had seen the wicked Duke of Marlow without incriminating himself. He wasn't certain how the man would manage, but he would tell her.

It did not matter what Gerard told Isabel, Justin assured himself. Susannah's hip brushed provocatively against his thigh with every step she took. He was hardly a saint. And he did not intend to change his way of life for anyone, especially for a female who had the audacity to reject his generous offer of marriage.

Chapter Ten

"Ah, yes, the blue is perfection for you," Madame Amarante said as she draped a measure of blue silk over Isabel's shoulder. "Here, you *must* see yourself."

When the small, dark-haired modiste stepped aside, Isabel glanced into the rosewood-trimmed cheval mirror that stood in one corner of her bedchamber in Marlow House. Bolts of silk, satin, velvet, kerseymere, and muslin spilled in colorful disarray across the ivory satin counterpane on the bed beside her. Pattern books lay scattered across the intricate pattern of ivory, rose, and blue in the carpet, amid lengths of lace and bolts of ribbon.

Madame Amarante and her five assistants had swept into the room an hour ago, transforming the elegant chamber into a dress shop. After telling the modiste the three Darracott ladies were in need of everything, Sophia had escaped the whirlwind that followed, abandoning Isabel and her sisters to the enthusiastic ministering of the modiste.

Phoebe glanced up from where she sat on the floor, studying a pattern book. "Oh, Isabel, I've never seen anything so pretty."

Isabel drew her fingers over the smooth material. She had never owned a silk gown. There had never been a need for anything this extravagant while she lived at Bramsleigh. She held the silk against her chest and swayed back and forth, while Madame Amarante fluttered about plucking at blond lace, chattering about trims and trains and matching shoes.

The scent of rose potpourri drifted from porcelain bowls set around the room, making Isabel feel as though she stood in the midst of a magical garden where fairies could turn a plain country mouse into a dazzling princess. No one would think she looked like a country mouse in a gown made of this. Not even the infuriating Duke of Marlow.

No matter how hard she tried to banish the exasperating creature from her mind, he haunted her. The beast invaded her dreams. He distracted her waking thoughts. She frowned at her reflection in the mirror. If it was the last thing she did, she would smother this demented infatuation.

Still, she could not help but imagine Justin's face when she walked into a room wearing an exquisite gown fashioned from this blue silk. In her fantasy he would fall helplessly under her spell. She, of course, would tell him to go straight to blazes.

She closed her eyes and smoothed her hand over the icy blue silk. Reality trickled in, like drips of icy water plunking upon smoldering coals. She could not possibly afford anything as expensive as the blue silk, not for herself, at any rate. Isabel glanced to where Eloise sat at the vanity, choosing the lace trim for one of her new gowns. Eloise would need gowns of silk when she entered society next year.

Isabel slipped the silk from her shoulder and laid it across the bed. "I'm afraid I don't think it suits me."

Madame Amarante's dark eyes grew wide. "You look divine in the silk. An angel."

Isabel rubbed the silk between her fingers. While she might justify their guardian spending a sizable amount on her sisters, she could not in all conscience allow him to do the same for her. Still, there might be a way to have the gown and appease her conscience. She left a bewildered Madame Amarante in her chamber and sought the duchess, convinced she had the perfect solution to a tricky situation.

Isabel entered the green drawing room expecting to find Sophia busy at her easel. Yet the only occupant of the room was certainly not the duchess.

Isabel froze on the threshold, excitement sizzling through her, searing the air from her lungs. Justin sat in a wing-back chair near the hearth, idly stroking Sophia's ocelot, who lay stretched across his lap.

Justin tilted his head and glanced at her. In the instant his gaze met hers, she realized her mistake. Although his eyes were the same gray-green as Justin's, they regarded her with the cool appreciation of a gentleman encountering a female he considered interesting. Not the searing stare of the devilish rogue who had very nearly taken her innocence.

"You must be Lord Huntingdon," she said, moving toward him, offering her hand.

His thick black brows lifted while a flicker of surprise entered his beautiful eyes. "And you are Miss Isabel Darracott." He lowered Perceval to the floor. The big cat curled into a fluffy ball near the hearth.

A clean citrus fragrance drifted around her as Clayton took her hand, the scent a sharp contrast to the smoldering scent of sandalwood that seemed so much a part of his brother. She smiled up into his face,

139

amazed by the resemblance he had to his brother. She had never before seen twins who shared identical features. Odd how one twin could turn her blood to fire and the other leave her with nothing more than a pleasant sensation of warmth. "It's very nice to meet you."

"The pleasure is mine." A whisper of curiosity filled his smile. "You surprise me, Miss Darracott."

"In what way?"

"My brother and I are often mistaken for one another. Yet you knew in an instant I wasn't Justin."

"I'm surprised you're often mistaken for one another. You're very different."

He frowned. "We are identical."

She studied his features, seeing the subtle differences in this man and his brother. With their sharply carved features, both were undeniably handsome in a blatant, decidedly masculine fashion. Both men also exuded a sense of command. Yet in each it was different. There was a quiet reserve to Clayton Trevelyan, a sense that he held the world at a safe distance. There was nothing safe about Justin. "Your features are the same, it's true. But your expressions are quite different."

"Only to those who know us well. Still, I understand you and my brother have had the opportunity to become well acquainted."

Heat crept upward along her neck. What had Justin told him? "He has spoken to you about . . . Did he mention he had . . . Did he tell you?"

Clayton smiled, warmth filling his eyes. "I understand you weren't impressed with my brother's marriage proposal."

"Your brother and I have different ideas concerning marriage."

"My brother can be a difficult man to understand,

Miss Darracott. There are few people who truly know him.''

''I know him as well as I care to.''

He laughed softly. ''I suppose you wouldn't accept him if he were on his knees before you.''

''I can't imagine your brother ever going down on his knees.''

Clayton shrugged. ''I doubt he can either.''

''My dear Isabel, I did not expect you to be finished so soon,'' Sophia said, as she entered the room. White India muslin rippled around her legs as she moved toward her. ''Have you grown weary of choosing your new gowns?''

Isabel's stomach tightened at the embarrassing situation in which she had been placed. ''I'm afraid I'm not having a great deal of success with Madame Amarante.''

''Is something wrong?'' Sophia took Isabel's arm. The subtle spicy, floral scent of expensive perfume spilled around Isabel as the duchess led her to a gilt-trimmed settee near the hearth. ''Is Amarante not to your liking?''

''No, Madame Amarante has been very obliging.'' Isabel glanced at Clayton, who remained standing near the hearth, regarding her with mild curiosity. It wasn't easy discussing her reduced circumstances, but it was necessary. ''Everything Madame Amarante has shown me is dreadfully dear. I thought I might purchase some material at a linen-draper and make my own gowns.''

Sophia blinked. ''Make your own gowns?''

''Yes.'' Isabel glanced down at her tightly clenched hands. ''I've become quite adept at sewing these past few months. I'm certain I could imitate the patterns Madame Amarante has shown me. It would save a great deal.''

''Sophia, you cannot tell me Justin is tightfisted

with his wards," Clayton said, his deep voice colored with a hint of humor.

Sophia waved aside the notion. "Justin told me to spend whatever was necessary for the comfort of the Darracott ladies."

Heat crept into Isabel's cheeks. "I would rather not be in his debt."

Sophia smiled at Isabel. "I would rather not be accused of ill-treating my wards. And I am more than certain Justin would not care to be called tightfisted."

"But Duchess, I—"

Sophia raised her hand, silencing Isabel's protest. "First of all, you are to call me Sophia. And secondly, my grandson can well afford to clothe you and your sisters properly. I hate to imagine what he squanders on his . . ." She hesitated, glancing at Isabel, a frown marring her brow. "On his other amusements."

Isabel knew precisely what the other amusements were. Justin might not have a mistress at the moment, but he would soon enough.

"Run along, child," Sophia said, patting Isabel's arm. "Choose the loveliest gowns. If you do not, you shall make Justin look a miser."

Isabel would not be cast in the same light as the women the duke kept for his amusement. "I would rather make my own gowns."

"You would rather. . . ." Sophia looked at Clayton, who had taken the chair across from her. "Explain to this child what it will mean to Justin if she carries through with her plan."

"I might explain it better," Justin said, from the threshold of the room. He fixed Isabel in a penetrating stare as he moved toward her. "If I knew what Miss Darracott had planned."

Excitement sparked through Isabel, evaporating the breath from her lungs. She lifted her chin, hoping she looked completely composed, while inside she trembled.

"The child expects to sew her own gowns." Sophia patted Isabel's arm. "I've tried to tell her you have no qualms about purchasing a proper wardrobe for her. But she insists on the strictest economy."

Justin paused in front of Isabel, gazing down at her as though she were some strange creature he had never glimpsed before. "Reluctant to spend my money, Miss Darracott?"

Isabel squeezed her hands together in her lap. "I prefer not to impose."

Justin's eyes narrowed with a look of suspicion, as though he didn't trust her or the words she had spoken.

"My dear child, if you tried to make all of the gowns you will need for the coming Season, you would never have time to enjoy any of the social events," Sophia said. "And you really cannot expect to make your appearance at the ball I'm giving in your honor dressed in a gown of your own fashioning."

"Ball?" Justin and Isabel spoke the word in startled unison.

"Of course a ball. How else would you expect me to present Isabel to the ton?" Sophia asked.

"But I do not expect to be presented to the ton," Isabel said.

Sophia shook her head. "My dear child, you are the ward of the Duke of Marlow. You cannot expect to live in London on the fringe of society. That reminds me, I suppose we really should present you to Prinny."

Isabel glanced from Sophia's smiling face to Justin's scowl, and back again. "I don't wish to put you to any trouble. And I understand giving balls and presenting girls to the regent as well as to the ton can be a great deal of bother."

"My husband died when we were young. I had only one child, a boy. I always longed for a daughter." Sophia touched Isabel's cheek. "Would you deny me the pleasure of sponsoring you?"

Isabel's heart pounded with the thought of entering society. In quiet times at Bramsleigh, she had often wondered what it might be like to dance at a ball given in her honor, to flit from one rout or musicale or party to another, to swirl through the glitter of London society. Yet the expense of it all would be far too dear. Especially for a woman well beyond her salad days. "Eloise shall be eighteen in November. I'm certain you would have a great deal more enjoyment in helping her enter society next year."

Sophia folded her hands in her lap. "My dear, I'm of an age when I cannot be certain I shall be around to see the next year."

Justin's laughter rumbled in the room. "You shall outlive us all, Duchess."

Sophia cast her grandson a dark look. "You are little help, my boy. You should be pointing out the advantages of entering society."

"I've never seen many myself." Justin sank into an armchair next to Clayton.

Isabel compared one brother to the other. It was like looking at a pair of masks, both sculpted with the same features—but one a portrait of cool reserve, the other smoldering sensuality.

"If Miss Darracott does not wish to enter society, I do not see why I should try to convince her to do so," Justin said. "And I certainly see no reason to present her to that overstuffed lecher."

"Perhaps we could avoid the formal presentation at court, since Isabel is hardly a chit straight out of the schoolroom," Sophia said.

Isabel squeezed her damp palms together. "Yes,

please let's avoid the presentation at court.''

"Still, we don't wish to insult Prinny." Sophia tapped her fingertip against her chin. "We could perhaps present her to him at the ball.''

Isabel's head pounded at the realization that the regent would actually attend a ball for her. "Could we perhaps avoid the entire idea of bringing me out this Season?''

"Consider it done," Justin said.

Sophia shook her head. "Clayton, kindly lend your sane voice to this discussion.''

Clayton smiled at his brother, a grin devilish enough to be worthy of the wicked duke himself. "I'm certain you would like to see your ward properly settled. How would you expect Isabel to make an eligible match if you keep her hidden away?''

Justin frowned at his brother, then planted his elbows on the arms of his chair. He clasped his hands, rested his chin on his knuckles, and pinned Isabel with a cool stare. "There is no hope for it, Miss Darracott. Once my grandmother has her mind set on something, no one can sway her. If she intends to put you on display this Season, on display you shall go.''

"I appreciate all you wish to do for me. But at my age, I really see no need to go to the expense and bother of bringing me into society," Isabel said, addressing Sophia in a calm voice.

"You sound as though you think you are some dried-up old spinster, ready to don a cap," Sophia said.

Isabel smiled. "I'm afraid I am.''

"Nonsense!" Sophia said. "With your face and figure, I shall have you married by the end of the Season.''

Isabel glanced at Justin, wondering what he thought of his grandmother's plan. He looked composed and utterly detached. Apparently the notion of the woman he had recently asked to marry him marrying another man did not move him. *Infuriating rogue!* "Please, there is no need to go to such bother for me."

"Justin, tell her to stop this ridiculous concern over expenses," Sophia said.

Justin smiled. "I'm afraid Miss Darracott has a very low opinion of my ability to act as guardian for her and her sisters. No doubt she is afraid I shall count pennies when it comes to their care."

Isabel bristled under his casual gaze. "I prefer not to be a burden."

Justin lounged back in his chair and rested his chin in the cup of his palm. "And I prefer not to quibble about food and clothing, Miss Darracott. It bores me. And I hate to be bored. The next I know, you'll be trying to find a position as a governess."

Isabel's eyes narrowed while fury heated her cheeks. "I can think of a few lessons I would like to teach to a certain arrogant member of the aristocracy, Duke."

"It would be interesting to see you try, Miss Darracott," Justin said, his deep voice low and deadly calm.

Isabel's skin prickled. She trembled with the effort to control the anger surging through her veins.

Sophia cleared her throat. "I expect you to choose the loveliest gowns, my child. You are my protégé, which means I expect you to shine. Amarante shall not lead you astray. Place yourself in her capable hands."

Isabel rose with all the dignity she could muster. "I shall endeavor not to embarrass you."

Justin watched Isabel leave, following the sway of muslin around her long legs. *Impudent little chit!* He rubbed his temples, trying to ease the pounding that had been centered there all morning. In his considerable experience with the fairer sex, he had discovered they were nothing if not predictable. Was Isabel really so different?

Women would marry a leper if he were rich and had a title. They loved to be lavished with presents. The more expensive the better. They adored being the center of a man's attention, and if they were not, they invariably pouted or fell into a fit of the vapors. If females were not essential for certain pleasurable pursuits, he would never bother with the money hungry she-devils.

Yet Isabel had thrown his marriage proposal in his face. And now the confounded female was actually worried about spending his money. The simple—if galling—truth was that Isabel defied his experience.

"Once I give her a proper town polish, she will be a great success," Sophia said.

Justin frowned. "She doesn't need a proper town polish."

"No?" Sophia smoothed the white lace at her cuff. "But she is a trifle provincial. Much too candid."

Justin coughed into his handkerchief. "Although it's an unusual trait in a woman, there is nothing wrong with honesty, Duchess."

Sophia frowned. "Are you catching cold?"

Justin wondered if the two soakings he had taken while at Bramsleigh had taken a toll on him. "It's nothing."

Clayton looked at Justin, an enigmatic smile curving his lips. "Have you ever had measles, Justin?"

"Of course I've had measles. Hasn't everyone past the age of twelve?"

"Not everyone," Sophia said. "As far as I remember, and I would remember, neither of you ever had measles.''

''I had them.'' Clayton grimaced. ''My first year in the army.''

Justin's breath stilled in his throat. ''I do not have measles.''

Sophia tapped her forefinger against her chin. ''Phoebe and Eloise both had them; Isabel said that's what delayed your return to town. Were you near the girls when they were ill?''

Justin swiped his handkerchief under his leaking nose. ''I do not have measles.''

Sophia lifted one finely arched brow. ''No. Of course you do not. Measles would not dare infect a man as ferocious as you.''

Justin glared at his grandmother. ''This nonsense about launching Isabel into society. You do realize you will be unleashing every fortune hunter in London after the girl. She inherits twenty thousand pounds upon her marriage.''

Sophia shrugged her slender shoulders. ''You shall be there to protect her. Without your consent, she inherits nothing.''

''Do you honestly expect me to trail after her like some bloody mastiff?''

Sophia lifted one golden brow. ''You are her guardian. I expect you to make certain the wrong sort of men stay away from her. I expect to see her properly settled by the end of the Season.''

Isabel married to another man. The thought settled with an unexpected weight against Justin's chest, as heavy as a millstone. He glanced at Clay and found his brother studying him, in that singular way he had of penetrating the defenses that kept the rest of the world out of his thoughts. *It does not matter one farthing to me, brother.*

148

Clayton grinned. *Certain of that, are you?*

"I'd better check on Isabel to make certain she orders what she needs." Sophia rose from the sofa. Perceval jumped up and followed her from the room.

With his left hand, Clayton brushed at the silvery gray cat hair on his dark gray coat. "Did you enjoy Vachel's last night?"

Justin rubbed his taut neck muscles. He still was not certain why he had done what he had last night. Susannah had been equally amazed, but, he suspected, not terribly disappointed. She had led him to the door of her bedchamber, but that was as far as he had gone. For some odd reason it had all seemed so damned artificial. After slipping a roll of bank notes into the bodice of her gown, he had left Vachel's without a backward glance. "I didn't see anything at Vachel's I wanted."

Clayton nodded as he picked more cat hair from his coat. "I can see why Isabel caught your interest. She has a special quality about her. You seldom meet a beautiful woman who is so unaffected. She is charming."

"Isabel had nothing to do with my not enjoying Vachel's."

Clayton glanced up from his coat, his gaze holding all the sarcasm missing from his voice. "Of course not."

"It was a long drive from Bramsleigh. And all that nonsense about theatrics put me off, that's all."

"I can see where it might."

Justin coughed into his handkerchief. "How did you find the Trenton musicale?"

Clayton smiled. "A dead bore."

Justin laughed. "I hope you have dropped this little idea of finding a bride from that list you had Sophia make."

"I am thinking of adding to it." Clayton plucked a few hairs from his sleeve. "I have a feeling that once the gentlemen of the ton get a look at Isabel, you are going to have a legion of besotted suitors to deal with. As her guardian, you shall have to consider her choices carefully."

An image of hundreds of panting fools salivating over Isabel filled Justin's mind. He squeezed his hands together, agitated by a nagging prickle somewhere in his belly. If he were not certain he was immune to the emotion, he would have believed it was jealously. "I pity the poor block who is foolish enough to marry that little termagant."

Clayton settled back against his chair. "I pity the poor fool who can't see his own feelings before it is too late."

Justin covered his mouth with his hand as he coughed. "I shall be brought to heel by no woman, Clay. I found no empty holes in my life before I met Isabel; there will be none after she is out of my life."

Clayton shrugged. "You know better than I do."

"That's right." Justin swiped his handkerchief under his damp nose. If it was the last thing he did, he would get over this affliction called Isabel.

Familiarity was the key, he decided. The more exposure he had to the disease, the less influence she would have on him. Women always lost their charm upon close inspection. He would all but move into his grandmother's house. He would see Isabel day and night. Each time she turned around, he would be there. In no time at all he would be cured.

Chapter Eleven

"Turn around slowly," Sophia said, waving her hand in a lazy circle. "Let me take a look at you."

Isabel complied, turning slowly, the diaphanous gauze of the sea green overdress floating out around the ivory silk slip that brushed her legs. The gown was Sophia's, one of many the duchess had dropped into her lap this afternoon. Several of Sophia's maids had been kept busy from that moment making minor alterations to fit the dresses and gowns for Isabel. She rested her hand over the swell of her breasts, amply revealed by the low neckline. "This is the fashion?"

"I suppose it seems a little revealing to someone who has been living in Bramsleigh, but it is quite the thing."

Isabel glanced doubtfully at her figure in the mirror. She had never worn anything this revealing in her life.

"I assure you, dear, all the ladies wear their gowns cut in this fashion."

"I still feel as though I am taking the clothes right off of your back."

Sophia dismissed Isabel's words with an elegant sweep of her hand. "Nonsense. I've never worn that gown, or any of the others I've given you."

Isabel could not imagine owning anything this beautiful without ever having worn it. "Never?"

Sophia laughed softly. "I shall let you know a secret about me, my dear. I have a dreadful habit of buying so many gowns in a Season that I never have a chance to wear all of them. I swear each year I shall not do it again. Then the next Season arrives, I see so many lovely things, and before I know it, I have once again purchased more than two women could possibly wear in any given year."

Although her father had been comfortably situated, Isabel had never been presented with any reason to indulge in such extravagance. The thought of what it all must cost set her head spinning.

"Besides, we can't sit at home waiting for Amarante to finish with your new clothes. There are a few select parties I think we shall attend before your ball. I want you to meet a few of my acquaintances. And we really must attend Lady Sefton's dinner next week. Maria shall be delighted with you. I think we shall give London a peek at you before the ball. But only a peek."

"I doubt they shall see anything exceptional."

"Nonsense. You shall delight them all. I must say Foster is an artist with hair. Don't you agree?"

Isabel glanced into the mirror, startled once again by her own image. Foster, Sophia's hairdresser, had appeared soon after Madame Amarante had departed early this afternoon. He had trimmed Isabel's wavy hair, allowing wispy curls to fall over her brow and graze the sides of her cheeks. The rest of the heavy mass he had coaxed into an intricate entwining of braids on the top of her head. The transformation utterly amazed her. She had never considered herself out of the ordinary, but tonight the woman looking back at her from the mirror looked like a fairy princess. "I hardly recognize myself."

Sophia squeezed her shoulders, the sweet scent of her perfume drifting around Isabel. "You look beautiful. Now come along; I want my grandsons to get a look at you."

What would Justin think of her now? Isabel wondered. Not that she cared, of course. Well, perhaps just a little. All right, she knew very well that she cared far too much what that infuriating male thought of her. Yet she couldn't seem to help it.

The rumble of masculine laughter rolled into the hall from the open door of the drawing room as they drew near. Her heart pounded as they approached the room where Justin and his brother were waiting for the ladies to join them before dinner.

Justin and Clayton were standing near the hearth, deep in conversation. They both turned toward the door when Isabel and Sophia entered the room. Although they had changed for dinner, donning black coats and buff-colored trousers, Isabel recognized Justin in a single swift beat of her heart.

Clayton smiled when he saw her, an appreciative look entering his beautiful eyes. Justin had an entirely different reaction. He frowned, his thick black brows drawing toward one another, his full lips pulling into a tight line. His critical gaze brushed from the coils of hair on top of her head to the green satin slippers peeking out from under her hem. The swift, brazen appraisal left her feeling certain he had found some fault with her.

She resisted the urge to touch her hair. It did not

matter what he thought of her altered appearance, she assured herself. Her world did not spin on Justin's axis. Still, she could not prevent the scalding tide of irritation washing over her.

Justin lifted his gaze and looked straight into her eyes, revealing, for an instant, the flame burning there. Isabel's breath evaporated from her lungs. Beneath that dark, sultry look, excitement sparked through her, warming her skin, shivering along her limbs. A grin tipped his lips, a glitter of amusement entering his stunning eyes. He knew. The man knew exactly how that glance had made her feel as giddy and tremulous as a schoolgirl. Oh, how she would love to wipe that smile off his handsome face.

Isabel managed a smile of her own as Clayton took her hand. "You look enchanting, Miss Darracott."

"Thank you," Isabel murmured, hoping no one would notice the turmoil Justin had caused with one smoldering glance.

Justin rested his arm on the mantel. "One of your gowns, Grandmama?"

Sophia flicked open her fan. "It never suited me. But it looks divine on our Isabel."

Justin's eyes narrowed as he lowered his gaze to Isabel's décolletage. "I suppose you had your maid remove a band of lace from the neckline."

Isabel touched the slim band of ivory lace edging the low neckline of the gown, her skin tingling as though Justin had touched her with the brush of his strong hands.

"Of course I did." Sophia flicked the fan back and forth beneath her chin, fluttering the golden curls framing her face. "Can't have her looking like an elderly matron."

Justin frowned. "What do you want her to look

like? A pastry on display for every salivating male within a mile?''

Isabel's neck tingled with the rise of her blush. ''I am certain the duchess would not allow me to wear anything inappropriate.''

''Precisely.'' Sophia closed her fan with a snap.

Justin's lips drew into a tight line. ''If you've chosen that kind of neckline for her other evening gowns, you can tell the modiste to start sewing in the lace.''

Sophia glared at him. ''I shall do no such thing. You will find gowns far more revealing in every ballroom in London. And well you know it, my boy. You might wish her to look dowdy, but I do not.''

''Don't allow my brother to bother you, Miss Darracott. The gown is fashionable. And you are lovely in it. Justin is just experiencing the pangs of a guardian who has suddenly realized how difficult it will be to keep all of your suitors under rein.''

Justin's nostrils flared, and Isabel could almost hear him wishing his brother to the devil. She smiled up at Clayton, perhaps a little too warmly, in gratitude for acting as her champion. ''Thank you, my lord.''

Clayton took her hand. ''I would hope you feel comfortable enough with me to use my given name. We are, in a way, family now.''

His touch was warm, the grasp of his large hand gentle. Clayton felt as safe and comforting as her own brother. Still, all the while she was painfully aware of Justin glaring at her, the heat of his displeasure scalding her despite the distance of several feet. ''I will, if you would do me the same favor.''

Clayton smiled. ''It would be an honor.''

Soon after Eloise and Phoebe joined them, they went in to dinner. Sophia sat at the head of the table, with her grandsons taking places on opposite sides. Clayton seated Isabel to Sophia's left, then took the place next to her. Although the width of the table separated her from Justin, Isabel thought the distance not nearly wide enough to provide any sense of calm. The man had the most uncanny way of making her feel as jittery as a cat in a room filled with snarling canines.

Based on the previous dinner she had experienced at Sophia's table, Isabel knew the chef was excellent, the food superb. Yet she scarcely tasted the delicate onion-flavored soup, or the salmon in butter and herb sauce. The delicate scent of burning beeswax candles mingled with the aroma of roasted duck in orange sauce. Still, the delicious repast might have been bread and water for all she took notice. Only Justin commanded her attention.

Several times she noticed Justin press his handkerchief to his nose and mouth, stifling a cough. She wondered if his two forays into the rain had given him a cold. Or . . . Phoebe and Eloise had had a cough just before they succumbed to measles. She dismissed that possibility. Justin had been quite adamant that he had no chance of contracting the illness.

Isabel managed to maintain a conversation with Clayton and Sophia, while she tried not to focus on the man seated across from her. Still, she failed. Time and time again she caught herself watching Justin. There was definitely something wrong with her, she decided. Only a besotted idiot would find the way a man touched a napkin to his lips utterly fascinating.

"I bought a book called *Avery's Book of London* at Hatchard's today," Phoebe told Justin, her excited voice catching Isabel's attention. "It lists all the curiosities, amusements, exhibitions, public establishments, and remarkable objects to see in London. I was hoping you might come with us to see the Tower tomorrow."

Isabel froze at her sister's innocent invitation.

156

Spending time in Justin's company would only exacerbate this blasted infatuation. "Phoebe, I am certain the duke has more important things to do than act as our guide to London."

Justin fixed Isabel with a cool stare. Light from the silver candelabra in the center of the table flickered against his face, illuminating the subtle tightness in his slight smile. "Few people are ever certain of what I might do, Miss Darracott."

Isabel held his cold stare, hoping none of her anxiety showed beneath his arrogant attempt to intimidate her. He might think her a country mouse, but she would not let this worldly lion frighten her. "I never realized you would be interested in escorting us all over London."

"Oh, we shall have such a wonderful time," Phoebe said, smiling up at Justin. "We shall see the menagerie, the mint, and look for headless ghosts."

"Headless ghosts." Justin glanced down at Phoebe, then cast a dark glance at Isabel.

Isabel returned a smile she hoped held more confidence than she felt. "Have you any interest in ghost hunting, Duke?"

"I am certain you could find no better guide than your guardian." Sophia smiled at Justin. "What time shall you be around to collect the ladies, Justin?"

Isabel held Justin's gaze, certain he would find a way to escape the disagreeable task. He certainly would not condescend to act as a tour guide, which was better for everyone. Oh, yes, it was far better to keep her distance from Justin Trevelyan.

A slow smile curved his lips. "I shall expect you to be ready by one, Miss Darracott."

Isabel twisted the linen napkin in her lap. He had agreed so he might irritate her. She forced her lips into a smile. "We shall be ready."

After dinner, as she walked with Sophia toward the drawing room, someone touched her arm. Before she even turned she knew whose warm, bare hand had brushed her skin; the sparks skittering along her nerves left no room for doubt. She paused in the hall and looked up into Justin's face.

"Would you care for a game of chess?"

His deep voice vibrated through her, scattering her wits like autumn leaves in a strong breeze. "Chess?"

Light from a wall sconce glowed behind him, casting his face in shadows. Yet it did not hide completely his devilish grin. "It's a game of strategy, played on a board of alternating light and dark squares. I thought you might be familiar with it."

Isabel stiffened at his sarcastic tone. "I am familiar with the game."

He coughed into his handkerchief. "Would you care to play?"

She frowned. "Are you feeling ill? You look a little flushed."

His lips pulled into a tight line. "I assure you, Miss Darracott, I am fine."

The arrogant rogue could not even admit to the smallest weakness.

"Do you care to play?" he asked, sounding bored with the idea.

She had been playing chess since she was five. She smiled up at him, thinking of how much she would enjoy beating him. "Certainly."

Later, in Sophia's drawing room, Isabel stared at the battlefield, deciding her next move. Until now she had thought herself a fairly accomplished chess player. At the moment, she was in danger of losing her throne to a man she would dearly love to strangle. He never took more than a few moments to contemplate the consequences of one of his moves. His play seemed reckless. Yet the strategy behind each move was ruthless in its perfection. She rested her fingertip on her remaining knight and searched for a way through Justin's defenses.

"You do realize this isn't an actual war. If you win, you shall not have the pleasure of throwing me into a dungeon."

Isabel looked up from the chessboard to the man sitting across from her. Justin was leaning back in his chair, grinning at her, obviously enjoying himself at her expense. Oh, how she would love to toss his arrogance into a dungeon and throw away the key. She slid her knight into position. "I might not have the pleasure of tossing you into a dungeon. But I would take a great deal of pleasure in beating you."

Justin glanced at the board. He moved his bishop straight into an unguarded position near her king. "I believe that particular pleasure shall have to wait. Checkmate."

Isabel clenched her hands into fists on her lap. He was without a doubt the most infuriating male she had ever encountered in her entire life.

"You would play better if you didn't allow your anger to get in the way."

Eloise and Phoebe had retired for the evening. Isabel glanced to where Sophia and Clayton were playing piquet at a table across the room. Since the chess table was nestled in one corner of the room, they were far enough away from the others to provide some privacy. Still, Isabel kept her voice low as she spoke. "I am not angry."

Justin lifted one black brow. "You are giving a fine performance, then. I suppose that's what misled me."

How could she explain her anger without betraying her treacherous feelings for the rogue?

"Since I am the one who was rejected, one would

think I should be the angry one.'' He coughed into his handkerchief. ''But I assure you, I bear you no ill will.''

''Under the circumstances, I could not imagine why you would.'' He would have to feel something more than lust for her to be angry over her refusal to marry him.

''I can only assume you are still angry over this morning.''

It took her a moment to realize what he meant. The man had a way of doing that to her, turning her brain to mush. ''You should know, I spent enough today to keep a small monarchy solvent for a year.''

He laughed, the sound a soft rumble from deep in his chest. ''I never realized buying a few gowns for a woman could cause such fury.''

''I suppose you have had a great deal of experience in buying gowns for your mistresses.'' She regretted the words the instant they were spoken. They sounded far too much like the words of a jealous female.

Justin glanced at her, a speculative gleam in his gray-green eyes. ''Is that what has your back up? Are you afraid I shall start thinking of you as one of my mistresses?''

An image of this man surrounded by a harem of beautiful women blossomed in her mind. She squeezed her hands in her lap. It was absolutely none of her concern, she assured herself. ''Nothing of the kind. I am simply not accustomed to being in a position to accept charity. Given the circumstances, I find it all the more galling.''

Justin's thick black brows beetled over the slim line of his nose. ''As you said a lifetime ago, I think it would be best for both of us to forget what happened at Bramsleigh.''

She forced her lips into a smile that felt brittle enough to break. "Of course."

"I would hope we can put the incident behind us."

She clenched her hands in her lap. "Consider it forgotten."

He rubbed his right temple. "As your guardian I have the right to bestow some amount of pin money. Consider the gowns a part of that."

"It is too much."

"I shall decide what is too much." He leaned forward, resting his arms on either side of the inlaid wooden chessboard. He kept his voice low as he spoke. "I am hardly a pauper, Isabel. And, in spite of what you care to think of me, I am not the sort of man who would have his wards run around in rags."

There was something defensive in his deep voice, something vulnerable in his eyes, something that made her wish she could strip away the sardonic mask he presented the world. "I did not mean to insult you."

He sat back in his chair. "You would do me the favor to stop regarding everything as charity. If I didn't think I could take proper care of you and Eloise and Phoebe, I would not have accepted your guardianship."

How many people would doubt his ability to be a guardian to anyone? From what Gerard had told her about the Duke of Marlow, most people regarded him as a scoundrel, incapable of taking responsibility for anything other than his own pleasure. What did Justin think of his own reputation?

Once again she caught herself wondering what might be hidden beneath his fierce facade. She had caught glimpses of a very different Justin Trevelyan from the harsh, arrogant aristocrat he presented to the world. She still bore the wounds from having ventured too close to the lion.

"It's getting late." He rose from his chair. An odd expression crossed his features, a look of utter surprise.

"Are you all right?"

"I am fine." He took one wobbly step, then sank slowly, missing the chair on his downward spiral. He whacked the carpet, landing on his bottom with a dull thud.

"Marlow!" Isabel hurried to his side. She knelt beside him. "You are ill."

"I am all right," Justin said, struggling to rise.

Isabel gripped his arm, staying him. "Don't try to stand. You might injure yourself."

Justin leaned against her side, his head lolling onto her shoulder. She slipped her arm around him and held him close. The unnatural heat of him radiated through her gown. "My . . . head aches."

Isabel smoothed the black waves back from his fevered brow. "You are burning up."

"I am fine. Just a little dizzy."

"Justin, are you all right?" Sophia asked.

Isabel glanced up as Sophia and Clayton came to investigate. "Has he ever had measles?"

Clayton grinned. "I believe he has them now."

Justin dragged his head from Isabel's shoulder. "I do *not* have the measles."

"Of course not. You are far too fierce to have measles." Sophia turned to Clayton. "Please take your brother upstairs to his old bedchamber. I will send someone for the doctor."

Justin pulled away from Isabel and attempted to stand. "I don't need a blasted doctor!"

Clayton grabbed Justin's arms and hauled him to his feet. He bent and tossed his brother over his shoulder. "Have a bottle of wine sent up," he said, marching toward the door.

"What the bloody hell do you think . . ." Justin's words dissolved in a low groan.

Isabel cringed at the tortured sound. When they had left, she turned to Sophia. "It's my fault he is ill. I should have kept him away from the girls, but he seemed certain he wasn't going to catch anything."

Sophia smiled. "There is nothing you could have done to alter his course of action. He has a stubborn streak wider than the Atlantic."

"Oh, he can be infuriating. But, to tell you the truth, I don't know how I would have managed without him when the girls were ill."

Sophia took Isabel's arm. "Then I shall not hesitate to call upon you to help in the sickroom."

"Of course."

Sophia patted Isabel's arm. "I have a feeling he is going to be a dreadful patient."

Chapter Twelve

You are the devil's spawn!

Blackness closed around Justin, pressing upon him, squeezing his chest. He leaned back against the door, not wanting to think of what hid in the darkness of the small room. He would not fall asleep this time. He would not let them bite him. Not this time.

Repent your sins. Fall on your knees and beg forgiveness.

The angry voice vibrated through the locked door. Justin closed his eyes against the blackness. He clenched his fists against the solid oak of the door, fighting the fear. He would not break. He would crawl on his hands and knees for no man.

You belong in hell!

Did he? What had he done for the Almighty to turn his back on him? But it was true. He was damned. Justin knew it. His own father could not stand the sight of him. Tears scalded his cheeks. His body shook with the effort to control his sobs, to keep them private. He would not give the man on the other side of this door the satisfaction of his tears.

It happens with twins. One is for the angels. The other for the demons. You shall burn in hell!

"No!" Justin could not get enough air. His breath came short and shallow, each gasp drawing a damp, musty taste across his tongue. Something stirred in the corner. He squeezed back against the door. "Let me out!"

When you beg.

Justin bit his lip, fighting the pitiful sobs he could not prevent. He would not beg. He would never beg. "Bastard! Bloody bastard!"

"Marlow!"

He broke the bonds of sleep in a rush, jerking upright, as though breaking the surface of a pool where he had spent too long beneath the water. His heart slammed against the wall of his chest. He gulped at the air, trying to pull breath into lungs that felt thick and heavy in his chest.

"It is all right."

A soft, feminine voice curled around him. A gentle hand clasped the taut muscles of his upper arm.

"You were dreaming. That's all. You are all right."

He turned his head toward that soft voice. A pale gray light slipped through the windows, faintly illuminating a slender figure dressed in white standing beside the bed. It took a moment for his blurry eyes to define her features. "Isabel?"

"Yes. It's Isabel." She smiled at him, warm and gentle. "Lie back. You have had a nasty dream."

A dream. Bloody hell! He thought the nightmares were buried. It had been a long, long time since they had plagued him. He fell back into a pillow of soft eiderdown. The soft white cambric of his nightshirt stuck to his damp skin. His head pounded. His body ached, as though someone had used him to practice his boxing skills.

She rested her hand against his brow, her skin cool and soft against his burning forehead. "How are you feeling?"

Like a blasted idiot. A grown man, still plagued by childhood terrors. God, he was pathetic. He looked up at her, searching for some sign of disdain in her eyes, finding only a gentle concern. "I'm hot."

"Would you like some lemonade?"

He tried to swallow, but his mouth felt as dry as parchment. "I would like a bottle of Irish whiskey."

"I am afraid lemonade is all I can offer."

"I'll take it."

She turned and filled a glass from a pitcher sitting on the table beside the bed. When he struggled to sit, she slipped her arm around his shoulders. She supported him while he drank. The crisp scent of lemons filled his nostrils while a tangy sweet taste flooded his parched tongue. After he drained the glass, she took it from his trembling fingers and lowered him back to the pillows.

"Better?"

Justin frowned. "You have a delightful sense of humor."

"I am afraid you are going to feel horrible for a few days." She dipped a cloth in water from the basin on the table, squeezed out the excess, and rested the cool, damp linen over his brow. Justin sighed from the momentary relief for his heated skin.

"I am really terribly sorry about this," she said.

"Are you the one who used me for boxing practice?"

"No. But I am the one who allowed you to tend to two girls with measles."

"Yes. This is entirely your fault. I am certain you arranged for Phoebe and Eloise to become ill while I was at Bramsleigh."

"I should have insisted you stay away from them."

He managed a weak smile. "And do you imagine I would have listened?"

She frowned. "I doubt you listen to anyone when you have your mind set. You can be dreadfully stubborn."

"It is one of my finer qualities."

She smoothed the counterpane over his chest. "Are you warm enough? Should I get another blanket?"

"Only if you intend to roast me alive."

She smiled, a glitter of mischief entering her eyes. "I have had that notion more than a few times."

"That hardly makes you a member of an exclusive club."

"No doubt. But few have had you in such a weakened state." She lifted her brows. "At the moment, you are very nearly entirely at my mercy."

He did not need reminding of his feeble state. The mighty men and women of the ton would howl with delight if they knew the Devil of Dartmoor had been laid low by a childhood ailment. They would be even more delighted to know of the nightmares. "I suppose Sophia put you up to playing nursemaid."

"You were there to help when my sisters were ill; it is only right I should be here for you."

He pulled the cloth from his brow. He felt as awkward as he had his first night at Almack's, and every bit as vulnerable—as though he had been stripped naked and tossed into a ballroom filled with women eager to evaluate every aspect of his masculinity. "I am not a child. There is no need to fuss over me like a mother hen. I assure you, I do not expect any ridiculous notions of guilt or duty from you. And you can certainly keep your pity to yourself.''

She studied him a moment, and he had the uncomfortable feeling she could look straight past the walls hiding his ugliest secrets. ''I thought you might like company,'' she said, taking the damp cloth from his hand. ''But if you would like me to leave, you need only say so.''

He did not. Still, he did not want to be the recipient of her charity either. ''What you do is entirely up to you. If you wish to stay, I have no objections.''

''Then you think you might tolerate my company for a while?''

''You may stay if you stop tripping over your guilt for something that was never in your control.''

She nodded, amusement tugging at the corners of her lips. ''I think I can manage.''

He released the breath he had been holding. ''Then sit, and stop hovering over me.''

She dampened the cloth in cool water and rested it over his brow before taking a seat in the armchair someone had placed near the bed. ''Would you like me to get a book from the library? I could read something to you.''

He did not want to be left alone. Not now. ''Perhaps later.''

''Do I run the risk of having my head bitten off if I ask you if there is anything you need or want?''

Unfortunately there was something he wanted, with an intensity even the illness could not dull. Pale morning light touched her face, glinting on the shiny curls falling over her brow, finding the tiny perfections of her features. He had once thought he would not have noticed this woman in a crowded room. Now he realized he had underestimated her charm in every way. When she had walked into the room last night, it had taken every ounce of his will to fight an insidious impulse to toss her over his shoulder, carry her off, and exorcise this idiotic infatuation by taking his fill of her.

"I wasn't trying to sound like a lion with a thorn in his paw. I apologize if I did."

She smiled generously in light of his stilted apology. "You have reason to be disagreeable, I suppose."

And more reasons than he cared to imagine for being infatuated with this woman. She was new to him. A different breed. One he had no inkling of how to handle. "I hope the girls aren't disappointed about our outing to the Tower being postponed."

She smiled. "Clayton is taking them this afternoon."

His muscles stiffened. "Is he?"

"I didn't think you would mind. I am sure you have seen everything in London."

"I have." But for some strange reason he had been looking forward to showing it all to Isabel and her sisters. "We had a tutor who insisted we see every historical cranny. He was fond of giving long, boring lectures." Almost as much as he enjoyed punishing his recalcitrant charge.

Isabel released her breath in a sigh. "I cannot imagine growing up in London the way you did."

"I didn't. When I was ten, my tutor brought us for a tour that lasted two weeks."

"When Sophia said this was your boyhood bedchamber, I assumed you had lived here most of the time."

"This was my bedchamber when my mother and father would come for the Season. They never left us behind in the country. After my mother died, my father stopped bringing us. He came here to live. Except for that one excursion to learn historical London firsthand, we stayed in Dartmoor, until my father sent us to Harrow.''

A shadow of a frown tugged at her features. "How old were you when your mother died?"

"Nine."

"My mother died when I was fifteen. It must have been even more terrible to lose her when you were only a child. I imagine you have a difficult time even remembering her."

"I have memories of her. A few." Each of them a precious relic from a place and time that seemed a fairy tale to him now. "She always smelled like spring flowers, and her voice was soft. Every night she would read to us until we fell asleep. I remember trying to stay awake just to listen to her."

"I'm surprised your father didn't bring you to London with him."

Justin shot her a sharp glance. "Why do you say that?"

"He must have been dreadfully lonely after your mother died. I would have thought he would want his sons near him."

He laughed, but the sound was less mocking and far more bitter than he had intended. "He wanted nothing to do with us."

She studied him, as though she were trying to fit together the pieces of his life. "Perhaps you reminded him too much of the life he had lost."

He closed his eyes against the pounding in his head. "I can see you have painted my father in some romantic, terribly tragic light."

"There must have been some reason why he abandoned you and your brother." She stroked her hand over his hair, gentle, soothing.

Justin swallowed a sigh of pleasure crawling up his throat. "I suppose we interfered with his social life."

Her hand stilled against his hair. "That would be too horrible to imagine."

Justin looked up at her, seeing in her eyes the ugly evidence of the pity he had heard in her voice. He had suffered enough conversation concerning his father. "Has Sophia overwhelmed you with all this talk about plunging you into society?"

Isabel withdrew the comforting touch of her hand from his hair. "She is like a whirlwind."

"She will pluck you out of one world and dump you into another. Make no mistake about it. The ton live in a different world from the one you left behind in Bramsleigh."

She nodded, her expression revealing her unease. "I do not wish to disappoint her. But I feel it is inevitable."

"In what way?"

"She has such lofty expectations for me. At my age, I have little chance of becoming the tremendous success she expects me to be."

Justin knew better. Isabel might not be the most beautiful woman the ton had ever seen, but she would turn more than a few heads. Something dangerous slithered inside of him when he thought of all the men who would be tripping over themselves trying to get near her. "You are an heiress. Every fortune hunter in London—and there are a legion of them—will be sniffing after your skirts. You need to take care."

She turned her face, staring out the windows. "I cannot imagine wanting to marry for the sake of money."

"Most people can."

She glanced at him. "I suppose you have had more than a few women throw themselves at you."

"I have. Although few play the game with me now."

"Since you have cultivated the title of the Devil of Dartmoor?"

Justin's chest tightened at the epitaph. "A poor reputation has its advantages. Before they realized I wasn't easy prey, at least three carriages would conveniently break down outside of my home every week. At the height of the craze I counted eleven. You could not imagine the extraordinary number of females who swooned from the heat of crowded ballrooms when they were just within my reach, so I might catch them before they collapsed to the floor. The last one who tried that particular tactic ended up in a crumpled heap at my feet. Strange, but that tended to curb the affliction."

She traced the outline of one of the pouncing gold lions in the blue silk counterpane by his side, the soft touch whispering along his thigh. "I can see why you might have grown a little jaded where it comes to women."

"Men are no better when it comes to a fortune. And to many, twenty thousand pounds is a fortune."

"I suppose there are men who will pretend to love and adore me all for the sake of my inheritance."

"It isn't a pleasant sensation when you suspect someone is interested in you solely for mercenary reasons. But you soon become adept at seeing the truth behind false smiles."

"And in the end you lock yourself away, far behind thick castle walls, which no one can penetrate."

"If you are smart, that is exactly what you do."

She looked up at him, her expression wiped clean of emotion. "And what if you see a mercenary where there isn't one? What if you are so busy protecting your heart that you abandon all chance of sharing your life with someone very special?"

Would she meet someone special? Justin wondered.

Her Tristan. A man capable of all those foolish romantic notions she demanded from a husband. A man who would earn the right to take her in his arms at night. A man who would spread all that soft brown hair across his pillow, touch her, hold her, and kiss those sweet lips. Justin clenched the counterpane in his fist, irritated by the ache of jealousy low in his belly. "You cannot trust any of them. Remember that."

"You make it sound as though every man in London is a scoundrel."

"Most of them are."

"Including your brother?"

Justin's breath halted with her sudden mention of his brother. "There isn't a better man to be found in the whole of England. Clay is a paragon, a war hero, a man who never makes a wrong step. Still, I doubt you and Clay are well suited."

She curled her hand into a fist on the counterpane beside him. "Why do you say that? Do you think I'm not good enough for him? Do you think I'm . . . tainted?"

The catch in her voice tore like talons at a conscience he had thought dead and buried. "What happened between us has nothing to do with this. You are still as innocent as the day you were born."

"Then why do you think I'm not suited for your saintly brother?"

"I recall you telling me you would only marry for a grand passion of the heart. You won't find that with Clay."

Her eyes narrowed. "I suppose you think I am incapable of arousing such passion in a man."

He held her angry stare, seeing the bitterness he had aroused in those beautiful eyes. He touched her cheek, her smooth skin cool against his heated fingers. "You have proof of the kind of passion you can ignite in a man, Belle. But it isn't enough for you.''

Warmth abandoned her smile, leaving an icy reserve in its wake. "I cannot imagine lust being enough for anyone."

"You underestimate the lure of it." He slipped his hand around the tightly clenched fist she held against the bed and lifted her hand to his lips. Her eyes grew wide as he opened his mouth against the inside of her wrist. He flicked his tongue over her skin, licking a faint salty taste from skin as smooth as satin.

She snatched her hand away from him, but not before he felt a ripple of excitement tremble through her. Her breathing came in short puffs as she stared at him. "I thought we had put all of this behind us."

He held her confused gaze, blood pumping hard and hot into his loins. "Have we?"

"If not, I suggest we do." She rose from her chair. "I'll see if there is anything of interest in the library I might read to you. Something elevating. Something that will take your mind off of your more primitive instincts."

Justin only wished something such as that existed. He watched her walk across the room, her usual grace spoiled by the stiff rod of pride running down her spine. The door opened before she reached it.

"You have company, my dear," Sophia said, as she entered the room. "Your cousin Gerard Witheridge is waiting for you in the drawing room."

Justin clenched his jaw. What the devil was wrong with him? He had lost his mind. He should not care if a hundred men were flitting around her. Only an insane man pursued a course that would lead to destruction. She did not want what he had to offer. He had nothing else to give. That should be the end of it.

Yet, for all the logic in the world, he could not seem

to purge her from his blood. He stared at the canopy over his head. What the bloody hell was he going to do?

Isabel drew her fingertip over the inside of her wrist. Strange, there was no mark. The touch of Justin's lips had been a flame against her skin; his kiss should have left a brand. Still, the brand was inside, where it did not show. Why couldn't the man just leave her be? Why must he touch her and kiss her and make her wish for things beyond her reach?

"Isabel?"

Isabel flinched as Gerard touched her arm. "What?"

Gerard's golden brows drew together over the thin line of his nose. "I am not sure you have heard a word I have been saying."

"Oh. I'm sorry; what were you saying?"

He released his breath in an irritated huff. "I thought you might like to go for a ride with me in the park."

She smiled. "I can't. I promised the duke I would read to him this afternoon."

Gerard set his cup and saucer on the tea cart beside the sofa. "Isabel, I do hope you aren't becoming overly attached to the man."

Isabel's back stiffened. "What makes you think I am in danger of that?"

"He is a libertine. Which means, for one reason or another, he has a fatal affect on women. I would hate to see you hurt."

"I appreciate your concern. But I am in no danger."

Gerard rolled his eyes toward heaven. "Although I hate to say this, you are a green girl when it comes to men of his breed. I would not want you to start imagining he would ever marry you."

Isabel clasped her hands in her lap and fought her rising irritation. "So you think he would never marry a woman like me? Am I really so unattractive?"

Gerard shifted on the sofa. "I did not mean to imply anything of the sort."

"Didn't you?"

"How you can think I do not find you attractive when I have asked for your hand, I cannot imagine."

"But Marlow would never ask to marry me?"

Gerard moistened his lips. "Devil Trevelyan has never shown the smallest predilection toward marriage. In fact, the man abhors it."

Yet he had asked for her hand. It took all her will to keep from blurting out that fact. She rubbed her fingertips over the inside of her wrist. "With the right woman he might change his attitude."

"Men like Devil Trevelyan do not change for the better."

Could a man like Justin change? She wanted to believe he could. In spite of everything, she wanted desperately to believe there might be a future with him. "He is not as black as you paint him."

Gerard rested his arm on the back of the sofa and leaned toward her. "The night before last I saw Devil Trevelyan stroll into a notorious house of ill repute. So if you imagine you have had any influence on him, you are mistaken."

Isabel's stomach tensed. "How do you know it was a house of ill repute?"

He leaned back. "It is notorious. Every man in London knows of Vachel's in St. James's Square."

She managed a smile. "Do you know it well?"

He pursed his lips. "How well I know Vachel's is not the issue. I am concerned about the influence that man might exert over you."

Get Four Books Totally FREE — A $21.96 Value!

▼ Tear Here and Mail Your FREE Book Card Today! ▼

PLEASE RUSH
MY FOUR FREE
BOOKS TO ME
RIGHT AWAY!

Leisure Romance Book Club
P.O. Box 6613
Edison, NJ 08818-6613

AFFIX
STAMP
HERE

"I am not as green as you might think, Gerard. I do not see saints in sinners."

"And I hope you will not be deceived by a devil, even if he is handsome enough to turn a woman's head and is as rich as a nabob."

Isabel remained in the drawing room after Gerard left. She sat on the edge of the sofa, fighting the urge to curl up into a tight ball. She felt bruised inside, as though Justin had beaten her with his bare fists. She squeezed her eyes closed, fighting the sting of tears she could not prevent.

This was foolish. She had no claim over Justin. No right to feel this desolate because he had sought comfort with another woman. Yet she could not stem the flow of pain. Images assaulted her: Justin surrounded by beautiful women, touching them, holding them, kissing them the way he had once touched and held and kissed her.

She forced air past her tight throat. It certainly had not taken him long to get over his disappointment. The first night in London he had managed to slip back into the pattern of his life, while she was left aching, devastated over his total lack of any real affection for her. Perhaps she was as green as everyone seemed to think she was. She had actually coddled a small infant of hope that he might one day realize he wanted her for more than the simple pleasures of lust.

A terrible thing, hope. At times you do not even realize you are holding it close to your heart, until the moment someone plunges a knife into it. She swiped at her damp cheeks with her handkerchief. Nothing could be gained by self-pity. She had managed well enough before Justin Trevelyan had charged into her life. She would not allow him to make a complete wreck of her.

She rose, stiffened her sagging spine, and marched

to the library. She had never believed in running away from a problem. She would not do so now. She would not give Justin Trevelyan the satisfaction of knowing how much he had hurt her.

When she entered the library, the portrait hanging on a panel between a pair of mahogany bookcases built into the wall drew her attention. Sophia had pointed it out to her the other day. Then she had been only mildly curious about Justin's father. Now, she wondered what type of man could abandon his sons after their mother's death.

George William Trevelyan glared at her from the confines of his carved rosewood frame. He seemed cold and appraising, so much so that she shivered looking up at him. She would guess he had been close to forty when the portrait had been painted, and from the bitterness in his expression, she supposed it was after his wife had died.

Although he had been a handsome man—slender, with golden hair, a fine straight nose, and sharply defined cheekbones—there was little of him in his sons. She suspected Justin and his brother favored their mother. Still, she wondered if the key to Justin's harsh outlook on life lay with this man. Why would a father abandon his sons when they needed him most?

"Did you have a nice visit with your cousin?" Sophia asked.

Isabel glanced to the door and found the duchess standing on the threshold. "Yes."

Sophia strolled toward her. "He is a very handsome young man."

Isabel smiled. "I suppose most women would find Gerard attractive."

Sophia paused beside Isabel and lifted her gaze to the portrait of her son. "Justin and Clayton do not really look like him, do they?"

"No, they don't."

"They look like their mother." Sophia sighed. "Ah, Lisette was one of the most beautiful women of her day."

"Is there a portrait of her?"

"It is in my son's bedchamber. I suppose I should have it moved, now that he is no longer here to enjoy it." Sophia tilted her head, frowning up at the portrait. "I have never particularly cared for that likeness of my son. He looks so very stern in it. Still, I suppose the painter could only bring to life what he saw. And by that time, bitterness was what the world saw in my son."

"I suppose he would have to be a bitter man, to abandon his sons after their mother died."

Sophia glanced at her. "He did not abandon them, precisely."

The glimmer of embarrassment in Sophia's expression triggered regret in Isabel. "I'm sorry. I didn't mean to imply he had not acted accordingly. I am certain the duke had good reasons for not staying with his sons."

Sophia turned away from the portrait. She walked to a large, claw-footed desk a few feet away. She stared into the polished mahogany surface a long while before she spoke. "My son married at an early age. He had just turned nineteen; Lisette was eighteen. But they adored each other. I agreed, with her parents, to allow them to marry. I had married when I was sixteen, so I didn't see any reason to make them wait. A year after they were married, Justin and Clayton were born. I thought life was close to perfection."

"How did she die?"

"The twins were a difficult birth. I am not certain that she ever truly recovered from it. It would have been best if she never became pregnant again, but she did. More than once." Sophia rested the tips of her fingers against the desktop. "She had several miscarriages. She died giving birth to a daughter. The dear little girl died several hours after her mother. We named her Anne."

Isabel looked up at Justin's father, trying to understand the man. "I don't understand why he wouldn't cling to his sons, instead of leaving them in the country while he came to London."

"Guilt over Lisette's death."

"Guilt?"

"He felt as though he had killed her. He could not look at the boys without seeing her. He withdrew from everyone. Overnight he changed from a warm, affectionate man into a bitter stranger who shunned emotion of all kind."

Isabel thought of the man Justin had become—his volatile emotions, his pride, his arrogance. The simple fact that he could keep her at a distance even when he held her so close that she couldn't tell the beat of his heart from her own. At least now she understood some small piece of the man beneath Justin's harsh mask.

"When George came to London, I asked him if the boys might come live with me, but he insisted I would not be able to cope with them. Justin had grown rebellious after his mother's death. He had always been a lively boy, but after Lisette was gone, he took to indulging in pranks. Harmless, really."

"I imagine he was trying to win his father's attention."

Sophia nodded, a sad smile on her lips. "Instead, George left the boys in Dartmoor, under the care of a tutor. Justin managed to scare him off, as well as three others in seven months. Finally George hired one of the younger sons of the parish vicar to look after the boys. His name was Roger Wormsley and he had great political aspirations. Wormsley thought he could gain my son's favor if he could manage to bring Justin under tight rein. His tactics were . . . brutal.''

Isabel rubbed her hands over her arms, feeling chilled in the warm room. She thought of the harsh mask Justin presented to the world, and wondered if it hid wounds that had never truly healed.

''Clayton wrote to me several months after Wormsley had become their tutor. He told me he was afraid Justin was going to die unless I took him away from Wormsley's influence.''

''He was afraid his brother might die?''

''You have every reason to look shocked. I was. I shall never forget. . . .'' Sophia hesitated, then cleared her throat. Still, her voice trembled when she continued. ''I found Justin locked in a pitch-black storage room in the cellar, a place where Wormsley often put him to think about his transgressions. Poor little darling, he was still bloody from the latest beating Wormsley had given him. And so thin. So frightened. Yet he looked at me with eyes that were far too old for such a young boy, far too hard, and said, 'No one will ever break me, Grandmama.' Later, I realized the warm, affectionate boy I had known had died in that cellar room.''

Isabel recalled Justin's hesitation that day at the cave. Might it have had something to do with what had happened to him as a boy? What had it cost him to descend into that blackened pit to rescue Phoebe? ''What happened to this Wormsley?''

''My son turned him off without a reference.''

''Nothing more?''

''What more could he do, unless of course he wanted to bring attention to his own neglect of his sons. He did not. Instead, he sent his sons away to

Harrow.'' Sophia looked at Isabel, unshed tears glittering in her eyes.

Tears burned her own eyes. Yet Isabel kept them from falling.

''I'm sorry, I should not have rattled on this way. It is just . . . I want you to understand Justin.''

Isabel managed a smile. ''I would like very much to understand him. He has this mask he wears. I think he feels safe behind it. But if you try to peek beneath the mask, he swipes at you with his claws.''

''He isn't really as harsh as he appears, even though he seems to cherish his disreputable reputation.'' Sophia settled herself into a chair near the desk. ''There are times when I wonder if he really enjoys being called the Devil of Dartmoor, or if he was told so often he was worthless and wicked that he believes it.''

''If he has never ruined the reputation of a young lady of quality, why do people consider him so dangerous?''

''If you have never seen it, you can only imagine what ambitious mothers and daughters will do to gain the favor of a man who possesses both a respected title and a fortune.'' Sophia gave a delicate shiver. ''I am afraid it can be quite vulgar. Justin has seen the English huntress at her vilest.''

''He mentioned something about carriages breaking down outside of his house.''

''And women swooning into his arms. Mothers trying to become my acquaintance, so they might gain an introduction to my grandsons.'' Sophia shook her head. ''A few years ago, Justin started playing this little game with females who were out to trap him. He would choose one at a ball or party, lavish her with attention; then the next time he saw her he would act as though he did not know her. Needless to say, the lady in question looked a fool.''

"What a dreadful thing to do."

Sophia raised her hand, her ruby ring catching the sunlight spilling through the windows behind the desk. "In his defense, he chose only the most aggressive huntresses, never a shy or unassuming girl. It was his way of defending himself."

Isabel shook her head. "He could have avoided them. It was his way of teaching them a lesson."

"You have never seen an English huntress on the prowl. It is a little like trying to avoid a hungry lioness when she has her mind set on devouring you. Still, they learned their lesson. Now most mothers and their daughters steer a wide berth around my grandson."

"I can understand why they would."

Sophia took Isabel's hands in a warm grasp. "I have always hoped that one day Justin might find a woman who could tame his wild ways."

"I wonder if such a woman exists."

Sophia squeezed Isabel's hands. "I have a feeling she might be very close."

Isabel glanced away from Sophia's perceptive eyes. No matter how embarrassing her foolishness might be, she had the uncomfortable feeling Sophia could look straight through her to the truth.

"I have never seen him look at a woman the way he looks at you," Sophia said.

A few hours ago, Justin had kissed her wrist. Yet she knew it meant nothing to him. She only wished it meant nothing to her.

"And the way he reacted to your gown last night. Mind you, a perfectly respectable gown on any other woman. Yet he wants you swathed from head to toe. He has definite proprietary notions about you, my dear."

Isabel refrained from telling the duchess precisely what type of notions Justin had about her. "I'm not certain that we want the same things from life.''

Sophia sighed. ''Ah, well, an old woman can hope to see one of her favorite grandsons married and settled. I would love to see his children before I die.''

Longing so potent it filled her entirely rose within Isabel. She dearly wanted children of her own. Unfortunately she had only ever met one man whose children she wanted to bear. And unless she was willing to share him with half the women in London, she would have to forget the beguiling notion of becoming his bride.

Chapter Thirteen

Justin frowned at the man who stood beside his bed. Miles Cranely was one of three gentlemen who had descended upon Justin's bedchamber this morning like vultures to carrion. "Put that blasted thing down. I swear, Cranely, one would think you had never seen anyone with measles before."

Miles dropped his quizzing glass. Average in height, slim, with light blond hair and refined features, Miles had the look of a drawing room ornament. Yet he took every fence with the rest of them. "A leopard. That's what he reminds me of. All covered with spots and roaring."

Lord Braden Fitzwilliam, Earl of Ashbourne, rested one broad shoulder against a post at the foot of Justin's bed. "Careful, Miles, I wouldn't step too close to this particular leopard. He might bite."

Oliver Newbridge chuckled softly. Thick, sandy brown curls framed a round, boyish face liberally

185

sprinkled with freckles. "Laid low by a twelve-year-old chit."

Braden, Miles, and Oliver were perhaps the only three people in London, apart from his family, who had the audacity to tease Devil Trevelyan. Fortunately, they had earned the right years ago at Harrow, where they had forged a bond of friendship with Justin and Clayton that had only strengthened over the years. "I'm glad I could provide some amusement for you."

Miles smiled. "I can think of several ladies who would like to compliment the chit for cutting you down."

Justin's stomach curled. The ton thrived on gossip, especially tender tidbits carved from the powerful and the wealthy. Although he had grown accustomed to the more obscene rumors about him, he did not care to have people laughing behind his back. "Have the three of you managed to tell all of London? Or will I be reading a notice about my ailment in the *Times*?"

Braden grinned. "Rest easy. We wouldn't want to get into the habit of exposing one another. A man has to have some secrets."

"And talk about secrets." Oliver plopped on the foot of the mattress and propped his back against the carved bedpost. "Why the devil didn't you tell us you were the guardian of three females?"

Justin leaned back against his pillows. "I didn't know until a few weeks ago. They were a bequest from my father."

Miles twisted the black ribbon of his quizzing glass, sending the lens spinning. "I can see where your father would find a certain twisted pleasure in saddling you with three females. Still, I am curious why you brought them to London. I would have thought . . ." He paused, his lips parted, his gaze riveted on something across the room.

Justin glanced in that direction and found Isabel standing in the doorway. Soft curls framed the perfect oval of her lovely face. Pristine white muslin draped her slender form. One look sent the blood pounding through his veins. Silently he cursed the blasted day he had met her.

"That answers my question," Miles said.

Oliver looked at Justin, his brows lifting over his gray eyes. "It seems Justin has been hiding something from us."

"I'm sorry," Isabel said, backing toward the hall. "I didn't realize you had guests."

"Don't run away without giving us a chance to meet you." Braden wasted no time at all. Of course, he had always appreciated a lovely face. Justin clenched the silk counterpane in his hand as Braden advanced on Isabel, a hawk swooping in for the kill. "You must be Miss Darracott."

Tall and powerfully built, with dark brown hair curling over his brow, and a face that might have inspired a portrait of heaven's Gabriel, Braden had cut a swath through the women of the ton. He feasted on both widows and bored wives with an appetite that rivaled Justin's. Yet, unlike Justin, Braden had no qualms about the hypocrisy of marriage. He had every intention of marrying and filling his nursery.

Isabel smiled up at him as Braden took her hand. "You have me at a disadvantage, sir."

"That's how he likes 'em," Miles murmured.

Justin suppressed the anger surging inside him. Only a fool allowed his emotions to betray him. He would not become a pitiful bufflehead who pined and whimpered over a female who had eluded his grasp. He was made of stronger stuff. In a voice he felt certain betrayed nothing but mild disinterest, he introduced his friends to Isabel.

"I do not wish to interrupt your visit," Isabel said, as Braden ushered her into a chair near the bed.

"You aren't. They were just leaving," Justin said.

Braden smiled at Justin, mischief glinting in his dark eyes. "Were we?"

Justin frowned. "Yes, you were."

"Miles, do you have to be somewhere?" Braden asked.

Miles shook his head. "I can't think of anywhere I would rather be."

Braden looked at Oliver. "Do you?"

Oliver propped his booted feet on the bed beside Justin. "I'm free for the entire morning."

"Well, we know Marlow has nowhere to go." Braden drew a chair next to Isabel.

Justin tapped his fingertips against the counterpane at his side and contemplated the ways he would wring Braden's neck. Oblivious to Justin's murderous thoughts, Braden turned the full force of his smile on Isabel. She would check his advance, Justin thought. Isabel was hardly the type of woman to be dazzled by the all-too-obvious charms of a master seducer. She had far too much sense.

"So tell me, Miss Darracott, why have we never met before?" Braden asked.

Isabel toyed with a long, shiny curl that had fallen over her shoulder. "How often have you been to Bramsleigh, Lord . . . ?"

"Ashbourne."

"How often have you been to Bramsleigh, Lord Ashbourne?" she asked.

"Never."

Isabel smiled far too warmly. "Then you have your answer."

Justin clenched his jaw. She was flirting with the rogue, encouraging a man who took *hello* as an invitation to bed. "Then it's your first trip to London," Braden said. "And how are you finding the metropolis?"

Isabel sighed. "I'm afraid I haven't seen much of it."

Braden leaned toward her. "If you should ever desire a guide, it would be my pleasure to show you the sights."

She tilted her head and glanced at Braden through her lashes. "That's very kind of you."

Justin clenched the counterpane in his fist. Yet he endured in silence while Braden and the others engaged Isabel in conversation, and Isabel flirted with each and every one of them. He had to endure, he reminded himself. He could not throw his friends out on their ears. Even if he itched to do just that. He could not pound his chest and warn every man away from Isabel. He had no claims on her, except for those of guardian.

Still, he did not like the predatory look in Braden's dark eyes. And he had a feeling it was only one of many such looks he would have to endure. For the first time in his life, he understood the desire to wrap a woman in cotton wool and hide her from the world.

After his friends had left, Isabel remained with Justin. Had he noticed her first attempts at what Sophia called the art of flirtation? As much as she would like to deny it, her performance had been entirely for Justin's benefit. In spite of her best intentions, she could not rip the man from her heart. The insufferable creature had made a lair there, and refused to budge. "Your friends are charming."

Justin glanced at her, his expression revealing nothing but a lingering boredom. "Are they? I hadn't noticed."

Oh, she could strangle the man. "You were very quiet. Are you feeling particularly ill this morning?"

"Not particularly," he said, his voice dreadfully calm.

Isabel lifted a book from the bedside table. She had worked diligently to provoke him. The very least the odious creature could do was show a hint of jealousy. Just the smallest shred of a proprietary notion. A tiny growl. Anything to give her foolish heart a glimmer of hope. "Would you like me to read to you? I believe we can finish Miss Austen's book this afternoon. I'm anxious to see how Emma manages to extricate herself from the tangle she has made."

"Silly, flirtatious women often find themselves in a tangle. You would do well to keep that in mind."

Perhaps he had noticed. She settled into the chair by his bed. "Sophia told me the art of flirtation is essential for any woman entering society."

Justin's lips drew into a tight line. "Did she?"

Isabel smiled. "As a matter of fact, she has been giving me lessons."

One black brow lifted. "She has?"

The dark current of anger in his voice sent a delicious tingle rippling through her. Perhaps her efforts were not entirely wasted. "Do you know there is an entire language associated with the fan?"

"Really?" he asked, his dark voice filled with sarcasm.

"You shall have to imagine, because I haven't one with me." Isabel lifted her right hand and spread her fingers over her lips. "If I should carry a fan in my right hand and unfold it over the lower half of my face, it means *Follow me*."

A muscle bunched in his cheek with the clenching of his jaw. "Remarkable."

She touched the tip of her right forefinger as though

she were touching the tip of a fan. "This means *I wish to speak with you.*"

"I suppose it would be too much simply to say it."

"Far too obvious."

"Of course, we wouldn't want to give the male of the species any clear signals."

"I'm told they are clear enough, if the gentleman is paying attention. I like this one in particular. If I were to place my fan behind my head..." Isabel rested her fingertips against her nape. Her heart pounded against the wall of her chest, each quick beat warning her against the path she was taking. Still, she took a hesitant step. "I would be saying *Don't forget me.*"

He frowned, a curious look entering his eyes.

She held his gaze, words straining for voice inside her. *Have you forgotten, Justin? Do you ever think of those few moments in the cottage? Do you ever wish you could hold me in your arms once more? Do you ever dream of kissing me? The way I wish and hope and dream about you?*

The look in his expression shifted, as though he could hear her every thought. The anger that had burned in his eyes altered into something more potent, a longing that mirrored her own. A warm current swirled around her, as though she stood waist-deep in a flowing river, the water drawing her toward him. He looked so vulnerable lying there, so handsome behind his spots.

It was not wise. It was in truth terribly foolish. Yet she could not suppress this need inside her. She wished she could throw her arms around him, hold him close, never let him leave her side.

"Isabel, I..."

"What?" she asked, after he hesitated for a long, anxious moment.

He pursed his lips. "What if the gentleman in question had never learned this silent language of the fan?"

"According to Sophia, gentlemen learn soon after entering society." Isabel pressed the tip of her finger to her lips, the gesture Sophia had told her meant *Kiss me*. "Do you mean to say you don't understand what this means?"

He lowered his eyes, his gaze coming to rest on her lips. His lips parted, then closed. He seemed to struggle with some inner demon.

Surrender to it, Justin. Touch me. Hold me. She rubbed the tip of her finger over her bottom lip. *Kiss me*. "Do you understand what it means?"

He tore his gaze away from her. For a moment he sat staring down at the tightly clenched fist he held against the counterpane. "It means a foolish young woman will find herself in more trouble than she can handle."

Isabel folded her hands on the book resting in her lap. Heat prickled the base of her neck. She only hoped the blush would not rise and betray her. "Sophia assures me that flirtation is quite acceptable. Even expected."

Justin looked at her, anger flaring in the depths of his gray-green eyes. "Unless you want to find yourself flat on your pretty backside with a man between your thighs, I suggest you refrain from flirting with men like Braden Fitzwilliam. He eats little girls like you for breakfast."

Isabel stiffened. "A gentleman would not force his attentions on a lady. And I'm quite certain Lord Ashbourne is a gentleman."

"As I recall it wasn't so long ago you very nearly lost your innocence to another man you assumed was a gentleman."

"That was different."

"In what way?"

She was not about to confess the truth, tell him she had made the monumental error of falling in love with a heartless rogue. She forced her lips into a smile. "I'm no longer quite that naive."

He held her gaze for a long moment, as though he were searching for something in her eyes. She met his look with all the composure she could scrape together, hoping he would not detect how frail her defenses were against him.

He leaned back against the pillows and closed his eyes. "I thought you were interested in finishing that book."

Isabel's fingers trembled as she fumbled with the pages, finding the place she had marked with a leather strip. When would she ever learn? If you tempt a devil you end up getting hurt.

Justin cinched the sash of his emerald silk dressing gown. The worst of the illness had passed, leaving him restless and tense. Days spent in Isabel's company had not improved his disposition. The chit had gone from flirting with him to treating him with cool cordiality. There were moments when he caught her looking at him with a warmth hot enough to blister, and others when her glance turned to frost against his skin. At times he felt certain she wanted him to touch her. Other times he was equally certain she could not stand the sight of him. He knew she was playing a game with him; all women played games. He just hadn't deciphered the rules. *The confounded little witch!*

Justin glanced at his brother, who stood near the hearth, frowning at him. "Did you find someone to do the job?"

Clayton rested his arm on the gray marble mantel. "Are you supposed to be out of bed?"

"The spots are faded, and I've had more than enough of lying about in bed."

"As I recall, once the spots were gone, I was in battle the next day. Fortunately, you only have to attend a ball in a few days."

Justin stalked to the windows. "Blasted ball. I don't know why Sophia feels she has to thrust Isabel into the stew of the beau monde."

"I suppose she sees no reason to keep her hidden away from the rest of the world."

Justin glared at the rain splattering against the windowpanes. "Every damn fortune hunter in London will be drooling over her."

"You underestimate Isabel, brother. I wager she will charm more than a few men who have no need at all for her dowry. She already has a following, and Sophia has only given London a few glimpses of her."

Justin knew far too well how easily Isabel could charm a man. He leaned his shoulder against the window frame and tried not to think of the infuriating little enchantress. Yet shoving Isabel from his mind had become a herculean task. "Did you find someone to do what I want?"

"I'm not sure anyone can do what you want."

Justin glanced at his brother. "I didn't think it would be easy. I thought you might know someone from your war days. Someone who knows how to go about finding information."

"This morning I spoke with a man I knew from the army. For the past year he's been working for Bow Street. If anyone can find out what happened that night and who did it, Sergeant Major Adler Newberry can."

"I want this handled as quietly as possible."

Clayton grinned. "Newberry knows how to keep secrets. He was a spy, after all. Still, I don't know if he will be able to pick up the trail."

"Someone knows what happened and who did it." Justin rubbed the taut muscles in his neck. He knew the odds were against him, but he had to try.

"Where is Isabel? I thought I would find her here."

Justin frowned at his brother. According to Sophia, Clayton had not only been keeping Eloise and Phoebe amused during Justin's illness, he had also been entertaining Isabel. "She is in the library, looking for something else to read to me."

"You have been keeping her busy these past few days."

"Not too busy to attend parties and dinners with you every night."

Clayton lifted one black brow, a glint of humor filling his eyes. "That's odd, I have never known you to be jealous over any woman before. Of course, Isabel is different from any woman you have ever known. Having a little trouble exorcising her from your blood?"

Justin did not even try to cover the truth. "Have you added her to your little list of prospective brides?"

"And if I have?"

The question hung between them, as pungent as smoldering wood. His brother married to Isabel. Unthinkable! Still, he could not sweep the thoughts and images from his mind—family gatherings with Isabel and Clay and their children. Sharp fangs sank deep into his belly, and this time Justin recognized the serpent of jealousy when he met it. His muscles tensed, a fine trembling gripping his insides. He actually wanted to knock his brother to the floor.

Clayton shook his head, a slight smile curving his lips. "You can sheathe your sword. Isabel considers me a friend, and I regard her in the same light. I have acted as her escort in your stead."

Justin turned toward the windows, appalled at the

jealousy raging inside him. "I'm beginning to believe in witchcraft."

"I pose no threat, but this town is filled with men who won't hesitate to try their best to cut you out."

"What do you expect me to do? I've asked the woman for her hand."

"Have you thought about actually paying court to her?"

Humiliating images flooded Justin's mind: Devil Trevelyan trailing after a slip of a spinster like a starving hound after a juicy morsel, snapping at every puppy who dared draw near his prize. He scowled at his brother. "I won't make a fool of myself for any woman."

Clayton released his breath in a long sigh. "Pride can also make a fool of a man, Justin."

"I got along fine before she barged into my life. I shall manage to get along fine . . ." Justin hesitated as Isabel swept into the room like a gust of spring wind.

"I found it!" Isabel hurried toward Justin, clutching a small leather-bound book to her chest. Twin flags of dusky rose rode high on her cheeks. Excitement glittered in her eyes. She looked flushed and pretty and so damnably desirable, Justin's chest ached. "Isn't it incredible?"

Justin would have used another word to describe the infatuation this woman held for him—diabolical.

"I never realized finding a particularly good book could be quite this exciting," Clayton said.

Isabel paused beside Clayton and smiled up at him. "I never expected to see this particular book again."

"What have you found?" Justin asked, annoyed by the easy warmth his brother shared with the witch.

Isabel stiffened at his brusque tone. She strolled to Justin and held out the book. "The old baron's journal."

"What the devil?" Justin plucked the journal from her hand. He flicked open the cover and read the inscription on the first page, the bold scrawl proclaiming the journal as the property of one Borden Caldwell Darracott, Baron of Bramsleigh, in the year 1649. "You found this in the library?"

"Yes. Father was so certain it would lead to the treasure. And now we can prove he was right."

Clayton joined them near the windows. "Treasure?"

"The Treasure of Bramsleigh. It's a story that has been passed down through my family. It's become something of a legend."

Clayton smiled at her. "And this journal is a piece of the legend?"

"It's said the secret to the treasure is in the journal. You see, back in 1649, the baron took his wife's jewels and hid them to keep them out of Cromwell's hands. One of the pieces was a beautiful emerald-and-diamond necklace. I've seen it in a portrait of the baron's wife."

"Sounds intriguing," Clayton said.

"I can't imagine how many of my ancestors have tried to find it. Father said one of his cousins was so obsessed with it as a boy, he actually hid in a sideboard when his parents were ready to return home from a visit at Bramsleigh." Isabel's excitement bubbled over in laughter. "Until last year, we never thought it possible to find the treasure. Then Father decided to enlarge the library, and one of the workmen found this journal hidden in a secret alcove."

Clayton frowned. "A secret alcove?"

"Someone formed it by building a second bookcase a few feet in front of the original one."

"That still does not explain why the journal was in the library here," Clayton said.

Isabel shook her head. "Father brought it with him to London. He wanted to work on the translations. It wasn't found among his things. We assumed it had been stolen, since both his and Stephen's rooms had been ransacked the night they were murdered."

"Your father must have left it with my father." Justin carefully turned the pages of the journal as he spoke. "Sophia mentioned that your father had been here that last night. My father died a few days later. The journal must have been put in the library after his death. I doubt anyone even realized it didn't belong here."

"We have to find someone to help with the translations." Isabel clasped her hands under her chin. "It's written in an odd combination of English, Latin, and Italian. Although I think I can manage the Latin, I don't know a word of Italian."

"I know a little."

Justin glared at his brother. "I know a great deal more."

A slow smile curved Clayton's lips. "That's true. Justin knows Italian as well as Latin. I'm sure he can provide all the help you need in translating the journal. If it interests him to do so."

Isabel looked at Justin, a certain wariness entering her eyes. "Are you interested?"

More than he cared to admit, he thought. "It could be amusing."

Isabel lifted her shoulders in a delicate shrug. "If you would rather not . . ."

Justin halted her words with a glance. "Shall we get started?"

She drew in her breath. "As you wish."

Nothing was as he wished it might be. But then Justin could not remember the last time one of his wishes had ever been granted. He had stopped making them a long time ago.

"I think my brother can manage without you for a few hours." Clayton took Isabel's arm. "I'm taking Eloise and Phoebe to the British Museum. I thought you might join us."

Justin met the humor in his brother's eyes with all the startling animosity inside him. "I'm certain Isabel would rather work on the journal."

"I'm certain you wouldn't mind allowing her a chance to see a little of London. She's been locked in this house every day since you took ill."

"And you've been left with the task of escorting my sisters everywhere." Isabel glanced from Clayton to Justin. "Still, I do feel uncomfortable dropping the journal in your lap, then running off."

And well she should, Justin thought. Before he could voice his opinion to her, Clayton was once again intruding between them.

"My brother loves solving puzzles. And I can assure you he needs no help with any of the languages. Although English does give him pains once in a while."

Justin's eyes narrowed.

Clayton's smile widened as he looked down at Isabel. "And I would dearly appreciate your company."

Isabel looked at Justin. "Would you mind?"

"I can't imagine why my brother would mind." Clayton fixed Justin with a challenging look.

Justin glanced away from them, afraid he might betray the turmoil inside him. "I can manage on my own."

"We will see you this afternoon," Clayton said.

Justin stared out the window as they left the room. Rain fell from a gray sky, distorting all it touched. The entire world seemed painted in shades of gray, even the shrubbery and flowers in the gardens below. He had actually wanted to strike his brother. Over a woman.

He closed his eyes and drew a deep breath. Somehow he had managed to allow this infatuation to get out of hand. It had to stop. He would not allow anyone to twist him into knots. Not even Isabel.

He returned to the sanctuary of his own home that morning, determined to slip back into his former life. Before he left Marlow House, his grandmother invited him to dinner. He declined. He could do without Isabel's company. There were other women in this world. Beautiful women. Desirable women. Women who could cure this affliction called Isabel.

Chapter Fourteen

Isabel sat in a chair near Gerard's mother, Henrietta, in the green drawing room of Marlow House. At the best of times, it took immense patience to follow the scattered threads of Henrietta's conversation; the woman flitted from one topic to another like an indecisive butterfly in a field of tempting flowers. With an infuriating rogue intruding into her thoughts, Isabel found it particularly difficult to follow her flighty cousin this afternoon. Justin had left without so much as a fare-thee-well. It was staggering to realize how little she meant to him.

Henrietta sipped her tea. "I was thunderstruck. Absolutely thunderstruck when Gerard told us you were coming out this Season."

"I have to admit, I was also a bit surprised." Isabel smiled at Sophia, who sat on a sofa across from Henrietta. "The duchess insisted."

"Really!" Henrietta's blue eyes grew wide. "How

remarkable! I would have imagined Isabel was far too old for such things."

The truth connected like a right to the jaw. Still, Isabel took no offense from Henrietta's customary candor. As much as she would like to deny the truth, she was hardly a girl straight out of the schoolroom. She was a woman old enough to don a cap. A woman who should have buried her dreams of romance and passion long ago. A woman who should certainly not coddle any hopes of ever reforming a maddening rake.

Sophia smiled. "It's a pity someone in the family didn't think to bring Isabel into society years ago."

"Oh." Henrietta thought upon this for a moment, her lovely face a study in concentration. "I suppose I could have done that."

"Any of her female relations might have," Sophia said gently.

Henrietta smiled. "It never occurred to me."

Sophia nodded. "I can see it didn't."

"Dear Isabel was always so busy managing Edward's household, I never once thought of her as a young girl. She was always so very practical." Henrietta tilted her head and gave Sophia a conspiratorial smile. "We always assumed she would one day marry Gerard. We still have hopes. They are so very well suited. So really there was no thought to bring her to London."

"Now that she has arrived in London, I am determined she shall enjoy the Season," Sophia said.

"Imagine, Isabel and my Anthea coming out in the same Season." Henrietta patted her daughter's cheek. "Although Anthea really should have entered society last year, I just know she shall be a tremendous success. Don't you agree, Duchess?"

Sophia smiled. "She is certainly a handsome girl."

A soft blush stained Anthea's pale cheeks. "Thank you."

There was no mistaking the resemblance between Gerard and his handsome young sister. They were both tall and slender. They had both inherited the golden hair and blue eyes of their mother. Yet, where Henrietta saw life as an endless garden of frivolity, both Anthea and Gerard perceived the thorns on every rose. Isabel suspected Anthea would rather spend her time exploring the dusty artifacts in London museums than plunge headfirst into the glittering pool of the beau monde.

"It was such a dreadful pity we had to leave London last year. We had no sooner settled in at Curzon Street, when . . ." Henrietta hesitated, her glance darting to Isabel. "Such an unfortunate occurrence with your father and brother, my dear."

Isabel managed a smile. "Yes. It was."

"Imagine, one night Edward and dear Stephen were having dinner with us. The next . . . Oh dear. So tragic." Henrietta sipped her tea. "And to think we were all deep in preparation for Anthea's coming-out. A death in one's family can be so disrupting."

"I am afraid Death has a poor sense of priorities," Sophia said.

Henrietta nodded. "Yes. It certainly does. Rumor has it your grandson is looking for a bride."

Isabel swallowed hard, forcing down the tea that had nearly choked her. She stared at Henrietta, who sat smiling at Sophia, completely oblivious to the turmoil she had ignited in Isabel.

"The strange thing about rumors is that one can never be certain when they are true," Sophia said.

"I certainly hope it is true. Lord Huntingdon is precisely the type of gentleman I wish Anthea to meet."

"Oh, and here I thought you were referring to my

eldest grandson.'' Sophia smiled sweetly. ''If you would like I can introduce you to Marlow.''

Anthea's cup rattled on her saucer. ''The duke!''

Henrietta threw her arm in front of Anthea, as though protecting her daughter from a charging bull. ''Oh, my goodness, no.''

Isabel's stomach tightened. In spite of her own irritation with the man, she still caught herself wanting to defend him.

Sophia lifted one golden brow. ''No? You wouldn't like to meet Marlow?''

Color rose in Henrietta's plump cheeks. ''I've met the duke.''

''I would be pleased to introduce dear Anthea to both of my grandsons. I'm certain Marlow in particular would find her delightful.''

The color drained from Anthea's cheeks. She looked at her mother in a silent plea for deliverance.

Henrietta pressed her hand to her heart. ''We never entertained any thoughts of Anthea and the duke. We certainly haven't such lofty expectations.''

Sophia settled her cup on her saucer. ''You mustn't underestimate Anthea's charm. My grandson has an eye for beauty.''

''Yes.'' Henrietta managed a smile. ''So I have heard.''

''Come back!'' Phoebe shouted in the hall. ''Don't go in there!''

An instant later Perceval loped into the room. Phoebe followed close behind, carrying a leather tether. ''Come back!''

The cat leaped from his pursuer, bounding straight for the sofa where Henrietta and Anthea sat. Henrietta shrieked. She shot to her feet, her cup and saucer plunging to the floor, sending a plume of tea into the air. Anthea screamed. Perceval recoiled, startled by the commotion.

"It's all right," Phoebe said, hurrying toward the cat. "He isn't going to hurt—"

"Leop . . . leop . . . leopard!" Anthea stuttered, pointing a trembling hand at the cat.

"He shall kill us!" Henrietta wailed.

Perceval bared his teeth at the shrieking woman, a deep-throated growl emanating from his tense body. With a high-pitched scream, Henrietta scrambled onto the tea cart, sending dishes scattering in all directions. She knelt there, screaming for help, while Perceval swatted at the dangling hem of her green muslin gown.

"Perceval!" Phoebe shouted, darting at the cat.

Anthea shot toward the door, screaming.

Perceval leaped to the sofa. Phoebe tripped, whacking the carpet with a thump.

"Help!" Henrietta screamed. "Someone save us!"

"Come here!" Phoebe shouted, scrambling to her feet.

Isabel grabbed her arm. "Don't!"

Phoebe turned to look at her. "But Perceval is frightened."

"He is much too upset right now," Isabel said. "He might scratch you by accident. Even if he doesn't want to, he could do considerable damage."

"Quite right." Sophia rose to her feet. "It is best to let him calm down right where he is."

"Do something!" Henrietta screamed.

Franklin Witheridge entered the room at that moment. He looked from his wife to the duchess, his dark eyes wide with amazement. "I found Anthea on the front steps, yelling for help."

Sophia smiled. "I do hope you calmed her sufficiently to keep the watch from storming my drawing room."

"I believe we are safe," Franklin said. "She is in my carriage. Where, by the way, is the bloodthirsty beast?"

"Oh, Franklin. Thank heavens you have come!" Henrietta wailed.

Franklin walked toward his wife. "Henrietta, what are you doing on a tea cart?"

Henrietta pointed toward the sofa. "Leopard! He'll eat us all!"

"Actually, he is an ocelot." Sophia frowned at her cat, who sat with his back pressed into the corner of her sofa, hissing. "And he generally prefers mice over people. Although he will take a good leg of mutton over anything."

Henrietta whimpered as she lifted a pleading hand toward her husband. "Save me!"

"I don't believe there is any danger, my dear." Franklin took her hand and helped her down from the cart.

Henrietta threw her arms around his waist and cowered in his arms. "He tried to attack me."

"I was playing with him, and he got away." Phoebe looked up at Sophia. "I'm terribly sorry, Duchess. I know you didn't want him in here this afternoon."

"Playing with him!" Henrietta stared at the girl. "You were playing with that ferocious beast?"

"He isn't ferocious," Phoebe said.

Henrietta lifted the tattered skirt of her gown. "Not ferocious?"

Franklin patted Henrietta's back. "I hope you will accept my apologies, Duchess."

"There is no need. Perceval is the cause of this trouble. I am sorry Henrietta and Anthea took such a terrible fright."

Henrietta turned her wide-eyed stare to Sophia. "He really isn't dangerous?"

Sophia smiled. "He only appears fierce. He is really as gentle as a tabby."

Henrietta pressed her hand to her neck, her gaze darting to the hissing cat. "A tabby?"

"Yes. Would you like a glass of sherry? It will quiet your nerves."

"No!" Henrietta gulped a breath. "We've taken far too much of your time this afternoon. Perhaps another day."

Sophia nodded. "Of course."

"We should be going. Anthea will be relieved to know her mother hasn't been devoured. Good day to you," Franklin said, before ushering his wife out of the room.

"He was always such an attractive man," Sophia said, after Franklin had ushered his trembling wife from the room. "So very athletic."

"Very different from Gerard," Isabel said. Although they were both tall, Franklin was dark and drawn with sturdier lines.

"Both are handsome in their own way." Sophia turned to Phoebe, who was kneeling beside the sofa, talking softly to Perceval. "Do wait until he calms down before you try to play with him. And have someone clean up this mess."

Phoebe smiled up at her. "I will, Duchess."

Sophia linked her arm with Isabel's. "Come take a turn with me in the gardens."

Air scrubbed fresh by the morning rain bathed Isabel's cheeks with the scents of evergreen and damp grass. They walked along the brick-lined path until they reached a stone bench nestled in a crescent-shaped nook of yew. They sat facing the fountain, where two frolicking Cupids tossed water at one another. For a long while the soft splash of tumbling water filled the companionable silence.

"What do you think of a match between the lovely Anthea and Justin?" Sophia asked.

Isabel's stomach clenched. "I think she is terrified of him."

Sophia nodded. "Still, he might change her mind. He can be charming. When it suits him."

Isabel knew far too well how charming the man could be. "I don't think they would be well suited."

"Perhaps not. Anthea is a little too severe. How about Clayton?"

"Perhaps. Yet, to be quite frank, I think Clayton would be better suited with a more lively female. His own disposition is so reserved."

"You're very perceptive." Sophia idly brushed her fingers over the wall of yew beside her, bending the supple green branches. "Clayton was once engaged to a spirited young girl. She was a trifle eccentric, but charming. Any room seemed positively brighter when she was in it."

"What happened to her?"

Sophia sighed. "Marisa decided she didn't actually want to marry Clayton."

Isabel looked up at the gray clouds swirling slowly overhead. "I can't imagine a woman changing her mind about wanting to marry Clayton. The more I know him, the more I admire him."

Sophia tilted her head and smiled at her. "Is there hope you may yet decide to marry one of my grandsons?"

"I hardly think Clayton is about to ask me to marry him."

"If he did?

Clayton possessed most of the qualities a woman could possibly want in a husband. He would be loyal and steady. Reliable. Faithful. He was handsome and intelligent, amusing and kind. Yet he was not Justin.

He could not set fire to her blood with a single glance. "I care for him as a cherished friend."

"Many successful marriages have started with far less than friendship."

Isabel knew she was a fool to fall in love with the wrong brother. Yet she could not change her heart. "I am certain Clayton will find someone much better suited for him than I am. He deserves a woman who can love him with all of her heart and soul."

"Yes. He does deserve all that." Sophia folded her hands on her lap. "Do you think Justin deserves the same?"

Isabel chose her words carefully. "I think we deserve what we are willing to give."

Sophia's lips curled into a knowing smile. "And you do not think Justin is willing to give a woman his love?"

A breeze drifted across the gardens, rustling the leaves of chestnut and oak trees, swaying the twin plumes of water from the fountain. "I think the duke and I have very different ideas of marriage."

"Before I die, I intend to see him properly settled. Mark my words, I shall hold his children in my arms. He will marry one day."

Isabel wasn't certain what she would do when that day arrived. Justin married to another woman. The thought latched onto her vitals like a hawk's talons sinking into a hapless mouse. Strange that she had never really thought of Justin married to another woman before. She had always thought of him as a solitary lion, prowling the streets of London, taking what he wanted. Yet one day he would take a bride. A woman who would hold him at night. A woman who would awaken to his smile. A woman who would bear his children. And would that woman always have to fear the day when her husband would stray? Would she care? Or would the woman he married be content with his wealth and his social position?

"I honestly believe the right woman can tame my wild grandson. Of course, she must possess the courage to try."

Isabel glanced away from the challenge in Sophia's eyes. It was easy to speak of courage when you were not the one risking your pride and your heart. Still, what kind of life would she have if Justin were to marry another woman?

It was foolish to imagine it. Yet a stubborn, reckless, demented part of her refused to let go of a certain beguiling question: Could she redeem a devil?

Justin spent the afternoon toying with the idea of rekindling an affair with one of his former mistresses, and ended by dismissing each of them as a bore. He plowed through the mountain of correspondence his secretary had left in a neat pile on his desk, and still he found no distraction from Isabel. That evening he dressed to dine at Vachel's, then sent his cook into a panic when he decided to dine at home instead.

He was still weak from the measles, Justin assured himself. It was the only reason he had no desire for one of Vachel's tarts.

Later that evening he walked into a saloon at White's, hoping for a little diversion from thoughts of a blue-eyed, sharp-tongued little termagant. He found three of his friends at a table near the hearth. Miles Cranely was the first to notice him.

Miles lifted his quizzing glass and peered at Justin. "I say, it's Marlow. I almost didn't recognize him without his spots."

"Careful, Miles, leopards are dangerous even without their spots." Braden poured wine into a glass and pushed it toward an empty chair between Miles and

Oliver. "You just missed your brother. He was on his way to Marlow House. Something about a chess game with a lovely lady."

"He always did have superior taste in his choice of companions." Justin sank into the leather-upholstered armchair and lifted his glass. He supposed that by this time Clay and Isabel were engaged in a game of chess. Sharing conversation, laughter. A now-familiar serpent slithered in his belly. He crushed it. Jealousy was a useless emotion. One reserved for fools who made the unforgivable mistake of losing their heads over women.

Oliver grinned at Justin over the rim of his wineglass. "Clayton certainly has been spending a great deal of time with your ward lately."

Justin's throat tightened. "Someone has to shepherd the chit around London."

"Spending time with a handsome female. Ah, the terrible tribulations of a guardian." Miles lifted his quizzing glass and studied Justin a moment. "You've got a new twist in that cravat."

Oliver turned and examined the cravat. "Half the young bucks in town will be sporting it by week's end."

Justin grinned. "They shall try."

Braden leaned back in his chair. "Clayton's looking for a bride. Maybe he intends to take Miss Darracott off your hands."

Justin frowned at his friend. He had come here to escape Isabel, not discuss her future prospects.

"I would say there are more than a few men who would like to take her off your hands." Oliver grabbed the wine bottle and refilled his glass. "Have you taken a look at the betting book?"

Justin clenched the stem of his glass. "They are placing bets on my ward?"

"On who shall usher her to the altar." Oliver sipped his wine, his gray eyes filled with humor. "Clayton, Hanley, and Witheridge are the favorites. Although there is a sprinkling placed on a dozen more. Even a few placed on you and Braden."

Justin eased his glass to the table, afraid he might snap the crystal. "The members of this club obviously have nothing better to occupy their minds."

Miles twisted the black ribbon of his quizzing glass, sending the lens spinning, reflecting the candlelight. "Word is she'll inherit sixty thousand when she marries."

Justin shook his head. By the end of the month, rumor would have her inheriting the Pavilion. "Does rumor also say I have to approve of her marriage or she inherits nothing?"

Braden rubbed the tips of his fingers together. "She is really something quite out of the ordinary run of things. It does not matter what she inherits."

Justin didn't care for the warmth in Braden's voice. "She is not exactly your style. I thought you were only interested in great beauties. Isabel is hardly a diamond of the first water."

"Perhaps she isn't the most dazzling woman in London." Braden opened his hands. "But she has a quality about her."

"I think she is lovely," Oliver said.

Miles nodded. "She has the face of an angel."

"And she has a good deal of sense. Most of the chits coming out these days are pretty little widgeons. They bore a man in a quarter of an hour." Braden swirled the wine in his glass. "I spent more than an hour at the Wheatons' Tuesday night, enjoying Miss Darracott's conversation. I have to confess, I could have spent all night in her company."

Sharp fangs of jealousy sank into Justin's belly. It

took all of his will to keep his features molded into a calm mask. When he had asked her how she had enjoyed the Wheatons' party, Isabel had not mentioned Braden. But then, they were not precisely on easy terms. "I suppose I don't have to remind the three of you that the lady is under my protection."

Braden laughed. "Never thought I would see the day when you would be guarding a chit's honor."

Justin fixed his friend in a narrowed glare. "Yet that is precisely what I am doing."

Braden tilted his head, his dark eyes filling with a shrewd understanding. "Does the wind sit in that corner, Justin?"

Justin lifted his wineglass. "I intend to see she doesn't fall victim to any careless flirtations, that's all."

"Even I know a lady of quality when I see one." Braden smiled at Justin over the rim of his glass. "I'm glad you are not in the race, dear boy. The field is already too crowded."

Justin sipped his wine. It didn't matter who took the chit off his hands, he assured himself. He would be a happier man once he washed his hands of her.

He spent a few hours with his friends. Yet their company did not ease the tension inside him. That night he lay for hours, staring up at the dark canopy above his head.

"Confound you, Isabel," he whispered to the shadows. "I shall not allow you to plague me."

Still, his will had little impact on his dreams. Isabel came to him as she did every night, tempting the devil with glimpses of heaven.

Chapter Fifteen

"I want this handled as quietly as possible." Justin fixed Adler Newberry with an appraising stare. The Bow Street runner sat in a leather wing-back chair across from Justin in the library of Justin's town house. "Anyone you hire to help must not know I am involved."

"No one but me will know, Your Grace." Adler rubbed his prominent chin, his expression growing pensive.

Beneath bushy dark brows, a pair of blue eyes regarded Justin with a shrewd intelligence belied by Adler's deliberate movements and unhurried speech. Tall and broad, with a thick nose that had been broken several times, he looked like a man who had participated in one too many prizefights. Yet, according to Clayton, this man had been an invaluable asset during his days as a spy in France. Since the end of the war,

Sergeant Major Newberry had plied his talent at Bow Street.

"I have to be honest with you. The trail is cold, Your Grace. I'm not hopeful we'll find anything more than what was found out last year."

"My brother has a great deal of faith in you."

Adler smiled, revealing a chipped front tooth. "The major is a fine man, he is. Still, I've never been one to work a miracle."

"Someone knows what happened and who did it. The type of men who did this are the type to boast about it. I want you to do everything in your power to find them."

"Aye, Your Grace. I'll do my best."

Justin rubbed his fingers over the coffee-colored leather covering the arm of his chair. "There is something strange about the entire incident."

"What is that?"

"Would common footpads attack a pair of gentlemen on the street, then proceed to ransack their hotel rooms?"

Alder's bushy brows lifted. "Strange indeed, Your Grace."

"There may be more than simple robbery and murder involved."

Adler folded the piece of paper Justin had given him. "I'll investigate the names on this list."

"Let me know if you discover anything. No matter how insignificant."

Adler stood. "I will, Your Grace."

After Adler left, Justin tried to work on the journal. Yet his mind kept wandering. Time and time again he caught himself staring out of his library window, wondering what a certain blue-eyed witch was doing. An hour later he walked through the front door of Marlow House, only to find Isabel not at home.

"Justin, I do wish you would stop your infernal pacing. You are disturbing Perceval. The silly cat is a hard enough subject without you aggravating him." Sophia grabbed Perceval's leather collar and coaxed the big cat to leap back onto the same pale green damask cushion that he had leaped from moments before.

Justin glanced at the portrait Sophia was painting of her ocelot. Painting was Sophia's latest whimsy. Her fancy took a different direction every three or four months. Her last had been making shoes. Unfortunately her talent usually fell far behind her enthusiasm. "If you are worried about aggravating the cat, don't let him see this."

Sophia cast him a hooded glance. "I wonder what has you in such a delightful mood this morning. Do you have a thorn in your side?"

The thorn in his side was not at home. Instead she was out, walking in the park with her sisters and his brother. Justin paused at the windows. He stared across Park Lane to the green depths of Hyde Park. In the distance, the smooth water of the Serpentine glowed silver in the sunlight. "I thought Isabel might like to work on that blasted journal today."

"Justin, it is only ten." Sophia glanced at him, a knowing smile curving her lips. "I didn't think you usually got out of bed before noon. Of course, you haven't been keeping your usual hours. Have you?"

Justin clenched his jaw, annoyed with the reason he was not keeping his usual hours. He was even more annoyed that his reason was not here. He turned away from the window and snatched the journal from a table near Sophia. He prowled toward the hearth, then threw himself into a wing-back chair. *Confounded female.*

He was not at all pleased with the fact that Isabel was not here when he wanted her. Worse yet, he did not like the fact that he wanted her at all.

"What do you think of a match between Isabel and Clayton?"

Justin's insides tightened. "Clay and Isabel are friends. Nothing more."

Sophia smiled at him. "Many a brilliant match has been based on far less."

"They aren't well suited."

"You do not think so?"

"I have it on good authority that she is interested only in marrying for a grand passion of the heart. That hardly makes her a good candidate for Clay's wife."

Sophia frowned. "I suppose she has been taking novels from a circulating library."

"I suspect it is her nature. She insists her parents shared such a remarkable relationship. They managed to fill her head with romantic notions."

"Love matches do happen, Justin. Your father and mother were very much in love. Your grandfather and I shared . . ." She stared at her canvas, a wistful smile on her lips. "He was an extraordinary man. In fact, the Trevelyan men are notorious for plunging into marriage for the sake of affection rather than good sense. What makes you think Clayton is incapable of providing Isabel with the type of romance and passion she wants?"

Justin smoothed his fingers over the leather cover of the journal. "Because he is still in love with Marisa Grantham."

"I suspected as much. It is a shame she cried off that engagement," Sophia said, her voice growing soft.

"Now you can understand why Clay and Isabel aren't well suited."

"Perhaps. Braden Fitzwilliam was paying a great deal of attention to her at the Wheatons'."

Sophia dabbed paint against her canvas, apparently oblivious to the storm of emotions her words had conjured inside him. "Braden pays attention to every attractive female he meets."

"And the women appreciate every moment." Sophia cast him a wicked grin.

"I doubt he will ever settle on one even after he is married."

"Excellent point." She swirled the tip of her brush through a dab of paint on her palette. "There is Gerard Witheridge. What do you think of him as a possible husband for Isabel?"

"I don't."

"He certainly seems intent on fixing her affection."

"If she were interested in Witheridge, she would have accepted him months ago. The puppy has been sniffing after her skirts long enough."

"Perhaps. Still, I suppose he could persuade her to change her mind. He is a dreadfully handsome young man. Although I find his manners at times a bit too stiff."

Justin rubbed the tip of his forefinger over a scratch in the dark red leather of the journal. Gerard Witheridge was a hypocrite who could preach against devouring the sins of the flesh while he was on his way to Vachel's to sample a few tarts. "He is a self-righteous prig."

"Precisely." Sophia laughed. "Still, we can be certain he is not after her inheritance. He was worth three thousand a year before his father gave him Bramsleigh. And when his father dies, he shall inherit seventy thousand pounds. We must consider him a worthy suitor."

"How do you know what he is worth?"

218

"I commenced inquiries the first day he came to visit. His parents, Franklin and Henrietta, live at Raynthon House in Hampshire. Henrietta came by to see Isabel yesterday and brought along Gerard's sister Anthea."

"They are probably trying to convince Isabel to marry their worthy son."

"I believe they are quite high on the match. Henrietta mentioned how happy they would be to have Isabel as a daughter several times."

Justin clenched his hand into a fist on his thigh. "How very accommodating of them."

"As it happens, I have been marginally acquainted with Franklin and Henrietta for years. You have met them, I am certain. They move in the first circle of society. She is a hen-witted little female, blond hair, blue eyes, very pretty in her time, though she has grown a bit plump. He is still a very attractive man, tall, athletic, brown eyes, with just a sprinkling of gray through his dark hair. He was once a notable in the Corinthian set."

"I am not surprised you remember him."

She crinkled her nose at him. "Do you remember meeting them?"

"Franklin Witheridge." Justin tried to place a face with the name. "I know him. He spends time at Jackson's when he is in town. I do not recall his wife. Perhaps I will after I see her again."

"Perhaps. At any rate, Gerard is the only male issue. He is four and twenty. He has five sisters, one of whom is married to Viscount Patrington. One is coming out this year; that is Anthea. Quite a handsome girl, though a little reserved. By the way, I received an invitation for her ball yesterday. The other three girls are still in the schoolroom."

Sophia dabbed her brush against the canvas. "Gerard is adequate with the ribbons, yet an undistinguished whip, which I am certain must disappoint his father. He attended Oxford, where he excelled in mathematics. He belongs to White's and Waitier's, as well as the Society for Analytical Study, which he attends every Tuesday evening. He never gambles. And he has never been linked romantically with any female.''

Justin stared at his grandmother. ''What type of snuff does he use?''

''A special blend of Martinique and Bordeaux from Fribourg and Treyer.''

Justin cringed. How many times had his own privacy been invaded by an English huntress? ''If the females of this town had been spies during the war, Napoleon would have been defeated years ago.''

''It is important to know all there is to know about any gentleman interested in your ward. We do want to make certain Isabel makes a proper match.''

''It is possible she will not find anyone who interests her.''

''I doubt that. Still, I suppose she should wait until after she has had a Season before she makes any decisions on marriage. When the gentlemen catch a glimpse of her at the ball, I am certain we shall have no lack of suitable candidates.''

''Blasted ball! You realize, of course, that your little plan to bring Isabel into society will only make matters worse. You will have all the puppies and fortune hunters in London sniffing after her skirts.''

''Yes. I expect she shall be a great success.'' Sophia smiled at him, her eyes filled with humor. ''I am depending on you to chase away any gentleman who would not be a good match for our Isabel.''

A match for Isabel. A man who would earn the right

to take her in his arms at night. A man like Braden Fitzwilliam. Justin shifted on his chair, irritated by the sting of fangs low in his belly.

"I do not suppose you have given any thought to offering for Isabel yourself?"

"Me?" Justin glanced at Sophia and saw the certainty in her eyes. Under that perceptive gaze, he felt as though he had a banner draped around his neck with his thoughts printed in bold letters.

"It would solve two problems, as far as I am concerned. I would like very much to see both you and Isabel properly settled."

"I have never regarded marriage as a solution to a problem." Until recently he had never considered it at all.

"You and Isabel get along well enough. She is lovely, bright, and charming. You might actually find you enjoy marriage with her."

He did not need reminders of all the reasons Isabel would suit him. Isabel's conversation was as lively as her mind. She could discuss horses as well as any man. She had, perhaps, a far too liberal view when it came to politics, but that only added spice to their arguments. And, as much as he wanted to deny it, memories of that one night in her cottage still haunted him. His dreams mocked him with images of Isabel. In dreams she came to him. In dreams he possessed her passion. Yet he had learned long ago that dreams were far removed from reality.

In the hall, the bright notes of feminine laughter mingled in harmony with the deep rumble of a man's, heralding the arrival of Isabel and Clay. Justin stiffened as they strolled into the room. They looked so damned comfortable together.

Isabel's smile faded when she saw Justin. Her lips drew into a tight line as she approached him, the warmth in her eyes sparking into something far more heated. She looked as though she wanted to strangle him. Justin frowned. What the devil had he done to deserve that scathing look? He did not have long to wait for the answer. After exchanging a few polite words with Sophia, Isabel invited Justin to take a walk with her in the gardens.

He glanced at her profile as he walked beside her across the terrace. She was clenching her jaw so tightly a small knot bulged in her cheek. The back of his neck prickled. An angry woman was far more difficult to handle than an angry man. A man might try to land him a facer. A woman would aim for something more private.

Her half boots tapped the brick-lined path. He matched her quick pace, following her past the Cupids frolicking in the fountain at the center of the shrub garden, to a far corner, where tall yew bushes shielded them from the house.

Isabel paused by a stone bench and fixed him with a chilling glare. "How dare you!"

Justin frowned. "I have dared a great many things in my life. Perhaps you could be a little more specific."

"Did you ever intend to tell me about your investigation into the deaths of my father and brother?"

Justin released the breath he had been holding. "For a man who was a master spy during the war, my brother has a loose tongue."

"Clayton thought I already knew about it. He was surprised you hadn't told me you hired Newberry."

He snapped a small branch from the yew, releasing a tangy scent into the air. "It is none of your concern."

"None of my . . . In case you do not remember, *my* father and *my* brother were murdered."

He twisted the supple green branch around his forefinger. "I didn't see any reason to raise your hopes. The investigation may come to nothing."

"I can understand why you may want to keep this from Eloise or Phoebe, but I am not a child."

Justin laughed. "You are a babe in the woods."

She released her breath in a huff. "I am not some silly sapskull who must be protected from every bump in life."

He tossed the branch to the ground. "Someone has to look after you, and I have been saddled with the task."

She marched toward him, closing the distance until he could feel the warmth of her skin radiating against him. A soft blush rode high on her cheeks, emphasizing the blue of her eyes. Sunlight shimmered on the curls framing her face, spinning light brown strands to gold. "You had no right to go behind my back."

The delicate scent of lavender swirled through his senses. He tried desperately to crush the desire slithering low in his belly. "I had every right to find the blackguards responsible for saddling me with a sharp-tongued termagant. Because of them, I am your blasted guardian. I can and will do what I think is best."

"I do not need a guardian. I am five and twenty—"

"And you have been hidden away in the country all of your life. Wrapped in cotton wool."

Her eyes narrowed into dark blue slits. "I told you once before that I could do without your help. All you need do is turn over my inheritance to me, and we need never see each other again."

Never see her again. That thought clamped like a vise around his chest. "This conversation is like a book. No matter how many times you read it, the ending is still the same."

"Trying to talk sense to you is like trying to discuss mathematics with that shrub," she said, pointing at the wall of yew. "You are the most stubborn, infuriating—"

"Stubborn! You are the most stubborn female I have ever had the misfortune to meet."

"And you are the most arrogant, infuriating, maddening brute. Oh, I could . . ." She thumped her small fist against his chest. "Blast you!"

"Confound you!" He grabbed her waist and lifted her straight off her feet. Before she could utter more than a startled gasp, he clamped his mouth over hers. She pounded her fists against his shoulders. He slanted his mouth over hers in a give-no-quarter, openmouthed assault, surrendering to all the pent-up frustration surging inside him.

She twisted in his grasp. He held her tighter, continuing the assault, flicking his tongue against her tightly clenched lips. He wanted to punish her for all she had done to him. The woman had no right to make him want as he had never wanted before. No right to haunt him day and night. No right to be so damnably desirable that he wanted to drop to his knees and beg for her favor.

He slid his arms around her, holding her flush against his chest. Her breasts seared him through the layers of their clothes. Heat flooded his loins. Memories flickered in his brain: Isabel warm and willing in his arms, opening to him, offering him all her sweet secrets. Hunger clenched his vitals. The need to punish dissolved in the heat she stirred inside him. From that molten pool rose a much stronger desire. He wanted to feel it once more, that glimmer of affection she had offered him on a rain-swept night a lifetime ago.

Open for me. He cradled the back of her head in his hand, his lips gentling against hers. She tensed against him, and then her lips parted, as though she could sense his need. She slid her arms around his neck. He allowed her to slip down the length of him. And still she held him, her lips moving against his, her tongue dipping teasingly into his mouth.

Lord, he had never tasted anything sweeter than Isabel's kiss. Longing more potent than aged brandy filled his every pore. His chest constricted, and an odd burning stung his eyes as a startling need pounded through him with each beat of his heart.

Love me, Belle.

The humbling need struck him like an open hand across his cheek. He broke away from her. She stumbled back and bumped into the bench. Her knees folded. Her bottom thumped onto the stone. She stared at him, her eyes wide and filled with the same confusion roiling through him.

He moved toward her, then checked himself. He would not touch her again. He could not. Not without completely betraying himself. If he were not very careful he would find himself on his knees before her. He felt exposed, horribly vulnerable to this woman. It took every ounce of will to shape his lips into a mocking grin. "That is one way to silence a woman."

Her lips parted. Yet it took a full twelve beats of his heart before she spoke. "Of all the spiteful . . ." She rose to her feet, her eyes narrowing with the same anger that colored her words. "This is not settled."

"You are mistaken, Miss Darracott. I never continue a discussion once it bores me."

She stiffened. "I wish to be informed of Newberry's progress."

He straightened the linen at his cuff. "If there is progress, I shall inform you of it. But I will not tolerate being bothered by daily inquiries."

"I shall endeavor not to bore you again." She

brushed past him and marched toward the house, her boots tapping the bricks.

He watched her leave, fighting the insane urge to chase after her like a blasted puppy. He leaned back against the thick wall of yew and dragged air into his chest. Still, he could not ease the tightness centered there.

Fool. Idiot. Imbecile! The words shouted in Isabel's brain, punctuating each tap of her boots against the bricks lining the path. How could any woman reach the age of five and twenty and remain as foolish as a five-year-old child?

Dear heaven, she had come close to admitting her own treacherous feelings for the rogue. Images flickered in her brain: Justin laughing while she poured her heart out to him. He would condemn her as a fool for rejecting his offer of marriage. He certainly would never offer again. Would he?

She paused as she neared the terrace. She could not face anyone. Not now. She slipped behind a crescent-shaped wall of yew and sank to the stone bench nestled there. A few feet away a robin pecked at the thick grass, oblivious to the woman sitting in abject misery nearby.

Isabel clasped her hands in her lap and struggled through the mire Justin had made of her brain. Even if he did offer her marriage, she would refuse the scoundrel. It was better to live her days as a spinster, to keep her pride, than to destroy herself for the sake of one impossibly intriguing male, she assured herself.

She leaned back against the wall of yew and watched the robin hop several feet across the thick green grass in his search for breakfast. The soft sound of splashing water in the fountain trickled through the yew, easing her tension. The only possible chance she had to survive with her pride intact was to bury these feelings she had for him. And bury them was precisely what she intended to do. It was her only possible course of action. She had no alternative. None at all.

Yet a part of her, a foolish, positively suicidal part of her, wanted to throw herself straight into Devil Trevelyan's strong arms. She thumped her fist against the bench. She had managed well enough before she had met the devil; she would manage well enough without him.

Chapter Sixteen

The scent of vanilla wafted from hundreds of burning wax candles in the ballroom of Marlow House. Candlelight flickered against crystal in chandeliers high above in the immense room, spilling light upon the crowd below. Isabel stood with Gerard near a potted palm in one corner of the room, stealing a moment of refuge from the crowd.

Every one of the 389 guests she had greeted with Sophia seemed intent on examining the Duke of Marlow's ward at close hand. Every woman wanted to evaluate her hair, her clothes, her carriage, her manner. Every man wanted to dance with her. Except one man. After a few brief words this evening, Justin had avoided her as though she had the plague.

Of course, Justin had no reason to waste his time with her, Isabel thought. Not when the room brimmed with beautiful women. Women as worldly and sophisticated as he was. Women who flirted outrageously with the notorious duke. At the moment, he was lavishing his attention on a beautiful blonde who had recently arrived. They stood on the landing leading from the entry hall to the three wide stairs descending into the ballroom, elevated for the entire room to see. As though he wanted to make certain she did not miss the little performance.

"I thought you intended to work at translating the journal with the duke," Gerard said.

"He is certain he can translate it without any assistance from me." She neglected to tell Gerard that the duke had as much desire to be near her as he did to have his fingers broken.

Gerard glanced past her, staring at the glass in a nearby French door as though it opened onto a magical vista. "When your father showed me the journal, I could scarcely believe my eyes. After all of these years, the key to a mystery was finally within reach."

Justin leaned forward and whispered something into the woman's ear. The blonde pressed her hand upon his chest and smiled an invitation Isabel could read from across the room. Isabel clenched her glass of lemonade.

"Has the duke found anything of interest in the journal?"

From across the room, Isabel glared at the infuriating duke. It did not matter, she assured herself. The man could seduce half the women in London for all she cared.

"Isabel," Gerard said, touching her arm.

She looked up at him. "What?"

Gerard frowned. "Has the duke found anything of interest in the journal? Anything at all about the jewels?"

She glanced toward Justin and that woman. Oh, she wanted to snatch every blond hair from that little tart's head. "The journal is a collection of observances and thoughts of the baron in the year 1649."

"Doesn't it have anything in it about the jewels?" Gerard asked.

" 'Find the dragon who guards the sanctum'."

" 'Find the dragon who guards the sanctum'? What does that have to do with the jewels?"

Isabel dragged her gaze from Justin and his blonde. "Marlow translated that phrase this afternoon. He believes it's a clue."

Gerard shook his head. "It doesn't make sense."

"Precisely. If the baron actually did place clues in the journal, that would have to be one of them. Since it does not make sense in any other context."

Gerard lifted his brows, a look of understanding dawning on his face. "There must be other clues scattered throughout the book."

"I would suppose." Isabel wished she could run to her room, close the door, and scream into her pillow. She had once thought finding a true passion of the heart would be the most exciting thing on earth. Yet if this was what came of it, this irritable, restless, homicidal feeling, then she wanted nothing to do with it.

"There you are," a tall, fair-haired man said as he approached her. "I was beginning to despair of ever finding you in time for our dance."

She had met Timothy Usherwood, Viscount Hanley, several times during the past two weeks. Not only was he one of the more attractive gentlemen who had asked to partner her this evening, he was also terribly charming. Perhaps a little too charming, but that did not matter. She handed her glass to her cousin, and took Hanley's proffered arm. If Justin could put her completely out of his thoughts, she would do the same. If it took her the rest of her life.

After the contredanse, Isabel hesitated only an instant when Hanley suggested they take a turn in the gardens. Since the duke indulged in countless flirtations, she saw no reason why she should not enjoy the company of an attractive male. And if she smiled a little too warmly, or allowed Hanley to walk a little too close, so much the better. She would show the infuriating duke she could also forget she ever felt a pang for him.

Another puppy sniffing at her skirts. Something dangerous coiled in Justin's chest as he watched Hanley lead Isabel from the dance floor. The man walked close enough to feel the brush of Isabel's skirt against his legs. Too close. And the way Hanley looked at her . . . Justin could almost see the drool at the corner of his smug mouth.

For the past few hours, Justin had kept his distance while one male after another fawned and salivated and made complete cakes of themselves over Isabel. He intended to keep his distance. He would not crawl on his belly to her. He would not join the salivating pack. When she realized there was not a man in the room who could stir her blood the way he could, she would be the one to come begging.

Until now, he had been satisfied with her behavior toward each panting fool. With each man who had dawdled in her company—even Braden Fitzwilliam— she had appeared cordial. Friendly. Yet he had detected nothing that would suggest she favored any of them in particular. Until Hanley. She was smiling up at Hanley in a damnable way.

"I have missed you." Lydia Holloway rested her hand on his sleeve.

Justin glanced down at the woman who had been one of his mistresses until a few months ago. Although she was small, a generous swell of pale breasts rose above her low-cut emerald satin gown. Her golden hair was piled high upon her head, with several plump curls lying upon one smooth shoulder. She reminded Justin of a porcelain doll, her cheeks rounded, her lips full and lightly rouged, her head empty. He knew from experience how enthusiastic the young widow could be in bed. Yet the knowledge left him strangely unaffected. "I thought Renshaw was keeping you company these days."

Lydia toyed with the top button of his black silk waistcoat. "He doesn't compare to you."

Not nearly plump enough in the pocket to afford her, Justin thought.

"I really shouldn't have anything to do with you, after the shameless way you sent me home from Italy."

Justin glanced at the diamonds glittering around her neck. The necklace had been his parting gift to her. No doubt she wanted a bracelet to match. He could not remember exactly why he had grown tired of Lydia, but he suspected she would remind him in a very short space of time. Trying to use her to take his mind off Isabel was proving useless.

Lydia tilted her head and smiled up at him. "It's crowded. I do not think anyone would notice if we slipped away."

Although those lovely lips smiled, her blue eyes remained cool and calculating. He caught himself comparing her smile to Isabel's and ended in thinking himself a fool to try. When Isabel smiled, her entire face lit with a warmth that could melt the frozen heart of winter. He had just witnessed that smile from across the room. It had been directed at Hanley.

Justin glanced across the room. Isabel was leaving by one of the doors leading to the terrace, with Hanley attached to her side. What the bloody hell did that blackguard think he was doing?

"Let's leave," Lydia said, her voice a soft purr near his shoulder.

He pulled his arm free of her annoying grasp. "The party is just getting started, Lydia. Enjoy yourself."

"But I thought—"

"I noticed Renshaw in the card room."

"Renshaw! But darling . . ."

Lydia's words dissolved in the collection of sounds in the room. Conversation and laughter collided with the music flowing from the minstrel's gallery. Yet Justin heard little above the pounding of blood in his ears. He marched across the room, brushing past people who tried to stop him for conversation.

Cool air heavy with the scent of freshly cut grass struck his face as he left the room. Several couples had ventured into the moonlight on the terrace. He prowled the shadows. Yet he did not find Isabel and Hanley on the terrace. He stalked into the gardens. When he got his hands on Isabel, she would regret the day she was born.

Music from the ballroom drifted past tall walls of yew, filtering into a secluded spot nestled in a far corner of the gardens. Unlike the path leading to the pavilion, here there were no lamps on wrought-iron poles chasing away the shadows, only the light of the moon.

Isabel sat on a stone bench nestled behind a crescent of sheltering yew, near the very spot where Justin had assaulted her the day before. She had brought Hanley here with a purpose: to erase those memories Justin had branded on her soul. Still, each passing moment in Hanley's company chipped away at those hopes. She smiled at the young man sitting beside her and tried not to think of the man she wished were with her in the moonlight.

"I never really believed in falling in love at a glance. Did you?" Hanley smiled at her.

She caught herself wondering what lay beneath Hanley's smile. Thanks to Justin she was ever alert to all the traps into which an heiress could tumble. Oh, how she wished she had never met the blasted brute. "I believe people can feel attraction in a glance. But love is an entirely different entity."

"When I saw you tonight, I felt as though someone had poured hot water over me."

"Perhaps you have a fever. You should get out of the night air." She stood, realizing the mistake she had made in flirting with him. Nothing would pry Justin from her thoughts. She had been a fool to try.

He shot to his feet and blocked her exit. " 'Shall I compare thee to a summer's day?' "

"I would rather you did not." She tried to step around him. He checked her move.

" 'Thou art more lovely and more temperate.' " He threw his arms around her and pressed his hands flat against her back.

She pushed against his chest. "Lord Hanley, I really—"

" 'Rough winds do shake the darling buds of May—' " His words ended in a gasp. One moment he was holding her; the next she was free and he was standing on his toes, suspended by a strong hand in his collar.

A tall, familiar figure stood behind Hanley. Moonlight spilled over Justin, carving his features from the shadows, illuminating a look of pure murder on his handsome face. Excitement crashed through her, like a storm-tossed wave against the shore. Isabel stumbled back and bumped into the bench. "Marlow!"

Justin glared at her. "You look surprised to see me."

Isabel shivered beneath that look. He appeared angry enough to kill something. "I thought you were occupied."

"Please!" Hanley's eyes bulged as Justin hoisted him higher. He clawed at his collar. "Can't . . . breathe!"

Isabel pressed her hand to her neck. "Do take care, Marlow! You are going to strangle him."

"Not tonight." Justin tossed Hanley toward the main path, like a cat tired of playing with a wearisome mouse.

Hanley crashed past the wall of yew, windmilling his arms to catch his balance. He stumbled several paces, then managed to right himself before hitting the brick-lined path. He staggered back, staring at the duke like a man who had come face-to-face with the devil himself. "I'm sorry, Marlow," he said, rubbing his neck. "I meant no disrespect."

Justin's lips curled into a chilling imitation of a smile. "Miss Darracott is under my protection, Hanley. Remember that the next time you or one of your friends decide to recite sonnets to her in the moonlight."

Hanley nodded. "Yes, Marlow. I will, Marlow."

Justin flicked the linen at his wrist. "Go."

Hanley sprinted to obey the soft command. His footsteps clattered against the bricks in his haste to escape any further punishment.

Isabel's heart pounded. She could not quell the exhilaration racing through her. In the midst of all those females who had flitted into his path this night, he had stormed after her. He had abandoned his plump little blonde in his quest to humiliate her in front of Hanley. "Do you mind telling me why you charged after Lord

Hanley like a barbarian wielding a club?''

Justin turned to face her, his expression set in harsh lines. "Did you want that young man drooling all over you? Is that the reason you came out here with him?''

Her spine stiffened. "Are you implying I did something inappropriate?''

Justin stalked her, invading the moonlight streaming between them. He halted in front of her, so close that his legs pressed against the blue silk of her gown. She held her ground, ignoring the sane voice inside her head screaming *Run!*

"You encouraged that blackguard." His low voice washed over her, thick with anger.

"What I do is of no concern to you.''

"Like hell it isn't. You are my ward. What you do reflects on me.''

"And you are worried I will tarnish *your* reputation?''

"You should be worried about *your* reputation.''

"I did nothing wrong.''

His eyes narrowed. "You were flirting with him.''

Heat crept upward across her neck. "I was not!''

"Bloody hell you weren't. I saw you.''

"Even if I was flirting with him, you have no right to say anything.''

"Like hell I don't. If I hadn't found you, that bastard would be halfway up your skirts by now.''

"Ooh." She stomped her heel on his toes.

He winced. "What the bloody—''

"I was about to do that to Hanley when you charged in, doing your best imitation of Genghis Khan.''

A muscle flickered in his cheek. "I will not have you flirting with every man in London.''

"If I wish to flirt, I shall.''

"No. You will not," he said, his voice low and as smooth as warm butter.

"I am old enough to—" Her words choked in a gasp as he wrapped his hands around her waist.

He plucked her off her feet. "Infuriating thorn in my side," he said, his voice a harsh rasp, his breath warm against her face.

She planted her hands on his hard shoulders, trying to look angry while her insides fluttered like demented butterflies. The flames of passion in his eyes seared the air from her lungs. "I demand you put me down," she said, her voice a breathless whisper. "Immediately!"

"Confounded woman!" he whispered, before tossing her over his shoulder.

Chapter Seventeen

The breath whooshed from her lungs as his shoulder connected with her middle. She clutched his coat, terrified he might drop her headfirst to the ground. "What are you doing?"

"Getting rid of a nuisance," he said, marching along one of the garden paths.

"A nuisance!" Pins tumbled from her hair, spilling the heavy mass over her face and down the back of his legs. She pounded her fist against his back. "Put me down!"

"Unless you want someone to notice you in this position, I would keep your voice down."

Isabel caught her lower lip between her teeth. She did not want to think of what gossip this little scene could cause. She clenched her eyes shut and prayed no one would see her in this humiliating position. "I will make you regret the day you were born," she said in a hiss.

"Of that I have no doubt."

Blood pounded in her temples. Each step he took drove his hard shoulder into her belly. With each stride her fury mounted until she could barely restrain a scream.

Through the pounding of blood in her head, she heard the gasps of servants as he carried her across the stone floor of the kitchen. She did not want to imagine what they must think of the sight they witnessed, or whom they might tell. She thumped her fist against his back as he started up the servants' stairs. "You will pay for this."

"No doubt."

"Put me down!"

He did not pause. Through the curtain of her hair, she saw the emerald-and-gold carpet lining the second-floor hallway. He threw open the door to his bedchamber and carried her inside.

"I warn you, I will not..." She gasped as he dropped her on her feet. She stumbled a few steps before she gained her balance. She pushed the hair from her face and glared at the rogue. Moonlight poured through the windowpanes, filling the room with a pale glow. Justin turned the key in the lock. The soft click ricocheted through her.

"What do you think you are doing?"

He tossed the key to the top of the tall mahogany armoire. "Making certain we don't have any interruptions."

The implication sizzled through her blood in a familiar, tingling excitement. Still, she would not be treated like an easy conquest. "I demand you open that door immediately."

He shrugged out of his black coat and tossed it over the back of a wing-back chair near the hearth. "I am not going to open that door until we have a few things settled between us.''

''There is nothing to settle.''

He tugged his cravat from his collar. The dark, sultry look in his eyes sent her heart into a headlong sprint. ''I'm afraid there is.''

Isabel glanced around the room, searching for an escape. She had to get away from him before she did something unforgivably foolish. She dashed for the door leading to the adjoining sitting room. He reached it first, placing six feet, three inches of powerful masculinity between her and freedom. The warmth of his body radiated against her, tempting her. She snatched at her retreating control. ''Stand aside.''

He locked the door and removed the key. ''Not until this is ended.''

She stepped back as he drew near. ''Precisely what do you mean, ended?''

He strolled past her and tossed the key to the top of the armoire. ''You are obviously a menace to every man who comes into your orbit.''

''A menace!'' She watched him flick open the buttons lining his black silk waistcoat, a delicious tingle spreading across her skin. ''How in the world am I a menace to the men of the world?''

He tossed the waistcoat on top of his coat. ''With your flirtatious ways, you are bound to draw blood sooner or later.'' He kicked off his shoes.

She glared at him. ''That is preposterous.''

''No, I think it is quite likely.'' He tugged the shirt-tails from his trousers. The warmth of his body had pressed deep creases in the white cambric. ''In fact, I seriously contemplated breaking Hanley's neck this evening.''

He was actually jealous over her. Isabel tingled with

240

the delicious realization. "It would seem *you* are the menace."

He grinned as he unfastened his shirt. "Since I have no intention of spending my days in exile, there is only one solution to the problem."

She crossed her arms at her waist. "That is?"

"I am going to take you off the market."

He pulled the shirt over his head and tossed the garment to the floor. Moonlight gleamed on the sleek skin of his broad shoulders. The shimmering light slid in a loving caress over the thick planes and angles of his chest, tangling in the black curls shading his skin. Desire played on her insides, like a hand drawing the string of a bow. Heat coiled and simmered low inside her. She could not surrender to this need. It was foolish. Insane. "I thought this was settled between us."

Justin moved toward her, his slow strides filled with the grace of a man in command of his realm. "You thought wrong."

Isabel backpedaled, afraid of what she might do if he touched her. "What do you imagine you shall accomplish by doing this?"

"A return to sanity. An end to this game you are playing."

"Game!" She hit a thick post at the foot of his bed. "I am not suicidal, Marlow. I certainly would not play any foolish games with you."

He stepped close to her, pressing her back against the bedpost. "I will not stand around watching you flirt with half the men in London."

Hard mahogany pressed against her spine. Yet she hardly noticed with the heat of blatant masculinity radiating against her. "I thought you were too busy with that plump little blonde even to notice I was in the room."

He dropped a kiss on the tip of her nose. "Jealousy suits you."

"No, it doesn't." She pressed her palms flat against his chest, intending to push him away. Heat bathed her skin. Her fingers curled against him, absorbing his warmth, the intriguing texture of crisp black hair. "I hate feeling this way."

He brushed his lips against her temple. "What way?"

She choked back a sigh. "Angry and jittery and so jealous I wanted to tear every yellow hair from that woman's head."

He plucked the few remaining pins from her hair and tossed them to the floor. "There is no sense in fighting this, Isabel," he said, sliding his hands through her thick hair. "You are besotted with me."

She leaned back against the post. "I must be out of my mind."

He slipped his arms around her waist and tugged her against him. "You are mine."

She slid her hands along his arms, over smooth skin, thick muscles shifting beneath her touch. "And you belong to no woman. Is that the way it is?"

His hands flexed on her waist. "I want you."

His dark voice stroked the longing deep inside of her. "Lust," she said simply.

His lips pulled into a tight line. "Look me straight in the eye and tell me you don't want me."

There was no hope for it. She wanted him, and the wanting would not go away in this lifetime. "I want more than you are willing to give."

"Damnation, Isabel, I want to make you my wife."

She rested her hands on his chest. "I doubt I should be very good at sharing my husband with other women."

He brushed his lips against her cheek. "I haven't

wanted another woman since the first day you barged into my life.''

His words stroked the tiny infant of hope she cradled deep inside her. He cared for her. She knew it, felt it as keenly as the blood surging through her veins. Yet she could not be certain if a man like Justin could ever truly belong to one woman. ''How do I know you will not change your mind?''

''Do we know anything in life as a certainty?''

She stroked his cheek; the dark pinpoints of his beard slumbered beneath the smooth surface of his skin. ''I cannot live a lie.''

''Would you choose a life without passion, Isabel?'' He slid his warm fingertips over her shoulder.

''You are speaking of a fire that flares, then dies.''

''If you deny this fire burning between us, you will go to your bed every night wondering what might have been if you had been brave enough to take what you want.''

A life without Justin. Days and nights filled with unfulfilled longing. Was giving him up worse than sharing him with other women? ''I want a real marriage.''

''With another man?'' He slid his hands upward over her back, the heat of his palms soaking through her clothing. ''Do you want another man's hands on you, Isabel? Do you want another man to hold you, to kiss you?''

She knew with the same certainty that she knew the sun would rise each morning that there would never in her life be a man who could stir her emotions the way this man could. ''You can be very cruel.''

''Not as cruel as you, my beautiful witch.'' He brushed his lips against her neck. ''Not cruel enough to turn my back on what we share.''

She slid her arms around his neck. "I'm a fool for wanting you."

He gripped her waist and drew her up against him. "You are mine. You know it."

For the moment she would not think of all the women who would try to steal his attention from her. All she could hope was to find a way to win his heart as well as his passion. "I suppose I should be glad you didn't hit me over the head with a club."

The tension melted from his expression. "I want you wide awake."

She brushed her lips above his right nipple, crisp curls tickling her nose, a lush, masculine scent filling her nostrils. "I wish I didn't want you. I wish I could ignore you."

"I will not allow it." He nipped the sensitive skin at the joining of her neck and shoulder, sending shivers skittering along her skin.

"Infuriating creature."

"Stubborn wench," he whispered as his lips brushed hers.

He slid his hands upward along her back, warming her through the silk and muslin of her clothes. He found the fastenings of her gown, slipped silk loops free of silk-covered buttons with the ease of a man who knew all the intricacies of undressing a woman. Her petticoat and chemise spilled open beneath his deft touch. He slid his palms over her shoulders, dragging a soft sigh from her lips as he peeled the garments from her shoulders. Silk and muslin drifted down the length of her body, brushing her skin, tumbling with a whisper around her ankles.

He lowered his eyes, his gaze skimming over her skin, so hot and hungry that the heat of it simmered deep inside her. She felt no shame standing naked under his gaze. In the light of that blatant male admiration, she felt tempting and beautiful.

"You have haunted me." He slid his hands down her arms and slipped his hands around her wrists. "Day and night."

"Have I?" Cool evening air brushed her bare back, while the heat of his chest warmed her breasts.

"What spell have you cast upon me, my beautiful witch?" He pinned her hands at the small of her back and lifted her up against him until her breasts pressed against his chest.

Isabel moaned at the sharp stab of sensation that spiraled from her breasts and shot straight to her belly. His heart hammered against her chest, racing, keeping time with her heart's own frenetic rhythm. "I'm not a witch. Simply a woman. A woman who cannot resist you."

He laughed, the dark sounds rumbling deep in his chest. "It is about time you came to your senses."

The scent of sandalwood warm from his skin swirled through her senses. "Arrogant, infuriating . . . magnificent man."

"Beguiling thorn in my side." He kissed the corner of her lips, then slid his mouth over hers, claiming her, driving any possible thoughts of resistance from her mind. Hunger and need filled his kiss, drugging her with his own heady brew of masculinity.

He slid his hands over her rounded bottom and lifted her against him. She wrapped her arms around his neck. Warm wool brushed her belly, her thighs. Through his clothes, the heat and strength of his arousal pressed wantonly against her, teasing her. She had never imagined her body could feel this way, as though every nerve had suddenly come to life beneath his touch.

He spread kisses down her neck, across her shoulder, all the while his hands moved up and down her back, over her hips, the pouting curves of her bottom, his long fingers flexing against her skin, as though he could not get enough of her. Women came easily to this man. She intended to be the last to warm his bed. If it killed her, she would drive all thoughts of other women from his mind.

His soft hair brushed her chin as he lowered his head, his lips closing over her breast. She tipped back her head, giving full rein to the pleasure surging through her.

A lifetime ago he had shown her a glimpse of passion, a flicker of stunning light. She wanted more. She wanted to bask in that light. She wanted the heat of it pouring over her flesh. She clawed at the front of his trousers, fumbling with the buttons until the flap fell open. His arousal pressed against the linen of his drawers. Three buttons freed him into her hands. She claimed him, dragging eager fingers over the length of him, reveling in the velvet heat of him, the steely strength of him.

A low growl rose from deep in his chest. He suckled her breast, tugging on her nipple, sending sensation after sensation pounding through her until she was whimpering, begging him for more. He slid his hands over her hips, her thighs, her belly, stroking her, inflaming her. She arched against him as he cupped the mound at the joining of her thighs.

"Burn for me, Belle," he whispered, slipping one finger inside her wet feminine passage. He clamped his lips over hers, dipped his tongue into her mouth, withdrew, again and again, matching the maddening rhythm of the slow thrust and withdrawal of his finger into her.

Everything she had imagined of desire or passion paled compared to this. Desire was not merely an emotion. Desire was a force: powerful, compelling, sucking her upward into a realm where pleasure reigned.

He slid the length of his arousal along her nether lips while his fingers played against her body. She clutched his arms as the pleasure rose and shimmered inside her, until her body shuddered with the sheer power of it. He lifted her in his arms and carried her to the bed. The silk counterpane caressed her as his weight pressed her down into the soft eiderdown mattress. He turned away from her long enough to strip away the rest of his clothes. Moonlight streamed through the windows, pouring over him, burnishing his skin.

She lifted her arms to him, welcoming him as the lover she had waited for all of her life. He came to her, holding her as though she were the treasure he had sought for eternity. He touched her everywhere—his hands, his lips, his tongue, caressing her, kissing her, tasting her. She trembled as he moved down the length of her body. He drew her slippers from her feet and tossed them to the floor.

She watched as he pulled the ribbon from her lace-trimmed garter and peeled the white silk stocking from her leg. Heat skittered along her nerves with the warmth of his hands on skin. He removed the other garter and stocking, then brushed his lips against her ankle.

"From the first day I saw you, I've dreamed of doing this," he whispered against her skin.

A low sigh escaped her lips as he slid his tongue upward along her calf. "I've dreamed of you touching me like this."

He turned his cheek against her thigh and grinned his devilish grin. "I would wager my dreams were more wicked than yours."

She licked her dry lips. "You have me at a disadvantage. Except for that one time in the cottage, I've never done anything like this.''

He turned his smiling lips against her inner thigh. ''I know.''

She leaned back against the pillows, tension drawing her insides taut as he drew upward, spreading kisses along her inner thigh. He threaded his fingers through the dark curls at the joining of her thighs, then touched her with his lips. She arched against him, startled by the intimate touch of his lips against her flesh. ''Wicked, indeed.''

''I want to taste you. All of you.''

He was right: never in all of her wildest imaginings would she ever have dreamed of anything this wicked, this wonderfully depraved. She tossed her head back and forth against the pillows, soft, inarticulate sounds spilling from her lips. Her body quivered beneath his touch, her mind whirling as sensation chased sensation within her. And then it came, that same dizzying pleasure he had shown her before. Her body shuddered with the force of it, the incredible joy of it.

As the last spasm shook her body, he plunged his shaft into her. Pain splintered through her. She gasped. Her body stiffened beneath him. She gripped his shoulders and prayed she would not do something unforgivably foolish, such as expire in his arms.

''Damn.'' He smoothed his hand over her hair, his expression drawn with concern. ''You are too . . . tiny. So tight. I should have realized. . . . I didn't think.''

He was accustomed to women who knew exactly what they were doing. Women who could accommodate his length and breadth without complaint. Heaven above, she would stay with this until the end, even if it ripped her in two. She felt him withdrawing, pulling away from her. She wrapped her legs around his hips. ''Don't you dare stop now.''

"Isabel," he whispered, his voice oddly strained. "There is no hope for it. No way around it. I cannot keep from hurting you."

The anguish in his expression tugged at her heart. The gentleness in this man poured over her, as warm as spring rain. She touched his cheek and smiled up at him. "I would suppose it is this way for most women the first time. And we've been surviving since the beginning of the world."

He swallowed hard. "Are you certain?"

She saw the turmoil in his glorious eyes, and knew with perfect clarity she would never in her life feel this way for another man. "The human race would have died a long time ago if women couldn't adapt to men."

He clenched his jaw and slid back into her. Her body stretched, hugging the velvet hardness of his arousal with only a slight sting. He kissed her, a gentle slide of his lips against hers while he slipped his hand between their bodies. He found the place where sensation hid. He celebrated that tiny bud, lavished it with attention.

She had not expected pleasure. She had hoped only to maintain her composure while he finished their coupling and found his release. Yet he conjured magic with his touch. He coaxed pleasure with his gentleness, until pain was nothing but a distant memory. Joy flickered inside her with each slow stroke of his body into hers, rising like bubbles in simmering water, collecting and coiling until it filled her.

She arched against him, following ancient instincts hidden deep inside, lifting to meet his downward thrusts. She pumped her hips upward, reaching for the pleasure, matching the ever increasing rhythm of his thrusts. She moved with him in a dizzying race, chasing pleasure until she slammed straight into it—a sudden burst of sensation, a lightning flash of splendor, a rapturous flight of release.

She clutched him to her with her arms and her legs, his name escaping her lips on a thread of breath. His body stiffened, a low rumble filling her ears, before he eased into her embrace.

A soft moan slipped from her lips and twisted around his heart as Justin slowly withdrew from her. He had never been with an untouched maiden before. Until now, he had not given much thought to any of the ramifications of virginity. Although he took a natural male pride in knowing no man had ever touched Isabel before, he had not been prepared for her pain. Still, all women started this way, he assured himself. He had not damaged her. Had he?

She was lying with her cheek against a plump pillow, her hair spilled across the blue silk counterpane, her eyes closed, her lips parted. Her breasts rose and fell with her deep breaths, her nipples lifting to him, taut and red from his kisses. He swept the length of her with his gaze, searching for signs of injury. Except for a few rosy marks where her skin had rubbed against his, she looked unharmed.

"Isabel," he whispered, brushing a soft curl from her cheek.

She turned her cheek into his palm, a low sound sighing deep in her throat. "Hold me, Marlow."

The tension in his chest uncoiled at her soft words. He lay beside her and took her into his arms. She snuggled against him, slipping her thigh between his, draining the last dregs of fear from his heart. "I think we know each other well enough for you to call me by my given name."

"Justin," she whispered, her lips moving against his neck. "Such a nice name."

"I'm glad you like it." He wrapped himself around her, experiencing an odd protectiveness toward this woman. For some unfathomable reason, he wanted to shield her from all the bumps and disappointments of life. He pressed his lips to her hair and breathed in the innocent scent of lavender.

He had never wanted an entanglement with a respectable female. He had not planned for this to happen tonight. He had planned to forget Isabel. Still, a man must make allowances for unforeseen calamities in his life. "It would seem you have survived without permanent damage."

"I hope I did not disappoint you."

"Disappoint me?"

She released her breath in a warm stream against his skin. "I know I'm not very accomplished at this, but I'm an eager student. Before long, I'm certain I can learn to please you."

He slid his hand down her back, smiling against her hair. No woman had ever worried about pleasing him before. "It could take a while. I'm afraid we might have to practice once or twice a day. Perhaps even more. Depending on your progress."

She pulled back and smiled up at him. "I'm a quick learner."

He wiggled his eyebrows at her. "In that case, I just might keep you locked in here for the rest of your life."

She slid her hand over his shoulder, the warmth of her palm soaking into his skin. "Do you always get what you want?"

It had been a long time since he had wanted anything he could not buy. He cupped her cheek in his hand. "Are you going to tell me you did not want this?"

She turned her face and pressed her lips against his palm. "You have the most infuriating way of turning my mind to mush. No doubt you shall drive me to distraction, but I would rather go insane with you than without you."

He pulled her close, sighing at the feel of her breasts nestled against his chest. "I always suspected you had a keen intellect."

She rubbed her cheek against his shoulder. "So it is my intellect that interests you."

"For some time now, I've been intrigued by very nearly everything about you."

She tipped her head and looked up at him, her expression revealing her surprise. "Careful. I might swoon with such shocking flattery."

"Sometimes I even manage to shock myself." He brushed the backs of his fingers over the softness of her cheek. Odd, but simply holding her this way was more satisfying than making love to any other woman he had ever known. "I never expected to marry. And here I'm about to be leg-shackled to a sharp-tongued little termagant."

She pressed her hand to her heart. "You have such a romantic way of expressing yourself."

He brushed his lips over hers. "I thought I expressed myself eloquently a few moments ago. But then, perhaps you need . . ." He hesitated as the door leading to the hall flew open.

Light from the wall sconce in the hall flowed into the room, slicing a golden wedge through the shadows. Sophia appeared and stormed through that golden light and then shut the door behind her. "Justin Hayward Peyton Trevelyan, I never believed you would sink to this level."

Isabel flinched, a low squeak escaping her lips. "Duchess!"

"Bloody hell!" Justin grabbed the counterpane on the opposite side of Isabel and tossed it over both of them, shielding their nakedness from his grandmother.

Sophia marched across the room, keys clanging on the metal ring she gripped at her side. "I could scarcely believe it when Hoskins told me he saw you carrying Isabel across the kitchen. As though she were a sack of potatoes!"

Justin tightened his arm around Isabel, holding her close to his side. "Isabel and I had a few things to settle between us."

Sophia paused beside the bed. Moonlight poured over her, illuminating the tight line of her lips. "Isabel, dear, has my despicable grandson harmed you?"

"No." Isabel clutched the edge of the counterpane just below her nose. "I'm fine."

"As fine as a woman can be after she has been assaulted by a brute." Sophia pinned Justin with a frosty glare. "What do you have to say for yourself, young man?"

Justin refused to cower under that glare. He was not a child caught putting frogs into his tutor's bed. "I have things well in hand, Sophia. You can run along."

Sophia crossed her arms over her chest. "Prinny is in the gold drawing room, waiting to meet your ward. We have a house full of guests. Did you think of what would happen if anyone knew what had occurred in here?"

Isabel drew a sharp breath. "Does anyone know?"

Sophia shrugged. "Aside from the servants, I cannot be certain."

"You can sheathe your claws, Grandmother. I plan to marry the girl."

"Of course you will marry her. And I will do my best to prevent a scandal."

Justin returned his grandmother's glare. "I don't

253

give a farthing what any of those blasted people down-stairs might think of me.''

Sophia drew a deep breath. ''You seem to forget we have Eloise and Phoebe to think of, as well as Isabel. You might not care what happens to your reputation, young man, but you will not besmirch theirs.''

''Oh, my goodness!'' Isabel sat up, clutching the counterpane to her chin, stripping the cover from Justin.

Justin snatched a pillow and clasped it to his naked loins. ''Grandmother, if you don't mind, I would like a little privacy.''

''You can have all the privacy you need.'' Sophia grabbed Isabel's clothes from the floor and handed Isabel the chemise. ''Put this on.''

Isabel scrambled from the bed. Justin frowned as he watched her slip into the garment. Sophia had yanked the reins out of his hands and he did not care for the direction in which she had steered them. ''Sophia, I have already decided we shall be married by special license.''

Sophia nodded. ''Of course. No one of any conse-quence bothers with posting banns. Come along, child. Let's see if we can repair the damage.''

Justin tapped his fingers against the pillow over his loins. ''We shall be married tomorrow morning.''

Sophia smiled at him. ''No, dear. You shall not.''

''What do you think you are going to do?'' Justin demanded, as his grandmother ushered Isabel toward the door.

''I am going to help this child get dressed.'' Sophia opened the door and peeked into the hall. ''Now, get out of bed. Get dressed. Get back to the party. And try to keep the regent amused until we return. I've seen to it he has a platter of pastries, but that will not keep him occupied for very long.''

* * *

Isabel hurried into her bedchamber, grateful that no one had seen her dressed only in her chemise. Sophia closed the door. "I've had fresh water brought up, just enough for the washbasin. There isn't any time for a long bath. By the time you have washed and dressed in a fresh chemise and petticoat, Alice should have the wrinkles pressed out of your gown."

Isabel could scarcely meet Sophia's eyes. Although she could not in all honesty regret the time she had spent in Justin's arms, she was ashamed she had not given her sisters or Sophia proper consideration before indulging herself. "I am so terribly sorry. I never meant to put you in this awkward situation."

Sophia patted Isabel's arm. "My dear child, my grandson put us in this situation."

"It wasn't entirely his fault. I am certain I could have convinced him to let me go, if I had only found the will to resist him."

"Isabel, you must know I am delighted you and Justin are going to be married. Why do you think I waited so long to come rescue you?"

"You waited?"

Sophia smiled. "Since Justin had already made a spectacle, I saw no reason to interrupt while you and Justin sorted through your difficulties. I thought it judicious to wait until the matter was settled."

"But the guests. The regent. The scandal! What are we going to do? I would never forgive myself if I harmed Eloise or Phoebe, or if I shamed you in any way."

"I think we can manage the damage. As long as we can keep that headstrong grandson of mine from indulging in the complete folly of an elopement, then I believe we shall survive with little more than a few scratches. But you must be strong. You must resist him if he tries to whisk you away.''

"I shall.''

"We will send an announcement to the *Gazette* in the morning. Under the circumstances, I believe a month is sufficient time for your engagement. It will allow us to prepare for a proper wedding and wedding breakfast. And from this point forward, we must be careful we don't toss another bone to the gossip mongers.''

Isabel nodded. "I shall not disappoint you.''

"I know you will not, my child.'' Sophia rolled her eyes to heaven. "Justin, on the other hand, shall do his best to vex me.''

Chapter Eighteen

"Clayton, take Isabel in to supper." Sophia slipped her arm through Justin's. "Your brother and I will be in directly."

Justin watched his fiancée walk away on the arm of his brother. Heads turned as she and Clayton made their way through the crowded ballroom. Male heads. Pride swelled in his heart at the same time that another, more caustic emotion roiled within him. He resented every lecherous glance cast in her direction. He had not thought it possible. In truth, he had thought the affliction would lessen now that he had actually bedded Isabel. Yet the fever had escalated.

Sophia tugged on his arm, ushering him in the opposite direction from Clayton and Isabel. She led him across the ballroom and out one of the French doors opening into the gardens. They plowed through squares of light spilling across the stone terrace from the French doors of the ballroom. She halted when

257

they reached a secluded spot on the far end of the terrace.

After glancing around to make certain they were alone, Sophia spoke. "Justin, these evil glares at every man who looks at Isabel must stop. I thought for one moment in the drawing room that you were going to rip Prinny's head off."

Justin leaned against the thick stone balustrade. "I thought of it."

Sophia lifted one finely arched brow. "May I remind you that they hang people for treason. Even dukes."

"I didn't like the way he was looking at her, as though she were a pastry he wanted to devour."

"If Prinny noticed your expression, you shall be quite out of favor with him."

"If I cared, I would not despair. The next time he wants advice about a horse, he will forget his displeasure."

Sophia tapped her closed fan against her open palm. "Do you realize you're acting like a pug protecting his favorite bone?"

Heat flooded his cheeks. He turned his gaze toward the gardens and hoped the moonlight would not betray the humiliating flush. "I never did like the idea of this blasted ball."

Sophia released her breath on a long sigh. "Now I understand why you wanted to keep Isabel hidden away from the world."

"I intend to marry her tomorrow morning."

"If you have any feelings for Isabel or her sisters, you will handle this affair with the utmost propriety. Rumors are already smoldering. You don't need to toss more coals on the fire."

"The gossip will cease to be amusing once we are married."

"But the stigma shall remain. It will follow Isabel all of her life. It will attach itself to Eloise and Phoebe. The Darracott ladies shall forever be associated with scandal."

A cool breeze swept across the gardens, rustling the leaves of the tall chestnut tree growing near the corner of the terrace. The soft sound seemed a thousand voices, each whispering behind his back. He had lived his life an object of speculation and gossip. He could tolerate more. But Isabel, the girls. He wanted to protect them from his own black shadow. "What do you want me to do?"

"Wait a month. Give me a chance to prepare for a proper wedding at St. George's."

"A month!"

Sophia tilted her head. Moonlight fell upon her face, revealing the curiosity in her eyes. "I am asking you to wait a month, Justin. It's hardly a lifetime."

It *was* a lifetime. Yet he still had enough pride to hide the true reason he wanted this marriage to take place as soon as possible. "You want to put me on display. Parade me down the aisle like a trained bear."

"Justin, what do you suppose people will think if you run off with that dear child?"

The truth: that he could not keep his hands off one infuriating little spinster. As galling as that might be, one possible alternative was worse. "I don't give a bloody damn what anyone might think."

Sophia lifted one golden brow. "You will refrain from using such language in my hearing, young man."

Justin swore under his breath. "I don't care to put on a spectacle for the ton."

"Justin, Isabel deserves a proper wedding, with her family and friends in attendance. She certainly does not deserve to be married in some shabby fashion, as though she were a secret you wished to keep hidden.

I will not have you tarnish her reputation by raising more speculation about her. We have Eloise and Phoebe to think of. I know you would never intentionally do anything to harm them.''

''I am planning to marry her, not set her up as my mistress.'' He knew how easily an engagement could be broken. Even though Isabel had given herself to him with unbridled passion, he still could not shake the fear that he would lose her. He kept thinking she would open those beautiful blue eyes, see him for the stinking, black-hearted scoundrel he was, and run screaming into the night.

''You are the girls' guardian, Justin. What would you think if some man stole Eloise or Phoebe away in the night?'' Sophia asked.

Justin looked at his grandmother. ''This is different.''

''Yes. This is far worse. The man in question is notorious.''

Justin's chest tightened. He did not need to be reminded of his reputation. He especially did not need for anyone to remind Isabel that the man in question was a rake, a libertine, a debauchee. She had denied him once because of his black nature; she could do it again.

''What are you afraid of, Justin?''

''Afraid?''

She smiled. ''I had forgotten, you are far too fierce to be frightened of anything.''

He knew fear. He had made its acquaintance at an early age. Fear was a cunning thing, able to slip through the cracks of any walls he had tried to build around it. As much as he wanted to deny it, fear had managed to coil around his insides like thin bands of steel, forged by Isabel's delicate hands.

"You are far too confident to imagine Isabel might cry off if you gave her a chance."

Justin curled his fist against the balustrade. "It would be her loss."

"It would also be yours."

"I would manage to survive."

Sophia studied him, and he knew the moonlight spared him no refuge from her perceptive gaze. "Under the circumstances, I certainly doubt Isabel will cry off. Even if you do drive her to distraction. There could be a child involved."

A child. The air settled in Justin's lungs as he realized his seed might already have found fertile soil in Isabel. "I suppose there is some merit in what you say."

"Do I feel the earth trembling?" Sophia asked.

Justin frowned. "I will give you three weeks. The amount of time it would take if we posted banns."

Sophia's lips flattened. "I suppose a month would be pushing your patience."

"Considering my opinion of a wedding at St. George's, a day will push my patience."

Sophia nodded. "It shall be hectic, but I believe we shall manage with three weeks."

"Don't expect me to have anything to do with this little spectacle except to show up at the church. I leave it in your hands."

Sophia patted his chest. "I think I can manage. And I know you can manage to behave like a proper gentleman with your fiancée. If you start to slip, think of Isabel. I doubt she would look kindly upon any blemish you may cast upon her sisters."

"I will manage." He could manage the role, he assured himself. He had to. He had no intention of giving Isabel an excuse to send him packing.

*   *   *

Could anyone tell by looking at her? Isabel wondered. If anyone had seen her draped over Justin's shoulder like a prize from the hunting field, they would certainly wonder what had followed. She stood by a potted palm in a corner of the ballroom, trying to look as composed and calm as possible. Every smile cast in her direction seemed a little too knowing. Had a plunge into the heated pool of passion scrawled an indelible brand upon her? She eased closer to the palm, seeking some shelter in the huge room. She wished she could hide. Yet she knew she had to face this mob with a smile.

"There you are."

Isabel jumped as Franklin Witheridge touched her arm from behind. She pivoted to face him, her hand at her throat. "Cousin!"

Franklin smiled. "I didn't mean to startle you."

Isabel shook her head. "I am afraid I'm a little distracted tonight."

"It's understandable. You have had quite an eventful night."

Isabel stopped breathing. "What have you heard?"

Franklin frowned. "I heard you were presented to the prince."

"Oh." Isabel forced her wooden lips into a smile. "Yes. The prince. He was very cordial."

"Gerard was looking for you earlier." Franklin smiled down at her. "We were afraid something had happened to you."

"I had a . . . mishap with my gown. It had to be taken care of before I could meet the regent."

"I am a little surprised the duchess did not arrange for a formal presentation at court."

"I really didn't want one."

Franklin nodded. "At your age, I can understand. I imagine that after a life at Bramsleigh, a ball such as this, in your honor, must seem a little overwhelming.''

"Yes. It has been an extraordinary evening."

Franklin smiled. "I have never seen you look lovelier, but then you must feel like a princess tonight.''

"I confess I do."

"Still, beneath all the finery, I am certain you are still the same practical young woman you have always been."

A practical young woman did not throw herself into the arms of a dangerous duke, she thought. She would never again be the same. Justin had altered her. She felt it. A certain change within her, memories of passion pressed into her every pore.

"I hope you will not forget a certain young gentleman who has hopes to make you his bride." Franklin patted her arm. "You know, Henrietta and I have always hoped to welcome you as a daughter."

Although she had never understood the reason they thought her so well suited for Gerard, she had always been aware of their sentiment. She had never tried to deceive them into thinking she would ever accept their son's generous offer of marriage. "Thank you. But I—"

Franklin lifted his hand. "Not another word on the subject. I am certain when the shine fades from all of this glitter you will see what is true and steady."

She thought for a moment of telling Franklin of her engagement. Yet she thought it better to inform Gerard herself. "Gerard is a fine young gentleman."

Franklin nodded, a look of pride filling his expression. "Excellent young man. By the way, he tells me you have uncovered a clue in the old baron's journal."

"Yes. A rather cryptic clue, I'm afraid. I hope the other clues are a great deal more straightforward than 'Find the dragon who guards the sanctum.' Or the treasure might remain hidden another century."

Franklin's lips turned down at the corners. "Gerard tells me Marlow is helping you with the translations."

"I am afraid he doesn't need my help. He is actually doing all of the translations."

"Hmmm. I wonder if that is wise."

"Why do you say that?"

Franklin shrugged. "It's quite possible he could decipher the clues, find the treasure, and keep it for himself. After all of these years, we really shouldn't risk losing it."

"I am quite certain I can trust him."

Franklin looked at her with the condescension of an elder dealing with a poor, deluded child. "Are you?"

Isabel squeezed her fan. "I have found the Duke of Marlow to be one of the most honest—the most honorable—gentlemen of my acquaintance. I would trust him with my life."

"Quite a testament, Miss Darracott," Eldridge Belcham said as he approached her. Although average in height, his habit of walking with a slight forward hunch made him look shorter. He had crimped his dark hair into tight curls and forced them into a disheveled look meant to lend a poetic cast to his pointed features. Yet the effort was wasted on a man who would never again see the better side of fifty.

Isabel squashed the irritation that rose in an instant whenever she saw this man. "Anyone familiar with the duke knows he is a man of honor."

"Interesting perspective." Eldridge glanced at Franklin and then back to Isabel. "I have been hoping to speak with you all evening. It's quite important."

Franklin accepted the hint and excused himself. Isabel flicked her thumb over the ivory spines of her closed fan as Franklin left her alone with Eldridge. "If you wish to speak to me about my father's collection,

Mr. Belcham, you will find I have not altered my decision.''

Eldridge glanced around the room. "Are you enjoying the ball?"

"Immensely," she said, irritation edging her voice.

Eldridge turned his dark gaze on her. "I wonder, have you heard the rumors?"

Isabel's throat tightened. "Rumors?"

Eldridge lowered his eyes, raking her figure with his gaze. "You really don't look any worse for your little adventure, Miss Darracott. Perhaps you even enjoyed it."

Isabel bristled beneath the improper perusal. "I have no idea what you mean. But I certainly do not appreciate your insolence."

He looked up, his small, dark eyes glowing with malice. "Did I mention I have been meaning to speak with you all evening?"

Irritation and anxiety coiled in her chest. "Mr. Belcham, if you have something to say to me, do get on with it."

"Earlier, I followed you and Lord Hanley into the gardens. I waited near the center of the gardens, hoping I might catch a few moments with you on your way back to the ball. Imagine my surprise when Marlow came storming after you. Of course, I had to take a peek to see what would follow."

The blood slowly drained from her limbs, leaving her shaky. She held Belcham's confident gaze and prayed she did not look as frightened as she felt. "The duke is very protective of his wards."

"Interesting way he has of showing it. Carrying you about slung over his shoulder."

Isabel twisted her fan in her fingers. "The duke and I had a small misunderstanding."

"Yes." He grinned. "Of course, I saw at once how

the situation might benefit me. I am a practical man, after all.''

''If you have a point, make it.''

''I want your father's collection, Miss Darracott. Give me the manuscripts and I will remain quiet about what I saw.''

''Blackmail?''

''I wouldn't use such a harsh term.''

Isabel squeezed her fan so tightly the spines snapped. ''I will not give you my father's collection.''

Eldridge leaned closer, spewing the scent of onions as he spoke. ''Think carefully about your decision, Miss Darracott.''

''Miss Darracott has a good deal of sense, Belcham. She always considers her decisions carefully.''

Isabel's blood surged at the sound of Justin's deep voice. She glanced from Eldridge's startled expression to find Justin standing behind her tormentor. Dressed entirely in black, except for a touch of pristine white linen at his neck and chest and another at his cuffs, he looked every inch as dangerous as his reputation. Tall, broad shouldered, a magnificent warrior ready to do battle.

Eldridge pivoted to face Justin. ''Duke! I didn't hear you approach.''

''I believe you were asking Miss Darracott to consider her decision when I approached. Since I am looking after her affairs, perhaps you would like to repeat what you have to say to me.''

''Ah . . .'' Eldridge swallowed so hard his throat clicked. ''We were simply discussing the possibility . . . I was hoping to persuade her to part with her father's manuscript collection.''

Justin stepped closer to the blackguard. Eldridge backpedaled straight into the palm. A feathery branch flopped over his brow. ''Her father's collection of manuscripts is under my protection, Belcham. They are not for sale. Do you understand?''

Eldridge stared at Justin from beneath the palm frond. ''Yes. I understand. Perfectly.''

Justin flicked the linen at his cuff. ''Have a pleasant evening, Belcham.''

Belcham turned and scurried away without another word. Still, Isabel doubted he would remain quiet, about anything.

''What did that little toad say to you?'' Justin asked, his voice low and dangerously dark.

Isabel stared down at her broken fan. ''He saw us in the gardens. He thought he could blackmail me.''

''The blackguard. I will make certain that little toad doesn't—''

She touched his arm. ''Please. Let it be. Otherwise you lend credence to his words.''

Justin frowned, twin furrows forming between his thick black brows, a look of discomfort crossing his features. ''I suppose I have provided enough fodder for the gossips tonight.''

''You were not the only person in your chamber tonight. I am as responsible as you are.''

''As I recall, I locked you in.''

''You would have released me if I had protested with any conviction. You're far too honorable to have done otherwise.''

An odd expression crossed his features, surprise mingled with an endearing glimmer of uncertainty. ''I suppose I should be happy for your habit of seeing saints where there are only sinners.''

Isabel had glimpsed the man behind the mask often enough to know him. Beneath the arrogant, insolent, cynical facade dwelt a man with a poor opinion of his own self-worth. ''Lately I have found I have a disturbing propensity for thinking you are one of the most kind, exceptionally generous, terribly noble, incredibly honorable men I have ever met.''

He stared at her for several moments. His lips parted, then closed and parted once more. ''Careful, Belle. If anyone hears you talking such nonsense, they might have you clapped into Bedlam.''

She smiled up at him. ''Sophia is certain we can emerge from this tangle without much damage if we are—''

''Isabel,'' Gerard said as he approached them. He cast Justin an uneasy look, then faced Isabel. ''I have been looking for you. You promised me a waltz, remember?''

''Of course.'' She glanced up at Justin. She wished she could run away with him tonight. Yet she had more than her own feelings to consider. She took Gerard's arm and allowed him to lead her to the dance floor.

Kind. Generous. Noble! Justin did not know if he should laugh or weep at Isabel's innocent insanity. He felt like doing both. She had a way of doing that to him, of muddling his brain until he was not certain of day from night. He watched Gerard Witheridge lead Isabel through the sweeping turns of a waltz. Her worthy suitor held her at a proper distance, while her lecherous fiancé drooled from a distance.

''I wonder if the good Mr. Witheridge has a chance in blazes of winning the delightful Miss Darracott,'' Braden Fitzwilliam said as he joined Justin near the edge of the dance floor.

Justin grinned at his friend. ''Do I detect a note of resignation in your voice?''

Braden shrugged. ''I admit, I entertained the notion of marriage to the lady. She has a wonderful candor about her. But I have realized the qualities I admire in her would make her unsuitable as my wife."

"Unsuitable?"

"Some men were never meant to be faithful to one woman. Some women were never meant to understand a certain proclivity a man might have for sampling more than one flower in the garden. If I were to marry Isabel, in time we would both be miserable."

The truth of Braden's words settled like a noose around Justin's neck. "I suppose you might change your mind if you were to marry a female who could hold your interest."

Braden's laugh rumbled above the sweet notes of the waltz. "I thought you knew me better than that. You and I are alike. The Almighty hasn't created a female who can hold our attention for long. Oh, I would try to mend my ways for her, but I would inevitably fail. The first time I strayed she would grow a little cool. The next, cooler still. In time I would turn any warmth in the lovely lady to ice."

Justin's throat tightened as though that noose were slowly squeezing the breath from him. "If a woman were to go into marriage with such a man, she would certainly know what to expect."

"Precisely. When I marry, I shall choose a female who understands the way of the world. One who will not break as easily as Isabel Darracott."

Justin turned his attention to the dance floor. It took less than three beats of his heart to find Isabel amid the crowd of dancers. She looked so lovely in the candlelight from the chandeliers above, so delicate, so damned innocent. The skin he had so recently touched glowed like ivory satin. Memories flickered in his mind, of long legs entwined with his, firm breasts brushing his chest. Blood stirred low in his belly. "Isabel is not as green as you think."

"She is as green as grass when it comes to men like us."

Do you always get what you want? Isabel's words echoed in Justin's brain. Ever since the first day he had set eyes on Isabel he had wanted her. He had chipped away at her resistance until it had crumbled. He wanted. He took. Blast his black-hearted soul, he wanted her still. Yet how long would his hunger last? How long before he was slipping away at night to spend the evening at Vachel's? How long before Isabel learned to hate him? The noose that had squeezed his throat slipped around his chest, constricting until his lungs ached. "She might surprise you, Braden. She might have a better understanding than you believe of men such as you and I."

Braden looked at him, his dark brows lifted in surprise. "Either one of us would make her miserable. As much as I hate to say it, the lovely lady needs a man like Witheridge. Someone steady. Boring. A man who will not break her heart."

"I am going to marry her."

Braden's mouth moved. Yet it was a full eight seconds before words followed. "I surmised she had captured your attention. Still, I never dreamed you would actually marry the girl."

"And what the devil did you think I would do with her?"

"Find her a suitable husband perhaps. Gad, man, your opinion of marriage is hardly a secret."

Justin clenched his hands into tight fists at his sides. "I have never pretended to be anything other than what I am. Isabel is going into this marriage with her eyes wide open."

Braden rolled the stem of his wineglass between his fingers, a frown carving deep lines into his brow.

"You have my best wishes, Justin. And my sincere hope your marriage shall be a success."

Justin could hear the doubt as clearly as he could see it in Braden's dark eyes. His friend did not believe for one moment that he and Isabel could make a success of their upcoming marriage. He glanced toward the dance floor and found Isabel among the swirling crowd. She had never wanted a man like Witheridge, he assured himself. She was not a naive little girl. She knew what kind of man Justin was, and still she wanted him.

Yet doubts pricked him, like a thousand needle-sharp thorns. If he had one shred of nobility he never would have touched her. If he had a scrap of kindness, he would have found her a decent man with whom to share her life. If he had a dram of honor he would have died before he hurt her. Yet he knew precisely what he was. He was a scoundrel. An unscrupulous libertine. A man who shuddered at the thought of losing Isabel. A man who would do everything in his power to keep her.

Chapter Nineteen

Isabel had always believed the direct approach was the best to take. The afternoon after the ball she sat alone with Gerard in the green drawing room of Marlow House and told him of her marriage plans.

"He is forcing you into this, isn't he?" Gerard took Isabel's hands in his.

"No one is forcing me into anything. I want to marry Marlow."

Gerard shook his head. "I don't understand. How could you want to marry a man like that. A libertine!!"

"Gerard, I realize the duke has a certain reputation, but I believe we can make a success of our marriage."

"I always thought, if I gave you time, we might . . ." Gerard dropped her hands and stood. His narrow nostrils flared as he stared down at her. "You would actually choose him instead of me?"

"Gerard, I always thought you wanted to marry me because it was what your parents expected. Not because it was truly something you wanted to do.''

"I always expected we would marry, that's true. But I do care for you.''

Isabel smiled. ''But you don't love me.''

Gerard released his breath in a long sigh. ''You have been reading too many Gothic romances, where the wicked duke mends his ways for the love of his life. In real life that doesn't happen, Isabel. In real life the wicked duke makes a mockery of his marriage and humiliates his wife.''

Isabel drew her finger over a gold leaf stitched into the green silk damask covering the arm of the sofa. She knew the chance she was taking with Justin. She also knew she would risk anything for a chance to spend her life with him. ''I have hope for my marriage, Gerard.''

Gerard knelt on one knee before her. ''Isabel, it isn't too late. I can purchase a special license. We can be married by the end of the day. Once you are under my protection, he wouldn't dare harm you.''

Isabel cupped his cheek in her hand, stunned by such recklessness in this staid and practical man. ''You deserve so much more than I could ever give you.''

Gerard sat back on his heel, his blue eyes growing wide. ''You're in love with him?''

Isabel nodded. ''I'm afraid I am.''

Gerard shook his head. ''My poor Isabel. I never realized you had fallen under that devil's spell.''

"I hope we shall remain friends, Gerard.''

Gerard took her hand in a firm grasp and smiled. ''My dear cousin, you may rely on me. Unfortunately, I fear you shall need a good friend in the future. I fear you are doomed to unhappiness.''

Isabel admitted to doubts about her future. It was quite possible Justin would destroy her. Yet if she did not marry him, she would live the rest of her days wondering what might have happened if she had only tried to tame her wicked duke.

Justin sat at the large claw-footed mahogany desk in Sophia's library, trying to decipher a centuries-old mystery. He stared at a page in the old journal, forcing his brain to translate the Italian and Latin sketched on the page, while his body did its best to betray him. He would not make a fool of himself for any female. He would not be ruled by lust. Only a weak man allowed himself to be ruled by anything other than his own intellect. In precisely nineteen days Isabel would belong to him. After the wedding he could, and he would, take her when he wanted her. Until then he could control this blasted ache in his loins.

Isabel's arm brushed his. Heat sizzled across his skin. He clenched his jaw. She sat close beside him in a lyre-back armchair, too close to allow him any peace. Her every breath distracted him. The warmth of her skin, the scent of her hair, the occasional brush of her arm against his, all tortured him, until his skin felt too tight to contain his desire.

Still, tonight, as every night since the ball, he had enough chaperones to keep him honest. Sophia sat with her embroidery hoop near the hearth. Eloise sat across from her reading a book. And Phoebe was perched on a chair to his left, watching his every move. He had not had a moment alone with Isabel in days.

He stared at the black ink scrawled in bold lines upon the page. It took every shred of his will to force his brain to concentrate on the task at hand. The blasted baron had couched his clues in a way that forced a seeker of the treasure to translate every bloody line in the journal.

He scribbled a few words on a piece of paper, then read them out loud. "In the dragon's breath you shall find the key to the lion's lair."

"What does it mean?" Phoebe asked.

Justin leaned back in his chair, burgundy leather sighing beneath his weight. "It means the old baron wanted to make certain we had a devilish time trying to find his treasure."

Phoebe grinned at him, excitement filling her eyes. "When can we go searching for it?"

"When we have all the clues," Isabel said. "Not before."

Justin frowned. "I wonder."

"What?" Isabel asked.

Justin met her curious eyes and wondered if he had ever seen a more beautiful shade of blue. "Even when we have all the clues, we still might not have a clear understanding of where he hid the treasure."

"If we have all the clues, why wouldn't we find it?" Phoebe asked.

Justin tapped his forefinger against the journal. "It's possible the clues point to landmarks or architectural features no longer in existence. From what I could see, Bramsleigh has been improved several times over the years."

"It has. Every baron has left his mark on the house," Isabel said.

"It would be dreadful if we could not find the treasure," Phoebe said. "Just dreadful."

"I have seen the original plans for the house," Isabel said. "They were found with the journal, in the alcove the workmen uncovered."

"The plans could help. We'll know more when we manage to uncover all the clues. No need to give up hope. When we have all the clues, we'll take a good look around Bramsleigh." Justin closed the journal.

"Aren't you going to keep working on it?" Phoebe asked.

"No, my little slave driver. I am not." Justin rose and stretched, easing the tension in his shoulders. He glanced at Isabel and tried not to think of all the days stretching out between this night and their wedding night.

Phoebe tugged on his sleeve, gazing up at him, a quizzical look on her small face. "When you and Isabel are married, will we live with you, or shall we stay here?"

The question caught him off guard. Odd, he had never considered the possibilities before. "I suppose it depends on what you would like to do."

"Well, you will have Isabel. And the duchess will be left all alone if we leave." Phoebe looked at Isabel. "If you don't mind, I thought I would stay here."

Isabel glanced at Justin. "That really isn't for me to decide."

"I asked the duchess this morning if we could stay with her," Phoebe said.

"If I had my way, Isabel and Justin would move in here with us." Sophia glanced up from her embroidery hoop and smiled at her grandson. "Yet I doubt we shall convince him of that. The very least he can do is allow me to keep you and Eloise. Wouldn't you say?"

"I see no reason why the girls shouldn't remain here." Justin looked at Isabel. What did she think of the situation? He should not care. He was their guardian. He could make the decisions about their care. Yet, strange as it was, he did care what Isabel thought. "What do you say?"

Isabel smiled. "I think the girls would be in wonderful hands."

Justin drew in his breath. "It's settled then."

After he bade the ladies a good evening, Isabel walked with him out of the library. Justin glanced over his shoulder as they started down the hall. "I'm surprised Sophia isn't following us. She seems determined not to allow me a moment alone with you."

"She wants only to make certain we don't give reason for scandal. Although I did hope we might play a game of chess this evening." Isabel smiled up at him. "Perhaps tomorrow?"

The warmth in her smile enveloped his heart, easing some of the fear lurking there. Fear he did not wish to acknowledge, yet could not deny. He paused and caught her chin on the edge of his hand. "I can think of other games I would dearly love to play with you."

She smiled, a glint of mischief filling her eyes. "I'm looking forward to future lessons."

A delicate trace of lavender drifted from her skin and teased his senses. He pulled her into his arms. The damp heat of her sigh brushed his lips before he kissed her, his lips settling over the softness of hers. She melted into his embrace, sliding her arms around his neck, returning the heat of his passion until he burned.

"Justin, dear, do give Isabel a chance to breathe."

Justin pulled back, startled by the amused yet firm disapproval in his grandmother's voice. He glanced down the hall and frowned at the duchess. "Performing this role of chaperon a little too strongly Grandmama?"

Sophia smiled. "A little late perhaps, but as strongly as necessary."

"Do I need permission to ask Isabel to come for a ride in the park with me tomorrow?" he asked, infusing his voice with as much sarcasm as he could gather.

Sophia crinkled her nose at him. "I'm afraid Isabel shall be occupied the next few days. We have a great many preparations for the wedding to attend to. And a precious small amount of time to do it in.''

"Sophia, you've kept her busy every day since that blasted ball.''

"Careful, Justin. You really shall give the ton something to gossip about. Imagine,, the Duke of Marlow so besotted with his fiancée he can't stand to have her out of his sight.''

His grandmother's words hit him in the chest with all the force of a charging bull. Heat crept up his neck and filled his cheeks. Justin turned and looked into Isabel's beautiful eyes. Was there a twinkle of amusement in those celestial depths? He could only imagine the amused stares that would be cast in his direction should he start trotting after his fiancée like a besotted puppy.

Sophia flicked open her fan and lazily began to fan herself. "Of course, if you would like to join us when the dressmaker comes to discuss the wedding clothes, you may. And of course the cobbler shall be by, and the milliner. Oh, if you would like to help us choose the menu for the breakfast, and make out the guest list, choose the invitations . . .''

"I would not.'' He straightened the linen at his cuff. He would not, under any circumstances, turn into a pitiable fool over any female. "I trust you and Isabel shall find it all delightful.''

Three days later, Justin barged into his brother's library. Clayton was standing near the window, staring out at the street below, where Justin had just run straight into Marisa Grantham on her way out of Clay's town house. He joined Clay at the window in time to see Marisa's carriage turn onto Brook Street.

Clay tilted his head and smiled at his brother. "Would you care for a whiskey?''

"What the devil was Marisa doing here?''

Clay crossed the room and opened one of the cabinets built into the wall. "She had some information she thought I might find interesting."

Justin drifted toward one of a pair of matching leather wing-back chairs near the hearth. "And did you?"

"Not particularly." Clay filled two glasses and joined Justin.

Justin accepted the glass from his brother's unsteady hand. "It must have been important for Marisa to come here."

"She thought it was." Clay drained his glass in three long swallows. "It was only some nonsense she heard at a party. Mari always had a fruitful imagination. I'm afraid it got the better of her this time."

Justin sipped his whiskey, the smooth liquor warming his throat and chest. "She is still as beautiful as ever."

"Yes, she is." Clayton turned away from him, hiding his expression. Yet Justin sensed the pain beneath the calm facade. Women could inflict wounds that never healed. If you let them get close enough. He drained his glass, scarcely tasting the mellow whiskey.

Clayton sank into one of the chairs near the hearth. "Have you had any word from Newberry?"

"I saw him this morning. He thinks he might have met a man who knows about the murders. He is going to meet with him again tonight, then report to me tomorrow morning." Justin sat in the chair across from his brother. "I may have provided him with another piece to the puzzle. Last night someone broke into my house."

"Was anyone hurt?"

"No. Although a window was broken, no one heard anything. The only room they bothered with was the library. And it does not look as though anything was

279

taken. Apparently they didn't find what they were looking for.''

Clayton frowned. ''Do you have any idea what they might have wanted?''

''I wonder if it might be a collection of medieval manuscripts.''

''Edward Darracott's collection? But that's at Marlow House.''

Justin held his empty glass in a column of afternoon sunlight slanting through the windows behind him. He twisted the beveled crystal, casting a rainbow of color against the blue-and-ivory carpet. ''I told Eldridge Belcham the collection was under my protection. I wonder if he assumed it was in my library.''

''If it is Belcham, he might look for it at Marlow House.''

''I have asked Newberry to supply Sophia with a new footman. Someone who will keep an eye on the ladies and the collection.''

Clayton rolled his empty glass between his palms. ''Do you really think Belcham would murder two men to get his hands on old books?''

''He is obsessed with them. Edward Darracott was his fiercest rival. Darracott was murdered before he had a chance to bid on a collection that was up for auction by the widow of a man who had recently died in an accident. Coincidence?''

Clayton studied his empty glass, as though looking for answers in the crystal. ''It makes you wonder why someone takes a notion to murder someone.''

Justin frowned, sensing something more beneath his brother's words than simple curiosity. ''Murders have been committed for far less reason than lust over ancient manuscripts. How many men have been murdered over the hand of a female?''

Clayton nodded. ''True.''

"I have told Newberry to have Belcham followed. If he is the blackguard responsible for the Darracott murders, I want enough proof to hang him."

"Have you told Isabel about this?"

Justin released his breath in a rush. "I haven't had a minute alone with Isabel since that blasted ball."

Clayton grinned. "The duchess has been keeping her busy."

Justin only hoped Isabel was too busy for second thoughts. He dug a long, silk-covered box from his coat pocket and tossed it at his brother. "What do you think of these?"

Clayton caught the black package in his right hand. He set his glass on the pedestal table near his chair and opened the long box. His black brows rose a fraction as his lips tipped into a devilish grin. "Six betrothal rings? I see you aren't leaving any room for doubt."

"I couldn't decide what Isabel might like." Justin neglected to say he had spent nearly three and a half hours poring over every ring and precious stone in three of the finest jewelry shops in London, before he finally settled on the six rings in that box.

In his search for the ideal ring, he had stumbled upon a square-cut emerald of such brilliance it seemed to glow with hidden fire, like Isabel. He had chosen it for her, imagining it on her slender finger. Yet before he left the shop, doubts had gotten the better of him. He couldn't be certain she would like it, so he chose a perfect oval-shaped diamond, for all the obvious reasons, a sapphire because her eyes darkened to a deep blue when he made love to her, a bloodred ruby for the fire she set in his blood, a pearl because it reminded him of her skin, and an aquamarine for the day she had saved his life. The mawkish reasons humiliated him almost as much as the indecision. Still, as he sat there thinking of Isabel's reaction, he could not ignore the anxiety coiling his insides into a tight ball.

"I thought I would just give her all of them," he said, hiding his anxiety beneath cool detachment.

Clayton glanced at him, the look in his eyes killing any hope Justin might have had of disguising his anxiety. "I'm certain Isabel would find any one of them a worthy gift."

Justin shrugged. "I have bought them now, so she can very well keep the lot. I won't set tongues wagging by sending them back."

Clayton closed the box. "I wasn't thinking, or I would have offered to give you Mother's betrothal ring before now. You can still have it for Isabel if you would like."

The ring Marisa had worn on her finger up until the day she had ripped Clay's heart from his chest. "No. You keep it. Give it to the lady of your choosing. These will do."

"I'm certain they will." Clayton tossed the box to his brother. "You're getting a charming lady—beautiful, intelligent. I have to admit, I envy you."

"Don't." Justin stuffed the long box back into his pocket. "I'm not sure I'm cut out to be a good husband. And I'm not sure Isabel is the type of woman who will tolerate living with a man like me for long. In a few years we'll see if I haven't managed to mess up the whole thing."

Clayton rested his chin on the steeple of his fingers. "Strange. I always imagined you would make a better husband than I would."

"You! Good heavens, Clay. You are a paragon. A bloody war hero. You have never made a wrong move in your life. Why the devil would you think I would do a better job as a husband than you?"

"Your fiancée is at least willing to go through with the ceremony."

"I didn't exactly give her much choice."

Clayton stared past Justin to the windows beyond, a dark gloom seeming to settle around him in spite of the sunshine. "You have an openness I have never possessed."

Justin frowned. "And you have the ability to fix your affection, something I have never had or wanted. You are steadfast and loyal. I'm a black-hearted libertine, who, if he had a decent bone in his body, never would have touched Isabel in the first place."

"Are you telling me you don't want to go through with the wedding?"

"I want her, Clay. And if marriage is the price I have to pay, I will pay it. I just hope . . ." Justin twisted his glass in the sunlight, watching colors spark in all directions.

"What do you hope?"

Justin released his breath on a shudder of air. "I don't want to hurt her."

"Then don't."

"A man like me doesn't change."

"He can, if he runs straight into something as unexpected as honest affection, a feeling so strong it sinks deep into his bones."

"Love?" Justin laughed, the sound bitter to his own ears. "I'm not capable of the emotion."

"You might surprise yourself."

Justin shook his head. "I know what I am. I only hope Isabel can tolerate me after the lust has burned itself into ashes."

Clayton smiled. "You shall do fine together."

"We'll have to, won't we? There's no hope for it now, except to make the best of it." And hope his bride could learn to accept him, and all the darkness of his soul.

Chapter Twenty

" 'Seek the lion's secret beneath his crouching form.' " Gerard lowered the paper and looked at Isabel from beneath raised brows. "That's it? The last clue?"

Isabel sat on the edge of the desk in the library of Marlow House. "The last of three."

Gerard dropped the sheet onto the desk. The parchment glided on a current of air before settling against the brown leather desk pad. "Are you certain there are no more?"

"Yes." Isabel lifted the journal from the desk, smiling as she recalled the deep resonance of Justin's voice as he read to her the last clue. Honestly, the man could read a treatise on farming to her and she would still be mesmerized. "The duke translated the last page of the journal last night."

"That's it then. We'll never find it. Not with those clues. They are meaningless. After all of this, we haven't a chance of finding the treasure."

"Perhaps we do." She slid her fingertips over a scratch in the dark red leather of the journal. "The clues must point to features of Bramsleigh as they were in 1649."

"The place has changed a dozen times since then."

"Father showed me a plan for the original house. It showed details of every room. It was in the hidden alcove the workmen found during father's renovation of the library, along with the journal."

Gerard frowned. "Hidden alcove?"

"Didn't I ever mention it?"

"No. I would definitely have remembered a hidden alcove."

"Someone, probably the old baron, had a narrow room made at one end of the library by building a second wall of paneling and bookcases several feet in front of the original wall, creating a hidden space between them."

Gerard pursed his lips. "And why didn't anyone tell me about it?"

"After it was uncovered, Father had the workmen put it back as it was. When he died . . . Well, I never thought of it."

"Do you know how to get into this alcove, or will we have to knock down the entire wall?"

"I'm fairly certain I can open it. Father showed me the original mechanism, which is hidden on one of the bookshelves. It releases a latch and allows you to pull open one of the bookcases."

Gerard smiled, a glimmer of excitement entering his eyes. "If the plans show us the house as it was, we should be able to decipher the clues."

"It will be interesting to see if there really is a treasure."

"Why not come with me to Bramsleigh today? We

could soon discover if there is any truth in the legend.''

Isabel smiled. ''Are you forgetting? I'm getting married in little more than a fortnight. I have a hundred things left to do.''

''I keep trying to forget it. When I think of you and that scoundrel, I—''

''He isn't a scoundrel. He is a very generous man.''

Gerard released his breath on a long sigh. ''I always thought you were so practical. But now I see you fooled by this man . . .''

Isabel tapped her fingers against the journal. ''Do you know Marlow launched an investigation into the murders of my father and brother? That is hardly the action of a scoundrel.''

''An investigation? Into the murders?'' Gerard stared at her, his expression a mixture of surprise and disbelief. ''I wouldn't be surprised if he told you he was investigating their murders to gain your sympathy.''

Isabel resisted the anger creeping up her spine. ''He didn't tell me. I found out about the investigation from Clayton.''

''Huntingdon. Then I suppose he really has launched this investigation. Still, I can't imagine he would uncover anything after all of this time.'' Gerard rubbed his chin. ''Has he?''

Isabel sighed. ''Nothing so far.''

''Well, I wouldn't coddle any hopes.'' Gerard took her hand. ''You do realize it isn't too late to change your mind.''

''It isn't too late to change her mind about what?'' Justin asked from the doorway.

Isabel jumped at the low rumble of Justin's voice. He moved toward her with slow strides. A dark gray coat molded his broad shoulders, buff-colored trousers hugged muscular legs, every inch of him declared raw, masculine power. His hair looked wind-tossed, the thick, silky waves curling over his brow. Isabel's skin tingled with the same heat that evaporated the breath from her lungs.

Justin paused beside the desk, so close his leg brushed her gown. He glanced from Isabel to Gerard, his gaze as cold as a blast of December wind. Gerard dropped her hand and stepped back, looking far too guilty to suit Isabel. Although her fiancé was an intelligent man, he was also volatile enough to come to daggers with little provocation. He had a natural, all-too-primitive proclivity for protecting what he thought of as his property. At the moment that included his fiancée. In time she hoped to pound a little sensibility into his thick skull.

Isabel stood and slipped her arm through his. Justin lifted one black brow in a silent question. "We were just discussing the last clue in the journal. Gerard was hoping we might go treasure hunting right away. I told him we must wait until after the wedding."

"Yes. That's it." Gerard sidestepped toward the door. "I was hoping Isabel would change her mind about waiting."

Justin molded his lips into a chilling smile. "The treasure has waited more than a century to be discovered, Witheridge. It can wait another few weeks."

"Yes, of course it can. Well, I'm certain you have a great deal to discuss. I won't interfere." He hurried from the room, leaving Isabel alone with Justin.

Justin caught her chin on the edge of his hand. He tipped back her head and smiled. "Is that puppy still trying to cut me out?"

In many ways arrogance hid uncertainty in this man. He might present a jaded facade to the world, yet the man inside was far more vulnerable than he would ever admit. She rested her fingertips against his lips. "Do you imagine any man could take me away from you?"

His lips curved beneath her fingertips as a warmth filled his eyes. "Still besotted with me?"

"Positively demented."

He sat on the desk and pulled her between his thighs. "I am glad to hear I will not have to return these," he said, drawing a long, narrow box from his coat pocket.

She took the box from his hand, the black silk warm from his body. "It isn't my birthday."

He shrugged. "We're betrothed. It's a betrothal present."

She opened the clasp and lifted the lid. Gems glinted in the sunlight spilling through the windows near the desk, sparkling at her from a bed of black silk. She stared at the stones, her heart crawling upward in her chest. "Rings," she whispered.

"I wasn't certain what you would like. So I picked a few," he said, his dark voice sounding far too casual, as though the present were nothing but the merest trumpery.

She pressed her hand to her hammering heart. "An entire bouquet."

"You don't have to wear them all. At least not at the same time."

She looked up at him, aware of the tears brimming in her eyes. He sat looking at her, all the uncertainty of a man feeling his way through the dark in his eyes. "They are all beautiful. But I wonder if you might do something for me."

He moistened his lips. "What?"

"Choose one."

He frowned. "You may have them all. There is no reason to choose one."

"I need only one betrothal ring. The ring you choose for me."

He set his jaw and stared into the box, like a student studying for a first in mathematics at Cambridge. After a few moments, in which he clenched and unclenched his jaw nine times, he made his decision. "The emerald," he said in a gruff tone.

She lifted the ring and set the box on the desk beside him. Round diamonds twinkled around the perimeter of an exquisite square-cut emerald, each capturing the light and reflecting the emerald's fire. "Would you place it on my finger?"

"I thought you did not have romantic notions," he said, sounding annoyed.

"I suppose I have a few."

He took the ring from her. She tried not to notice the way his hand trembled as he placed it on her finger. "There, the deed is done."

"Thank you." She looped her arms around his neck and kissed him, a quick glide of her lips over his. Yet not quick enough to spare her from the sudden heat flashing through her, like flames through dried kindling. She leaned back in the circle of his arms and smiled. "Do you know what I wish?"

He slid his hands over the curves of her bottom and drew her into the heat of his loins. "Tell me."

She shifted her hips, rubbing wantonly against the tempting ridge of his arousal. He sucked air between his teeth. She leaned against him, her breasts snuggling into the hard planes of his chest as she whispered against his ear, "I wish we could make love. Right here. Right now."

He flexed his long fingers against her bottom. "If I didn't think one of your sisters or my grandmother might come barging in at any moment, I would slip your lovely, long legs around my waist and oblige you, my beautiful, wanton wench."

"I dream of you at night." She nuzzled the skin beneath his ear, smiling as he sighed. The warmth of him surrounded her, soaking through her gown. Yet she wanted to feel that warmth against her bare skin. "I imagine your hands on my skin, your lips, your tongue. I imagine your bare chest rubbing against my breasts, the hair on your legs tickling my inner thighs, your huge—"

"Keep it up, wench, and I'll forget my attempts at restraint." He nipped her shoulder. "We could end up giving someone a show they would not soon forget."

She pulled back and looked into his beautiful eyes. Could he see her heart in her eyes? "I'm looking forward to our lessons, my darling."

He kissed her chin. "I have to admit, I'm looking forward to them as well, my gorgeous witch."

A few weeks ago, if anyone had told him he would be conducting business on a regular basis before noon, Justin would have laughed. Yet here he was, sitting in his library at half past nine in the morning, listening to Adler Newberry relay the information he had gained in his meeting with an informant the night before.

Justin stared at the initials carved into the back of the gold watch Newberry had handed him a moment ago. "This Billie Leggott told you he knew what happened to the owner of this watch?"

"He said he would tell me everything, for a price."

Justin leaned back in his chair. He glanced from the watch to the man sitting across from him in a matching leather armchair. "What does he want?"

Newberry lifted his brows. "A hundred pounds."

"Do you think this man is involved in the murders?"

"Hard to say, Your Grace." Newberry rubbed the side of his forefinger over his thick lower lip. "But from all I can gather, he's never been involved in anything more than minor thefts. I doubt he added murder to his accomplishments."

Justin smoothed his thumb over the back of the watch, where laurel leaves surrounded the initials. He had little doubt the timepiece had belonged to Edward Carlyle Darracott. "When are you going to meet with him again?"

"Tomorrow night."

"I want to be there."

Newberry's thick dark brows pulled together over his crooked nose. "Your Grace, I'm meeting with him at the Cock and Cur pub on the docks. It's not exactly a fit place for a duke."

Justin smiled. "You might be surprised at the places this duke has been."

Newberry pursed his lips. "Your Grace, not meaning to show any disrespect, but if I'm worried about keeping someone from slitting your throat, I won't be able to do a decent job of getting information out of Billie Leggott."

Justin laughed softly. "I think I can manage to protect my own throat."

Newberry released his breath on a suffering sigh. "It's your decision, Your Grace."

"Don't worry, Newberry, I won't get in your way. I just want to see this man, hear what he has to say, see the expression in his eyes when he says it."

Newberry nodded. "As you wish, Your Grace. I'll be 'round to fetch you at eleven tomorrow night."

"I'll be ready."

A few moments after Newberry left, Fromsby entered the library to announce the arrival of a female visitor.

"Who is the lady?" Justin asked, slipping the watch into his coat pocket.

"She would not give me her name, Your Grace. But she insisted it was urgent she speak with you."

He could not imagine a lady coming by his house at this time of the morning. For that matter, ladies, unless they wanted to become infamous, did not come by his house at all. "And you say this is a lady, not a dirty dish?"

Fromsby nodded. "She arrived in a black town coach with no markings, yet of fine quality, as were the horses. From her dress, her manner, her speech, she is quality, Your Grace."

Justin frowned. "You've never seen her before?"

"If I had, Your Grace, I would not be able to discern it. The lady is wearing a headdress with a veil over her face. Her footman and driver are both in black livery and wearing wigs. Perhaps to disguise their identity. Apparently the lady does not wish to be recognized."

"Mysterious."

"Yes, Your Grace."

A few months ago, he would have welcomed a mystery lady into his home, and more than likely into his bed. Now, with his wedding quickly approaching, he acknowledged a certain wariness for women who appeared mysteriously on his doorstep. Still, his curiosity got the better of him. "Show her in, Fromsby."

Justin rose and rested his arm on the mantel, preparing himself for the mystery lady. If she was here to make trouble, he would soon make her regret the day she walked across his threshold. A few moments later Fromsby showed her into the room.

White silk draped her slender figure. She was taller than average, somewhere near five feet, five inches. Her white turban headdress hid her hair. A heavy white veil shrouded her features. She obviously wanted no one to know she was paying a visit to Devil Trevelyan. Yet there was something familiar about her. Something about the way she moved. When she bumped into the arm of a sofa, he had a strong suspicion of her identity.

Justin dismissed Fromsby. When he and the woman were alone he spoke. "Do you intend to tell me who you are, or shall I guess?"

"It's dreadful looking through this," she said, lifting her veil. She smiled at him. "Did you know me?"

"Marisa. I thought it was you, but I wasn't certain."

"You have such a wicked reputation, Justin. Even if I brought my mother as a chaperone, I would be the topic of gossip for weeks." Marisa Grantham came toward him, offering her hands.

Justin took her hands in a firm grasp. "And did you give any thought to my reputation?"

Her eyes sparkled with humor beneath dark, slanting brows. "When did you start to worry about your reputation?"

"When I became guardian to three females."

"Oh." She crinkled her slim nose. "I hadn't thought of that."

"And did you think of what my fiancée might think if someone told her a mysterious woman was seen at my house?"

She smiled, a dimple appearing at the right corner of her mouth. "I'm certain you can set her straight."

"You have such faith in my powers of persuasion."

She laughed. "Justin, you could charm a devoted man-hater like my Aunt Cecilia to run away with you, if you put your mind to it."

He smiled, thinking of Marisa's prudish spinster aunt. "Fortunately, I've never set my mind on that particular course."

"I must say, I'm glad to hear you care about what your fiancée might think. There are so many dreadful rumors about your engagement. I thought they were all a lot of humbug. No woman could ever trap you into doing anything, particularly marriage. And as for you forcing *her* into marriage . . ." She waved her hand in an elegant gesture of dismissal. "Nonsense. You have never needed to force a female into doing anything, except perhaps to get her out of your house. By the way, have I wished you happy?"

Justin took her arm and led her toward one of the leather armchairs near the hearth. "I suspect you didn't come here this morning to wish me happy."

"No." Marisa sat on the chair and arranged her gown around her. "I came here to ask you to talk some sense into your brother's stubborn head."

Justin rested his arm on the mantel. "This concerns the same thing you went to see him about yesterday?"

She nodded. "Did he tell you about it?"

"Only that you overheard something at a party."

She released her breath on an agitated sigh. "It is like him to take such news with such dreadful composure. I suspected he would do nothing about it. That is why you simply must help me hammer some sense into his head."

"I might do better if I knew what this was all about."

"Murder."

Justin blinked. "Murder?"

She plaited the fringe of her white paisley shawl as she continued. "I was at the Merrivale ball the other night. Do you remember their maze?"

"Not as interesting as the one at Hampton Court. But suitable for rendezvous."

"Precisely. Well, I noticed Lord Hanley leading one of my nieces into the gardens, so I followed."

Justin rubbed his chin, thinking of his own encounter with Hanley. "Acting as chaperon these days?"

Marisa tilted her head and smiled at him. "It shouldn't seem so strange, a woman of my years."

"A woman who still has half the men in London dangling on a string."

She shrugged. "Amazing what men shall do for the sake of a fortune. Even dangle after a woman who is all of seven and twenty."

Justin suspected Marisa would still be pursued, even if she were not worth a considerable fortune. She had a vivacity that drew men like stallions to a mare in season.

"I suppose I should have donned a cap years ago, but I enjoy parties far too much to put myself on the shelf."

He rested his chin on his palm. "I'm surprised you didn't choose a husband from your legion of suitors years ago."

She lowered her eyes, hiding the expression in the golden brown depths. "Some things don't turn out the way we plan. Life is funny that way."

Justin watched her plait the fringe of her shawl while he resisted the urge to demand the reasons she had ripped his brother's heart to shreds. Another man perhaps? A married lover who refused to leave his wife? "You were saying that you had followed your niece and Hanley into the gardens, where you found what?"

She glanced up at him. "Heard."

"All right. What did you hear?"

"I entered the maze, looking for Hanley and Beatrice. Beautiful girl, though perhaps a bit overwhelmed with every eligible gentleman in London paying his court to her. At any rate, I reached the center without finding them. I had started back, when I heard a man mention Clay's name. Something in his tone made me pause. They were directly on the other side of the shrubbery, so I had no trouble at all hearing them. Although your brother seems to think I heard it all wrong.''

Justin took a deep breath. ''Marisa, what did you hear?''

Marisa twisted the fringe she had just braided. ''Two men plotting to murder Clay.''

''What the devil! Murder him?''

Marisa nodded. ''One of them said, 'We shall have to get rid of Huntingdon; he could spoil it all.' The other agreed. He said they would have to be careful, one wrong move could expose them. But he would arrange to have the threat *eliminated*.''

''Did you find out who they were?''

Marisa shook her head. ''They moved on. By the time I found my way out of the maze, they were gone. But I'm certain I would recognize the one man if I ever heard him again. He was very distinctive.''

''What did Clay say about this? Did he have any idea who these men might be, or what they might have been talking about?''

''He is certain it is all some misunderstanding on my part. He knows of no one who would like to murder him.'' Marisa smiled sweetly, her eyes flashing fury. ''I, on the other hand, can well imagine wanting to strangle the man.''

Justin studied her lovely face. ''You're worried about him.''

She shrugged. ''Of course I'm concerned. I heard them. I know they were serious.''

Was there something more behind her natural instinct to protect an old love? Did she still have feelings for the man she had jilted? Even as the thoughts formed he dismissed them. Apparently becoming engaged had warped his brain, planted some insidious romantic notions.

Marisa rose from the chair. "You have to speak with Clay. He must take care. We have to look for these men. They have to be stopped."

He nodded. "I'll speak with him."

She smiled. "If anyone can talk some sense into him, it's you."

He took her hand. "I'll do my best to resolve the problem."

Three hours later, Isabel sat at the small gilt-trimmed writing desk in the morning room of Marlow House, reviewing the menu for the wedding breakfast, blissfully oblivious to the rumors about her fiancé, which were spreading through London faster than the plague.

"Isabel, are you busy?" Eloise asked as she entered the room.

Isabel dropped the menu on a pile of invitations to various parties and balls and musicales that had arrived in the morning post. "What is it?" she asked, rising from her chair at the sight of her sister's pale visage. "Are you feeling all right?"

"I'm fine."

Isabel pressed the back of her hand to her sister's brow. "You don't feel overly warm."

"I'm not ill. I'm . . ." Eloise turned away from Isabel and walked to the windows. "I need your advice."

Uneasiness gripped the edges of Isabel's stomach as she watched her sister. "About what?"

Eloise stood for a long moment staring out at the gardens before she spoke. "If you had heard a rumor, a terrible rumor about someone you admired, and that rumor might be very important to someone you loved, but you knew this rumor would hurt this person dreadfully, would you tell what you had heard?''

Isabel joined Eloise at the window. "What have you heard?''

Eloise glanced at Isabel, then turned her troubled gaze back to the gardens. "I was shopping with Anthea and Henrietta this morning.''

"Did Henrietta say something to upset you?''

"Not exactly. We stopped for cake and tea at a little shop. We were there no more than ten minutes before two friends of Henrietta's descended upon us. Belle, they were so excited about what they had heard, it was as though they had been given a wonderful present they had to share.''

The uneasiness twisted into a tight knot of dread in Isabel's stomach. "What did they say?''

"It's about the duke.''

Isabel nodded, her body growing numb. "I assumed as much.''

"They said he has a mistress.''

Isabel's chest constricted. The room darkened; Eloise's face blurred in her vision. She gripped the edge of the window frame for support. "A mistress?''

"They said she dresses all in white, with a veil to cover her face when she visits him.'' Tears spilled down Eloise's cheeks. "Oh, Belle, the way they talked, it was a game to them. They were so excited, trying to decipher who this woman might be. I expected Henrietta to tell them who I was, but she just kept saying she knew it would happen.''

Isabel struggled to regain her balance. She felt as though she were walking a narrow ledge—with one false move she would take a long tumble. It could not be true, she assured herself. Justin would not have taken a mistress days before his wedding. He had not grown tired of her already. Had he? "People love gossip, Eloise. Especially gossip about a man as wealthy and powerful as the duke.''

''Do you think they made it up?''

Isabel slipped her arm around Eloise's waist and walked with her to a nearby sofa. ''I think it's wise not to believe too much of what you hear.''

''He wouldn't do it.'' Eloise sank to the pale yellow silk damask cushion. ''I simply cannot believe he would do anything so vile. And I told them as much.''

''Thank you for defending him.'' Isabel sat beside her sister. ''For a very long time people have looked for the duke to behave in the worst possible fashion. They want to believe he is a devil. It will take them a long while to realize he isn't the vile creature they think he is.''

Eloise dabbed at her cheeks with her lace-trimmed handkerchief. ''Then you aren't going to call off the wedding?''

Isabel swallowed hard, forcing back the bile that had etched an acidic path up her throat. If Justin truly had taken a mistress, then she was a fool for believing she could make a real marriage with him. ''This must be a misunderstanding.''

Eloise threw her arms around Isabel's shoulders and hugged her close. ''He wouldn't humiliate you this way. I know he wouldn't.''

Isabel closed her eyes. If only she could be so certain. She had to learn the truth. No matter how much it might hurt. Was she wrong about him? Had she fooled herself into seeing what she wanted to see? Was he every bit as wicked as his reputation? If Justin was the type of man to take a mistress only days before his wedding, he was not the type of man she wanted as her husband. ''You mustn't worry about me, Eloise. Everything is going to be fine.''

*   *   *

Gunfire cracked through the large gallery. Justin lowered his pistol. A thin cloud of sulfurous smoke hung in the air, stinging his nostrils, distorting his vision. Still, he could see the hole his bullet had made. His aim had been to the right, about a finger's width from the heart of his target.

"Marisa came to see you this morning?" Clayton asked. "All dressed in white? With a veil over her face?"

Justin handed his pistol to one of his footmen for reloading. "She is concerned about you."

Clayton aimed his pistol and fired. The bullet plowed into the heart of the target. "You know how dramatic Marisa can be."

Justin lifted his other pistol. "She heard two men discussing the need to eliminate you."

Clayton handed his spent weapon to his footman. "How many times have you said you would like to murder someone? Yet I don't recall you ever having carried out the threat."

"She seemed to think it was serious."

"She has always had a lively mind." Clayton picked up his other weapon and fired. The bullet slammed into the target a hairsbreadth from the first shot.

Justin smoothed his thumb over the ebony handle of his pistol. "You can't think of anyone who might want to murder you?"

"Not offhand."

"Perhaps it is nothing. Still, it might pay to be careful."

Clayton grinned. "Why do you suppose I thought we should visit Manton's this afternoon?"

Justin glanced at his brother's target. "A blackguard who would plan a man's murder probably would not come at him straight on."

Clayton leaned against the wooden shelf separating the marksmen from the target area. "Aside from hiding for the rest of my life, there is nothing much I can do about it."

"Have you considered trying to find the men Marisa overheard?"

"What? Trail after Marisa at every function of the Season, eavesdropping on conversations, hoping she can identify the voices of two men she heard through a hedge?"

Justin smiled. "She might be able to find them. And you may become acquainted with the lady again."

Clayton cringed. "In less than a week Marisa and I would be at daggers. Not to mention the gossip we would stir. Thank you, but I've already stuck my head into that particular guillotine."

Marisa had cried off their engagement without warning. Justin thought of the days remaining before his own wedding. He felt the weight of the single sheet of parchment he had received this afternoon, like a stone in his pocket.

The missive from his fiancée had been formal, as cold as a letter to an attorney. *I need to speak with you at your earliest convenience. There is a personal matter of some importance that needs to be resolved before May 18.* May 18, their wedding date. What the devil did Isabel need to speak to him about? Last night she had assured him all the preparations were well in hand. He did not like the feel of this. It felt too much like a woman who had suddenly come to her senses.

Justin avoided the inevitable confrontation with Isabel the rest of the day. And, as the day wore on, his doubts mounted. He vacillated between self-assurance that her note had nothing at all to do with a wish to cry off their engagement, to a bitter certainty she had at last opened her beautiful eyes.

Instead of having dinner at Marlow House, which had become his custom, he ate alone at home. He would face the issue on his own terms. He had a few ideas of how he could keep Isabel off balance. None of them the least bit noble, or honest, or fair. Yet this was a battle. And he did not intend to lose.

After dinner he paced his library, glancing every now and then at the note Isabel had sent him. If his plan leaned precariously toward that of a desperate man he chose to dismiss the notion. His reasons for preventing Isabel from leaving him were certainly not of a mawkish romantic nature.

Isabel was a woman. One of countless he had known and bedded. Certainly he had never enjoyed a sexual encounter quite as much as he had with her, but it was, after all, lust at its apex. The desire would wane. True, he had grown fond of her, but he was not fool enough ever to lose his black heart to *any* of her sex. He wanted her to go through with the wedding because he had no intention of becoming an object of ridicule for the ton—that was the sum of it. No woman would humiliate him the way Marisa had humiliated his brother. He would make certain Isabel was at that church on May 18, if he had to use every devious trick he could devise. He smiled. Devil Trevelyan would not be outwitted by a slip of a spinster. She would never realize what hit her.

Chapter Twenty-one

"Don't take another step, or I'll shoot."

Justin froze, trapped in a column of moonlight spilling through a window of the bedchamber, like a fly in amber. The light struck his back, casting a soft glow on the slender figure standing near the bed. Silver glinted from the shadows, moonlight reflecting on the pistol she held pointed at his chest. "Isabel, if you fire that weapon you'll have everyone in the entire house awake and in here."

"Justin?"

"Who the devil did you expect?"

She lowered her weapon. "What are you doing here?"

"You said you had something to discuss with me."

She moved toward him. "I didn't expect you to creep into my bedchamber in the middle of the night."

"I didn't creep. I never creep."

"I thought you were a burglar. Perhaps the same

burglar who broke into your library.'' She paused a
foot in front of him. Moonlight spilled across her, revealing the silver-handled brush she was holding, the
weapon she had used to hold him at bay.

''What would you have done if I were a real burglar? Brushed my hair until I cried for mercy?''

She scraped her thumbnail across the bristles. ''It
served the purpose.''

He tilted his head and studied her appearance, curious at how a proper young lady dressed for bed. Her
hair fell over her shoulder in one long, thick braid.
Chaste white cotton draped her figure. White lace
brushed her chin and hid her wrists. White ruffles
spilled around her ankles. Covering her from chin to
toes, the nightgown hid everything but a mere hint of
the lush curves of her breasts and hips. Still, the blood
stirred in his loins. He had the uncomfortable feeling
this woman could wear chain mail and he would still
find her one of the most alluring females he had ever
seen.

He clenched his teeth in recognition of the danger
this woman represented. If he weren't careful, he
would be trailing after her like a pitiful, besotted
puppy. ''Do you always wear a sack to bed?''

Her lips pulled into a tight line. ''For your information, this is not a sack. It is a perfectly respectable
nightgown.''

''I cannot say I have seen many perfectly respectable nightgowns. Nor can I say I want to.''

She lifted her chin, a militant gleam in her eyes. ''I
suppose the ladies who have shared your bed slept in
something a little more revealing.''

He smiled, enjoying the trace of jealousy in her
voice. ''The women who have shared my bed didn't
do a great deal of sleeping.''

The corners of her mouth tightened. "I should have known."

"And as for attire, they wore nothing. Except a dab of perfume here." He brushed his fingertips over the pulse point in her neck, feeling the quick throb of her heart. "And here." He drew the tip of his forefinger over the pearl buttons running down the center of her gown, grazing her breasts with his fingers. "And . . ."

She stepped away from him, but not before he felt the heat of her startled sigh against his chin. "Thank you, but I can do without a demonstration of where your mistresses apply scent."

He closed the distance between them, stepping so close the white ruffles at the hem of her gown brushed his polished boots. Need pumped through his veins with each squeeze of his heart. "Do you know what I want to do?"

She stepped back. "There is a matter we need to discuss."

He lifted the end of her thick braid. Her little discussion could wait until he was finished, until he burned like a flame in her blood, until he was certain she could not in this lifetime turn away from him. He was master here, as she would soon learn. "I want to find all the places you've dabbed lavender water against your skin."

"Justin, we—"

"With my tongue."

Her mouth opened, then snapped closed. She took a moment, as though marshaling her defenses before she spoke. "I feel this is of grave importance."

"Yes, it is." He tugged on her braid, drawing her toward him like a mare on a tether.

She poked the end of her brush against his chest. "I insist we—"

"Make love?"

"Justin, we really must . . ." Her words evaporated as he slid his hand down the length of her arm, from her shoulder to her wrist.

"Yes, I think we really must," he said, curving his fingers around the delicate bones of her wrist.

"Don't distract me."

"Is that what I'm doing? Distracting you?" He lifted her wrist, the lacy cuff falling back from her skin. She drew a sharp breath as he touched the tip of his tongue to the soft skin of the inside of her wrist.

She pulled her wrist from his grasp. "You know very well what you're doing."

"I know very well what I intend to do."

She slid the tip of her tongue over the contours of lips he had tasted a thousand times in his dreams. "Justin, I really must insist. . . ."

"Insist?" He slipped his fingers around her arms and drew her near. "What do you insist? That I make love to you until you burn?"

"Will you please listen to me?" She strained against his hold. "The matter I wish to discuss—"

"Isn't nearly as important as this." He lowered his lips to hers.

She stiffened as he slid his arms around her. The rejection struck him as sharply as a fist to the jaw. Fear trickled into his blood, a bitter poison threatening to destroy him. What if she had come to her senses? What if she realized the monster she was getting in this bargain? What if she took away all the warmth he had found in her arms?

No matter how much he wanted to deny it, he needed her warmth to chase away the icy despair creeping like a thick, enveloping frost over his vitals. He fought the overpowering urge to fall to his knees at her feet. His chest tightened with the humiliating image: Devil Trevelyan begging for a scrap of this woman's affection.

He slanted his lips over hers in an openmouthed, straight-out assault. He would not beg. He had never begged in his life. Even when he was trapped in the darkness. Even when the rats had come. He had never begged.

She pushed against his shoulders, struggling to free herself. He tightened his arms around her, holding her close against his black, aching heart. She could not do this to him. She could not waltz into his life and make him want as he had never wanted before, only to turn her back on him. He would not allow it. He slid his tongue over the tight seam of her mouth, silently demanding she open for him. She had to open for him. A small voice whispered from a shallow grave deep inside him: *Please*.

For a moment he feared it was truly ended. Then he felt it, the melting of her resistance, the slow shift of her body in his arms, her breasts snuggling against his chest, her hips easing against his. He wanted to toss back his head and howl in triumph. Yet he could not stop kissing her. He could not stop the need pounding in his loins. He growled deep in his throat, a dark, primitive sound filled with his need.

She slid her arms around his neck and held him, as though she were afraid someone might rip him from her arms. Let anyone try and he would send him straight to blazes. He dragged his lips over her jaw, down her neck, while he slid his hands over her back. Cotton warm from her skin scraped his palms, denying him the sleek satin of her skin.

He slipped his hands between their bodies, yet the delicate little loops fastening tiny pearl buttons mocked his trembling fingers. In frustration he gripped the edges of her nightgown and yanked the gown apart. Buttons popped from the soft white cotton, hitting his chest.

She gasped and pulled away from him. "Why did you do that?"

He grinned. "Your perfectly respectable nightgown has far too many buttons."

She backpedaled, clutching the edges of her gown together. "We can't do this. Not until . . . I really have to know—"

"Do you know how much I want you?" He stalked her.

"Do you?" She bumped into the side of the bed. "And here I was thinking you might be having second thoughts about our wedding."

He stepped close to her, so close the warmth of her skin bathed him through his clothes. "Second thoughts? What the devil gave you that idea?"

She laid the brush on the bedside table. "Apparently people believe you have taken a mistress. A woman who dresses all in white when she comes to your house."

"A woman who . . . Bloody hell! And tell me, do you believe I have taken a mistress?"

She fiddled with the lace at her neck, keeping her gaze on the silver-handled brush. "I don't want to believe you have grown tired of me so quickly."

"Yet you aren't certain."

"No. That's what I wanted to discuss with you. I wanted to know the truth." She looked straight up into his eyes. "Have you taken a mistress?"

He stared at her, her words taking a moment to soak into his befuddled brain. "I think I should resent that question."

She twisted the tattered lace at her neck. "I would prefer not to have asked it, but I really must know."

He had not realized until this instant how much he

had come to rely on her peculiar notion of his character. Now he could not deny the tightening in his chest at the possibility she no longer thought him an honorable man. "Would you believe me if I told you I hadn't been intimate with another woman since the day you barged into my life?"

Her eyes widened in obvious surprise. "Of course I would believe you."

He frowned. "You would?"

"You would never lie to me."

He stared into the open honesty of her expression, awed by her twisted trust in his honesty. "You believe I could take a mistress days before our wedding, but I'm honest enough to tell you the truth about it?"

"You hate lies of any kind. I know. You told me so the first day we met."

He shook his head. "You amaze me, Miss Darracott. Utterly amaze me."

She cupped his cheek in her hand, all the turmoil he had suffered since reading her note mirrored in her eyes. "Then you aren't having second thoughts?"

"Hell and damnation, woman! Do I look like a man having second thoughts about this wedding?"

All the tension drained from her face. "No, I suppose you don't."

"And don't think I shall take it graciously if you try to cry off. I won't be made a fool by any female. This wedding shall take place as scheduled. Do you understand?"

"Yes, I understand. The wedding shall proceed without any more nonsense from me."

He felt his lips tipping into a smile and quickly crushed it. "It makes me wonder how you ever managed to take care of yourself and your sisters, the way you run around taking foolish notions to heart."

"I hadn't realized the notion of you taking a mistress was so foolish."

A cat-in-the-cream smile curved her lips, triggering a warning bell in his head. Too late. Like a spark from flint, he saw the flaw in his carefully laid plans to coerce his fiancée to the altar. The infuriating little chit would think she wielded some horrible power over him. She would soon believe she could lead him about by the nose. The day any female got the better of Devil Trevelyan would be the day it snowed in hell.

"Since we've had your little discussion, I shall leave you to your dreams." He turned away from her and marched toward the door. He intended for this marriage to go forth under his terms. He would be the master of his house. The chit would see she could not slip a ring through his nose.

"And have I managed to change your mind about finding all the places I've dabbed lavender water against my skin?"

Her soft voice coiled around him like a silken ribbon. He halted a few feet from the bed, trying to ignore the erotic images blossoming in his head. A man must stick to his principles, especially when he maintained only a precious few. "I find it's later than I expected. I told Fitzwilliam and the others I would meet them at White's."

"Oh, I see. Pity, really. Since I have insulted you, I thought you might give me a chance to apologize properly."

Apologize? A host of images flooded his brain, battling with his better judgment. *Do not look at her. Do not hesitate. Walk out of this room. Now.* "Another time."

"I suppose I should get out of this tattered nightgown."

He hesitated. In spite of all the warning bells ringing

like Notre Dame in his head, he glanced over his shoulder, just as Isabel peeled open her innocent white nightgown. Heat shifted like smoldering coals in his belly as he watched the white cotton spill from her slim shoulders and drift downward, dragging his hungry gaze with it. Cotton slid over the lush curves of her breasts, her hips, the long length of her legs. The garment fell with a sigh around her ankles. The sane voice in his head dwindled to a gasp.

He lifted his gaze, slowly tracing the play of moonlight upon her skin. She stretched like a cat in the sun, lifting her arms, arching her shoulders back, the movement shifting her breasts upward. They rose and fell with each soft breath she took, taut pink nipples lifting to him in silent invitation.

"I really wish you would stay," she said, sliding her hand over her belly. "I feel as warm as melted butter inside."

He tried to swallow, but all the moisture in his mouth had disappeared. His rod pushed against the barriers of his clothes, eager to make a fool of him.

She lay upon the white sheets of her bed, a pale pearl in the moonlight. "You have the most uncanny way of making me feel wicked and wanton. I find myself thinking of the most extraordinary things when you are near."

He moved toward her—he could not help himself; he was a puppet drawn by the invisible strings she tugged. He paused beside the bed and tried to appear composed. "Such as?"

"I would like to learn every strong line of your body. Every curve. I would like to explore you, with my fingertips, and with . . ." She drew her hand upward over the outside of his thigh. "My lips."

His breath tangled into a knot in his throat. He did not try to talk, afraid of the sound he might make.

"I want to kiss you everywhere. The way you kissed me that first time."

She drew her fingers over the thick ridge of his arousal, caressing him through the layers of his clothing. Sensation stabbed along his nerves.

She smiled up at him. "Take off your clothes, Justin. Let me make love to you."

He swallowed hard, and still his voice was husky when he spoke. "I don't know; you have questioned my honor."

"Not precisely." She dragged her nails over the cloth covering his arousal.

He sucked in his breath. "What would you call it?"

"Being practical. A woman needs to know if the man she intends to marry still wishes to marry her. Still, since you were insulted, you should allow me to make it up to you in some way."

Many ways sprang to life in his head. He tried valiantly not to surrender to the temptation. A man must remain in control.

"Is there anything I might do to make amends?"

He watched her pale fingers work the buttons on his trousers, his defenses unraveling beneath her gentle assault. "I suppose there might be a few things you could do."

"Shall you tell me?" The flap fell open, exposing the white linen of his drawers, and the solid evidence of his desire for her. "Or shall you leave me to my own imagination?"

He leaned toward her as she slipped her hand into his parted trousers. "Surprise me," he whispered, brushing his lips against her temple.

She flicked open the buttons of his drawers. "I warn you, my imagination has been taking the most wicked directions these days."

He grinned as the barrier gave way beneath her touch. "I'm shocked."

"Not as much as I have been." She took the heated length of him in her cool hands.

Her soft sigh collided with his. He clenched his jaw, fighting the low moan of pleasure crawling up his throat.

"I have always been a practical female." She traced the thick ridge of his arousal with her fingertips. "If anyone had told me I would one day fall under the spell of a wicked duke, I would have told them they should depart for Bedlam. Yet here I am, bemused, besotted, bewildered."

"Bewitching." He managed the single word, incapable of another intelligible sound.

"Bewitched is more to the point." She took his hands and pulled him until he sank to the bed beside her. The soft skin of her belly brushed the tip of his aroused flesh, dragging a wayward moan from his lips.

She rubbed her breasts against his shirt. A soft moan slipped past her lips and penetrated his blood. "I cannot make it through a single hour of any day without thinking of you."

Her words rippled through him, like a breath of summer gliding over a frozen pool. He watched, entranced by this female as she undressed him, slipping the cravat from his neck, dealing with the buttons of his shirt, his waistcoat, stripping away his coat, pulling the garments from his body. She slithered down the length of him, then sat back on her knees at his feet. She tugged off his boots, his socks, tugged on his trousers and drawers. He lifted his hips, allowing her to strip him bare. He watched her, entranced as she slid her hands up his thighs, as she pressed warm kisses against his skin.

She was a witch casting her spell. A siren luring

him. A woman learning the power she wielded over her man. Still, he could find no will to resist this sweet seduction. No chance for mastery. No desire to command. He felt like clay in her hands, not knowing how she would shape him, not caring what she made of him.

"So many intriguing textures," she whispered, drawing her cool hand upward, along his calf. She turned her head, her soft lips pressing against his inner thigh. "So incredibly warm."

He tipped back his head, groaning at the insidious pleasure darting along his nerves as she flicked her tongue against his skin. She moved upward, touching him, kissing him, tasting him. He clutched the sheet in both hands, fighting for some semblance of control. He had bedded countless women, paid for the services of the most accomplished whores in England, France, and Italy, and none of them had ever turned his blood to liquid fire the way this woman could.

She straddled his hips. He nearly came apart at the soft brush of damp feminine curls against his heated flesh. "I'm yours, Justin. In every way," she whispered, as she slowly took him into the warm haven of her body. "I love you."

Her soft words twined around the stone that had grown around his heart, squeezing the barrier and threatening to shatter it. He knew better than to believe in any female's romantic notions; they never lasted. Yet he could not prevent the warmth from settling in his chest.

He arched his hips in time to her rhythm, following her lead, something he had never in his life done before. Yet it was strangely arousing, surrendering to this woman, delivering himself into her hands.

He pulled her toward him, until he could brush his face against the plush warmth of her breasts. He licked the valley between, drank the silvery light from one taut pink nipple, then lavished his attention on the other. She grasped his shoulders, her breath escaping with soft, inarticulate sounds as he suckled like a babe at her breast.

She rode him, arching her hips, meeting his every upward thrust until she was shuddering with pleasure, until the delicate contractions of feminine release tugged on the length of him, coaxing him to join her. With a soft moan he surrendered to the pleasure, joining her in a moment of supreme joy, where all the cares of the mortal world dissolved into dust.

She fell against him and pressed her lips against his neck. He abandoned himself to her embrace. The fragrance of lavender mingled with the scent of their lovemaking, swirling through his senses. Her warmth bathed him, touching him deep inside, finding the remote frozen wasteland where he had buried his dreams.

Isabel hugged the sheet against her breasts, watching as Justin dressed near the bed, listening as he told her about his morning visitor. She had not realized it would be so easy to become accustomed to being with a man. She had not expected to feel as though he were an essential part of her, as vital as her every breath. Yet here she was, lying in bed with nothing but a sheet to cover her, wishing she could trade the soft brush of linen against her breasts for the rasp of the black curls covering Justin's broad chest. "So Marisa was the mysterious lady in white."

Justin tucked his shirt into his trousers as he spoke. "She thought I could help convince Clay to take the threat seriously."

"Do you suppose the threat is genuine?"

He sat on a chair near the bed and tugged on his

boots. "I doubt it. I can't think of anyone who would want to murder my brother. Now, if she had heard someone plotting to murder me, I might take her more seriously."

"A jealous husband? A discarded lover?"

Justin chuckled. "You have a realistic view of the man you're about to marry."

"Practical." Isabel brushed her hand over the empty mattress beside her. "Do you have to leave so soon?"

Justin shrugged into his close-fitting black coat. "Do you want to see Sophia flay the skin right off of my back?"

"No. I want to sleep in your arms."

He glanced at her, his expression revealing a flicker of surprise before his lips drew into a devilish grin. He could hide a hundred emotions behind that smile. He could conceal the uncertainty he would swear he never felt. Yet she had glimpsed the man behind the mask. Earlier, if she had not seen the apprehension in his eyes, if she had not heard a current of uncertainty in his deep voice, she might never have believed Justin Trevelyan could be concerned about her intentions to end their engagement. Perhaps it was due to pride. Yet she believed he actually cared more for her than he was willing to admit. It was enough to give her hope she might in time tame her wicked duke.

The mattress dipped as he sat on the bed beside her. "Be careful, my beguiling witch," he said, stroking his hand over her hair. "If you keep looking at me like that, you shall soon get your wish. And in the light of day, when Sophia finds me here, I will tell her you seduced me into this fall from grace. Try explaining that to the duchess."

She certainly never dreamed she would one day seduce a man. Yet she had. And in doing so, she had

316

discovered a heady sense of power. "Will you come to see me tomorrow evening, after everyone has gone to bed?"

He laughed softly. "Insatiable little wench, aren't you?"

She toyed with the top button on his waistcoat. "You have no one to blame but yourself, for being so handsome, so incredibly virile. I'm afraid I shall have a difficult time keeping my hands off of you when we are married."

He lifted his brows in mock shock. "I shall have to warn the servants to stay clear when you get that hungry look in your eyes."

She slipped the ebony button through the black silk of his waistcoat. "For quite some time now, I've come to believe you are the man I've been waiting for my entire life."

He lifted a lock of her hair and allowed the strands to slide through his fingers. "Romantic notions."

She suspected he enjoyed her romantic notions more than he cared to admit. "Come to me tomorrow night."

"Tempting wench." He kissed her brow. "I'll try, but I'm not sure I'll be back in time."

She frowned. "Where are you going?"

"I have an appointment with the man who had this." He slipped his hand into a pocket of his coat, withdrew a gold watch, and handed it to her. "Do you recognize it?"

Isabel turned the watch over in her hand. Flickering light from the lamp on the bedside table glowed in the gold. Even before she read the initials carved into the back, she recognized it. "It's my father's."

"I thought it was."

She looked up at him, her heart thudding against

317

her ribs. "Tomorrow night you're going to meet with the man who had this?"

"He might be able to lead us to the blackguard who murdered your father and brother."

"Do you think he had anything to do with the murders?"

"It's hard to say. It's one of the reasons I'm going. I want to see this man for myself."

Chills whispered across her skin. "He could be a murderer."

He pulled the counterpane over her. "You're cold."

"You aren't meeting with him alone," she said, drawing her arms out from beneath the ivory silk counterpane. "Are you?"

"Newberry is going with me." He smoothed his fingertips over her brow, as though he wanted to smooth away her worried frown. "No need to worry. I can take care of myself. And Newberry will have a few men in place to watch our backs."

She slid the pad of her thumb over the back of the watch, the initials rough against her skin. "I would like to go with you."

"We aren't meeting at the British Museum. We're meeting at a public house on the docks in the middle of the night. The last thing I need is to worry about keeping some bastard from harming you."

She gripped the black wool of his sleeve. "You will be careful?"

He slid his arms around her and held her so close she could feel the beating of his heart against her chest. "Nothing will keep me from making you my bride."

She smiled against his neck, dismissing the anxiety coiling in her belly. Justin was a strong man, capable of defending himself. Nothing would happen to him.

Everything would be fine, she assured herself. "I'm going to hold you to that promise, my wicked love."

Justin sat in the window seat of his bedchamber, staring into the garden behind his house. It was an ordinary garden. Ivy climbed the brick walls enclosing the perimeter where several chestnut and elm trees rose from a stretch of thick grass. Yet tonight, filmy scarves of fog drifted over the grass and coiled about the bases of the trees, lending a strange, preternatural quality to everything the mist touched.

In some ways Isabel was like that fog. When she touched him, all the ugliness in the world faded from his sight. When she held him in her arms he caught himself believing all the silly romantic notions that filled her beautiful head. She made him believe he could slay dragons. When she looked at him he wanted to become the man she thought he was.

Isabel loved him. He had known it before she had confessed her feelings. A woman like Isabel would never give herself to a man without believing in that great romantic myth. What he hadn't realized was how much he needed her to believe in that ephemeral, all-too-elusive emotion. Yet he did. He needed to see that smoldering warmth in her eyes when she looked at him. He needed to feel the warmth of that affection seep into his pores. He needed to drink the sweetness of that warmth from her lips.

Some men were never meant to be faithful to one woman. Some women were never meant to understand a certain proclivity a man might have for sampling more than one flower in the garden. If I were to marry Isabel, in time we would both be miserable.

Braden's words echoed in his memory, spreading a chill across Justin's skin. How long before the blackness of his soul extinguished all of that compelling warmth he had found in Isabel? How long before he shattered her every illusion? How long before he taught her to hate him? Despair rose inside of him, closing around his heart like a vise.

He closed his eyes. "I don't want to hurt you, Isabel. I never want to hurt you."

Yet how could a devil hope to redeem his soul?

Chapter Twenty-two

The next afternoon, Isabel received her cousin Gerard in the green drawing room at Marlow House. He sat beside her on a sofa near the windows, studying the watch Justin had given her. "I suppose it could be your father's watch."

"It is Father's. I'm certain of it."

Gerard frowned at the gold timepiece. "Still, it doesn't mean Marlow shall find the blackguards who murdered your father."

"He'll find them."

Gerard looked at her, a frown carving deep lines into his brow. "You have a great deal of faith in the man."

Isabel smiled as he handed her the watch. "The duke has an uncanny way of getting precisely what he wants."

"I've noticed. He managed to convince you he is a worthy man." Gerard rose and walked to one of the windows overlooking Park Lane. He stared through a square pane, his back stiff, his hands clenched into fists at his sides. "And now he has set out to solve a case of murder. There is positively no end to the duke's prowess."

Isabel joined him at the window. "He is not the same as his reputation. He is really a fine, honorable man."

"I wonder of what quality is the devil's honor?" Gerard leaned back against the casement. "You seem to be certain he shall make a suitable husband for you. I'm afraid I can't share your confidence."

Memories from the night before curled around her like a warm embrace. "The duke and I shall manage nicely."

He touched her cheek, a wistful smile curving his lips. "Dear, practical Isabel. I never expected to see stars fill your eyes."

"Neither did I."

"I'm afraid they are blinding you to the truth."

She shook her head. "I know what I'm doing."

He slid his thumb over the curve of her jaw. "There is still time to change your mind."

"Nothing could make me change my mind."

Gerard withdrew his hand. "And would you change your mind if you knew your gallant fiancé has taken a mistress?"

"What a bother!"

Gerard lifted one golden brow. "I would say it is."

Isabel waved away his words. "I don't mean it's a bother that he has taken a mistress."

"Not a bother? Isabel, is that man slipping something into your tea?"

"No. Of course not."

"It must be a drug. Some herb to muddle your brain."

"Don't be absurd."

"Then he has mesmerized you. Otherwise you would send the scoundrel packing."

Justin had her under a spell, but he had used nothing more than his own nefarious charm to do it. Isabel drew in a breath filled with the fragrance of the dried roses sitting about the room in porcelain bowls. "The duke has not taken a mistress."

Gerard rolled his eyes. "It must be a drug."

Isabel clenched her teeth. "I asked him about the rumor. He told me it wasn't true."

"You've heard about the mysterious lady in white?"

"Yes. And I know Justin has not taken a mistress."

Gerard nodded. "Drugs and mesmerism."

"Justin would not lie to me."

Gerard sighed. "The man is not worthy of you, Isabel. He shall make you unhappy. I swear, I would like to put an end to him before I would see him hurt you."

"You're wrong about him, Gerard."

"I hope you are right Isabel." He smiled, a cool, sarcastic curve of his lips. "And the rest of London is wrong."

Isabel glanced out the window. Sunlight slanted through the clouds hanging above the park, slashing misty gold columns upon the waters of the Serpentine. She had to believe in Justin. She had to believe she could make a place in his heart. Otherwise her life would become a fair imitation of Hades.

The acrid scent of burning pipe tobacco mingled with the stench of unwashed bodies and spilled ale in the main room of the Cock and Cur. The low din of male voices raised in conversation and laughter filtered through the smoky haze, reaching a round table against the far wall. Justin ran his thumb over the chipped rim of his glass of rum and studied the man sitting across from him at the table.

Billie Leggott was younger than he had suspected, no more than five and twenty. Although just below medium height, he looked quick and strong. A man capable of murdering two unarmed men?

"Mind you, ol' Harry ain't no murderer." Leggott's dark eyes shifted from Newberry to Justin. "And I ain't neither. Never sent no gent t' the boneyard, I ain't."

"Very noble of you." Justin twisted his glass on the scarred oak tabletop. "You said you had information about what happened to the man who owned the watch you gave to my friend."

Leggott flicked his tongue over his lips. "The deal was fer a hundred. Where's me blunt?"

Justin pulled a packet from his coat pocket and slid it across the table. Leggott snatched it and pulled it open. After a moment he frowned at Justin. "There's only fifty 'ere."

Justin smiled. "If I'm satisfied with your story, you can have the rest."

Leggott narrowed his eyes. "You wouldn' be tryin' t' cheat a man, would ye?"

"Earn your money."

Leggott eyed Justin as though assessing his opponent. Justin did not flinch. He did not blink. He met Leggott's look with icy calm, while inside he fought the urge to take the man by the neck and shake him until he told the truth.

Leggott blew a resigned sigh between his lips. "A chum o' mine tol' me about this job a swell paid him te do. Strange gent, Harry says. Never showed his face. And even stranger what he asked 'im te do."

Murder was not precisely strange for this part of the

city, Justin thought. "For what did he pay him?"

"Search the hospitals, steal two dead bodies, both men. And he was to be real particular about size and 'air color and that. Then he was to kidnap two fine gentlemen and ship 'em off on a prison boat."

Justin's breath constricted in his lungs. "Someone paid Harry to steal the bodies of two dead men. And to kidnap two gentlemen?"

"We . . . I mean 'e, Harry, was to make the dead men look like it was the two swells he'd kidnapped. Had to bash in their heads, 'e did. The bodies I mean, not the gents." Leggott smiled, revealing stained, chipped teeth. "Harry made extra money from the captain, selling him the two swells. The captain said they can always use more convicts in New South Wales."

Justin's blood pounded with the possibilities swirling in his head, possibilities he was almost afraid to believe. "And you're certain one of the men you shipped to New South Wales was the owner of the watch?"

Leggott grinned. "Aye. Harry made sure the gents weren't takin' nothin' of any value on their trip. Says the gent who paid him t' do the job wanted it all t' look like they was killed fer their blunt."

If it was true, and Justin had no reason to believe it wasn't, then Edward and Stephen might still be alive. Who the devil would go to such lengths to be rid of Darracott without shedding his blood? He thought of Isabel and all this could mean to her and her sisters. He had to find the truth. No matter what it took, if Edward and Stephen were alive, Justin had to bring them back home.

"Now, where's me blunt? Ye said I was t' ave it when I tol' ye what 'appened."

Justin pulled a packet from his coat and tossed it at

Leggott. "If you can tell me who hired Harry, I'll make it five hundred."

Leggott's eyes widened. "Wish I could, I do. But, seein' ye ain't the kind o' gent who would take kindly t' a lie, I can't 'elp. Never seen 'im. I mean Harry, he ain't never seen 'im."

Justin rose from the table. He intended to see punished the man responsible for putting Isabel and her family through this hell, no matter what it took. "If you think of anything that might identify the man who hired you, I mean who hired Harry, you know how to contact my friend here."

Leggott nodded his head. "Aye, sir. I will, sir."

Justin and Newberry left the pub and walked a short distance to the town coach Justin had waiting. When they were inside, Newberry spoke. "I think he's telling the truth, Your Grace."

Justin leaned back against the black velvet squabs. "I doubt he is smart enough to make up something that bizarre."

"I have my men watching him, Your Grace. We know where to find Harry as well. At your word, we can take both of them into custody."

"Not yet. I have a feeling Leggott and his chum will try to collect on the five hundred. I want them trying to figure out who the man is who hired them."

Newberry smiled. "Aye, Your Grace."

Justin stared out the window, blind to the dark shapes of buildings drifting past his gaze. What should he tell Isabel? Her father and brother might be alive. They might also have died during the voyage or soon after arriving in New South Wales. Prison ships were notorious. No one really cared what happened to a convict.

Still, he knew how much Isabel valued the truth. She had a right to know what he had learned this night.

It would take months to discover if her father and brother were still alive. No matter what the outcome, Justin would be with her when they learned the fates of Edward and Stephen. No matter what, he would cushion any possible blow as best he could.

After he dropped Newberry off at his home, Justin directed his driver to take him to the alley behind Marlow House. He had an appointment to keep with a beautiful termagant.

Isabel slid her hand along the naked curve of Justin's hip. She smiled against his neck, reveling in the weight of him pressing her down into the soft eiderdown mattress. A little more than an hour ago he had slipped into her bed and awakened her with a soft kiss. What had followed rivaled her most delicious dreams.

He released his breath in a warm sigh against her temple. ''Am I crushing you?''

She took his earlobe between her teeth and tugged. ''I can endure a great deal more of your crushing.''

He laughed softly against her hair. ''My wanton wench.''

She trailed her fingertips along his spine. ''My wicked darling. It is entirely your fault that I cannot get enough of you.''

He hooked his arm around her waist and rolled to his side, taking her with him. She snuggled against him, sliding her knee between his thighs, pressing her breasts against his chest. He stroked the damp hair from her cheek, a gentle smile curving his lips. ''I thought you wanted to hear all about my meeting tonight.''

''Somehow you managed to distract me from it.'' She traced the line of his collarbone with her fingertips. ''Did you learn anything?''

''Billie Leggott had an interesting story to tell. It's

possible . . .'' He rested his hand on her shoulder and rubbed his thumb back and forth against her skin. ''Isabel, it's still too soon to be certain. But your father and brother might be alive.''

Isabel stared at him, stunned by his words. ''What did you say?''

''It's possible both Edward and Stephen are alive. They may have been sent to New South Wales, as convicts. Two other men might have been left in their stead.''

She gripped his arm, her heart pounding so hard she felt dizzy. ''You have my head spinning. Please, tell me everything.''

Justin stroked her shoulder as he related the events of his meeting with Billie Leggott. ''Tomorrow I'm going to send my man of affairs and five of Newberry's men to New South Wales. If your father and brother are alive, we'll find them.''

It was all so incredible, she could scarcely believe it. ''Who would hire a man to make it appear as though two murders had taken place? Why would anyone do something like that?''

''Someone who wanted Edward and Stephen out of the way, but who didn't want to resort to murder. Can you think of anyone who might have benefited from the 'deaths' of your father and brother?''

Isabel struggled to gather the scattered fragments of her wits. ''Belcham may have wanted to get rid of Father, but not dirty his hands with his blood.''

''Possibly. Was there another heir, besides Franklin Witheridge?''

''No. But I cannot believe Franklin or Gerard would be involved in something so vile. And it isn't as if my cousins need money.''

Justin tucked a curl behind her ear. ''According to Sophia, both Franklin and Gerard are flush in the pockets. I haven't heard anything to the contrary. If one of them had a penchant for gambling, I might understand. But they don't.''

"The only one I can think of who might want to be rid of my father is Eldridge Belcham. His lust for those manuscripts may have completely muddled his reason.''

Justin slipped his arms around her and held her close. "Isabel, I don't want you to mention this to anyone. Especially your sisters. If your father and brother were sent to New South Wales on a prison ship, they may not have survived the voyage or the treatment they received once they arrived at their destination.''

Isabel nestled close against him, trying to chase away the chill inside her. They had to be alive. Please let them be alive, she prayed. "Thank you for telling me the truth, Justin.''

He slid his hand over her hair. "I didn't think you would be satisfied with anything less.''

She pressed her lips to his shoulder. "I hope you always feel that way.''

His arms tightened around her. "I had better go.''

She pulled back to look into his eyes. "I'll be glad when you can stay all night. I want to sleep in your arms. I want to awaken to your smile.''

He kissed the tip of her nose. "I'm not sure I smile in the morning.''

She nipped his chin. "I'll have to take measures to see that you do.''

Justin stepped out of his coach in front of Clayton's town house. A cool breeze threaded with the scent of burning coal bathed his face. Tongues of fog coiled around the street lamp in front of the house, shimmering yellow in the flickering gas flame. One of the four black geldings hitched to his coach snorted and twitched, his harness jangling in the eerie silence of the thickening fog.

If he hadn't already returned, his brother would soon be headed home from an evening of bride shopping at the various balls in town. He needed to talk with Clay about Leggott's story. He wanted to test a few of his ideas about who had shipped the Darracotts to New South Wales. As he approached the house he glimpsed movement in his periphery. Instincts screamed a warning that came a heartbeat too late. Justin pivoted in time to see a flash of powder reflected in the fog. The crack of gunfire slammed into his ears. A bullet plowed into his side, searing his flesh. Pain flashed along his nerves, buckling his knees. He pitched forward, onto the sidewalk.

"Your Grace!" Lynam, his coachman, and one of the footmen rushed to his side.

Justin struggled into a sitting position. "Go after him!"

"Davies has gone running after the bastard," Lynam said.

As Justin tried to stand, pain knifed through him, snatching the breath from his lungs. Blood swam before his eyes. He fell back against the fence, dragging air into his burning lungs. He clamped down hard on his will, forcing back the darkness creeping over him. He would not swoon. He never swooned.

Lynam rested his hand on Justin's shoulder. "I don't think you should try to get up on your own, Your Grace. Let James and me help you inside. I fear you shall swoon."

"I am not going to swoon, Lynam." Justin leaned back against the wrought-iron fence in front of his brother's house. He clutched his hand against his arm and side, his palm sliding against the damp warmth of blood. "I never swoon."

"Aye, Your Grace. If you'll put your arm around my shoulders, I'll be getting you into the house." Lynam slipped his arm around Justin and helped him to his feet.

Pinpoints of light danced in the darkness filling Justin's eyes. "Bloody hell," he whispered, as he swooned.

Chapter Twenty-three

Come to me, Justin.

Isabel's words drifted through the fog hanging like a gray veil in Justin's mind. He felt a soft tug on his vitals, a gentle coaxing toward the image of the woman filling his mind. Isabel stood on the cliffs of Bramsleigh, her unbound hair drifting in the breeze, her hand outstretched toward him. She was smiling at him. Beckoning him to her arms. He turned his head on the pillow. The scent of freshly washed linens dried in the sun filled his nostrils. Yet he craved the scent of lavender.

"Isabel," Justin whispered.

"I am glad to hear it's my name you have chosen to call in your sleep."

Justin pried open his eyes. Sunlight flooded his sight. A figure sat in relief against the bright light. Justin blinked, clearing his vision until Isabel's face came into focus. She sat on a chair by the bed, smiling at him. Sunlight tangled in the curls framing her face, spinning gold from the brown strands. Eyes that would make a summer sky envious regarded him with a warmth that stroked him, filling all the dark, hollow places deep inside him.

"How are you feeling?" she asked, stroking her hand over his hair.

"As though I have been dragged behind a curricle for a few hundred miles." Justin rubbed the bandage that slashed across his chest. Another white strip of linen bound his upper arm.

Sophia left the window seat to stand beside Isabel's chair. "The surgeon said you were a very lucky man."

Blood pounded like a hammer against the inside of his skull. "He isn't looking at things from my perspective."

Sophia squeezed his hand. "The bullet went straight through. It carved a piece out of your arm and took some flesh off your side, but none of your bones were shattered. With a few days' rest you should be fine."

"In that regard, I shall bow to the surgeon's appraisal."

"The surgeon left a vial of laudanum," Isabel said. "Would you like some?"

Justin grimaced. "If I want to muddle my brain, I will do it with whiskey. At the moment my head feels as thick as a brick."

Sophia tilted her head, a mischievous smile curving her lips. "There are those who would say that is a fairly natural condition for you."

Justin grinned at her. "Is there something around here to drink? I feel as though I've been chewing cotton wool."

Isabel stood and filled a glass from a pitcher on the bedside table. She shifted a pillow behind him as Justin struggled into a sitting position. Her arm brushed his bare shoulder. The innocent touch shot through him like a spark from flint. He looked up at her as she handed him the glass. She looked completely unaware of how she had set his blood pounding with a single touch. Lord help him if she ever realized the power she could wield over him.

He drained the glass, savoring the barley water as though it were fine wine. "Never thought I would appreciate barley water."

"Clayton said you would be thirsty," Isabel said, taking the glass from his hand.

"He would know. He has had experience." Justin gingerly rubbed his throbbing arm. "Where is my brother?"

"He went to speak with Marisa Grantham," Sophia said.

"He went to see Marisa? Why?"

Sophia clasped her hands at her waist. "Clayton has some strange idea he might have been the actual target last night, and not you."

"Clay the target." A chilling dampness broke out over his skin, while a weight pressed against his chest. "I hadn't considered that possibility."

"He said Marisa had overheard someone discussing his murder at a party several days ago," Sophia said. "Why didn't anyone bother to tell me about it?"

Justin held Sophia's steady gaze. "At the time he didn't take it seriously."

Sophia's lips tightened. "I cannot imagine why anyone would want to murder Clayton."

"Neither can I." Justin leaned back against his pillow. "I hope Marisa can help find the key to the puzzle."

"Before another attempt is made." Sophia glanced at Isabel, then at Justin, a look of concern marring her features. "I will have some toast and tea prepared.

You'll feel better after you eat something.''

Justin stared after his grandmother as she left the room. Someone might want his brother dead. Until now he had not truly accepted the possibility. He could easier believe someone wanted him dead. He would rather they were after him.

''Are you certain you didn't hire someone to take a small bit of flesh here and there?'' Isabel asked.

Justin looked up at her, curious about the direction of her thoughts. ''I must look as though I've lost my wits.''

The mattress dipped as Isabel sat on the edge of the bed. ''I suppose it would be a rather extravagant way to postpone our wedding.''

He took her hand. ''I will be there for the wedding, my beautiful witch. And the wedding night.''

She stroked her hand over his hair, her fingers gliding softly against his scalp. ''I intend to hold you to your promise. No matter what. You see, I've grown rather fond of you.''

''Rather fond?'' He lifted her hand to his lips.

She nodded. ''The truth is, I'm having a terrible time imagining life without you. So I'm afraid you shall have to take care. I should dislike it immensely should you get yourself killed.''

''No one is going to murder my brother or me. I will see to that.''

She brushed her lips against his brow. ''The man who did this might try again.''

He squeezed her hand. ''Don't worry, Belle. No one shall rescue you from my wicked clutches. I intend to stay around for the next forty or fifty years.''

''I'm glad to hear it. I rather like being in your wicked clutches.''

He slipped his hand around the back of her neck and drew her down to him. Her breath brushed his lips before her mouth settled over his. He tasted her fear for him mingled with the sweet affection he had come to depend upon. He wasn't certain why the Almighty had sent Isabel to him. Surely a mistake had been made. An angel did not belong with a man like him. Yet she was his. And he would fight anyone and anything to keep her.

Later that morning, Isabel was surprised to have a visitor at Clayton's town house. She entered the drawing room and found Franklin Witheridge standing near the windows, staring down into the street below. He turned when Isabel entered the room.

"Cousin, this is a surprise," Isabel said, moving toward him.

"I stopped by Marlow House to see you this morning and the butler told me you were here." He took her hands. "I understand Marlow was shot last night. Is he all right?"

"He'll be fine." She stared up at him, stunned by the rapid spread of the news. "How did you find out about the shooting?"

He shrugged. "Servants. You cannot keep any secrets in London. I heard it from my valet, who heard it from one of the maids, who no doubt heard it from one of Huntingdon's servants. According to rumor, he was shot by the jealous husband of one of his mistresses."

Isabel pulled her hands from his grasp, her anger rising at the injustice of the gossip. "I'm amazed at how easily people assume the most vile things about Justin."

Franklin lifted his dark brows. "Are you so certain it wasn't a jealous husband?"

"Justin doesn't have a mistress."

Franklin smiled at her, the kind of smile reserved

for naive children. ''Perhaps it is best to keep your eyes closed to such things.''

She refrained from telling him she thought it best to keep one's nose out of other people's concerns. Unlike her cousin, she refused to be rude. ''If there is nothing else, I would like to return to Justin.''

Franklin rubbed his chin. ''Actually, there is something of grave importance I need to discuss with you.''

''What is it?''

''I really do wish there were some way to convince you to marry my son instead of Marlow, but I suppose your mind is set.''

''I'm afraid it is.''

Franklin nodded. ''Yes. I suspected as much.''

Isabel found her thoughts wandering. Although Justin had fallen asleep a short while ago, Isabel preferred to sit and watch him sleep than to converse with her cousin. ''I'm sure you'll understand when I say I really would like to return to—''

''Gerard informs me Marlow's investigation into Edward's death has taken an unexpected step forward. He said you have recovered Edward's watch.''

''Yes. Justin is hopeful the man who had it might be able to answer a few questions about what happened that night. He hopes to see the men responsible brought to justice.'' Isabel refrained from telling Franklin about Leggott and his incredible story.

A frown carved deep lines into his brow. ''I never realized Marlow would be so interested in uncovering the details of the murders. He has proved most troublesome.''

''I'm not certain I understand. Why would his investigation be troublesome to you?''

''Because of what he might discover.'' Franklin pulled a pistol from his coat pocket. Sunlight glinted on the silver barrel.

"Cousin!"

"I had hoped you would marry Gerard. It would have made things much easier," Franklin said, gripping her arm. "Come along, Isabel."

Isabel twisted her arm, trying to break free. "You cannot think to force me to marry Gerard."

Franklin poked the muzzle of the gun against her ribs. "Be practical, Isabel. Do you imagine I would actually kidnap you for my son?"

Isabel tried to swallow, but her mouth was as dry as dust. "Why are you doing this?"

"I need your help."

Isabel stared at him, thoughts colliding in her startled brain. "My help?"

"According to Gerard, you know where I might find the original plan of Bramsleigh. You will find that plan for me, then help me find the treasure."

"You are doing this for the treasure?"

He squeezed her arm so tightly that pinpoints of pain prickled along her nerves. "Do you know how very long I've sought it? All of my life."

Isabel strained against his grip as he ushered her toward the door. "I'm not going anywhere with you."

"Careful, my dear. You shall cause notice. And I would be obliged to shoot anyone who got in my way." He slipped his pistol into his pocket, holding it pointed at her through the claret-colored wool. "Do you understand?"

Isabel stared at him, the realization of his deadly intent seeping like acid into her veins. If she weren't careful she could get someone killed. "Yes. I understand."

Franklin smiled. "Very good. Now you shall come along with me, like a good girl. And no one shall be harmed."

Isabel allowed him to lead her out of the drawing

room, down the stairs to the entry hall, and out into the street, where his traveling coach was waiting. Franklin threw open the door of the coach, pushed her inside, and then climbed in behind her. Isabel fell against the burgundy velvet squabs as the coach lurched forward. Franklin settled into the seat across from her and rested his pistol against his thigh.

Isabel rubbed the red marks Franklin's fingers had left imprinted on her skin. She glanced from the pistol to her cousin's face. She recalled her father once mentioning Franklin's obsession with the treasure, ever since he was a lad. Franklin had once hidden in a sideboard when his parents were ready to return home from a visit at Bramsleigh—all so he might continue his search for the jewels. "If you kill me, you won't have anyone to show you where the plans are."

"I could take a hammer to the walls of the library. It would take longer, and be a great deal more trouble, but I could manage." Franklin smiled at her. "Still, I would prefer to do this the easiest way possible. I had hoped I might find the treasure before you and Marlow even finished the translations. Now I can see that I would have needed your help even if I had been able to find the journal in his library."

"You were the one. You broke into Justin's house. Didn't you?"

"I had gone through a great deal of trouble to get that journal from your father. When Gerard told me you intended to marry Marlow, I thought it best to liberate the journal from him. Still, when I didn't find it, I decided to allow you to translate it; then I could look for the treasure after you had done all the work. Fortunately Gerard told me about the plans you had found. Those plans may be just the key I need."

"Was it you last night? Did you try to murder Justin?"

Franklin shook his head. "As much as you would like to deny the truth, I have little doubt that last night a jealous husband or an angry mistress decided to spill Marlow's claret."

Isabel refused to debate her fiancé's honor with this blackguard. "You had my father sent away so you could get your hands on the journal."

Franklin chuckled softly. "It would seem Marlow has made more progress than I suspected."

Isabel could scarcely breathe. "Then it is true? Father and Stephen are alive?"

"They were when I had them shipped off to New South Wales. I cannot say what happened after that."

"How could you do it? How could you ship them off to be treated like slaves?"

Franklin drew his fingertip over the barrel of his pistol. "I could have had them murdered, Isabel. Perhaps I should have. I shall allow no one to get in my way. I have been looking for that blasted treasure all of my life. I will find it."

The icy determination in his dark eyes left no room for doubt. She shivered, even though it was warm in the coach. She sank back against the squabs. Her father and Stephen—dear heaven, they were alive. She chose to dwell on that thought rather than the daunting possibility that she might not survive her cousin's obsession. She glanced out the window, watching a row of gray stone town houses pass in her vision. When Justin learned she had disappeared, he would come looking for her. He would find her. She was certain of it.

"Justin!"

Justin bolted upright in bed, eliciting a sharp stab of pain from his side. He grabbed his side and stared at the woman standing beside his bed. "Sophia! What the devil—"

"He has kidnapped her."

Justin dragged his hand through his hair. "What are you talking about? Who has been kidnapped?"

"Isabel."

His heart lurched. "What has happened?"

Sophia twisted her handkerchief in her hands. "Franklin Witheridge came to speak with Isabel this morning. One of the footmen saw them leave and get into a traveling coach. She hasn't returned."

"How long ago?"

"Nearly an hour ago. I went to Witheridge's house and questioned his wife. I couldn't make much sense out of what she was saying, with all the weeping she was doing. I'm afraid I did frighten her a bit."

"Frighten her?"

"I told her you would pay a call if she didn't tell me what Witheridge had done with Isabel. It had a most extraordinary affect on her." She smiled. "Your disreputable reputation has some advantages."

Justin shook his head. "What did she say?"

"She kept babbling about some treasure. From what I could gather, Franklin has been obsessed with some treasure since he was a lad."

"Bramsleigh." Justin grabbed the covers to throw them aside, then realized he was wearing bandages and nothing else. "Send Lindsley to me, with a set of Clay's clothes. And have Clay's traveling coach made ready."

Sophia gripped his shoulder. "Justin, perhaps we should wait for Clayton. You look dreadfully pale."

"I'm not about to lie around waiting for Clay when that bastard has Isabel. Either you send Clay's valet to me with some clothes, or I will get them myself."

Sophia nodded. "Very well. I will send Lindsley to you."

Justin clenched the blue silk counterpane in his hand as his grandmother hurried from the room. Anxiety pressed against his chest, as thick and heavy as a boulder. He wanted to toss back his head and scream. He wanted to take Franklin Witheridge by the neck and choke the life out of him. If he harmed Isabel, Justin would tear the man apart with his bare hands.

Isabel walked beside Franklin down the long hallway leading to the library at Bramsleigh. Their footsteps tapped against white and black squares of marble, the sound hitting the oak wainscoting and echoing with a hollow ring against her ears. She had never seen her home this way, so empty, so lifeless. Gerard had sent all the servants to London for the Season. In each room they passed, Holland covers draped the furniture, turning each piece into a shapeless mound of gray. It all made her feel isolated.

"Come now, Isabel, shake those blue devils." Light from the taper Franklin held flickered over the gray specters of shrouded furniture as they entered the library. "If you do as you're told, I won't harm you. And just think, I can actually help return your father and brother to you and your sisters."

The scent of dust rustled from the canvas covering the carpet of the library as they crossed the dark room. "I suppose I shouldn't dwell on the fact that you are the one responsible for them being taken from us in the first place."

Franklin used his taper to light a branch of candles near the hearth as he spoke. "Think of it this way: at least I didn't have them murdered."

She paused near the bookcase concealing the hidden room. "If I can believe you."

Candlelight glowed against his face, illuminating the chilling curve of his smile. He lit the wall sconces. "At the moment, the only thing you need to believe is that I shall be most upset with you if you don't lead me to the treasure."

Isabel managed a smile in spite of the dread curling like icy fog along her spine. "By now Justin knows you kidnapped me. If you harm me, he will punish you, cousin. There will be nowhere you can hide."

Candlelight glowed on the pistol he slipped from his pocket. "Dear Isabel, there are ways of dealing with men like Devil Trevelyan. And I am not above using the most severe methods. You should hope your fiancé does not decide to leave his bed to find you until I am well away from here, with the treasure in my hands."

The murderous gleam in his dark eyes held a grim determination that left no doubts in her mind. Franklin would murder Justin with the same cold calculation he had used to have her father and brother shipped off to New South Wales. He would not allow anything to get in his way.

"Make it easy for all concerned." Franklin chucked her under her chin. "All I want is the treasure."

Although she would dearly love to kick the man, she knew it was useless to try to overpower him. She was far too practical to risk anyone's life for a handful of jewels. She turned and tugged down the cover shrouding the bookcase. "The workmen found a room behind here. The entire bookcase opens like a door."

Franklin ran his hand over the edge of a smooth oak shelf. "How does it open?"

"There is a lever concealed in a recess on—I believe—this shelf." Isabel slipped a volume of Shakespeare's sonnets from the far end of a middle shelf. She ran her fingertips over the bottom of the shelf above it, searching for an indentation and the concealed lever. When she did not find it she slipped the book back on the shelf, then removed another on the shelf above it.

"I would imagine we have only a short time before Marlow comes barging in here," Franklin said, his voice a low rumble near her ear. "If you want to keep him healthy, I would hurry."

She glared at him. "I'm trying."

He smiled. "Do better."

She ran her trembling fingertips over the bottom of the shelf. When her fingertips sank into a narrow recess, she nearly collapsed with relief. One strong tug released the lever and the hidden lock. "There," she said, stepping back. "You should be able to open it now."

Hinges creaked as Franklin dragged the bookcase open, revealing a narrow alcove where a bookcase sat back between carved oak panels on either side of it. "Which book has the plans?"

Isabel pulled one of the thick leather-bound books from the bookcase and blew the dust from it. She carried it to a nearby table and laid it upon the gray canvas cover. "You do realize it's possible we won't be able to find it."

"I've waited all of my life to find it. If I have to knock this house down with my bare hands, I will find it."

Isabel glanced at the mahogany tall-case clock in one corner of the room. Although it had stopped marking time, she was aware of each passing second. As much as she wanted Justin to find her, she wanted even more to keep him safe. She could only hope Franklin got what he wanted and left before Justin found them.

Franklin pulled a folded sheet of paper from his coat pocket. He pulled it open and read the first clue.

" 'Find the dragon who guards the sanctum.' We need a dragon. Find one.''

Isabel searched through the plans. In a matter of minutes she had found not one dragon, but thirty. "The old library. This shows dragon heads carved into each cornice of the bookcases."

Franklin looked around, his eyes wide, his expression one of a man in shock. "All the cornices have been replaced."

Isabel stared into the secret alcove, where candlelight flickered against the dusty oak shelves. At each end of the bookcase, a dragon's head loomed out of the cornice. "Not all of them."

Franklin pivoted, his attention drawn to the old bookcase. "It has to be one of those."

Isabel rose as Franklin grabbed an armchair and hurried toward the bookcase. She stepped back, toward the door. If she could get away from him, she could run to the caretaker's cottage.

" 'In the dragon's breath you shall find the key to the lion's lair.' " Franklin planted the chair below one end of the bookcase and faced her. "Come here."

"You don't need me any longer."

"I will decide when I'm finished with you. Now get up there and see if you can find anything in the dragon's mouth."

His obsession bordered on lunacy. She could very well get herself killed if she didn't do what he wanted. She closed the distance and climbed onto the seat of the chair. Stretching, she reached above her until her fingers slid against the carved dragon's tongue. She hesitated a moment, thinking of what might be living in that cavity. She had never had much tolerance for spiders.

"Time is passing, Isabel."

And Justin might be drawing close. She closed her

eyes and stuck her fingers inside the open mouth of the dragon. Dust coated the smooth oak carving. She rubbed her fingers all around the inside. "Nothing."

"Get down."

When she complied, Franklin moved the chair to the opposite end. "Try this one. And you'd better find something this time."

"What if there isn't anything to find? It could very well have been one of the other dragons."

Franklin's eyes narrowed. "It has to be here."

She stepped onto the seat of the chair and plunged her fingers into the dusty opening. She slid her fingers all around the cavity. At first she felt nothing more than dust-encrusted wood. Then, as her fingers cleared a path, she felt something else. A recess and a smooth piece of metal that felt like the lever she had found in the bookcase. She slipped the tip of her finger beneath the lever and pried it upward. The lever slid open. Hinges creaked to her right.

"We've done it," Franklin said.

One panel of the alcove had slid away from the wall. Isabel climbed down from the chair as Franklin swung the panel wide open. He grabbed a branched candlestick from a nearby table and held it in front of the opening. Candlelight plunged down a steep staircase and collected in a puddle of gold on the stone floor at the base of the stairs.

"Go," Franklin said, shoving Isabel toward the stairs.

She did not like the looks of it. Too many unpleasant things liked to inhabit dark places. Not to mention the unpleasant man standing behind her.

Franklin squeezed her shoulder. "You're wasting time."

Isabel sucked in her breath. She gripped the metal railing and started down the stairs. A cool dampness enveloped her as she sank deeper into the pit. At the base of the stairs she pressed back against the smooth stone wall. A thick, musty smell filled her every breath. Franklin paused beside her and raised the candles. A narrow passage led to two storage rooms. In the second they found a stone statue of a crouching lion perched on a low stone pedestal. The entire piece was about the size of a full-grown mastiff.

" 'Seek the lion's secret beneath his crouching form,' " Franklin said, setting the candlestick on the floor. He tried to lift the lion off its perch. It wouldn't budge. He bent and examined the connection of the lion to the base. "It has to be here."

Isabel looked back along the passageway. How long before Justin came? She stared at the statue, searching for an answer. "Try twisting it."

Franklin hooked his arm around the lion's body and twisted. Stone scraped against stone as the lion swung away from the base, revealing a cavity hidden in the pedestal. He lifted the light and stared into the opening, a man who has found his greatest desire. He stuck his hand into the cavity and withdrew a large leather pouch. He ripped it open. Isabel stepped closer, drawn by the legend come to life. Candlelight spilled into the pouch, setting ablaze the jewels nestled in the leather.

"I always knew it was real," Franklin whispered.

"You have your treasure; now leave." Franklin could be dealt with later for his crimes. At the moment, Isabel was more concerned with making sure he didn't kill anyone.

Franklin looked up from the jewels. Candlelight glinted in his eyes. "I intend to do just that."

Isabel turned and headed for the doorway. She did not want to spend any more time than necessary in here.

"I'm afraid I can't let you leave here, Isabel."

She froze at the click of a pistol being cocked. She turned to find Franklin with his pistol pointed directly at her chest.

Chapter Twenty-four

Justin hurried along the hallway leading to the library at Bramsleigh. Pain burned like smoldering coals in his arm and side. Still, he scarcely noticed. Franklin's coach was in front of the house. They were here. And the light spilling into the dark hallway would lead him like a beacon to Isabel. She was all right, he assured himself. Franklin had no reason to harm her. The bastard wanted the jewels. Nothing more. Yet he could not ease the anxiety gripping his heart like a vise.

The light flowing from the library dimmed, as though someone were extinguishing all the candles. Justin paused near the door. A moment later Franklin stepped into the hall. Light from the taper he held carved an arc in the shadows, catching Justin on the fringe of the golden glow. He paused when he saw Justin, his expression, illuminated by candlelight, revealing only a mild surprise. "Marlow. This is a surprise. What are you doing here?"

Justin stalked the man. "Where is she?"

Franklin's brows lifted. "She? Who are you looking for?"

"You know bloody well who I'm looking for." Justin paused in the circle of candlelight, a foot away from Witheridge. "Where is Isabel?"

"Isabel?" Franklin set the single candlestick on a table against the wall. "Is she missing?"

"Don't play games with me, Witheridge. I'm in a dangerous mood." He stared into Franklin's dark eyes without trying to hide all the barely restrained fury burning inside him. "Tell me where she is."

Witheridge eased his hand into his coat pocket. "I saw her this morning, at Huntingdon's house. I had heard you were injured last night. Do you think something has happened to her?"

Justin caught the glimmer of candlelight on steel. Before Witheridge could aim his weapon, Justin struck, bringing his hand down sharply against the other man's wrist. Witheridge gasped. The pistol dropped from his hand and clattered against the floor.

"Damn you!" Witheridge muttered, lashing out with his fist.

Justin blocked the blow with his forearm. The impact vibrated through his arm, jabbing his wound like a poker to coals. In that instant of stunned pain, Witheridge found the advantage. He connected with his left, hitting Justin's chest. The breath exploded from his lungs, and Justin staggered back and hit the wall.

Witheridge lunged for the pistol. Before he could raise the weapon, Justin lashed out with his foot. The tip of his boot rammed into the bottom of Witheridge's chin. Witheridge's head snapped back. The back of his skull cracked against the oak-paneled wall, followed by the distinctive click of teeth against teeth. A low moan trickled from his lips as Witheridge slumped headfirst against the floor.

Justin snatched the pistol from Witheridge's limp hand. He grabbed the man's shoulder and rolled him to his back. "Witheridge," he shouted, slapping the man across the cheek. "Wake up, damn you!"

His only response was a feeble moan.

Justin straightened and shoved the pistol into his coat pocket. He grabbed the candlestick from the table and rushed into the library. The faint glow of his candle flickered on gray Holland covers. "Isabel!"

His desperate cry died against the heavy canvas covering the bookcase-lined walls. Silence closed around him. He rubbed his aching side, his fingers sliding against a damp warmth. The wounds were bleeding again. Isabel had to be here, somewhere.

He tossed aside a cover shrouding a sofa, looking for any sign of her. What if he had lost her? What if the bastard had killed her? The thought stabbed him more sharply than the wound in his side. She was only a woman, one of many he had known. Yet the thought of a life without Isabel made him want to toss back his head and scream.

He refused to believe she was gone. He refused to believe she had chipped away the stone surrounding his heart only so it could be shattered with her loss. Witheridge had sent Edward and Stephen away but he had not murdered them. He would not have murdered Isabel. She had to be here. Somewhere.

He walked through the room, tossing aside the Holland covers. Witheridge had come here looking for that blasted treasure. He had brought Isabel here to help find it; Justin was certain of it. Where could she be? As his mind formed the question, his gaze fell on a bookcase at the far end of the room.

The faint light of his taper brushed against the

wood. As he drew closer he saw the bookcase tilted out away from the wall, revealing an alcove behind it. Isabel had mentioned a hidden alcove.

He lit the candles of a branched candlestick he found on a table near the alcove. A chair sat at one end of the bookcase, just below a dragon. What was the clue? ''The key is in the dragon's breath,'' he whispered.

The clues to the treasure—if he followed them he might find Isabel. Blood swam before his eyes as he stepped onto the seat of the chair. He gripped the bookcase, dragging air into his lungs, trying to clear his head. When the dizziness passed he reached into the dragon's mouth. His fingers slid into a recess and against a cool wedge of metal. When he pried the lever upward, he heard a soft click to his right.

Justin stepped from the chair and pulled the panel wide open. He lifted the branched candlestick and stared straight down into hell. Terror coiled around his chest, as thick and tight as a steel band. ''Isabel!'' he shouted, his voice ricocheting in the cavernous darkness.

Through the pounding of blood in his ears he heard her voice echo against the stone below him, calling his name. Alive! She was alive. Joy and relief rose inside him, colliding with the solid wall of his fears.

''Justin! I'm locked in a storage room.''

Trapped in the darkness. He gripped the railing, his palm growing slick against the metal. Memories stirred inside him, taunting him.

You are the devil's spawn!

A shaking commenced deep inside him, where the horrific remains of his boyhood memories rose like demons from their resting places.

''Justin!'' Isabel's voice broke through his paralysis.

Damn the weakness! He forced his legs to move, taking the steps, descending into the pit. Candlelight flickered on the stairs before him, shaping an oasis in the darkness. He paused at the base of the stairs. The stone walls seemed to close around him, pressing against him and squeezing until he could scarcely draw a breath.

"Justin!" Isabel shouted. "I'm here. At the end of the passage."

Her voice penetrated his fear. "I'm coming for you."

He clutched the candlestick, forging his way through the narrow passage until he reached the closed door at the end. His hand trembled as he pulled back the bolt and threw open the oak door. Candlelight poured into the small room, bathing Isabel in a soft glow. He caught a glimpse of her frightened expression before she launched herself at him.

"Justin!" Isabel barreled into his arms with such enthusiasm she knocked him back against the wall. She clung to him, her arms tight around his waist, her cheek pressed to his chest. "I knew you would find me. I knew it."

He rested his cheek against her hair and closed his eyes against the darkness. He held her close, absorbing the trembling of her slender frame. The slight scent of lavender chased away the mustiness of the passage. Words clawed at his throat. Words that whispered of all the things he had felt when she was lost to him. He wanted to tell her how relieved he was to hold her again. How much he cared. The nightmarish fear he had of never seeing her again. Yet he could not form a single syllable. All he could do was hold her close, and silently thank the Almighty for saving his soul.

* * *

Isabel paused on the threshold of her former dressing room in Bramsleigh Hall, her breath tangling in her throat at the sight that greeted her. Justin stood near the washstand, pressing a cloth against the wound in his side. His coat, waistcoat, and shirt lay over the edge of the copper bathing tub. Candlelight from the wall sconces slid in a golden caress over the sleek skin of his shoulders. The golden light poured down the intriguing valley of his spine and rippled with the thick muscles shifting beneath smooth skin. It was still difficult to believe this magnificent male would soon be her husband.

He turned, his lips curling into a devilish grin when he caught her staring at him. "Find some bandages?"

She moistened her dry lips. "I found some ointment at the cottage. Mrs. Tweedbury always kept it for cuts. I ripped a sheet into strips."

Justin's dark brows lifted as his gaze lowered to the pile of linen draped over her arm. "Do you have plans you haven't told me about?"

"What do you mean?"

Justin pulled the chair out from the vanity. "You have enough linen to wrap me up from head to toe."

She smiled. "I suppose I got a little carried away. Has the bleeding stopped?"

"It appears to have." Justin sank onto the seat in front of the vanity.

Isabel draped the pile of linen over the top of the vanity beside the Bramsleigh jewels. Emeralds, diamonds, and rubies glittered in the candlelight. Yet the glitter seemed tarnished when she thought of what lust for those jewels had cost her family. She opened the jar containing Mrs. Tweedbury's herbal remedy, crinkling her nose at the strong scent of the stuff. "This might sting a bit."

Justin sucked in his breath as she spread the pale

green ointment over the slash in his side. "What the devil is in that stuff?"

"I'm not sure. But it always seemed to help scrapes and cuts heal without infection."

A muscle bunched in his cheek as she smoothed the ointment over the gash in his arm. He closed his eyes. "The remedy might be worse than the affliction."

"I'm sorry, I didn't mean to hurt you. The sting will go away in a short while." She lifted a strip of linen and placed it gently over the bright red gash in his side. "Hold it here for me."

He covered her hand with his, the warm contact sending sensation skimming along her skin. She eased her hand from beneath his and drew the strip of linen over his chest, slashing white across springy black curls. She crushed the desire stirring inside her. He was a wounded man who had endured enough exertion for one night.

"Lift your arm."

He complied, thick muscles shifting in his arm as he raised it from his side. She slipped the bandage beneath his arm, trying not to notice the warmth of his skin as she guided the bandage around him.

"You look as though you've recovered from your little adventure."

Isabel shivered when she thought of that dark little cell where she might have spent eternity. Cold and dark and quiet, except for an occasional scurrying sound that she had not wanted to think about. Locked in that black cell, she had felt completely isolated from the rest of the world. One thought had burned in the darkness; one thought had kept her from shattering into a thousand pieces: Her faith that Justin would find her.

"I'm fine, thanks to you." She leaned toward him as she smoothed the bandage across his back. His breath brushed her cheek, sweet as spring rain. The warmth of his skin bathed her. A familiar heat coiled and twisted low inside her. She fought to cool it. He needed his rest. He certainly did not need a demented female coaxing him into a lusty tumble. "If Phoebe were here I'm certain she would think you every bit as heroic as a knight of King Arthur's court. At the risk of sounding like a woman with terribly romantic notions, I must say I would have to agree with her."

His smile seemed unbelievably shy. "I shall have to remember how little it takes to impress you."

She brought the bandage around his other side, thinking of a young boy who had been locked in a similar cell time and time again. Alone and frightened. Trapped in darkness. She understood what it had cost Justin to come into that pit to rescue her. She also understood how little he cared to discuss his own heroism. "What shall we do with my cousin?"

"I don't suppose we can just leave him in the cellar."

Isabel took little comfort in knowing her cousin was now occupying the same storage room he had banished her to. She drew the bandage once more around Justin's chest. "I keep thinking of poor Anthea and the other girls. A scandal would ruin them."

"We could ship him off to New South Wales without telling anyone." Justin brushed his lips against her shoulder.

She swallowed the sigh crawling up her throat. She should not encourage the man. "As fitting as that might seem, I would hate to put his family through the same ordeal he put us through." She slipped another strip around his chest and tied it in place.

"We'll wait to see if your father and brother are all right. If they are, we'll allow your father to decide Witheridge's ultimate fate. Until then, I thought I might send the blackguard on a little trip."

Isabel slipped a strip of linen around his arm. "Not New South Wales?"

Justin shook his head. "I have a sugar plantation on Jamaica. I understand my manager can always use another hand in the field."

Isabel stared at him. "Are you serious?"

"He deserves far worse for what he did."

Isabel wrapped his arm and then used another strip to tie the bandage in place. As she worked, her thoughts centered on her father and brother and the treatment they might now be receiving. "I suppose Henrietta can always say he is away on business."

"His family won't be harmed." Justin slid his hand down her back, the warmth of his palm soaking through her gown. "You do nice work."

She lifted her gaze as she felt the hooks of her gown give way beneath his deft fingers. The look in his eyes halted the breath in her throat. Desire and need, uncertainty and conviction. She saw all of this and more in his eyes. "The surgeon said you needed rest."

He grinned at her. "I can think of something else I need more."

"We shouldn't," she said, as he slipped the gown from her shoulders. "Your wounds—"

"Are scratches. Nothing compared to the ache I have for wanting you."

Her gown tumbled to the floor. Her resistance crumbled. She had no chance for redemption against the temptation of Justin. "Are you sure?"

"More sure than I've ever been of anything in my life." The dark sound of his voice held a sweet, aching quality that whispered to the longing deep inside of her.

"We must be careful," she said, sliding her hands over his bare shoulders.

He slipped his hands around her waist and drew her

between his thighs. "Honestly, Isabel, if you don't let me make love to you, I fear you shall cripple me."

She cupped his cheek in her hand, the black stubble of his beard teasing her palm. "In that case, I don't see how I could possibly deny you."

Thick black lashes lowered as he turned his face, the warmth of his breath spilled across her wrist, the softness of his lips pressed against her palm. "Never deny me, Belle."

It was not within her power to deny him. She hoped it never was. She hoped he never gave her reason to turn away from the warmth they shared.

He pressed his lips between her breasts and released his breath in a slow exhalation. The heat of his sigh spread like warm honey across her skin. "I made a startling discovery tonight."

The dark ring of his voice resonated deep inside her. "What did you discover?"

He slipped his fingers beneath the straps of her chemise and petticoat, and slowly peeled the garments from her shoulders. "I discovered you've become essential to my well-being."

Isabel trembled with the confirmation of all the hopes she had cradled deep inside her. "Have I?"

"As essential to me as my every breath." He slid the garments down her arms, his palms grazing her skin with heat.

The soft muslin slid over her breasts, her belly, her hips, her legs. "I am shocked. That sounded dangerously close to a romantic notion."

He smiled as he drew her onto his lap. "There are times when I shock myself."

Amazing, she thought, as she caught their reflection in the cheval mirror that stood in one corner of the room. Rosewood framed the image of a naked woman sitting astride a man's lap. A wanton portrait. Erotic.

Arousing. Practical, dependable Isabel. Deliriously happy Isabel. She smiled at her image, as shocked at her own sense of freedom as she was at the feel of his arousal pressing against her most private region.

He slid his open palms upward over her back, drawing her near, until he could capture her nipple with his mouth. Sensation splintered through her, setting a thousand fires in its wake. The heat of his aroused flesh seared her through the smooth wool of his trousers. Soft wool stroked her inner thighs, cradled her bottom, teased her skin. Her entire body came alive, shimmering with desire for this man.

He rubbed his cheeks back and forth against her breasts, softly abrading the sensitive tips with his rough beard. She gasped with the exquisite sensation. The musky scent of sandalwood swirled through her senses, intoxicating her. She slipped her hands into the thick waves at his nape, her fingers sliding through the silky strands, her fingertips finding the warmth of his scalp, as she held him close to her breasts.

He slipped his hand between their bodies and flicked open the buttons of his trousers. His arousal pressed against the linen of his drawers. She watched, her body crying with need, as he unfastened the buttons. As the linen fell away, his hardened sex reached for her.

"I love you," she whispered, as she took him deep inside her.

"Always love me," he whispered, his voice betraying a powerful, aching need.

"Always."

She tossed back her head, her unbound hair brushing her naked back, a soft sound rising inside her, escaping in a sweet song of pleasure. Although she could not say what it was, there was a subtle difference in this joining, something that dipped beneath the surface of the pleasure she always found in his arms. Something that wrapped around her with a warmth more powerful than the sun. Something that filled her with a stunning joy.

She moved to his rhythm, abandoning herself to this man, as he lifted her from the bounds of reason and into the realm of pure sensation. When the last shiver of pleasure shook her body, she collapsed against him, resting her cheek against his bare shoulder.

Justin slid his hand over her shoulder. "I love you, Isabel."

The words had come so softly she was not certain she had truly heard them, or if they were merely a wish her heart had whispered. She lifted away from him and looked down into his beautiful eyes. "Did you say something?"

He laughed softly, the sound husky and more than a little shaky. "I said I love you."

She cupped his cheeks in her hands. "Say it again."

He grinned at her. "I love you, my beautiful witch. I love you, my infuriating termagant. I love you, my delectable bride to be."

She tried to prevent the tears from rising in her eyes, but they refused to listen to her practical plea. "You can't imagine how very glad I am to hear you say it."

He slid his thumb over the tears streaming down her cheek. "When I thought I had lost you, I realized that the rest of my life, all the days and nights that stretched out in front of me, would be empty."

She stroked the hair, back from his forehead, silky strands of ebony curling around her fingers. "You thought you might miss me?"

"I thought I would go mad without you. I realized how much I love you."

She dropped a kiss on his lips. "Was it so very difficult to say?"

He released his breath on a long sigh. "It's a strange feeling."

She patted his shoulder. "I hope you grow accustomed to it. I rather like hearing you say it."

He slipped his arms around her and pulled her down against his chest. "Then I shall grow accustomed to saying it. I'm not certain what I did to deserve you, but I'm not going to question it. I'm just going to adore you for the rest of my life, and consider myself the luckiest devil on earth."

Isabel strolled with her father through the shrub garden at Marlow House, her arm linked through his. Her brother strolled on the path in front of them, flanked by Phoebe and Eloise, both girls bombarding their brother with questions. Edward and Stephen had arrived in London this morning, transported from New South Wales in luxury upon Justin's yacht.

Edward patted his daughter's hand. "I wish I could have been here for your wedding."

She smiled up at him. "I'm glad you shall be here for the birth of your first grandchild."

Edward glanced down at Isabel's rounded belly. "I never gave up hope of seeing you and the girls again. And now I find I have a new son, a grandchild about to make an appearance, and the Bramsleigh jewels have been recovered. It seems, in ways, that I've been gone a lifetime."

"You are back now. That is all that matters." Isabel paused near the fountain in the center of the garden, the sound of splashing water cascading around them. "I'm curious. Why did you leave the journal with the duke?"

Edward stared at the water tumbling from the hands

of a pair of playful cherubs. "He showed a great deal of excitement about finding any clues it might have held. I told him we would work on the translations together."

She rubbed her palm over his arm. "You were trying to help him through the last days of his life."

Edward nodded. "Somehow I have a feeling George is watching from above, smiling at what his son has managed to accomplish."

"I would like to think Justin's father would approve of our marriage."

Edward squeezed her hand, a wide smile curving his lips, lines crinkling at the corners of his blue eyes. "That last night I was here, George and I talked a long while. He regretted a great many things in his life. He said how much he wished Justin would marry one day. He confessed he had always hoped one of his sons would marry one of my daughters."

Isabel looked up at the sky, where wisps of clouds drifted over pale blue. "You know, at one time I think it would have killed Justin to have done what his father had wished. But, I think he's beginning to forgive him. I think he's made his peace with him. I'm very glad."

"You seem very happy."

She noticed Justin walking along the brick-lined path, his long strides chipping away at the distance between them. "I'm more happy than I have ever been in my life."

"I have sent a message to my manager on Jamaica," Justin said as he joined them. "As you requested, I have told him he shall have Witheridge's services until next June."

Edward chuckled softly. "Thank you, Justin. For everything, not simply dealing with my cousin. You have given me and my son back our lives. You have taken care of my daughters through a difficult time. And you have made Isabel a very happy woman. I am truly grateful."

Justin slipped his arm around Isabel's shoulders. "I assure you, Edward, it was entirely my pleasure."

Edward nodded sagely, and with a wink he left Isabel and Justin near the fountain while he joined the rest of his family. Isabel rested her head on her husband's shoulder and watched her father take a place beside Eloise.

Justin ran his hand over her arm. "Have I neglected to tell you today how very much I love you?"

She tipped her head and smiled up at him. "I believe you mentioned it this morning, in bed."

"Strange, but I feel this odd need to tell you again." He kissed her brow. "I love you, Isabel."

She slipped her arms around his waist and held him as close as her rounded belly would allow. "Always love me, Justin. As much as I love you."

He hugged her close to his chest. "Always."

Epilogue

The scent of lavender wafted from hundreds of burning wax candles in the ballroom of Marlow House. Justin stood on the edge of the dance floor, watching his eldest daughter glide over the floor in the arms of Lord Vernon Richardson, Marquess of Hempstead. Justin did not care much for the way the young man was looking at Lisette, as though she were a pastry he wished to devour.

Isabel slipped her arm through his. "You look as though you would like to strangle someone."

Justin frowned. "That blasted puppy is holding our daughter too close. It's a waltz, not a wrestling match. I have half a mind to march out there and—"

"Darling, Hempstead is a respectable young man. Sophia assures me he is every bit as responsible and worthy as his father was."

"I'm not at all sure why we had to have this blasted ball."

She stroked his arm. "Because your daughter is eighteen. And it's time for her to enter society. We can't keep her wrapped in cotton wool."

He glanced down at his wife. Candlelight poured from crystal chandeliers high above the immense room, finding golden strands in the soft curls framing her beautiful face. Giving birth to five children—all daughters—had not destroyed the allure of her slender curves or her ability to drive him to madness in bed. "Can't we?"

She rested her hand on his chest, over the heart she owned. "Only if we want her to be miserable. And I know you don't want that."

Nineteen years of marriage to him, and the female still had the power to stir his blood with a single touch of her hand. She had been his only lover since the day she had barged into his life. And he had not regretted his monogamy for a moment. She smiled up at him, and, in spite of his every attempt to the contrary, his anger melted beneath the warmth of her smile. "Am I behaving like a demented, overprotective sapskull?"

She lifted up on her toes and kissed his cheek. "You are behaving like a concerned papa."

"The bloody room is filled with rakes and roués."

"Lisette has more sense than to be taken in by the wrong sort of man." She leaned against him. "I hope each of our daughters is fortunate enough to meet a man just like their papa."

Five daughters—he wondered if he would survive. He slipped his arm around Isabel's shoulders and held her close, not caring if they drew curious glances from their guests. Members of the ton had long ago realized the Duke and Duchess of Marlow were a hopelessly amorous couple.

He turned his gaze to Lisette. Her ebony curls swayed against her slender back as she flawlessly followed her partner's lead. The knots in his stomach slowly unraveled as he realized his little girl had grown into a woman every inch as beautiful as her mother, and every bit as practical. "She is a sensible girl."

"Yes, she is. She told me she shall not marry until she finds the one and only man for her."

He grinned at his wife. "Where did she get such romantic notions?"

Isabel patted his chest. "From watching us, my love."

AUTHOR'S NOTE

In doing research for my books I always come across interesting facts. For those of you curious about the proper forms of address for an English Duke or Duchess, it actually depends on your position in society. If you were a member of the gentry or the nobility you would address the Duke or Duchess as "Duke" or "Duchess," unless of course you were on intimate terms with them. In some instances you may also address a Duke by his title. If you were below the gentry you would use "Your Grace." A little bit of trivia that may come in handy the next time you are presented to a Duke or Duchess.

I hope you enjoyed spending time with Isabel and Justin. If you are wondering what happens to Clayton and Marisa, their story comes to life in my next book, *Saint's Temptation*.

What happens when a man who shuns emotions collides with a woman who embraces every exuberant moment of her life? Marisa Grantham ended her engagement to Clayton Trevelyan without an explanation. Seven years later, she and Clay are thrown together in a search for a murderer. Vivacious, passionate, and more than a little eccentric, Marisa drives the staid Earl to distraction. Still, Clay has no hopes of solving a dangerous mystery without her help. The years have not dimmed the attraction these two opposites have for each other. Perhaps this time they can find a way to overcome the obstacles keeping them apart. *Saint's Temptation* should be available in December 1998.

For excerpts from my books, a glimpse at my current project, and a little about me, visit my web site at: www.tlt.com/authors/ddier.htm. You can also send me E-mail at: DebraDier@aol.com.

I love to hear from readers. Please enclose a self-addressed, stamped envelope with your letter. You can reach me at:

P.O. Box 4147
Hazelwood, MO 63042-0747

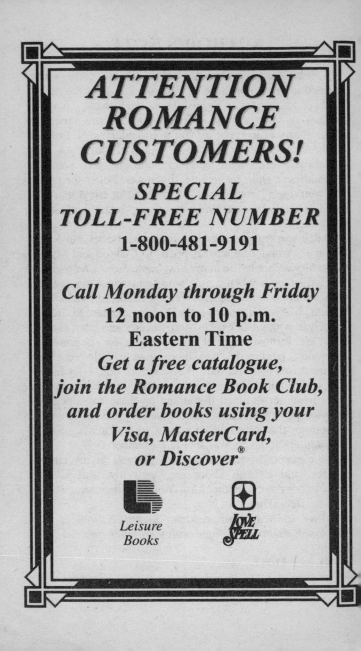

DEVIL'S HONOR

DEBRA DIER

LEISURE BOOKS NEW YORK CITY

For Denny, Sally, Beth, Dani, Dennis and Chrisdin.
You make it a joy to be part of the same family.

A LEISURE BOOK®

March 1998

Published by

Dorchester Publishing Co., Inc.
276 Fifth Avenue
New York, NY 10001

ISBN 0-8439-4362-9

The name "Leisure Books" and the stylized "L" with design are trademarks of Dorchester Publishing Co., Inc.

Printed in the United States of America.

THE CRITICS LOVE
DEBRA DIER!

DEVIL'S HONOR

"An 'I couldn't put it down!' novel."

—Lisa Ramaglia for America Online

MACLAREN'S BRIDE

"Debra Dier will delight readers with her delicious love story. Meg and Alec are a passionate pair and the Scottish setting is truly romantic! Ms. Dier has written a thoroughly enjoyable novel that readers will love!"

—*The Literary Times*

"Debra Dier's delightful drama is definitely a historical romance reader's dream."

—*Affaire de Coeur*

"The talented Ms. Dier captures the English/Scottish animosity to perfection and weaves an exhilarating tale that will touch your heart and fire the emotions. Great Reading!"

—*Rendezvous*

LORD SAVAGE

"Exhilarating and fascinating!"

—*Affaire de Coeur*

"Kudos to Ms. Dier for an unforgettable reading adventure. Superb!"

—*Rendezvous*

"Sensual, involving and well written, this is another winner from the talented pen of Ms. Dier."

—*The Paperback Forum*

A REDEEMING PASSION

Justin touched her cheek. "I have no intention of ever entering that constrictive hypocrisy known as matrimony, Belle. If you have any thoughts about trapping me with your innocent wiles, consider yourself warned. You will get hurt."

Isabel stepped back. "You cannot abide to have anyone think you honorable. Or generous. Or kind. Everyone must be a little afraid of you. You certainly wouldn't want anyone to know you are really very amiable."

"Amiable?"

"You are very dear, actually."

"Dear?" He stared at her, his heart pounding an appalling rhythm against the wall of his chest. Did she think he was some stripling lad? A drawing-room ornament? Some puppy sniffing after her skirts? He cringed at the insipid thought. The blood pounded so loudly in his ears, he could scarcely hear her next words.

"You're also incredibly chivalrous and terribly gallant."

"Enough!" He wrapped his arms around her waist and hauled her up against his chest and off the floor. He clamped his mouth over her startled lips, intent on teaching her a lesson. He would show her just how dangerous he was. Heroic. Chivalrous. Gallant! He was a scoundrel. A rake. A libertine with no hope of redemption. And this kiss would prove it.